OPEN
BAR

OPEN BAR

A Novel

Dan Schorr

Copyright © 2025 Dan Schorr

All rights reserved. No part of this publication may be reproduced, distributed, or transmitted in any form or by any means, including photocopying, recording, digital scanning, or other electronic or mechanical methods, without the prior written permission of the publisher, except in the case of brief quotations embodied in critical reviews and certain other noncommercial uses permitted by copyright law. For permission requests, please address SparkPress.

Published by SparkPress, a BookSparks imprint,
A division of SparkPoint Studio, LLC
Phoenix, Arizona, USA, 85007
www.gosparkpress.com

Published 2025
Printed in the United States of America
Print ISBN: 978-1-68463-256-5
E-ISBN: 978-1-68463-257-2
Library of Congress Control Number: 2025906211

Formatting by Kiran Spees

All company and/or product names may be trade names, logos, trademarks, and/or registered trademarks and are the property of their respective owners.

This is a work of fiction. Names, characters, places, and incidents either are the product of the author's imagination or are used fictitiously. Any resemblance to actual persons, living or dead, is entirely coincidental.

NO AI TRAINING: Without in any way limiting the author's [and publisher's] exclusive rights under copyright, any use of this publication to "train" generative artificial intelligence (AI) technologies to generate text is expressly prohibited. The author reserves all rights to license uses of this work for generative AI training and development of machine learning language models.

1
Serena

*A*GE DOESN'T MATTER. *Especially with someone as mature as you.*

Serena allowed these toxic words to marinate in her mind as she reached into the top right drawer of her mahogany desk and withdrew a stick of cinnamon gum from the open pack. She would have preferred one of her peppermint lozenges, but sometimes they gave her short-lived sneezing fits, and there wasn't time for that. Instead she delicately peeled back the gum wrapper, then shoved the spicy stick into her mouth, which had remained agape since she'd read those same words on yet another document three minutes ago.

She slowly began to chew and savor the needed pop of soothing flavor while glancing at the beautiful campus outside her second-floor office window. Red brick buildings, lush green fields, stone paths, and the immaculate new student center that would open soon, after the undergraduates returned en masse and this sparsely populated summer world once again burst into frenzied activity.

For the past forty-eight hours, Serena had pored over hundreds of documents buried in the legal department's electronic archives. One father's call had initiated her search while simultaneously plunging her into a cauldron of unbearable guilt. Now it was time to get other people involved.

But who? It was undeniable the university president was complicit, so who should she contact? Who could she trust? For the past decade, the general counsel had approved all the settlements and nondisclosure agreements. The Title IX coordinator position had been vacant for nine months. Who else was there? The board of trustees? The police? The hacks on the Mountain Hill City Council?

Maybe Drew. Possibly she could trust him.

Before reaching for the phone, she decided to look things over just one more time. The manila folders were stacked neatly in front of her, the papers in each one appropriately sorted and stapled and labeled and highlighted. She opened the first, stared at the documents, then turned to the next folder, with the new name and legal agreements from three years later. The similarly sickening allegations, the same odious language.

Age doesn't matter. Especially with someone as mature as you.

She steeled herself for what was about to come. She knew the university would try to cover it up, just as they had for years. But she wouldn't let it happen this time. She was going to stand up and sound the alarm and protect these girls and stop this monster.

Serena punched in Drew's extension.

"General counsel's office," came Drew Kosick's young, enthusiastic voice.

"Drew, it's Serena. Are you alone?"

"No, I have a couple of people here. Is something wrong?"

"I'm coming over. Clear your office."

"I can't. We're in the middle of something important. Can we meet this aft—"

"No." She clicked off the call, grabbed her bag, and headed for the door.

Serena then stopped and turned back to look at her office, wondering if she'd ever see the inside of this space again. The chances were good she'd be swiftly escorted off campus and terminated for accessing confidential documents without authorization. Should she take a minute to collect a few things? She already had copies of the relevant files at home. She looked around and saw her family photos and assorted books, including the latest Caleb Lugo novel that she hadn't yet begun reading. On the wall behind her desk, the framed undergraduate diploma she'd earned twenty-five years ago from this university hung proudly.

No, she couldn't allow material possessions to slow her down. She needed to get moving *now*.

Out the door, down the steps, into the suffocating August humidity, as her white blouse began to stick to her back. Across the central campus hub, down a few blocks, faster and faster she walked until the auburn hair that usually brushed across her forehead was matted with sweat.

The moment Serena stepped into the building, she was enveloped by a blast of merciful air-conditioning. She rode the elevator to the fifth floor, then burst into Drew's office.

She didn't bother to knock, just swung the door open and announced, "Sorry, I need everyone to leave." Then she saw it was only Drew, looking startled as he stood there in front of his desk. Tall, lanky, thin faced, brown haired, and wearing the university-approved male professional summer attire of jeans and a polo shirt. Serena looked around the room and said, "I thought you had people in here."

"I did. I asked them to come back later. I hope this really *is* important."

She closed the door and stared at him for a beat before speaking. "For the past ten years, Rob Dempsey has been molesting girls in the university's youth summer softball program."

Drew's face looked frozen for a few seconds, then he blinked. "Oh my God. How do you know this?"

"One girl's father called me two days ago, and that led me to find many other credible complaints in university records. Many. *Very credible.*"

Drew looked down at the metallic paper shredder next to his desk. He ran a few fingers across his chin as his head momentarily twitched. Finally he looked back at Serena and said decisively, "We have to tell Tim."

Naturally he'd first think of Tim Durso, his boss. Mountain Hill University's general counsel.

"He knows," she answered. "He's known for years. He signed off on settlements and NDAs with some of the families to keep this quiet."

Drew shook his head in disbelief. "That's not possible without others finding out."

"I have the documents. It all happened with the support of the president. And our beloved athletic director."

"Fuck. Are you sure?"

"Yes. The father's name is Darren Tyrell. He called me in tears, barely able to finish a sentence. His daughter Ali is twenty-two now, and last week she told him that when she was fourteen and attended the softball camp, Rob got very close to her, became a real mentor, and had her perform oral sex on him at least four times."

Drew grimaced. "Did he force her?"

"Does it matter? She was fourteen. He was forty."

"It's wrong either way, *obviously.*" He paused for a few seconds, then said, "But I think it does matter. Doesn't it?"

"Drew, the father cried as he told me how his daughter held this in for so long. She moved back home recently, and he could tell she was struggling with something. He got her to start seeing a therapist, and after a while, she told her father what Dempsey had done to her. And he finally understood why for years she hadn't slept well, couldn't keep up in school, and had trouble making friends. He cried as he told me he'd failed his daughter, totally failed to protect her."

"That's horrible," he answered quietly, then closed his eyes. Serena wondered what he was thinking. Was he considering the horrors of the sexual abuse itself or that he'd been ignorantly unaware of the cover-up around him?

Did he feel any of the culpability that ravaged Serena now? A crucial part of her job was to protect people from exactly these types of atrocities, but she'd been inexcusably ignorant. She'd battled irrational guilt over trivial issues her entire life, but there was nothing irrational about her feeling responsible for this tragic failure.

"And you know what he said to this girl?" Serena asked, struggling to keep her voice steady as Drew's eyes popped back open. "When he was grooming her in *our* youth softball program, telling her how much potential she had, instructing her and all the others to affectionately call him 'Uncle Rob'? He asked if she'd ever been with an older guy, and he said, 'Age doesn't matter. Especially with someone as mature as you.'"

Nervous disgust flashed across Drew's face. "We have to tell Tim. Right now." He picked up his office phone, but before he could initiate the call, Serena grabbed it away. She shook her head as she placed it back in its cradle.

"Tim investigated the first complaint almost ten years ago. And five others since then with very similar allegations. Two investigations involved girls who wouldn't agree to be interviewed, so Rob Dempsey was found not responsible. But get this, their families received settlement payments"—Drew closed his eyes again—"right before the girls said they wouldn't cooperate. Four other accusations were dismissed as inconclusive because of the whole 'he said, she said' bullshit. But you know what three of these girls separately reported that he said? Three girls, not counting the one whose father I spoke with two days ago."

"Age doesn't matter?"

She nodded. "Especially with someone as mature as you."

"Christ."

"So that's four girls over the course of a decade, all independently reporting he said *the same thing* before he molested them. Four girls who didn't know each other! And despite that powerful corroboration, because he's so fucking prominent in the softball world with all the championships and accolades for his underprivileged girls program, the university simply directed him not to be alone with any females under eighteen without another adult present. And to attend some bullshit training classes about proper coaching protocols. Doubtful any of that was ever enforced. He was allowed to keep coaching! Who knows how many girls there are who never reported. How many he's doing this to now. And all this was kept from me!" She paused before she reminded Drew, "Tim's part of the cover-up."

Drew looked down at the phone. She sensed he wanted to pick it up, and she readied herself to again snatch it away. He then stared back at her, his mouth moving silently for a moment before he finally uttered, "So what should we do, Serena?"

"I don't know, but as deputy general counsel you're the highest-ranking legal person who doesn't appear to be compromised. Your name wasn't on any of the paperwork, so I'm assuming you had no idea about any of this."

"Of course I had no idea! I never would have let this happen if I'd known. We have to go to Tim. That's the proper protocol. We'll approach him together, and we'll both make sure it's not ignored this time. As the father of two young daughters, I care *a lot* about—"

"Okay, yeah, yeah," she interrupted, rolling her eyes. "Daughters. Caring. Got it."

She shook her head. She'd hoped for more from Drew. Just as she'd hoped for more from the university. But everyone was just looking to cover their own asses. "You know what," she said, "forget I brought this to you. When these things go public, people always ask who knew what when, and how they responded. Your solution is to go to the guy who's been covering this up. I just thought of a better idea." Serena turned around and reached for the door.

"Wait! Where are you going?"

She opened it, and then glanced back at Drew. "He's holding practice right now. I'm putting an end to this myself. I'm not letting him spend another minute with these girls." Then she surged out the door and headed to the nearby stairwell, hearing urgent footsteps behind her as she rushed down the stairs. Back into the hot summer air, she briskly moved down the main walkway toward the nearby athletic center and the two neighboring ballfields.

Drew came running up beside her, breathing heavily. "You can't do this. Please, Serena. Don't. What happened before is unacceptable, but this isn't right either." She kept walking, looking ahead and ignoring him. "Think! They'll fire you."

Serena already knew that possibility. And the idea of losing her job made her queasy. Her daughter Kayla was a rising sophomore on a full ride because Serena was a longtime employee. If the university fired her, suddenly having to pay the exorbitant college tuition as a single mother would plunge her family into financial calamity. But she couldn't let that deter her.

"That would be quite a story," she shot back without breaking her stride. "Terminating me for disrupting the work of a pedophile. He's literally the wolf in sheep's clothing, and I'm the only one who gives a shit!"

"I care, Serena! You know I do. That's why you came to me. But this is crazy!" he pleaded.

She just kept walking, her mind full of determination.

They charged down the hill amid the smell of late summer and freshly cut grass, and there in front of them were two beautiful, perfectly manicured ballfields, with the brown dirt infields at opposite ends of the wide green expanse facing each other. Now about forty yards from the closest diamond, she could see a small figure swing a bat and make contact with a pitch as a loud *ping* pierced the air, and the yellow ball tumbled down the third base line. The girl dropped the bat and sprinted in her purple-and-white camp uniform to first base as the fielder at third swept up the grounder and flung it across the diamond.

Serena continued her march toward the field with Drew hustling right behind her. The camper playing first base held one foot on the bag while she stuck out her other leg and reached as far as she could. As the ball smacked into her outstretched glove, the runner's right foot hit the base. Meanwhile, Serena was still moving, not as fast as the speedy teenager, but similarly getting increasingly closer to her destination.

"Safe!" declared a confident and assertive male voice, and Serena's head immediately focused on the man standing in the middle of the infield wearing a purple MHU baseball cap, gray athletic shorts, a purple-and-white MHU softball T-shirt, and a silver whistle hanging from a black lanyard around his neck.

Rob Dempsey's strong arms and hands began clapping, and a smile spread across his handsome middle-aged face. "Way to run it out, Jamie! Excellent fielding, Marissa! Love that throw. Really tough play and you almost got it there in time! Great stretch at first, Iyanna. I've been coaching softball a *long time* and you girls are really, really—"

"This practice is over!" Serena hollered from shallow left-center field as her sweaty frame grew closer to the infield, and she noted that Drew's vigorous attempts to keep up with her abruptly stopped as the words left her mouth. "Right now! Over!"

The players turned toward her, those on the field and in the dugouts, with looks of surprise and confusion. The coach turned in her direction too with a quizzical expression.

"We're in the middle of practice here, ma'am—"

"Maybe you didn't hear me." She was now fifteen feet away and closing in. "I said this practice is over."

"I'd say everybody heard you. Who are you?" he responded, looking her up and down.

"Serena Stanfield. Human resources director," she announced as she tried to catch her breath. A few feet away, Drew shook his head and seemed intent to speak, but no words came out. All around, the players stared at Serena. Near the third base dugout a couple of girls held up their phones.

"What's this about?" Dempsey asked, leaning in toward her and clearly growing more agitated as they met on the infield grass, now just a couple of feet apart.

"End this practice now," she ordered. "Then follow me."

He pointed at her and snapped, "You don't talk to me like that. And you don't interrupt this practice. Get off my field *now*."

She was about to respond when the petite shortstop with a crimson ponytail extending from her MHU visor called out, "Yeah, get off the field, bitch!"

She glanced at the girl, opened her mouth to answer, and then shook her head and turned back to Dempsey. "You want to know what this is about, Coach?" She then stepped closer to him and whispered, "Age doesn't matter. Especially with someone as mature as you."

Dempsey stepped back a couple of paces, looked down, pulled off his cap, then raked his fingers through his thick, graying hair. His face looked somber and uneasy as he stared into the distance and then responded in a low voice, "You need to speak with Tim Durso. He already looked into those lies."

"Oh, I know he did," she said emphatically, nodding her head. "I know all about how Tim 'looked into' them. And let me promise you something, *Uncle Rob* . . ."

"What's that?"

She stared at him intently, trying with maximum effort to establish the eye contact he was earnestly resisting.

"Tim won't save you this time."

There was one more adult present, standing near home plate. She recognized him from the online team softball photos as Cole Malinowski. Early thirties, well-built, a former MHU standout baseball player. Serena had read that Rob Dempsey took him under his wing long ago, with Cole serving for most of the past decade as assistant coach and assistant director of the softball camp. Cole stayed where he was but kept shifting his weight from side to side. Serena could see the young coach didn't know what Dempsey expected of him.

Serena trained her eyes on him, as one of the key questions she'd wanted answered, ever since she first uncovered the sordid actions of the university's pedophile softball coach, engulfed her brain.

Cole, what have you known about all this? she thought. *For all these years and all these girls, you were right by his side. While he sexually abused his players and damaged their lives, how much were you aware of while you did nothing? While you remained absolutely silent.*

2
Troy

TROY ABERNATHY uncomfortably considered what he could do to stay employed, to survive the next seemingly inevitable wave of layoffs, not wanting to return to random tasks at his uncle's restaurant in Astoria. His current corporate position was psychologically debilitating, with each day bringing an assortment of toxic interactions that drowned him in constant apprehension and sleepless nights. But the even greater fear that overwhelmed him was not having this job at all.

He was barely hanging on, while young professionals at other companies basked in success, as reflected by their flood of self-congratulatory LinkedIn posts announcing new positions, impressive promotions, and thought-provoking interviews on cutting-edge podcasts. 30 under 30, 40 under 40, "honored and humbled to be recognized" this, and "excited and grateful for the new opportunity" that.

For many, attending this fancy New York City charity fundraiser would be a thrilling sign of achievement, but for Troy it was yet another professional obstacle course littered with land mines. He tried to innocuously blend in, but he was so out of his element among the rich and well-connected attendees, for whom the $1,500-a-plate cost was just the tip of their expenditures. The real funds would be brought in through the silent auction, followed later by the live auction, as people bid on luxurious trips, products, meals, and precious, donated celebrity experiences.

When he last looked at the silent auction area, an exclusive dinner for ten personally cooked by a famous television chef had been bid up to $36,000. Staying at a movie star's home in Lake Como for a week was now listed at $75,000. If Troy could bid on one item, it would be the private poker lessons with top pro and human rights activist Priya Varma, but forking over two-thirds of his annual salary while he squeaked by paycheck to paycheck and feared termination wasn't in the cards.

Troy suddenly sensed that one of the evening's land mines was just in front of him, as a man a few feet away approached the event's aloof host, who was notoriously annoyed by autograph and photo requests. "Could I bring my family over for a picture with you?" the man asked nervously. "It would mean so much."

Troy immediately knew this guy was the father of one of the scholarship kids, because of course he was. The wrinkled dress pants, maybe the only remotely nice pair he owned. The white button-down shirt, a little too tight around the stomach, probably purchased several years and twenty-five pounds ago. The hair with too much gel, surely overapplied because of overexuberance to make sure he looked professional and appropriate for this big, once-in-a-lifetime event where he knew he didn't belong. And let's not even get started on his posture. Or the salmon-colored tie.

The father's question had been directed at Caleb Lugo, the world-renowned author and philanthropist, the star of the show, who'd created the foundation that was holding this elegant gala purportedly to benefit the education and development of young writers.

Caleb had been moving past the man, headed elsewhere in that purposeful way that famous people do to avoid banal conversation with fans, but now he stopped and turned. Fifty-five and aging gracefully with salt-and-pepper hair and just the hint of forehead wrinkles, he sighed with transparent annoyance and opened his mouth to respond, while his eyes actively searched the room. But instead of addressing the question, he settled his gaze on Troy and snapped, "Hey, are you with C&R?"

Troy could see the author immediately knew he must be a junior associate with the firm, because of course he was. Professional looking with his conservative haircut and average suit and tie, but clearly not one of the polished, wealthy guests who populated the grand ballroom. If it weren't for his corporate investigations firm buying tables to support clients' charities, Troy would never be invited to such events. And this week two managing directors were suddenly laid off, so the company needed a couple of warm bodies to fill the ten seats.

Troy was probably the only person in the firm who hadn't been staffed on one of Caleb's assignments. But he had heard enough about working for this man to know that when his time came, he should expect to be spoken to with disdain, repress all frustration or even outrage, then bill his time accordingly.

"Yes, sir," Troy responded with a smile. "I am. Can I help you with something?"

Caleb threw an arm around Troy's shoulders and steered him away from the father, who looked on with awkward disappointment. Meanwhile, Caleb's head jerked right and left as he scanned the room. "I shouldn't have ignored him like that, but I have a bit of a serious situation." It wasn't an apology. There was no remorse. "Where's your boss? I need to talk to him." He dropped his arm from Troy's shoulders and added, "Right now."

"He's definitely here," Troy said as he searched the attendees without success. "I'll find him for you. No, wait, I'll call him."

Caleb began touching Troy's shoulders again, one hand on each this time, staring intently at him with palpable concern in his eyes. "I've *tried* calling him. He's not answering his goddamn phone. You'd think after all the millions I've fucking pissed away with you people, I could get my calls answered!"

Millions. For thirty years. Longer than Troy had been alive.

Caleb wasn't a typical C&R client. The firm worked mostly for Wall Street investment banks, corporate litigation practices, and international businesses with FCPA compliance issues. Not condescending writers swimming in personal problems.

But Caleb's money qualified him to be a client too—his money and the fact that he'd hired the firm in its earlier days when they were hungry for business. Caleb had just published his first novel at the time and initially wanted to interview investigations experts as research for his next work. From there the relationship grew.

Caleb Lugo's issues were constant, highly profitable, and not the typical investor due diligence or government-appointed monitorship assignments. Instead, young professionals with Ivy League degrees might find themselves wheeling an empty baby carriage by an Upper East Side restaurant to see if they could catch Caleb's estranged wife consuming alcohol in violation of a family court order, or surveilling his college-aged daughter's boyfriend to see if . . . well, the firm was never told what they were supposed to be looking for. But they were instructed to look, and the firm was well paid, so they looked.

Millions. It wasn't just the books that made him an extremely wealthy man. There were the movie rights, the two network TV series, and the latest adaptations of his tales on Netflix.

"Well, it's loud in here. He probably can't hear the—"

"This is urgent," the author interrupted. "I'm supposed to address the room in a few minutes, and I have to speak with him before that. Do whatever you have to do."

"Absolutely, Mr. Lugo. I'll get him right away." He contemplated lightening the mood with an additional comment. Maybe something like, *I work for an investigations firm, so I'm good at tracking people down*. But Caleb's intensity and Troy's own common sense told him to just focus on the mission, so he stepped back from the man's embrace and started quickly working his way through the crowd, looking in all directions, as he called his boss's phone.

"You've reached Anderson Davis at C&R Investigations. Please leave your name, number, and—"

He tapped his phone and slid it back into the left inside pocket of his suit jacket. When he looked up, another phone was being waved in his face.

"Troy! Have you seen this MHU video?" came the young female voice of his fellow junior associate, Julia McGinnis.

"Yes. Have you seen Anderson? Caleb wants him. It's urgent."

"I grew up near that campus. Oh my God, I *love* when the girl yells, 'Get off the field, bitch!' Would it be unprofessional if I made that my ringtone?"

Julia was generously imbibing from a glass of white wine while looking professionally attractive in her gray business suit, her blonde hair pulled neatly back. She placed her right index finger against her chin, squinted her brown eyes, and looked off into the distance while slightly bobbing her head, as if she were contemplating the answer to the deep question she had just posed.

"You shouldn't drink so much here," he warned as a waiter carrying a tray of shrimp cocktail brushed past him. "We're all one step away from being laid off as it is."

They were all working in this stressful, precarious environment, needing to justify their salaries on a daily basis. And his situation was more dire than others thanks to his subpar background—the youthful mistakes and lack of family connections or a prestigious educational pedigree. For Troy, the hardest part of breaking into this corporate world was getting a foot in the door. Thanks to Julia, he now had one leg planted inside, and hopefully one day he'd find a way to repay her. But if he lost this job, it would be no easy task finding another with as much potential.

He was drowning in uncertainty. It was an open secret that C&R might soon be sold to the DePalma Capital Partners private equity firm. Would that be a cause for celebration or distress? Would that help save their jobs or lead to a massive RIF? All unclear.

But Julia didn't seem to share his concerns. "I bill a ton of hours and get paid shit." She scrunched her nose and forehead. "What crazy motherfucker's gonna lay me off?" Then she gestured around the room, using her wine glass like a laser pointer. "Might as well take advantage of the open bar . . ."

Unlike most of their junior colleagues, Julia was staffed on some bank monitorship that allowed her to easily bill fifty to sixty hours a week, enough to satisfy what C&R's managing directors expected of junior associates. Troy nodded apprehensively and anxiously scanned the crowded banquet hall for Anderson as he responded, "Most of us don't have the luxury of working on a project where we're so highly utilized."

"What's your favorite Caleb Lugo novel?" Julia asked.

"I haven't read them. I started one once."

"I've read them all," she said with a sudden ultra-dramatic tone. "My favorite might be the one where there's a murder in a small town and the residents are all full of dark secrets. I also liked the one about the divorced guy having a midlife crisis. He reevaluates all his past relationships and discovers his true self in the process. A real heartwarming, life-affirming journey of self-discovery and self-acceptance. A stirring story about what we choose to keep from our past and what we choose to leave behind."

He continued searching the room, wishing his intoxicated colleague would help. "Please, Julia, I really need you—"

"Or maybe my favorite is his novel about life and loss and second chances and the meaning of friendship and how sometimes the love you need is found when you least expect it." She waved her hand in a flourish as some of her wine spilled onto the parquet floor. "Oh, also there was one that was a magical, sexy, big-hearted romance where the impossible becomes possible. A moving portrait of what happens when we choose to love someone not in spite of who they are, but because of it. And the new one, *Don't Spend It All in One Place*. A bittersweet story about a family that struggles with grief but together turns it into something beautiful. An exhilarating exploration of accountability and redemption."

"I can't tell if you're being serious or sarcastic."

She took another long sip from her glass and then looked at him, wide-eyed. "Neither can I!"

Was that Anderson in the distance? Troy saw an older figure on the other side of the room with a slight build and gray hair. But before Troy could step in that direction, the man turned around. Not Anderson.

Troy looked intently at Julia. "Where's Anderson? Caleb's frantic. Says it's an emergency."

"I saw him on the balcony a little while ago talking with Emma. Anderson had Tara from HR give her a PIP today because her utilization was down last quarter. She's fucking devastated."

I wish you had just told me that earlier, Troy thought as he took off toward the balcony. He reached the end of the ballroom and stepped out through the doors into the hot August air, and he was quickly immersed in the lights and sights and sounds of Midtown Manhattan on a Friday evening from thirty stories above ground.

"Anderson," he called out to his seventy-year-old boss, who stood by the railing, wearing a sharp, trim pin-striped gray suit with matching paisley tie and pocket square.

"Troy," Anderson responded, "meet Gillian Fenton. Chief of sex crimes for the Brooklyn DA's office and board member of the Sixteen Foundation."

Caleb Lugo's foundation. The official name origin story was that he wrote his first full-length novel at sixteen years old. Word around the C&R office was that he was sixteen when he lost his virginity. Maybe both were true. If so, clearly a noteworthy year.

"Very nice to meet you," he said, shaking Gillian's hand. She was probably twenty years older than Troy and looked confident and relaxed in a dark blue pantsuit. "I love SVU," he added supportively, eliciting a sigh and a perfunctory, unimpressed nod from her.

"So as I was saying, Gillian," Anderson said, now pretending Troy wasn't there as he turned his attention back to her. "I've been wanting to follow up with you for a while, but—"

"I'm very sorry to interrupt," Troy broke in, and instantly saw the flash of annoyance on Anderson's face that Troy was all too familiar with. Would this lead to an imminent blowup? Probably not in front of others, so Troy would most likely experience the consequences when he least expected it.

Another absurdly long assignment handed to him late on a Friday afternoon with an arbitrary Monday due date. A caustic email castigating his work performance, with little or no basis in fact. Every time Anderson's name popped up in his email inbox, or appeared on his phone's caller ID, he felt an intense swirl in the pit of his stomach, not knowing what the consequences would be when he opened the message or answered the call. An older generation would no doubt tell him to just suck it up and pay his dues like they did, and not let it get to him. And in fact he was pretty much doing those first two things.

Did his boss know how much he hated him? Probably not. Troy believed he was pretty good at acting as if he liked people whom he hated, which he felt was actually a pretty marketable skill.

Now, with Anderson stirred to annoyance, Troy knew he had to talk fast. "Very sorry," he continued, "but Caleb's looking for you. He says it's *urgent*."

"Okay, where is he?"

"Back in the ballroom."

Anderson turned to Gillian. "My apologies, but when an important client *demands* your time . . ." He held both hands face up and tilted his head, looking remarkably like the shrugging emoji. "But it's not that bad, actually. Maybe I can convince you to cross over and enjoy life on our side. You've certainly paid your dues in government." Then he smiled his recruitment smile. And she smiled back graciously, with apparent sincerity and interest.

"Okay," Anderson ordered Troy. "Take me to him."

They worked their way through the main room, and Anderson followed Troy as the young associate fought through the crowd, scanning all over to see where the author was currently located. But before Troy could find him, a hand firmly grabbed his right arm and roughly swung him around.

"There you fucking are," Caleb hissed with agitation. "Do you treat all your clients like shit? Or just me?"

"Mr. Lugo, I'm sorry I wasn't quicker, but I rushed to find Anderson, just like you asked. And then we were looking for you."

"You know," Caleb said to Anderson, "there are dozens of fine investigations firms in New York. I think they'd all be happy to take my money. And when I call with an emergency, I bet they'll fucking answer!"

"Sorry, Caleb," Anderson responded quickly. "I was on the balcony and cell reception was very poor."

The author shook his head and gestured for them to follow him to a corner of the ballroom. He then looked at the two men with concern in his eyes and lowered his voice. "Can you conduct research in Spain? Urgent research?"

"Yes, absolutely," Anderson answered.

"I mean *really* conduct research in Spain. For *real*. As in, you have a guy who can do it and he can do it right now. Not 'Sure, Caleb, we can handle it,' and then you make a hundred calls to start figuring out if you actually can."

Troy knew Anderson had no idea. He was a senior managing director, head of the flagship New York office, not someone in the weeds of vetting subs and understanding all aspects of C&R's global research capabilities. He glanced at Troy, and Troy jumped on it.

"Yes, we have a great resource in Spain. I've used him many times, and I can hopefully have him working on whatever you need by morning."

Caleb cleared his throat. "Okay, look. Last year in Barcelona, I met a Spanish model at a book tour thing. Said she was a big fan of my work. We spent some time together there. Totally innocent. We didn't even kiss. Then she came to New York a few months ago."

C&R generally avoided work involving personal, potentially intimate relationships. Troy's colleagues were white-collar corporate investigators, not sleazy ex-cops dumpster-diving for dirt or trying to catch a spouse *in flagrante delicto*. But Caleb was an important client with deep pockets. And the last quarter hadn't been great. Nor the one before that.

"What happened in New York?" Anderson asked.

"*Nothing*. Nothing happened. That's the thing. I'd tell you if something had, you know that. She was just in my apartment one evening for a little while. We had a couple of drinks. *Nothing happened.*"

"Okay," Anderson said. "So how can we help?"

"Her name's Bianca Velencoso. I have her phone number, and that's about it. You'll see there's a lot about her online. She's known for modeling and a few small acting gigs. I need your best investigators to find out everything you can on her. Everything." He paused briefly to anxiously dart his eyes around them and then continued, "Because she's saying I groped her and wouldn't let her leave my apartment."

"Saying to who?"

"The police. They just reached out to my lawyers and these cops want to question me *tomorrow*. It's a fucking nightmare. She's probably looking for money. Or maybe a bigger platform, and she thinks making a bullshit claim against a celebrity author is the way to get it. We need to know everything there is on this woman so we can show she's not credible. Before this becomes public and I'm totally fucked. Before these cops decide to arrest me."

"Mr. Lugo," Troy began explaining, "I recommend we start by researching all available public records. Media, social media, litigation, criminal proceedings, business interests, property, judgments, liens, things like that. We can also conduct source inquiries with people who know her to identify potentially adverse information, but I'd suggest first doing the public records research because it's more discreet and maybe that will give us leads to act—"

"Hey, kid," Caleb interrupted with annoyance. "I don't need to know how you make the fucking sausage, okay? Just get cooking."

"Understood. I'll get on this immediately."

"Good. I expect an update tomorrow. Here's her name and phone number." Caleb slipped Troy a piece of paper. "Okay, it's time for me to speak," he added, and Troy watched the writer head toward the dais at the front of the room.

Anderson turned to Troy. "You've really used the Spanish sub many times?"

"A few. He did a decent job."

Anderson sighed, which Troy knew meant he was irritated with that answer. But Troy felt he had to play it straight with his boss, even if not so straight with the client.

"Do you believe that story?" Troy asked as he pulled out his phone to contact the sub.

"Her name might actually be Bianca Velencoso," Anderson replied gruffly. "Who the fuck knows about the rest."

Troy nodded. It was too late in Madrid to call, so he tapped an email to his resource. He prayed the guy wasn't on vacation, or slammed with other work, or off the grid for some random national holiday.

It would be disastrous for C&R to have to tell Caleb the next day that research had not started immediately. Troy would have to set his phone alarm for 3:00 a.m. to see if he had an email response, and then call Madrid immediately if needed. What time would it be there then, 9:00 a.m.?

He was halfway through drafting the email when he heard the roar of the crowd and looked up. Gillian, the criminal prosecutor from the balcony, stood at the center of the stage's dais, talking into the microphone, smiling broadly. "You know," she began, "I'm not used to speaking in front of an audience without starting with 'Ladies and gentlemen of the jury,' so please bear with me." The assembled laughed politely, and she continued, "It's just amazing to see across this room so many wonderfully impressive boys and girls, just entering their teens, their lives full of hope and promise. I've lost count how many of them wrote in their scholarship application essays or told me personally tonight that you, Caleb, tremendously inspired them. Inspired them to read. Inspired them to write. Inspired them to tell their truth to the world. Thank you, Caleb. From all of us: *Thank you.*"

The crowd applauded as Caleb walked up to Gillian, hugged her, and grinned with appreciation while shaking his head in what Troy assumed was simulated disbelief at how powerful and moving this moment was.

"You've always been there for these kids," she declared. "And you've always been there for me. So I'll always be there for you. Always."

Then Caleb was in front of the mic, gazing out at the crowd of the rich and successful, as well as the young writers and their parents.

"I reject the idea that I have inspired you," he said as he focused on a few of the teenagers on the floor below him. "I reject it because the truth is . . ." He paused, and Troy recognized how obvious it was where he was going. It was all so preordained at this point. The finish, the reaction, the swoon of the crowd in appreciation. "The real truth is that it is *you*, my children, who *inspire me*."

Applause. Adoration. Cheers that swelled for thirty seconds and then held at the crescendo as Caleb nodded and extended his arms in the direction of some of the scholarship winners and clapped enthusiastically. The passionate clamor still filled every inch of this Manhattan ballroom, with no sign of dying down anytime soon, when Troy completed his urgent email to Madrid and pressed send.

3
Megan

As a relatively new member of the Mountain Hill City Council, Megan Black knew she should be consumed with the sickening, bombshell allegations that had just surfaced from the city's prestigious university. She was flooded with media inquiries and messages from furious constituents, and she struggled to get her head around the situation. What exactly had been going on at that school and for how long? If the allegations were true, how had it been allowed to continue for years?

And most importantly, who was going to provide support and justice for those who had been abused, and ensure this never happened again in their city?

But Megan also had another crisis to confront. A crisis that was over a decade in the making.

Her friend's lawyer had texted eight days earlier:

Evina's appeal denied. So sorry. One of us should go tell her. She shouldn't hear it from someone in prison. Please call to discuss ASAP. I wish as a member of the city council you had the power to just make this all go away.

City council.

Megan recalled that big night at home the previous year, when she and her husband called their two middle school–age sons into the kitchen and with a ludicrously dramatic tone asked them to sit for an "important discussion." Of course this immediately freaked them out, with their older son asking who died, and the younger speculating about whether they were getting divorced. Her husband smiled with reassurance as he said, "No one's dead or divorcing. This is a serious family conversation about something significant your mother is considering. Something I'm very, very proud of her for, and I think you will be too."

They then proceeded with utmost gravity to talk about how, because of her involvement with the PTA and strong advocacy for lighting and road improvements on Route 48, she had been asked by some key local figures to run for city council. She had left her job at the accounting firm years earlier to focus on raising their children, but for the past few months she felt it was time to return to her career. She had put together a résumé, created a LinkedIn profile, started reaching out to contacts, and attended a few networking events. But then she was presented with a more intriguing and possibly rewarding path.

She and Alan told their boys that this was a big *family decision*, that they all had to *make together*, because that's how they rolled, because this might change *their lives too*, and they wanted to make sure everyone was *absolutely comfortable* with how tough a city council campaign could be.

So laughable in hindsight, with their voices and demeanors conveying an intense seriousness as if she was thinking of running for fucking president. That's how big this seemed then. What a leap it appeared to be, how exalted she believed this position was. That was before she actually ran, and won, and became fully aware of the clowns that inhabited the council, with their petty grievances and turf wars and transparent efforts to steer funds and patronage jobs to their supporters.

For the past eight months, she'd been one of them, with her reputation inevitably and increasingly tied to how citizens viewed the dysfunctional council as a whole. Therefore, to many residents in the City of Mountain Hill, she was now a clown too.

She was new to politics but learning how it all worked, or didn't. Unlike many she encountered, she really wanted to help people. More and more she became convinced that to actually affect people's lives, she'd have to escape local government and seek higher office. It was too soon for that, but if she worked hard and built support, in three or four years she could maybe consider running for state assembly. Or possibly state senate. Although even those positions wouldn't give her the power to help Evina Jansen, who needed her assistance right now.

In seventh grade Megan's locker had been right next to Evina's, and they rode the same bus home. Megan had been the lonely new kid after her parents moved to Mountain Hill, but Evina took her in, sat with her at lunch, and talked to her on the bus.

In no time they became inseparable, and even when they attended colleges in different states, they called each other every week, went out late together in their hometown on semester breaks, and roomed with each other when they studied abroad in London their junior year.

The only thing that came between them was *him*, the boyfriend Evina started seeing in her early twenties. Handsome, charming, a litigation associate at a local law firm, Logan Young looked great on paper, and Evina seemed so excited to be dating him. But from his earliest days in Evina's life, Megan winced at the warning signs. There was rarely a night out without him becoming excessively intoxicated and belligerent. He was obsessively jealous and controlling, never letting Evina go anywhere at night without him, and interrogating her any time she made small talk with a bartender or was remotely friendly to a male waiter.

During fleeting moments when she was alone with Evina, Megan told her this guy wasn't good for her, that no boyfriend that insecure was going to turn out to be a good partner. But Evina shrugged and said that for the most part he was kind and really loved her.

Megan became increasingly alarmed by the endless cycle of breakups and reunifications, the repeated signs that he was physically hurting her, which Evina would always explain away as innocent injury. The sprained wrist suffered in a "kitchen accident," the bruise by her left eye caused by a "clumsy fall," the burn on her neck from her "curling iron."

The day Evina announced her engagement, Megan feigned happiness, then went home and cried for her friend. And clearly, Logan knew Megan wasn't his ally. On the wedding day, he grabbed Megan's wrist and pulled her toward the back of the ballroom. Feeling the force of his hand on her, experiencing the confident control he so casually exercised, sent a rush of dread through her body. Her best friend had just vowed to spend her life with this bully, and Megan hadn't been able to prevent it.

He dragged Megan to a quiet spot outside the bustle of the reception and delivered a cold stare. "I know you think I'm wrong for Evina, but I want you to know that I love her very much."

She nodded, letting these words soak in. It wasn't the right moment to push back. She wasn't going to ruin her friend's wedding.

"So I'm asking you politely to stop undermining our relationship," he then added. "She's happy, and that should make you happy. But it seems like it's just making you jealous, and that's not right. You really need to find a man of your own, Megan."

Over the next five years, she was with Evina through it all. The ever-escalating series of beatings, the four times he was arrested for domestic abuse, the four times the charges were dismissed because Evina refused to cooperate and recanted her initial allegations. Megan tried to provide support as her friend wrestled with misplaced self-blame, fears of retaliation, her husband's repeated promises that he would never harm her again, and Evina's hope that Logan could one day keep his word if he just stopped drinking.

Meanwhile, Megan repeatedly urged her to leave the relationship. Begged her to do so on so many occasions. When Evina showed up at her apartment four years after the wedding, pleading for help, wearing a torn nightgown and bleeding from her temple, Megan was horrified but also perversely relieved that this latest violent incident would mean an end to Evina's marriage.

But a week later, she was back with him, and texting Megan with excitement that she was pregnant. Megan was right there in the hospital after Evina gave birth, holding her friend's baby in her arms, and then two years later holding Evina as she sobbed because child protective services had taken her daughter away after several reports of violence in the home.

The night that Evina was arrested the following year, Megan was her first phone call. "He's dead," her friend told her, and Megan immediately sensed the whole story. Evina had finally stood up to this man, finally defended herself. Such a relief that he would never hurt her again, just as a whole new nightmare was beginning.

By this time Megan and Alan had met, married, and had two children of their own. When the trial commenced almost a year later, Megan barely saw her family for six weeks, as she sat in the front row every day and strategized with Evina's lawyer in the evenings.

Evina took the stand and explained that her life with Logan had been a succession of horrors. She detailed stories of his frequent drunkenness, his violent nature. "He often told me I was ugly," she said quietly, looking down at her hands in her lap, "and he'd hit me in the face when he said it. I was too much of a pig for anyone else to want me, he claimed."

Throughout the trial Megan often looked at the jury. They were so hard to read, she thought, except for that dark-haired woman at the end who winced whenever Evina described something violent.

Evina told the jury her husband also abused their two-year-old daughter, that he slapped her across the head if she got in his way, and shook her furiously when she cried. He'd once beaten her legs with a switch after the little girl knocked over a beer he had placed on the coffee table.

Evina's court-appointed lawyer let her go on sharing the dark details of life with Logan, and then Megan could sense she was readying for the most difficult part of her testimony. The attorney took a step closer to her as he said, "Can you tell the court about the night of your husband's death?"

Evina coughed nervously and looked quickly at the jury box, then back down at her hands. "He came home around two a.m.," she said. "One of his friends had won two thousand dollars on a scratch-off lottery ticket and taken his whole crew out for drinks to celebrate. So Logan was even drunker than usual. He kept ringing the doorbell over and over because he lost his key. When I opened the door, I asked him how he misplaced his key, again, and that did it. He went crazy."

Evina's voice became higher and louder as she continued, now telling her story faster. "We were in the kitchen, and he shoved me so hard I fell backward over a chair and heard a crunch in my neck. I tried to stand up, and he came at me, yanked me to my feet, and hurled me against the wall. I slid down and crumbled into a defensive ball on the floor, and then he grabbed me by the T-shirt and pulled until he'd ripped it right off me. He was screaming in fury, his face just inches from mine. Calling me worthless, disgusting trash. And he had the same look in his eyes as when he'd beaten me six months earlier. Back then he'd been drunk and angry, just like this, and he started punching me, really punching me hard, with his fists. On my chest, my neck, my head, my face. Again and again and again. I barely survived that time."

Evina looked at the jury box. "So I knew what was about to happen. He was going to kill me this time. So when he turned away for a moment, I grabbed a kitchen knife and plunged it into his back. Next thing I knew, I was lying over his crumpled body, desperately trying to save his life by holding towels firmly over the wound to stop the bleeding."

Megan watched in support as Evina detailed how, after it was clear he had died, she summoned all her remaining strength and dragged his body into their car, drove thirty miles, and dumped him into a ditch. "I don't know what I thought was going to happen then," she testified. "I had no plan. I was terrified. Then his body was found the next day and he still had his wallet with his ID in his pocket. I had crossed state lines, so this was a federal crime, and law enforcement came right for me, seized the car, searched the house, found the knife. But this was no premeditated murder. I swear. This was a frantic effort to survive when he was intent on killing me."

Megan scanned the jury again, praying they interpreted the entire scene as a desperate act of self-defense, a last resort of a woman who saw no other way out. Megan thought Evina had been convincing, very credible and sincere. But the faces of most of the jury members looked stoic. Even the dark-haired woman's face revealed nothing. One elderly woman began to subtly shake her head with incredulity for just a second. Long enough for Megan to start shivering in panic.

The prosecution team argued Evina hadn't acted in self-defense because she stabbed him in the back, and she showed "consciousness of guilt" by trying to dispose of the body. They asserted that if she really had been abused for all those years, she could have just left. Then his family testified that she was lying about him ever hurting her, that Evina was a manipulative, dishonest woman who falsely accused him of domestic violence and then brutally murdered him.

When the guilty verdict was read and Megan watched Evina collapse onto the floor in anguished sobs, she wanted to rush to her friend and comfort her. But to the court, Evina was now a convicted murderer. As distraught tears streamed down her own cheeks, Megan watched her best friend escorted through a side door in handcuffs.

For the past eight years, Megan lived through various appeals, hoping one would be the legal answer for which they yearned. As each court coldly rejected their attempts at overturning the conviction, Megan visited Evina in prison every Tuesday, making the two-hour drive no matter what was happening in her life, regardless of the weather or other potential commitments. And Evina made it clear that, besides her lawyer, no one else was visiting her.

Even though Megan saw Evina every week, on this visit following the latest, and supposedly final, legal setback, Megan was still jolted by the sight of her friend who seemed to have recently aged another decade and now appeared to be well into her forties. She looked shapeless in a cement-colored prison jumpsuit. Her dark hair was streaked with gray, and the skin around her eyes was deeply creased.

They sat across from each other in a large, open room with rows of dark wood tables, each with a short partition separating visitors from the inmates they were there to see. At five different locations throughout the visiting area, signs with bold-faced type displayed a list of rules, such as that feet had to always remain on the ground, open-mouthed kissing was not allowed, and only one short embrace would be permitted during each visit, either upon arrival or departure.

"I know," Evina said, closing her eyes and shaking her head. "I already know."

"I'm so sorry," was all Megan could come up with at first, not sure what real comfort she could provide now that Evina's last legal option was obliterated.

"I can't live like this any longer," Evina said in a voice so quiet that it sent a shudder through Megan's chest and neck. She clearly remembered one of their conversations from several years earlier, when Evina had first told her about some of the worst aspects of incarcerated life.

"The people here . . ." Evina had started to say, before trailing off.

Because of Evina's murder conviction, she had been put into a unit with other women who were deemed to be the most dangerous and potentially violent. Evina had talked with Megan about her constant fear that she would be the target of physical violence by another inmate. Evina's prison life had been a near-constant series of harassment and desperate attempts to maintain a low profile and avoid anything that could be remotely seen as seeking a conflict with anyone else.

"Are inmates threatening you? Hurting you?"

"It's not just them. It's some of these correction officers too. They treat us like their property. They touch us whenever they have the opportunity. Wherever they want. Because they're in charge."

"You need to report that," she had advised.

"It's not the type of thing you can report. I'm at their mercy twenty-four seven. The consequences of reporting would be even worse," Evina had said, staring at one particularly intimidating-looking correction officer near the far wall.

I can't live like this any longer. As Megan continued to contemplate those words, for a little while Evina seemed to want to say something but didn't. Megan stayed silent. Finally, Evina looked back at her friend. "I have one option left, and it's the longest of long shots. I've exhausted all possible appeals. But I can apply for clemency."

"From who?" Megan asked. "The governor?"

"No, it's a federal crime, so only the president can grant that. My lawyer submitted the paperwork two months ago. It's based on the fact that I'm a domestic violence survivor unfairly sentenced to decades in prison for defending myself."

"How does the process work?" Megan asked. It sounded like an impossible leap to get the most powerful person on the planet to care about Evina's plight.

"I need to get the support of someone who has the ear of the president. I'm not asking for an exoneration or even a pardon. After eight years in hell, I'm just trying to get my sentence commuted. But you need to first have someone powerful care about your case. I've written to everyone. Politicians, reporters, bloggers. Even some celebrities who care about these issues. All ignored me. Unfortunately I don't have a Kardashian on my side..."

Megan nodded and tried to make sense of this angle. One person had the ability to instantly grant Evina her freedom. But that person, for them, felt impossibly out of reach.

"You're in politics now," Evina said. "Do you have a connection in Washington? Anything would be better than what I have now."

No one potentially helpful came to mind right away. Not even close. She was a local official with less than a year in office, so far in every way from the White House.

I can't live like this any longer, Evina had said. And Megan remembered once reading an online article about suicide by incarcerated individuals that explained that with no easy access to drugs, weapons, or individuals to assist, prisoners often had to resort to crude and painful methods to end their lives, and the thought of that terrified her.

She looked at her friend with sorrow and helplessness. She wanted to project strength, and hope, but her voice was full of inadequacy as she told Evina, "I can't think of anyone who might be helpful, but let me ask around. I don't even know where to start, but I'll do everything I can to figure something out."

A week later, Megan now sat outside the Washington, DC, office of her congressman, Aaron Montgomery, and scanned the photos that plastered the waiting room walls. Countless shots showed him smiling next to constituents or other politicians. Next to an American flag was an enormous shot of Congressman Montgomery shaking hands with the president.

They'd had an appointment in his Mountain Hill district office, but then delays with passing a continuing resolution to keep the government funded required all representatives to remain in the nation's capital instead of flying home for August recess. Rather than reschedule, she'd jumped on the next available flight.

She opened the large folder she kept stuffed with paperwork pertinent to Evina's case—news articles, trial transcripts, the Petition for Commutation of Sentence that Evina had filed with the US Department of Justice's Office of the Pardon Attorney. The top of the first page of DOJ's petition form prominently proclaimed *To The President of the United States*, and Megan wondered how many of those forms the president ever became aware of.

Just as she began to feel overwhelmed by the bleakness of her chances, Aaron Montgomery strode from his primary office flashing a warm smile. He was tall, early forties, and handsome, with his suit jacket off and his starched, white button-down shirt rolled up at the sleeves, projecting the image that he was hard at work.

"Megan," he gushed, extending his hand. "It's so great to see you again."

Aaron had held this seat for a decade, winning it during a special election in his thirties. When Megan ran for council as an underdog against some more seasoned local activists, she had met with Aaron and asked for his support. He hadn't endorsed her, but Megan sensed he had a favorable opinion of her because he remained neutral in the race, when his backing of one of the other candidates likely would have crushed her chances.

He'd also connected her with a former DC politico to run her campaign, and he privately offered her some advice that had been instrumental in her victory: "Have a winning message that galvanizes voters, and stick to it. People will try to throw you off your talking points, but don't let them. Just keep repeating your message."

It sounded a little superficial at the time, the type of oversimplistic politician-speak that she wanted to avoid. As Alan pointed out, she really wasn't a "stick to the talking points" type of person. But she decided to follow Aaron's advice.

She rallied people around the problems in the underfunded school district and the council's failure to address the perilous road conditions on Route 48. She kept pounding those issues, repeatedly and consistently, without getting sidetracked by anything else. And the strategy worked.

Megan rose and Aaron kissed her cheek, then placed a hand on her back as he led her toward another room, where a leather chair and an enormous oak desk radiated power and success. He then walked toward two olive-fabric chairs near a glass conference table, and they sat across from each other.

"First, I really want to apologize," he started.

"For what?"

"I didn't get to read any of the materials you sent over. And I meant to have a staffer review them and brief me, but that didn't end up happening either."

She nodded, taking in this unsatisfactory beginning. Megan needed to appear gracious, not exasperated and disappointed. Although if she was too amicable in her response, he might think this issue wasn't massively important. The true surprise was less that he hadn't perused Evina's documents, but that he had been so honest about his failure to do so.

"Besides the budget vote and MHU, this week has been jammed with a lot of constituent demands. Do you know the McGinnis family?"

"I don't think so."

"Oh, you should. Big supporters of mine and other candidates they like. Huge fundraisers. And between you and me, sometimes huge pains in the ass. But it's good to deliver for supporters like them when they ask for things, and today . . . they're asking for things. So I'm trying to help them." His eyes opened wide. "But not in a quid pro quo way, of course."

"Of course," she said with a wave, pretending that concept was ludicrous.

"The MHU stuff is consuming almost all my time today," he continued. "I'm sure it's the same with you. Constituent outrage and concerns, media requests, calls for resignations, everything. The allegations are so horrible. And of course very sad."

"Absolutely. Tragic."

"Right. Although that softball field video is also kind of funny in a messed-up way, you know?"

But she didn't find it amusing at all. And she didn't feel like feigning that she did. So when he chuckled, she just returned an ambiguous raise of her eyebrows in response.

"I can't believe the president hasn't resigned yet," she then replied. "The university president, I mean. Not the one down the block."

He smiled at her attempt at humor. "So tell me about this woman. Evina Jansen?"

She perked up a little at the fact that he got her name right.

"Yes, Evina Jansen." Megan had repeatedly rehearsed her elevator pitch, and now was the time to deliver. "She grew up with me in Mountain Hill. Extremely kind person. She ended up in a violent relationship with a terrible man who manipulated and brutally assaulted her for years. He even physically abused their infant daughter, all while threatening to kill Evina if she ever left him. She finally stabbed him in self-defense during one of his drunken attacks, and she was wrongly convicted of murder in federal court. She's served eight years in prison and she's barely surviving. Physically wasting away, extremely depressed. But she has decades left in her sentence.

I'm asking for your help because she's a true victim and she deserves ... she *needs* ... to have her sentence commuted by the president."

And this time, I am referring to the one down the street.

Aaron shook his head slowly. "Just when you think Rob Dempsey is the worst human being you're going to hear about today..."

"Evina's final appeal was denied. Now her lawyer's filed this clemency petition, but we're afraid it's not going to go anywhere. She's reached out to various people and organizations who help with this type of thing, but she's gotten no traction. No assistance. She's doing very badly now. She's suicidal. If there's anything you can do to get this on the president's radar..."

He scratched his chin as he considered her plea. "Commutations are popular these days. It's not like a decade ago when people wanted everyone locked up. And this one does check a lot of boxes." He extended one finger after another as he listed the assets of Evina's situation. "Female. Mother. Abuse victim. Already served a significant sentence. I assume she's been a model inmate..."

His phrasing seemed crass. Too clinical and calculating and cold. But if that's how she earned his support, it was fine for him to prioritize the political angles and benefits along the way. After all, didn't she phrase her plea in a manner to appeal to such interests? The whole thing was unsavory—perpetuating the concept that if you know the right person, you can escape incarceration while those without connections languish for decades. But she couldn't change the system, certainly not now, and it wasn't like she was some huge power broker anyway. She was just a woman with a plan to try to help her friend who was experiencing severe injustice.

"That's the current political reality," Aaron continued. "The hot topics are women's issues and freeing the unjustly imprisoned. When I was first elected, these things were barely talked about. But if you want to be successful in politics today, you need to be seen as supporting those issues. And you need to have your finger on the pulse of how fast the world is changing. There's a new reality for everything that you must understand if you're going to go anywhere."

"I'm not sure what you mean."

"Well, for example, while old-school politics was about crafting a strong apology if you got caught doing . . . whatever . . . modern politics is about never apologizing, never admitting mistakes, never looking weak. Instead, you double down and show strength or they'll tear you apart."

Megan nodded. But as much as she appreciated the political guidance, she was determined to keep the focus on Evina. "I think presidential clemency for Evina Jansen would be extremely helpful," she asserted, in her mind thinking *helpful for Evina*, but knowing full well that it would be largely heard by the congressman as *helpful for you*.

"This might be your lucky day, Megan. The president needs my vote on this budget very badly. It's going to be extremely close. I think I can horse-trade a little and maybe get this done."

She was stunned into momentary silence, terrified to embrace the momentous possibility of this statement. Then she succumbed and allowed the warm rush of hope to surge through her being.

"That would be extraordinary."

"Do you think . . ."

"Think what?" she asked.

"Do you think she'd be okay doing a media appearance with me after? After her release?"

"Absolutely. I'll make sure of it," Megan quickly promised, despite having no idea whether Evina would be comfortable with that. Now wasn't the time to haggle over details. If the president commuted Evina's sentence and she declined to speak with the news media afterward and give Aaron his sought-after positive exposure, Megan would deal with the consequences of her unfulfilled promise at that time.

Aaron rose, so she stood too. Was the meeting already over? "I have to get back to the budget negotiations and the MHU fallout," he said. "But my staff and I will promptly review everything you sent. This sounds like quite an unfair situation, so I'm happy to help. You know I don't back down once I put myself out there, and I'll fight for this. Tell Evina Jansen that as long as I'm her congressman, I'll fight for her."

"Thank you so much," she replied. "If you can do this, we'd both be eternally grateful."

And no matter what his motives, she felt this last sentence of hope and appreciation deep in her gut because it was unequivocally true.

4
Serena

SHE KNEW THEY WANTED to fire her. Hell, they might even want to kill her. And they certainly would do one or both of those things if they thought they could get away with it. But for now the two men just seethed and stared during breaks from their berating.

Serena generally disliked confrontation, but unfortunately couldn't escape it now. Having all this unmitigated animosity directed at her was greatly unsettling, and they knew that. As she stood in the center of the room, her stomach rumbled, her head started to pound, and she tried to figure out if she really needed to use the restroom again, or if the sensation was just a function of nerves.

"Why didn't you pick up the fucking phone?!" shrieked university president Carey Westbrook as he paced in front of his desk. His moon face was even more crimson than usual. "Or just come to my office! You should have let me know what you found before you charged onto the damn softball field like a fucking lunatic. I got you this job, supported you all these years, and now you use it to completely fuck me over! My God, what you've done . . ."

Carey was sweating, taking deep breaths, clearly in full panic mode. General Counsel Tim Durso stood nearby, calmer, resigned. Only minutes earlier he too had ranted, but now he silently took deep breaths. Maybe with forty years on the job, he'd saved enough for retirement. Possibly with the death of his career in sight, he was moving quickly through the stages of grief and had already made it to acceptance.

Then there was the fourth person in the president's office, Drew Kosick. Because he'd been on the field when Serena blew up all their lives two days earlier, he'd been invited to this soiree. But so far he'd been more or less mute as he observed from a corner of the office.

"What would you have done if I'd come to you?" Serena challenged.

Carey stopped pacing and shook his head in disbelief as he spoke with arms flailing. "I can sure as hell tell you what I *wouldn't* have done! I wouldn't have launched this shit into the world with a viral video! We would have *talked* about it. We would have looked into the alleged misconduct and figured out the truth!"

Serena focused on the sweat stains around the neck of Carey's blue dress shirt. He was a nationally prominent university leader who was reportedly on the short list for a presidential appointment to head the National Endowment for the Humanities. A potential stepping stone to an actual cabinet post. Her actions had likely ended all that.

Serena kept her voice steady and looked straight at him. "My understanding is that you already knew everything I knew. It appears you were aware of the repeated allegations, the botched investigations, the settlements, the NDAs, all of it. I'm the HR director, and you hid all this from me for years! So I didn't see any point in going through the chain of command."

"Okay, let's all stay focused," Tim interjected. "At this point, we need to come together with one voice. One plan. Right away, we need to announce we're launching a comprehensive investigation. Obviously, I can't be the one to oversee it, and Serena, neither can you. So it's going to be led by Drew. Serena, we want you to sign off on that immediately. Let's get out in front of this whole mess."

Serena looked at Drew, who glanced away, then down at his

scuffed brown shoes. She turned back to Carey and Tim. These were desperate men. The board of trustees and the governor would probably call for Carey's resignation by sundown. And Ali Tyrell, whose father's call had spurred Serena to act, had announced a press conference with the other Coach Rob survivors for later that week. Carey and Tim issuing a statement that they took these allegations seriously and supported an investigation would be publicly viewed as a highly inadequate attempt to salvage their jobs and reputations. Even if Serena, as the female whistleblower/HR director, endorsed their plan. Which she wouldn't.

She shook her head. "No. And no offense, Drew, but it has to be independent. An outside firm, with excellent credentials and subject matter experience. No ties to the university. Unfettered access to whatever information and witnesses they request. That's the only way, if you want to save yourselves."

Which, she knew, it actually wouldn't. But it was the correct thing to do. And there was no way they could ever, would ever agree to that, because such an investigation would reveal overwhelming evidence that Rob Dempsey sexually assaulted girls at this school for years, and that Carey and Tim both knew about it, and failed to act.

Correction: They acted.

They acted to cover it up, to cover *him*, because they knew it might greatly harm the university's reputation if people knew what he'd done. They trusted him to start behaving, to have learned his lesson. But after the third allegation? The fourth? The fifth? All these settlements, all the NDAs. They were both complicit, and any competent, independent investigation would show that. It was all unavoidable. She had set things on an inevitable path to the truth coming out. Then there would be the civil litigation exposure, and the possible arrests of university officials on criminal charges.

"Serena, you owe us this," Carey insisted. "After the damage you caused to this institution. You say 'independent' as if it implies some objective third party coming down from the heavens. But in reality we'd end up with some ambitious outsiders constantly widening the scope and digging for as much embarrassment as they can. They'd look at us like targets for their trophy case while billing millions of dollars. You know Drew, you trust Drew. That's why you went to him. You need to sign off on this plan with us, then we'll issue the public statement immediately. That's my decision as university president, and you have to respect and support that."

But she knew that by the next morning Carey Westbrook would no longer hold that title. The board of trustees would appoint an interim president, as she had seen done at other institutions following much smaller scandals. And while current leadership no doubt wanted to hide the truth, it was textbook crisis management 101 for a *new* leader to demand a truly independent inquiry because they could be unafraid of the consequences while projecting transparency. For them, an independent investigation meant having someone else do the really hard work without the new president needing to take blame for anything that was uncovered from before their watch.

So she was being threatened by a corpse, who she felt confident would maintain little or no power to haunt her from the grave.

Inside her tote bag on the floor, Serena's phone began buzzing for what must have been the third or fourth time since the start of the meeting. She wondered if it was her daughter Kayla, who Serena had asked a few days ago to help find a sexual misconduct speaker for new student orientation. But unless it was an emergency, Kayla would most likely text, not call.

Serena reached down, grabbed her phone, and looked at the screen. *No Caller ID.*

"It's my daughter," she lied. "I need to take this. And again, the answer's no."

She quickly headed out the door with the phone pressed to her ear.

"Serena Stanfield," she said, bounding down the steps and out onto the college green.

The caller quickly explained that she was an athletic director from a university in Colorado. She sounded relieved that Serena had answered.

"I'm so sorry to keep calling," the woman said, "but I need to speak with you immediately."

"About what?"

"Cole Malinowski. MHU's assistant softball coach. We're set to hire him as our head coach. To oversee our teams, our camps, everything. We interviewed him three times and conducted an exhaustive background check, including speaking with his direct supervisor."

"Supervisor? You mean Rob Dempsey?"

"Yes," the woman replied meekly. "That was before any of this came out. We were planning to announce Cole's hiring tomorrow, but now we're concerned about going forward. I'm calling to ask if there's anything we should know before we finalize his hire. I haven't seen him mentioned in any of the news coverage. Is he allegedly involved in any of the misconduct?"

Serena had to be careful. Was this really an athletic director on the other end of the line? It was nearly impossible to know who to trust. And while she didn't want to malign their assistant coach without evidence, she also wouldn't help him take a new position of authority over women and girls, when odds were he either knew about Dempsey's actions or was negligent in his failure to perceive them and intervene.

"I can't reveal confidential information," she replied, as she entered her own building and began walking up the stairs. All the stress and physical exertion made her breathing labored as she continued. "But there's going to be an independent investigation to look into the softball program and beyond. My recommendation is to hold off until that investigation is completed."

Despite what the current president had said, an independent inquiry was destined to be required. And she wasn't going to be complicit in the typical "pass-the-trash" antics in which one institution quietly allowed or even encouraged another to retain their worst offenders.

"How long will that investigation take?" the athletic director asked. Serena pictured the woman's face, tense and anxious. "I'm not sure we can wait. Our president wants the position filled, like yesterday."

"There's no way to know," Serena answered, and then tried to end the call. "But we're literally in the middle of a firestorm here, so I need to—"

"Can I ask which firm will be investigating?" the woman interrupted. "My bosses are going to ask."

She was back in her office, entering and closing the door behind her and collapsing into her chair as she reached for a bottle of water on her desk. "I'm sorry, but I can't provide that information. The university will publicly announce the name of the investigative firm at the appropriate time. Hopefully soon."

5
Troy

"I NEED YOU, Troy. Get in here," Julia said as she grabbed his arm and yanked him into the windowless lactation room off the hallway of offices and suites. Human resources had created the space ostensibly as a show of support for their employees balancing career and family. But the female associates were young and not yet having children, while the managing directors were all male, so the room was never used for that designed purpose.

During Troy's orientation tour almost three years earlier, Julia had pointed to the room with the comfortable-looking blue sofa, a wood table with a small green melancholy plant, and a painting of a duck on the opposite wall. "This is where the associates cry by themselves when they can't take this place anymore," she had noted matter-of-factly, and kept moving down the hall.

Now she pulled him in and closed the door, so they were suddenly alone in this small space. "I thought we were just friends now," he said, lightly referencing the ridiculous idea of them hooking up there in the middle of the day.

"I don't have time for silly banter," Julia replied quickly. "Rain check."

"I don't either. I have to talk to Anderson immediately about this Spanish research."

"Did the sub get back to you?"

"Yeah, he sent me his preliminary findings this morning," he answered. There had been no instant response to his email. But the 3:00 a.m. phone call had connected him with the guy, who said he would commence research on Bianca Velencoso immediately and provide an update within the next two days. "But nothing helpful. She's a young model, doing young modeling things. A lot of work as an extra. Career highlight seems to be two lines of dialogue on a *Money Heist* episode. Caleb's gonna freak out."

"I've worked on a few matters for him," she said. "Freak out, he does."

"This is my first. Maybe this time he'll fire the firm. And I'll be blamed. I need to talk to Anderson. How about I find you afterward and you can tell me whatever's going on?"

He wanted to stay out of trouble, survive each day, and keep this job. His best moments were when he was just alone in his cubicle, conducting database research and writing reports, not having to interact with any of his arrogant and dysfunctional supervisors.

Sometimes he would have to tag along to second seat witness interviews, typing on his laptop the various questions and answers posed by a managing director, and then writing up interview summaries and reports for clients. Other associates resented that they were never able to conduct such interviews themselves, but Troy had no such complaints. Too much could go wrong, and at this point in his tenuous tenure, it just wasn't worth the risk.

He turned to grab the door handle, but Julia seized his arm again.

"I need your help. It can't wait."

"All right. Quickly."

"You know how I was a college intern on Capitol Hill?" she started to explain.

"Yeah."

"I worked for my local congressman, Aaron Montgomery. My

parents are tight with him. Big financial backers of his campaigns ever since he was in the state legislature."

"Never heard of him."

"He's kind of a backbencher. But my parents think he's the shit. They say he's going to be governor one day. Yesterday he resigned his congressional seat to become interim president of Mountain Hill University."

"Tough time to be taking over that place. The softball coach stuff alone will be a nightmare."

She nodded and then started talking with increased urgency. "Right, so he's putting out an RFP for a firm to do a large-scale independent investigation of the coach's conduct and any cover-ups and failures to respond appropriately by campus officials. Lot of pressure from some elected leaders and the board of trustees to get this started ASAP. Interviewing everyone who's ever been in that softball program. Going back years. All staff. All administrators. Comprehensive report. We're talking hundreds of interviews. RFP responses are due in five days."

At this point Troy was only half listening. With every minute his anxiety about delivering bad news to Anderson escalated. "Okay," he said, "but we have no quals in that area. We're not getting it."

"Listen. Montgomery wants to show my parents he's delivered for them in a big way before he declares for statewide office."

"Like awarding this investigation to their daughter's firm?"

"Exactly. He and his staff know the history of the C&R name, and in a lot of places that's still very powerful because, thankfully, they don't know how fucked up things actually are here. My parents already heard from his chief of staff, and she wants to set up a meeting. They want our team to fly out there tomorrow, and they're asking which MDs are going to lead it. I have this great connection, but of course as a twenty-seven-year-old associate, I don't have the stature to bring in a high-profile, complicated sexual misconduct investigation. I need to involve one of the MDs. But I know whichever one I tell—"

"Yep."

"—will just totally fuck me over."

Troy had seen it before, although not on such a potentially massive scale. Associates generally didn't bring in business. That was the role of the MDs. Associates wrote the proposals, conducted the research, then drafted and compiled whatever documents were needed. They were judged on how many hours they billed and how well they were utilized. Their value basically came down to that number.

The associates were young, unestablished, and not connected to big-time players as the older managing directors were, so they rarely got origination credit or any of the big money that came with it. Managing directors did. Meanwhile, this project could be enormous, just as the firm was in a tailspin, when a large piece of revenue could instantly turn someone from the next to be laid off into a C&R hero.

"Not sure how I can help," Troy said.

"How do I bring it in without those assholes stealing all the origination credit?"

"Let me think about it."

"No time. Has to happen now."

Troy very much wanted to help her. For multiple reasons he yearned to come through for Julia in a huge way, to demonstrate his gratitude, his support, his regret. But he also had his own career predicament to confront.

"I need to see Anderson about Caleb Lugo. Come with me," he suggested. "Maybe he can help."

She shook her head, and her face contorted in disgust. "You know what he did to Emma?"

"Not all the details, just that he had Tara from HR give her a PIP she didn't deserve. Very on-brand for him. I really don't know what to say. They're all vultures. They're all desperate."

She looked at the painting, and Troy wondered if she was trying to find some wisdom from the simple image of the duck floating contentedly on a lake, the reflection of the sun aglow around it. After a long pause she turned back to him. "Okay. Let's go see your vulture."

He followed her along the gray carpet and past the cream-colored walls dotted with photos of the firm's founders, Brandon Crawford and Anthony Roberts. The two men had years ago sold off their ownership for hundreds of millions to a parent company that soon flipped the venerated firm to another parent company that flipped it to another. The most recent owner was supposedly heading into bankruptcy, hoping to unload the company to private equity firm DePalma Capital Partners. Nevertheless, C&R was still a respected name in the industry, and as with the Roman Empire shortly before it fell, the firm continued to carry a lot of cachet in certain circles.

They passed a couple of burly guys from the Security Risk Management team, then arrived outside Anderson's office, a large space with a grand window that faced the Chrysler Building. The MD offices all had one glass wall facing the hallway that was transparent enough to reveal how many people were inside but opaque enough to obscure their identities. Two shapes were standing in the office, and the movement of their arms revealed an animated conversation.

Just before Troy could knock on the door, he heard a semi-hushed, annoyed male voice. "*You* don't get to decide who inherits his clients. That's bullshit."

Then he heard Anderson respond, "I'm dividing them fairly. He barely had any clients anyway. We should have RIF'd him a long time ago."

"But you're still not making the call on all of them. No fucking way."

Troy turned toward where Anderson's assistant was usually

parked across from the office, but the chair was empty. Before he could decide what to do next, Julia reached across him and knocked on the door. The conversation inside went silent, then there were footsteps, and Anderson opened the door.

"I'm sorry to interrupt," Troy said, "but I need to talk to you about the research in Spain."

"Okay," Anderson responded. "Come in."

He and Julia entered the office and saw the desk adorned with photos of Anderson's grandchildren and other relatives. Luke Holloway, a managing director three decades younger than Anderson, stood looking perturbed in a gray suit, his eyes staring intensely at Anderson from behind black-framed glasses, his blond hair a little askew. Anderson closed the door behind them.

On the wall across from the desk, a mounted, muted flat screen showed a national news network covering a press conference with a crowd of people standing behind a microphone on what looked like the lawn of a college campus. A dark-haired woman in her twenties spoke emphatically and tearfully, as the chyron below read *Ali Tyrell and "Uncle Rob" Survivors Hold Press Conference*.

Luke didn't acknowledge Troy and Julia, but kept his eyes on Anderson. "We need to finish our conversation."

"Give me a minute," Anderson said. "This is urgent. For Caleb Lugo." Then he turned to Troy. "What did we find?"

Troy shook his head. "Nothing adverse so far. She's an actress. Does some modeling. Bit parts here and there on TV."

He braced for Anderson's response. His moods were like a pendulum, able to swing from kind and ingratiating to rude and insulting in a second, depending on the issue and sometimes seemingly dependent on nothing at all. Everyone in the room knew it, and the air sat thick as they all waited to see which Anderson they were going to hear from.

This research assignment wasn't just a "check the box" task. It was far more than pre-transactional due diligence that the client needed to be able to cite for regulatory compliance, the kind of investigation that made the client happy when it uncovered nothing. In this case, failure to dig up helpful information would likely be viewed by Caleb, and therefore Anderson, as a cataclysmic failure.

But Anderson simply nodded quietly, appearing only slightly disappointed. "Okay, have our sub keep digging. We have enough on her to satisfy Caleb for the moment."

Troy looked from Anderson to Julia and back to Anderson. "We do? What do we have?"

"Emma came up with some good intel," he said cryptically.

Troy wanted more information, but Anderson's impatient gaze made clear that this part of the conversation was over. "Okay, understood," Troy said, though he didn't understand at all. When had Emma been assigned to this project and why? Usually anyone conducting research at C&R knew who else was involved so they could be most efficient and not overlap their efforts. This was strange.

Troy looked again at Julia, and only then did Anderson seem to notice she was in the room.

"Can I help you?" he snapped.

Julia glanced at the television and then at Troy. She didn't appear to be seeking Troy's assurance or guidance but instead was silently communicating, *Coming here was your idea, so if this blows up in my face I'm blaming you.*

"I have a strong lead for getting C&R the Mountain Hill University investigation," Julia announced.

Anderson looked surprised, then skeptical. For a few seconds he didn't speak as he pursed his lips in contemplation. "Okay, let's talk," he said. "Luke, Troy, give us the room."

Troy turned to the door, but Luke didn't move. He then shook his head instead. "I'll join you for this conversation, Anderson."

"I'll update you after."

Then they were all silent, motionless, all four of them standing in place. On the muted television screen, the woman appeared to speak vociferously as people around her gestured and shouted. Troy had never seen Anderson's authority challenged like this, and he anticipated a volcanic response. But Anderson just turned to Julia and commanded, "Tell me what the story is."

Troy wasn't sure if he should leave, but Anderson was no longer asking for that, and he sensed Julia would want his moral support. Maybe Anderson now preferred he stay, since he was a potential extra hand to quickly draft proposal materials and arrange logistics. Not a threat to seek origination credit as Luke surely would.

"I worked for the congressman who just became MHU president," Julia explained, with a glance toward the television screen. "My family's very close to him. The university's issuing an RFP that's due in five days, and I was told C&R has been invited to submit, that we might even have the inside track with the right team. The RFP is being run by some guy in their legal department, Drew Kosick. All communication is supposed to go through him, and any other contact with university personnel is prohibited, technically. But the new president's chief of staff wants to set up a meeting with our team and the president."

Anderson's eyebrows shot up. "When?"

"Tomorrow afternoon."

Troy knew what Anderson was thinking. Multimillion-dollar assignment, just when MDs were being laid off left and right, just as the firm was desperately trying to show strong revenue for a sale to DePalma Capital Partners. Luke might be an asset here, as he had a lot of experience with RFPs, but if his enhancements provided the firm with a 20 percent greater chance of winning the project in return for a 50 percent share of the origination credit, basic mathematics told Anderson not to involve his fellow MD. Better to build a team on his own, keep it close to the vest, and involve junior associates for all the legwork.

But Luke was still in the room, certainly not leaving now, not when this huge steak was hanging in front of them to salivate over.

"So," Julia continued, "obviously this isn't about who gets the credit. It's about the firm. We're a team. It's about helping the client. Through a terrible situation."

God bless her, Troy thought. *She's just going to come out and fucking say it.* She had a confidence and directness unlike any other associate.

Meanwhile, Anderson and Luke stared at her, waiting to hear what she would utter next. No need to offer a perfunctory "of course" in response to her prelude of platitudes. They were too far in their careers for that, too desperate to seize this opportunity.

"But I'd like to understand how origination credit would work," Julia added, and then flashed an amicable smile, appearing to try and take the edge off any tension that might result from her remarks, but also letting them both know that, unlike other C&R associates, she wasn't afraid of them. Especially not while she was holding this gorilla of a business opportunity.

Anderson didn't delay, and uncharacteristically didn't show any offense. "Julia, I'm glad you brought that up. Obviously, I'll make sure you're *very* much recognized for this opportunity. If this investigation comes in, that will be reflected in your year-end bonus, and I'm sure you'll receive an appropriate salary increase."

"Can you be more specific?" Julia pressed. "I'm concerned my contribution may be lost in the shuffle, because the project will obviously be *so large* and intense and all-consuming. I've seen stuff like that happen. Although I'm sure it's never intentional."

Anderson displayed compassion and support, although Troy doubted he felt either. "Any specific compensation has to go through Tara from HR and get sign-off from our regional business head, but I understand your point. If we get this assignment, I'll start that process right away."

Troy watched Julia nod and he wondered how she would respond. It was a vague, unenforceable promise, just like so many others that had never come to fruition. Yet Troy felt she had no choice but to agree and hope Anderson would actually follow through.

"I completely understand that you need approvals before promising me anything specific," she said.

"Thank you, Julia."

"So why don't you let me know when you have those approvals, and then I'll connect you with the university president for this multimillion-dollar engagement."

Troy's mouth dropped open, and he had to clutch his jaw to make sure it wasn't actually hitting the floor. Luke's body stiffened in surprise at Julia's insubordination and then he displayed the subtlest of grins.

Anderson was having none of this, as he walked closer to Julia, glared, and pointed a finger in her face. "I'd like to know what fucked-up logic is telling you it's a smart move to threaten me. Because I'm pretty sure that was the dumbest fucking thing you've ever said in your life!"

Troy sensed Anderson wanted to strangle her, and there was a nonzero chance he actually would try. "I'm sure she didn't mean it that way," Troy said in hopes of defusing the situation.

"I'm not making a threat," Julia explained. "I'm just saying I have a great opportunity for the firm, and I want to make sure I'm not ignored when the origination credit is assigned."

"I told you I'd look into your compensation if we're retained."

"And I'm sorry, but I don't feel comfortable connecting the firm with the MHU president unless there's something more solid."

"Comfortable? You don't feel *comfortable*?!" Anderson paused and took a breath, but it did nothing to calm him. "I've gotten rid of many associates for far less than this shit you're trying to pull. So listen to me carefully. You think I won't terminate you because of this big lead you supposedly have. And for now, you're correct. But if you don't *immediately* do everything in your power to get us this investigation, I'll fire you for cause today."

Julia stood there in silence, not moving, looking back at Anderson and refusing to blink.

"She'll help," Troy asserted. "We'll both get to work on it now."

"Is that right?" Anderson asked Julia. "Because this lead is now the only thing keeping you employed. If it doesn't work out, with or without your assistance, then you're fucking gone."

She remained quiet and stood up straighter, her body language showing she wanted to hold firm as Troy implored her with his own intense stare to capitulate. Finally, she did.

"I'll help."

"Smart decision," Anderson replied. "Now give me five minutes to clear my schedule. Then let's all meet in conference room B and figure out how we're going to get this thing. I've already been speaking with Gillian Fenton from the Brooklyn DA about joining C&R. Her background would be perfect for our proposal."

Seconds later Troy and Julia were walking toward the conference room. "That was a *horrible* idea to go to him," she whispered accusingly.

"That was a horrible idea to *say that* to him."

"They're going to bill millions on this. I'm not going to let him take it all from me. I'm just not."

"But how? What can you do?"

For now, Julia just shrugged as they passed the lactation room and kept moving down the hallway.

6
Megan

Two hours after leaving her congressman's office, Megan had stood in the security line at Reagan National Airport and felt her phone buzz in her bag. She looked at the screen and saw it was Evina calling from prison. Megan was cutting it close to her flight time, but she had to answer. She knew from past experience that Evina could only call when the one phone on her unit was free, and it might be a while before she had another opportunity.

"Hello, this is a prepaid call from Evina Jansen, an inmate at the Fox Lake Correctional Institution," the all-too-familiar computerized voice began. "This call is subject to monitoring and recording. To accept charges, press 1."

Megan quickly pressed 1. "Hi, Evina. Can you hear me?"

"Yes, Megan. How did it go?" Evina's voice sounded higher than usual on the crackly recorded jail line. Megan imagined her biting her nails down as she waited for news.

"He said he'll help. I think he means it."

"Wow," Evina gushed. Then for a few seconds she went silent, and Megan just heard the usual background noise of the prison's staticky connection. When Evina spoke again, her voice trembled. "That's, that's incredible."

Right away Megan feared she'd jumped the gun. Maybe she should have worded the news differently, dialed back the expectations. She couldn't bear the idea of setting up Evina to be crushed again, and she feared what another dead end might do to her dear friend.

"But please understand," Megan said as boarding announcements blared in the background and a double stroller with two toddlers nearly collided into her. "I don't know him well. I can't be sure he'll follow through. I'll keep pushing, but getting the White House to seriously consider this request, having the president grant clemency . . . those are heavy lifts, even for a congressman."

"But he said he'd help?" Evina was hooked. She was hopeful. Megan decided to just let it be, to allow her friend some happiness.

"He did." That was true. Megan closed her eyes and tried to will Aaron Montgomery into following through.

"*Thank you*, Megan," Evina said, in a tearful whisper. "And please send my appreciation to Congressman Montgomery. I'm so thankful he's trying to help."

The next evening, Megan attended a heated city council meeting about the earthshaking university revelations. Seven city council members sat around the large horseshoe-shaped table at the front of the room, with the great seal of the City of Mountain Hill hanging above the gray-bearded city council speaker who presided from the middle, directly facing the audience. Megan sat at one end of the horseshoe because she was the council member with the least seniority.

The university president had resigned earlier that day, and various members of the community waited in line behind a tall microphone stand for their opportunity to voice their opinions about this crisis. The first few speakers focused on the horrific nature of the allegations and the heartbreaking abuse reportedly suffered by the girls in their university's summer softball program. Their impassioned comments were met with vociferous nods of agreement by the city council members and those in the audience.

But then the conversation topic morphed into what the university should do next to address these claims, and any semblance of unanimity was immediately fractured.

"I'm calling for the immediate appointment of an independent investigator who won't be under the control of university leadership," one woman who Megan recognized from the local historical society declared. "No one from the university can be trusted. The investigation needs to be completely independent."

From the eight long, dark brown wood rows where local residents and reporters sat, Megan heard a smattering of applause. But she also noted numerous people shaking their heads in robust disapproval.

Were they university employees? Family members of staff? Ripping the school apart for an intensive investigation would be very risky for them.

Who would be found responsible for knowing too much, or for knowing too little when they should have seen more? How many litigants would come out of the ground with salivating lawyers demanding seven-figure settlements, draining the school's endowment and treasury?

This could necessitate massive cost-cutting measures, termination of important educational programs, staff layoffs, reforms, restructuring. Savage tarnishing, maybe irrevocably, of the university's prestigious reputation that was the source of pride for so many Mountain Hill residents. And a potential catastrophe to the local economy that was so dependent for jobs, commerce, government grants, and much more from their beloved school and all its programs and activities.

What if it got so bad, the financial consequences so extreme, that the institution actually needed to fold? Unlikely, but not impossible. The potential carnage prohibited anyone associated with the school or this city from feeling secure.

Megan knew that those fears, that sense that addressing the allegations in a more discreet manner might be the safer route, had directly led to this monstrous situation festering for years. Resulted in so many girls, many of them now young women, being sexually abused because people were afraid of the extreme fallout that might result from doing the right thing.

"The lack of leadership over the past decade while this coach abused these girls is unconscionable!" the woman proclaimed. "The university can't be trusted to conduct its own investigation. It's essential that we have an objective review."

One of her fellow council members declared the investigation should be conducted by Dunaway & Horowitz, the law firm that had served the school for over two decades. But then another argued this was exactly why that firm should be disqualified, because they'd been paid by MHU for years and had a clear conflict of interest. "We need a major investigative firm, with years of experience and a reputation for impartiality. With no prior connection to the university."

Megan tried to concentrate on the various comments from constituents and council members, but as horrible as the MHU allegations were, her mind was primarily on Evina. After so many years, maybe she was finally on a real track toward freedom. Megan just couldn't focus on this debate about process—who should investigate, how should an investigator be chosen—which at times seemed to gloss past the real issue of widespread sexual misconduct on campus.

Just get someone good, she thought. *I don't care where they're from.*

She was exhausted from her travel to DC and consumed with Evina, so she hadn't really been focusing on the proceedings when one of the residents ended her short speech by musing, "So hopefully Aaron Montgomery won't let political and financial considerations derail what's best for the victims. Now that he's been named university president."

Megan froze upon hearing these words, and as she absorbed them she became overwhelmed with a panicked rage. Could this possibly be true? She seized her phone from her bag, her chest in knots. But before she could look online for confirmation, she saw the breaking news notification announcing his resignation from Congress that had been sent twenty-five minutes earlier.

She needed to stay at this meeting and appear engaged, but it took all her effort to remain fixed in her seat. She'd seen the unseemly side of politics before, but this was unbelievably cruel. Aaron had promised to use his congressional position to advance Evina's cause, and now suddenly he would no longer be a congressman.

Why hadn't he told her before resigning? Did he have a plan to assist from his new role? Almost surely not. With his resignation from Congress, he was taking on a new job, with daunting, highly controversial obstacles. And presumably leaving the old ones behind.

"Councilwoman Black, you've been relatively quiet this evening. What's your opinion?"

The question had come from the city council speaker, putting her on the spot when she hadn't been paying attention. Was this intentional? Regardless, the room fell quiet as everyone waited for her response. Her pulse quickened as she recognized she had no idea what had just been said, and tried to come up with a response that wouldn't reveal her ignorance.

"Let's give Aaron Montgomery a chance to formulate his plan," she said. "I think it would be disrespectful to tell him what to do before he's barely had a chance to take office."

A few seconds of silence followed, as council members and residents stared. Were they expecting her to say more? Had they seen through her attempt to appear poised and focused on the meeting and not reveal how truly rattled she was inside?

Thankfully the discussion then moved on to other attendees, and her mind went back to anxiously considering her next steps and how she should break the news to Evina. Or would Evina already know, from whatever news sources she was allowed in prison?

As deferential as her comment had just been toward Aaron, she was intent on using a starkly different tone once this meeting ended and she was free to call him and express how furious she was. When the council speaker finally announced that the evening's business was concluded, she dashed from her seat toward the exit, hoping to reach it before any citizen or reporter could intercept her.

She entered her car and, once safely inside, called Aaron Montgomery's cell number, which he had given her when they had first met a year earlier. She turned on the engine of her parked vehicle to initiate some air circulation on this humid night as she listened to four rings and then the beginning of his outgoing voicemail message.

"Aaron, it's Megan Black," she started quickly, knowing she had a lot to say and limited time before she reached the maximum voicemail length. "I need to speak with you. Tonight. You said you'd push for Evina Jansen's petition and then you resigned without even telling me! She's in *prison*, Aaron. She's an innocent woman who defended herself from an abusive husband. She's a real person. It's not right to make a promise like that and then leave us hanging. Is there someone else on the Hill who can lead the push for this? I don't care how busy you are with your new job, *I need to talk with you immediately.* Call me when you get this, no matter how late it is."

But he didn't call back, even when she left him another voicemail the following day. Megan was determined not to let Aaron's disingenuous promises permanently derail her efforts. She and Evina had faced setback after setback for years, and always pivoted to the next plan, never giving up. So she wasn't going to act as if Aaron was the only person who held a solution in his hands.

It was now two days after the council meeting, and the best strategy she could think of was to try to use her position as a council member to build public support for Evina's clemency petition. Maybe getting local attention and some positive news coverage could help galvanize people, and then she could work to have the issue picked up statewide, and then nationally.

So she had Aimee Guzman, the council's MHU undergrad communications intern, put out a press release announcing a media availability for that afternoon with the headline, *City Councilwoman Megan Black Calls for Presidential Commutation of Unjust Prison Sentence for Mountain Hill Domestic Violence Victim.*

Megan stood in front of the council's moveable podium on the steps of City Hall, with Aimee at her side. Aimee was looking down at her iPhone and furiously sending a few messages.

"*The Courier* just said they can't attend," she informed Megan, shaking her head as her fingers flashed across the keypad. "Sorry, I was hopeful about them being here."

Megan took this in, looking out at the street of pedestrians moving through the downtown, going about their business, none of them there to see her presser. So embarrassing to be standing there without an audience. Worse than embarrassing, since the cause was so grave. It was another deflating gut-punch and she felt like a failure. She should have asked local domestic violence groups to send attendees, or at least gotten her own family to show up, so she and Aimee wouldn't be alone.

"So no media's coming?" she asked the twenty-one-year-old for guidance. As young as Aimee was, Megan had quickly learned how savvy the intern could be with understanding the media. "We couldn't even get one local blogger?"

What about everything Aaron had said about women's issues and freeing people from incarceration being huge topics these days? Why wasn't that all working here?

"Sorry, no," Aimee replied. "They're all obsessed with the university scandal right now. That's all anyone cares about."

"We need to figure out how to make people care about *this* issue."

Aimee put her phone down on the podium and looked up at Megan. "I have a communications professor who says it's not about making people care about your issue. It's about connecting your issue to something people already care about. Rather than trying to get the media to cover your cause, you shape your cause into something the media's already covering."

Megan scratched two fingers across her right eyebrow as she considered Aimee's suggested strategy. "You're saying that because people care about the university scandal I need to tie Evina's situation to that?"

Aimee nodded. "Like, did she attend school there? If she's an alum, then—"

"She's not."

"Well, both situations involve victims of abuse. Maybe that's an angle."

"I just don't see a real connection," Megan said, feeling demoralized and ineffective. "I get what you're saying, but if we're going to link Evina's petition to the Rob Dempsey mess, we'll need more than that."

"My point is that all the media wants to cover right now is the university. Seems like everything else is being ignored," Aimee said. "So let's figure out how to connect Evina's case to MHU. Let's find a hook."

Megan couldn't immediately think of any "hook" as she looked out from the podium at the empty area reserved for local reporters. Now she had an interesting theory from an undergraduate professor without a practical application for the theory. But she appreciated Aimee's support, and right now Megan desperately needed her enthusiasm.

She also really needed to speak with Evina. They hadn't talked since Aaron's resignation, and she assumed Evina would be taking that hard, as was she. Megan had to get to the prison where she could look Evina in the eyes, and by then Megan would need to be armed with some convincing words of encouragement.

"Okay, let's keep thinking about a university angle," Megan instructed. "For now, let's get out of here."

"Do you want to make a media statement?" Aimee asked.

"To who?"

Aimee held up her phone. "I'll record it. We'll put it on social."

"It'll look pretty lame holding a media availability without any media."

"I'll frame it tight," Aimee explained. "No one will be able to tell."

7
Serena

"I've thought a lot about shooting this coach in the fucking head," Darren Tyrell said from across the conference room table, his chest rising beneath the charcoal-gray quarter-zip sweater that revealed a stark white T-shirt beneath. His eyes were intense and his large build intimidating, Serena thought. She couldn't tell if he was about to cry, as he had during his initial phone call to her, or explode in anger and tear the room apart. He stared at her and added, "Him and everybody else who let this happen to my girl."

His daughter Ali sat beside him, not saying a word. She'd spoken passionately during the news conference the previous day, but now she sat silent, looking despondent as her father expressed his outrage, his horror, his thirst for justice. Ali was in her mid-twenties, with short black hair and heavy eyes, still tightly wrapped in the denim jacket she'd been wearing when she arrived despite the August heat outside.

Serena wasn't surprised by Darren's outrage, but she was startled by his words. This was the language of a man who wasn't going to wait much longer for justice. Rob Dempsey had sexually assaulted his daughter, and he was finished with promises of action.

"That makes two of us," she said against her better judgment.

Serena instantly knew this response was potentially disastrous, so she quickly added, "But I won't, of course. And neither will you, right? We need you to give us a chance to get to the bottom of all this and help law enforcement hold him and others accountable."

This was why she had asked for this in-person meeting. It would take a little time to get the university's investigative firm in place, and she wanted to start building rapport and form positive connections with the sexual assault survivors. If Ali and the others didn't cooperate with the investigation, the full truth would never be revealed. Law enforcement would surely go after Rob Dempsey, but the horrible misdeeds of those who covered for him might stay buried. She was determined not to let that happen.

Darren looked into the distance, and then next to him at his daughter, who broke her silence. "My father called you without my approval. He wanted to report what happened to me, and I don't blame him for that. But I'm not sure I want to relive this trauma by speaking with some so-called investigator from the university. I don't know why I should give this school another chance," she said. "Why would I trust anyone here? When I was a camper, I trusted, and now I'm paying for it . . . every day."

"That's understandable," Serena responded supportively. "The university hasn't earned your trust. I'm working to change that. I want everything investigated completely so everyone—and I mean *everyone*—who allowed this to happen for years is held accountable."

Who was everyone? Certainly the former president, general counsel, and athletic director. Their culpability was already crystal clear, but others had to have known, such as assistant coach Cole Malinowski.

Serena looked at Ali, then at Darren. What could she say to convince them the university wanted the truth? "Ali, Darren," she said, "please give me a chance. I'm outraged by all of this. From the second I heard about the accusations, this has been all I've thought about."

Then she focused directly on Ali. "I'm going to fight to expose everything that was done to you and the others, to help you heal, and make sure nothing like it ever happens here again." Serena searched their faces for some recognition of what she'd just said, maybe a glint of belief or support. Nothing. So she added dryly, "I think it's fair to say my passion for the matter has gone pretty viral."

She was being praised in some circles as a whistleblower, the person who had finally revealed to the world the evils occurring on this campus. That crazy video had helped foster this image, showing an angry, sweaty, middle-aged woman berating a man for sexually assaulting vulnerable girls.

"Yes," Darren replied. "That's why we're both here, listening to what you have to say."

"We have a new president," she explained. "Soon we'll have a new general counsel and athletic director. The university's going to retain an outside, independent firm within days and give the investigators unfettered access to witnesses, documents, everything. They're going to coordinate with law enforcement, and they'll conduct their own expert investigation that'll be comprehensive, transparent, highly professional, and untainted."

"We'll see," Ali replied skeptically. "You know what happened to one of the other girls? She was fifteen, and she reported Coach Rob to some counselor here. She was told, 'Oh, you can file a formal complaint, but it's a really grueling, emotional process. Very taxing. You should give it a lot of thought because sometimes going through that can be extremely stressful and not worth it in the end.'" Serena grimaced. "She was *fifteen*! She didn't file a complaint. She started flunking all her classes. And she stopped playing softball, the game she loved and was really good at. And she's still dealing with the trauma from this place five years later. She has all sorts of addiction problems and I'm trying to help her."

Serena's mind was on fire with a desire to help this unnamed young woman, to add her to the growing list of people who deserved justice and healing. And who could help build a case against Rob Dempsey and the others. "What's her name?"

"She doesn't want me to reveal her name."

"Who's the counselor she spoke with?"

"I don't know."

This was exactly the daunting problem that was eating away at Serena every moment. Knowing that so many people ignored these girls' plights and yet continued their own lives and careers, unscarred and without repercussions.

"I have a meeting with one of the potential firms in a few minutes," she said. "We're going to vet a few and choose the strongest one. Then I hope you'll give them a chance. Not for the school but for everyone who's suffered and is still suffering."

Ali and her father stood without saying anything. Darren quickly shook Serena's hand while Ali headed for the door. Just before walking out of the room, she stopped and turned back to Serena with accusing eyes. "*If* I decide to talk to these investigators, and *if* I tell the others they should do the same, and then these investigators fail us, I'm going to let everyone know. *Everyone.* The media keeps asking for my reaction to the university's response, and I'll tell everyone who'll listen how this school failed us again. How *you* failed us." Then she turned and headed down the hall, followed by her father.

The last part was so personal, so direct and searing, Serena felt tears begin to burn her eyes. Her lungs were tight, and she tried to remain calm as she realized it had been a while since she'd taken a breath.

Twenty minutes later, Serena stood in a windowless conference room in the school's main administrative building. Paintings of former university presidents covered the walls. The wood table could seat ten comfortably, but right now there were just two men in the room.

Drew stood by the door, looking unusually professional in a suit and tie, and he faced the new university president, Aaron Montgomery. The former congressman was in his mid-forties and handsome in a choreographed way, with unusually white teeth and perfect hairline.

Drew glanced down at the phone he held and announced, "C&R is here. They're early."

"Bring them in," Aaron said with authority.

Drew nodded and walked out the door, leaving Serena alone with her new boss, whom she'd met only briefly that morning at a staff meeting. She forced a smile.

Both Serena and Aaron remained standing. He smiled back and said, "It's quite a coup to get senior people from a firm like this to fly out here on such short notice. The RFP you and Drew drafted looks great."

"Thank you. It seems like a few top firms are interested in submitting before the deadline."

Aaron pointed a finger toward the door. "They're the ones. You don't get a better name than C&R. Sends the right message to all our constituencies. Should get the city council to chill out a little. Let's meet them and then get this rolling."

"Well," she replied, "we obviously need more than a name. Justice for these young women . . . and our school's survival are both literally on the line."

How serious was this new president? Was he committed to the university conducting a comprehensive, transparent investigation, or was he just another administrator guided by the university's financial and political interests?

Serena couldn't read him. This politician from Washington, bailing from Congress to take an extremely well-compensated job back home with the aspiration of saving the local institution from existential crisis. He was already trying to do an end-around the RFP process, not a great sign. And she didn't love the idea of using a firm that specialized in corporate investigations, often involving complex financial, research, and cyber expertise. That was all high-profile and impressive, but not exactly aligned with investigating a softball coach who had—

There was a knock on the door, and Drew walked in, followed by two men and a woman, all dressed in expensive suits and trendy, immaculately shined shoes. They carried smooth, brown leather briefcases. These were clearly New Yorkers.

"Anderson Davis," said the oldest one as he reached out his right hand and greeted Serena first, then Aaron. He had the weathered face of a man in his early seventies. Serena guessed he was late in his career but still eager for the next challenge, or at least that's the vibe he successfully gave off.

Next to him stood a younger man, in his early forties probably, with an enthusiastic grin and ingratiating eyes peering out behind his glasses. "Luke Holloway," he announced as his hand clasped Serena's and then Aaron's.

Then the woman spoke. "I'm Gillian Fenton," she said to both Serena and Aaron at once and then shook their hands too. "It's great to meet you."

"Gillian is our proposed project leader," Anderson explained. "She just joined C&R after twenty-seven years prosecuting sex crimes in New York City. The last ten as chief of the division."

Gillian smiled modestly. "I'm very comfortable around a complex misconduct investigation or inside a courtroom, but I'm new to this corporate meeting thing. And I'm not used to giving presentations unless they start with 'Ladies and gentlemen of the jury,' so please excuse any faux pas."

Everyone responded with a little chuckle and Serena felt a sense of warmth flow over her. Suspicious as she was of new people, high-priced consultants in particular, she couldn't deny the visceral reaction she felt in Gillian's presence. She might be exactly what they needed—a tough but caring former sex crimes prosecutor who would be instinctively, skillfully, and passionately driven to help fix this place.

They all settled into chairs around the conference table, and the C&R team presented their proposal with a comprehensive PowerPoint slide deck on the room's large screen. For someone without business experience, Gillian provided a flawless game plan, covering potential investigative scopes, anticipated challenges, interview strategies, preliminary document requests, and estimated timelines. Then she explained how she would seamlessly coordinate the concurrent jurisdiction with law enforcement. She talked about her experience over nearly three decades of investigating and prosecuting child sex offenders, working with survivors and their families, and earning the support and trust of victims who had experienced horrendous trauma.

Her two male colleagues barely spoke, simply nodding and watching as Gillian detailed how she planned to lead an experienced team to thoroughly and transparently uncover and document years of alleged abuse. How she would work to determine who was aware all these years, who should have spoken up, and who might have covered up, all the while protecting due process for everyone who might be implicated. She would evaluate the university's policies and procedures, why it appeared they weren't followed, and what needed to be done going forward.

As she neared the end of her presentation, she turned off the screen so everyone focused solely on her. "Fighting sexual misconduct has been the cause of my life and career for twenty-seven years," she said. "I've investigated it and prosecuted it in the trenches of New York City. And I'd be honored to bring that experience and commitment with the C&R team to help this great university uncover the truth, right some of these wrongs, and rebuild your institutional trust and reputation for the future."

Then they were all shaking hands again, and when Serena was face-to-face with Gillian, holding her hand in a friendly embrace, she just had to say, "Thank you very much for coming out here and sharing your expertise. I hope we have a chance to work together."

"I would love that," Gillian replied.

Aaron appeared to have made his decision already. "We'll be in touch *very soon*," he declared with a knowing look that said the university's search was over. The C&R team was headed for the door when Aaron added, "One more thing. Please tell Julia McGinnis I say hello."

8
Troy

Troy clicked on the link in Julia's text, and for the second time in two days, an article from the *New York Dispatch* popped up. Yesterday's story had detailed that, according to unnamed sources, police were investigating a sexual assault claim against noted author Caleb Lugo by a Spanish model named Bianca Velencoso. It sent shock waves through media, social media, and the C&R office. Caleb issued a firm denial.

But this new article had a different tone:

Model asked for film role from Lugo before molestation claim, earns major bank as sex worker.

Troy quickly read the first two paragraphs:

> The Spanish model who accused author Caleb Lugo of sexually assaulting her tried to use the threatened claim to score a movie role in an upcoming Netflix adaption of his best-selling novel Don't Spend It All in One Place, sources told The Dispatch. Meanwhile, Bianca Velencoso has earned significant funds from hardcore sex work via raunchy online site OnlyFans and elsewhere under the pseudonym Scarlett Espinoza.
>
> Although she was careful not to reveal her face on camera

in the numerous extremely NSFW photos and videos obtained by The Dispatch, *the images have been confirmed to be of Velencoso, based on a unique small birthmark on her left breast and her use of the same online screen name on other platforms.*

He was sitting in his work cubicle, with not-that-high walls separating him from other C&R employees who weren't anointed with their own offices. There wasn't much privacy, and he'd always been careful to avoid viewing explicit content at work. This was about a C&R client, so it was presumably okay. But what if someone just observed him looking at the images without understanding the context?

He lowered the phone into his lap and hunched over, trying to obscure the screen from anyone who walked by. He knew this action made detection less likely, but also greatly inflated the appearance of impropriety if someone did take notice.

The first photo showed Bianca's tanned, toned body from the waist up, apparently on a runway somewhere, seductively pouting as she gazed into the distance. A very small, light blue bikini top covered part of her breasts. Next to the image was a cartoonish magnifying glass, within which was an enlargement of Bianca's left breast, and a red arrow pointed to a brown birthmark visible just below the bottom edge of the bikini.

The next photo showed a headless naked female body, similarly shapely and attractive, appearing to lie on a bed with her right hand extending down to her crotch as her torso arched back. Small black bars had been added by the site to cover each nipple, and another one obscured the fingers that were presumably touching herself. The photo featured another magnifying glass, this one zooming in on the same birthmark.

He wrote back to Julia, *Anderson must love this.* Then he added, *WTF, did they study the breasts of every woman on OnlyFans until they found her?*

He looked at a screenshot embedded within the article, which purported to be from a now-defunct website affiliated with "Scarlett Espinoza." The text from the site read, *My preferred verification is to hear from two ladies who you've spent some time with during the last year. Sorry, but I'm unable to accept agency referrals.*

He was trying to understand what that meant when Julia responded to his text.

We need to talk. Meet me ASAP.

He rose and moved past the other cubicles toward the main hallway, and after ten seconds he saw Julia in the distance, approaching from the other direction. They walked toward each other, then he stopped at the lactation room and held the door open for her.

"Emma says this article's a major problem," she said once they were inside.

"For who?"

She shrugged. "I'm sure Caleb's happy, but Emma says this whole situation is really bad. She was here with me a few minutes ago, then had a panic attack and left. I tried to follow her, but she told me she needed to be alone for a little while and could meet later outside the office."

Troy looked at her, confused, trying to piece this all together. "But what is she worried about?"

"I don't know. We have to talk with her after she calms down. Did your Spanish sub find this stuff?"

"No. He found nothing of any use, so I have no idea where this is coming from. What's happening with MHU?"

"I have no fucking idea." Julia clenched and unclenched her fist and then exhaled deeply. Her voice was full of frustration as she stood in front of Troy and fumed, "They flew out there yesterday. Took Gillian with them. No one's telling me anything. I *knew* this would happen. And you said I should go to Anderson anyway. This is exactly what I was afraid of."

"We haven't even been retained yet. You don't know if you're being cut out."

"Exactly. I *don't* know. I don't know anything. That's messed up considering I got C&R in there. So far all I have for my efforts is Anderson's threat to fire me. You know how big this investigation is? And he's going to take all the origination credit. No way he's telling our CEO a fucking associate handed him this opportunity." Her phone buzzed in her hand, and Julia looked down before announcing, "It's Emma. She wants to meet now."

He looked at his own phone: 4:07 p.m. "I have a DD due tomorrow morning."

"Finish it tonight. She wants to talk. Right away."

He still had to complete some last bits of research for a due diligence assignment, plug it into the report template, and proofread it before sending to the managing director in California who had given him this matter. He needed to look for red flags in the background of some filthy rich tech entrepreneur only three years older than Troy who was about to be bought out by the client for millions. Troy couldn't help wanting to find some damaging information, to tank this deal, to help knock down another arrogant tech prick. But so far everything checked out clean.

"Okay, where?"

"The Gin House."

They left lactation central, turned down the hallway, then went out the glass double doors and into the elevator. Once outside, they made their way down Lexington, then cut over to Third, through the Midtown businesspeople and assorted bustling New Yorkers before arriving at Emma's usual watering hole.

The bar was getting crowded as New York's young professionals were starting an early summer happy hour. It was one of countless establishments around the city that had been ironically styled as Prohibition-era speakeasies. Inside the nondescript doorway, the interior of the main room was anchored by a long bar of brushed steel. Countless whiskeys and other liquors lined the dark walls, and chandeliers that looked to be snatched from 1920s banquet halls hung from the tin ceilings.

"There she is," Julia noted.

At a small round table, Emma sat with her back against the wall and sipped from a black straw submerged in a grapefruit-colored drink. A large green tote bag sat agape on the floor next to her, her short brown hair looked unusually disheveled, and her eyes appeared tired and reddened.

Julia dropped into a seat and looked around for a waiter. "Drink up, everyone," she instructed. "I'm expensing this."

"Expensing to what?" Troy asked as he sat down. Associates didn't have expense accounts, and there was no client matter to bill this to.

Troy watched Julia narrow her eyes in disapproval at his lack of temerity. "They're going to reject my expense after I handed them MHU? I don't think so."

A woman came by to take their orders.

"Another Campari orange," Emma said despondently, her gaze unfocused.

"Oban, please. Neat," Julia said. "Troy, what do you want?"

"Club soda for me. I have to finish a report today."

Julia looked up at the waitress. "He'll have a club soda. And dump some Ketel One in it." The waitress grinned and then shuffled off to the bar. Julia looked at Emma. "Can you tell us what's going on? We want to help."

Emma's hand shook as she grasped her straw and looked at neither Troy nor Julia. She seemed to be addressing someone only she could see. "I've done something really bad," she said, slowly lifting her glass. "And now I don't think I can live with myself. That fucking place broke me."

"Talk to us," Julia said in a soft voice. "We'll figure it out, whatever it is."

Emma took a long sip of her drink, then set it back on the brown wood table. The restaurant was filling up around them, and Troy hoped the noise of so many conversations would make their discussion unintelligible to others.

"So I did all that pro bono work with Matthew over the past year. For the Innocence Project. All that investigative research into potentially wrongful convictions."

C&R had sent a holiday video the previous year to clients, employees, and business partners touting the idea that the firm wasn't just about making a profit—which Troy had found amusing because the company was, in fact, not making a profit—but was committed to social justice and helping better the lives of the less fortunate. The work for the Innocence Project, led by then-MD Matthew Crane, was a central part of that.

Emma continued, "Then Matthew's RIF'd last week because he wasn't originating enough new business, and next thing I know I'm called in to meet with Tara from HR, and Anderson is there too, and they tell me my utilization is too low, so I'm being given a formal reprimand and a PIP. They say I have a month to turn things around or I'll be gone too."

The waitress returned and set down their drinks. Emma drained the rest of the one she'd been working on and placed the glass on the tray.

"But you've been slammed with work for as long as I can remember," Troy interjected.

"Yeah, but I was told the current review by our parent company, which we all know is being done so they can package us for a sale to DePalma Capital, doesn't count pro bono for utilization stats. Only client billable work. So I'm like, really shocked, and I say no one has ever told me this before. And I explain that Matthew promised me the Innocence Project stuff would count toward utilization."

"And?" Julia asked.

"Anderson just shrugs and says in this condescending tone, 'Well, as you know, he's no longer with the firm. Is this representation you're citing in writing anywhere?' And of course it's not. So now all of a sudden I'm on the list of people about to be tossed overboard."

"He's an asshole," Julia consoled her.

"It's not just him. I explained again how hard I've worked. That we did all this great stuff that gave C&R a lot of positive exposure. And Tara was just stone-faced, looking at Anderson for direction. They weren't even really listening to me. So I'm trying to stay calm and I say, 'Can't you just give me a warning? Why does this have to be a formal, documented thing?' Because that's going to really hurt my career. And he just responds, 'This is your warning, Emma. Would you prefer to be exited from the firm right now? The performance improvement plan *is* your warning.'"

Emma lifted her drink, and her hand was now shaking even more than before. "You can't let this get to you," Troy advised. "I know it sucks. Last year I got a twenty-five-hundred-dollar raise in January, and then at the end of the year my bonus was reduced by three thousand. It's infuriating. Maybe this craziness will pass once there's a sale. They're all panicked about it falling through if it doesn't look like they're getting their financial house in order, and that means layoffs, RIFs, PIPs, everything. The C&R name is the big draw, but they can't sell unless they show a trajectory toward better financials. Hopefully the sale happens soon, and then maybe we'll have some stability and sanity."

"Right," Julia confirmed, placing a hand on Emma's arm. "We'll get through this together."

Emma looked directly at her and then Troy for the first time. "There's a lot more. It gets much worse."

Julia stuck one finger in the air as the waitress walked by, to indicate they needed another round.

"You confronted him at the Caleb Lugo event," Troy prompted.

"*Confronted* is a big exaggeration. I was too much of a fucking wimp to *confront* him. But I tried to talk to him. I said I'd worked really hard this past year, that there may have been a misunderstanding about what counts and doesn't count for utilization. I explained that I really want to keep this job. Because I *need* to keep this job."

Julia leaned forward. "And?"

"We were out on the balcony. He clearly didn't like that I was bothering him, especially at that event. He was a real dick about it and told me he couldn't withdraw the PIP, that it was already issued, and those things can't be taken back because of HR procedures. Which is of course bullshit. So I just left and started crying outside and walked all the way home. But an hour later my phone rang. It was Anderson. Said he had an idea to make sure I have enough billable work so I'm not RIF'd at the end of the month."

"How?" Troy asked.

"He told me he had an emergency assignment for an important client, and he knew I was really good with social media research, that I knew all the best scraping tools, and was really smart. Totally different tone than before. He said the work was confidential for now, even within the firm. But he told me if I did a good job it would go a long way to helping him make the case to others that I was needed here."

"And the assignment was . . ." Troy already knew the answer, but he wanted to hear Emma say it.

"Research on Bianca Velencoso," she answered sullenly. "For Caleb Lugo. Anderson wanted anything I could find on her. So I worked all night, fucking looked everywhere, and she was just this normal, young, up-and-coming Spanish wannabe model. But then I figured out that in high school she posted on some Spanish blog using the name Scarlett Espinoza, and her comments there matched some of the content on her Bianca social. Same references to the same kinds of things, like pop stars, fashion. Posting the same times and days under her real accounts as this screen name. So I knew it was her. My Spanish teachers would be so proud... She stopped using the Scarlett name for a few years but then picked it up again, so that's how I found her. She thought the handle anonymized her so she could discretely do sex worker shit through OnlyFans and her website, and until now I guess it did. But now Caleb's people told it all to *The Dispatch*."

"How is that relevant to him allegedly sexually assaulting her?" Troy asked.

"It's not," Julia answered. "But it's enough to make sure she won't be taken seriously. And all the SWERFs who love his novels and devour them with their book clubs will stand by him. This whole thing goes away."

Emma went on like a parishioner at a confessional. "Yeah, I doxed her. I found all this info to make the world see her as a whore. And I did it to save my job, so in reality *I'm* the fucking whore."

"Look, you can't blame yourself," Julia said soothingly, while moving her grasp to take Emma's hand in hers. "We're investigators. Finding adverse intel is part of the job, even if it feels bad at times."

Emma silently moved her hand away from Julia's touch and held it up to indicate she wanted to prevent any further comments. She then shook her head. "I'm not done." Troy decided to start drinking his vodka soda.

"So I pulled another virtual all-nighter and then in the morning I was in his office, exhausted and telling him what I found," Emma explained. "He was thrilled. Said to me in this highly patronizing way that he always viewed me as having so much potential, and it's great to see me finally beginning to realize that. Then he handed me a handwritten list of seven women and said, 'Now let's see what you can find on *them*.'"

"Who were the women?" Julia asked.

"He only gave me their names, but as soon as I started digging, it was clear they were all in Caleb's orbit. Some actress who appeared in a film adaptation of one of his books. A PR person for his publisher. An aspiring singer who was a former staffer at the Sixteen Foundation. All young women. All entertainment, media types who crossed paths with him. And get this, when I can't identify anything helpful on any of them, he tells me to find all available photos of these women that show they're, as he says, 'perhaps not the most upstanding members of society.' He says he wants modeling photos, especially nude pics—anything sexual. The more explicit, the better. Anderson says the goal is to get images and videos that will, in his words, 'embarrass and discredit' them. At this point it's so obvious: Some of them—maybe all of them—are making claims against Caleb, so Anderson wants dirt."

"But what does any of that prove?" Troy jumped in. "Sexy photos of an actress? A singer? So what?"

"Doesn't have to prove anything. Just needs to damage their credibility. Anderson said Caleb and his lawyers want these images. And he said my continued employment depended on whether I was successful. I knew it was wrong, but I got back to work, and I actually found some pretty graphic stuff on a few of them, especially from early in their careers, buried in random places online. I told Anderson I'm concerned some of these were probably posted without their consent by angry ex-boyfriends as revenge porn."

"And what did he say?" Julia asked.

"He said, 'Obviously I don't condone these being posted without their consent, but it's not *our fault* they're out there. These will be very helpful to our client. And from the looks of what they're doing in the photos and videos, these women aren't exactly innocent victims.'"

Troy tried to understand this last comment. "What did he mean by that?"

"By that he meant he's a fucking asshole," Julia explained.

"I was still terrified of losing my job," Emma continued, "so I put them all in a file and sent them to Anderson yesterday evening, knowing he and Caleb were going to use what I found to embarrass and blackmail these women into silence. Then I went home and bawled my eyes out, knowing I'm a complete sellout." Emma set her elbows on the table and ran her fingers through her hair. "I'm a total piece of shit."

"You're not a piece of shit, Emma," Julia said. "That place does things to people. The *place* is shit. We need to say something, all three of us."

"Absolutely," Troy added. "We have your back. Let's all go to HR together."

Emma nearly spat out her drink and then shook her head in disdain. "Are you crazy? No one from HR cares. They do what they're told by Anderson and senior management."

"This is misogynistic bullshit," Julia said, "and he's making you part of the problem. You need to speak up, and we'll go with you. We have to present a unified message about this firm."

Emma nodded and stirred her drink. "You're right, I needed to speak up. So I did this morning."

"I don't understand. To who?" Troy asked.

"*The New York Times*."

Julia's mouth dropped open. "Wait, *what*? Tell me you didn't." Troy and Julia exchanged a look of shock.

"One of the women commented on Instagram that a *Times* reporter reached out to her about Caleb Lugo. So I pieced together who the journalist was, and I called her. This reporter's a real crusader, exposing terrible things done by powerful people. She reminds me of Emily Kinum. Turns out she's been researching sexual misconduct accusations against Caleb for months. She's doing a huge feature. She didn't know about most of the women on our list, so I gave her a pretty good roadmap for her article. If I hadn't done that, I wouldn't be able to live with myself."

Julia's face went cold. Troy had only once before seen her look so furious, and he felt his throat constrict. In her attempt to soothe her guilty conscience, Emma had tossed a grenade that was about to incinerate their entire world.

"You have to call the reporter back and retract everything. Right now!" Julia ordered.

Emma didn't look at her. She seemed to be talking to the invisible person again. "I can't do that. I finally realized all these things I just accepted as inevitable are actually unacceptable. I had to do something."

"You leaked *confidential client info!*" Julia seemed to be trying to both scream and keep her voice down. "That's disgusting!"

Now Emma looked straight at Julia. "Let's be clear: I leaked nothing. All I did was say to the reporter, 'Hey, I hear you're looking at this. These are names of women you might want to contact.' The rest is up to them. Nothing's on the record, so there's nothing to retract. I didn't even give her my name. And I blocked my number!"

"Think, Emma," Julia huffed as she slapped the table. "Caleb's a well-known C&R client. This is going to tank the MHU deal! No way they hire us to look into their Uncle Rob scandal if we're the firm working to protect a serial sex offender!"

"*This* is what matters? Whether we land another client?!" Emma shot back.

"It sure as hell matters to me! I brought MHU in!"

"You said yourself they're screwing you over for origination credit!"

"And I'm going to raise hell about it."

As she said this, Troy nervously noted that much more than just origination credit was at stake. When Julia had tried to stand up to Anderson, he promised that if the MHU investigation went away, so would Julia.

"With all due respect," Emma responded as she pushed her chair back from the table and crossed her arms, "I doubt that. You're more talk than action when it comes to confronting the big boys. You'll just passive-aggressively expense a few drinks while brooding about MHU for the next year."

"*You* of all people have the *nerve* to question whether I'll stand up for myself?!"

"Guys," said Troy. "Let's keep the focus—"

"They'll bill millions, then throw you a couple thousand extra in your December bonus," Emma interrupted. "Then we'll be sold, and the new owners won't know or won't care what you helped originate before they took over. You're never getting anything real from this. You know that."

Julia's eyes were on fire. "No, I'm planning to fight for this," she insisted. "I'll call the university president if needed. I have his cell. You think Anderson has that? Doubtful."

"When is this running?" Troy asked.

Emma looked from Julia to Troy. "I don't know. They work on these investigations for months."

"Emma, please. You need to call the reporter back," he urged.

"And say what? *Just kidding*? Forget it. It's done. And yeah, I'm freaked out about it, but I don't regret it."

Julia rose and held her glass in the air, squeezing it in her right fist. Troy wondered what she was going to do. Throw it at the wall? Toss the drink in Emma's face?

"We've always had your back, Emma," she said instead. "Always supported you. I know you feel *all sad* about how you were treated. That's no excuse for being so fucking weak that you have to take us down with you. You need to call that reporter and try to undo this. And you need to understand that what you did was unbelievably, appallingly selfish. And really fucking stupid."

She slammed her glass down, and scotch splashed onto the table. People nearby turned and stared. Julia opened her purse, pulled out a few bills, and threw them down into the puddle of whiskey. Then she turned and stormed out of the bar.

Troy wanted to follow, but first he looked back at Emma. "Seriously, you need to get in touch with that reporter again. If there's a big takedown of Caleb, and it comes out that C&R went after those women..."

"I already told you. I didn't mention anything about C&R. The reporter has no idea what we did."

Troy leaned in close to her. "It's *The Times*, Emma. You don't think they'll figure it out? Then what happens when our clients find out confidential information was leaked to the media? How many of them will drop us then? And that toxic reputation, that stink, will stay with all of us as we try to find new jobs. Every other firm will look at our résumés and say, 'Oh yeah, you're from the firm that leaks.' We might as well burn *can't be trusted* on our foreheads."

Emma's eyes grew wide. "But—"

"And what if this article tanks the sale of C&R? That means we don't get new ownership, and our best case scenario is we're stuck with the same shit executives running the company. And *then* we're even more at their mercy because they'll know nobody else will hire us."

Emma closed her eyes in exhaustion. She rubbed her temples, then opened her eyes and said, "You can disapprove of what I did. But I needed to do this so I could live with myself. And I can't tell a reporter to forget the names of women she's probably already reached out to by now."

Troy could see this was going nowhere, but as he stood to leave, he gave it a last attempt. "Listen, Emma, if you care about the rest of us, you'll try. You'll call her right now. Please." Then he turned away and headed out into the light, hoping he could somehow summon the necessary focus to return to the office and finish his report.

9
Megan

MEGAN'S MIND wasn't in the room with her body. As she worked her way around the reception hall packed with $1,000-a-plate donors, ten to a table, she was wracked with guilt that she'd filled her friend with false hope. She needed to see Evina as soon as possible. But first she had to get through this event.

Local elected officials held court in tight clusters. Some attendees wandered the length of the room, trying to find someone important to talk to, or they studied their phones to appear busy while they waited for someone to pay attention to them. Others convened around the bar area, with a few clearly trying to make back their 1K by expeditiously throwing back drink after drink.

Megan thought about how misleading these gatherings were. Back when she started attending these functions, she'd been amazed by how many people cared about local issues. Then she learned most of them showed up for reasons having nothing to do with ideology or public policy. Their jobs were tied to the local machine, their businesses dependent on vendor contracts from various campaigns, their social lives intertwined with local committee meetings and district leader activities and campaign happy hours.

Forty-five minutes. That was how long she figured she needed to stay, to show support for the event's organizers without making painfully clear how desperately she wanted to leave. She had wanted to head to the prison today, but she understood if she was going to keep her seat on the city council and set herself up to seek higher office, she had to attend tedious fundraisers, stay at least forty-five minutes, and make sure the right people knew she'd been there.

She moved around the room, shaking hand after hand. Because right now, she was one of the people a lot of attendees were there to meet. She was a relatively new city council member, and the people paying $1,000 a seat wanted access to that.

A tall, bald man in a wrinkled suit waved a piece of paper in front of her. "Councilwoman Black," he gushed with breath that reeked of gin, "I have this letter I sent to the mayor. About the lighting on Route 48."

"That's my issue," she quickly assured him. Megan had been extremely vocal about the need to address the city's winding roads that were made even more treacherous by poor illumination and countless potholes. "That's one of my top priorities. I ran on that."

"I *know* you care. But nobody else does. That's why I support you. The mayor's office just sent back some form letter. I wrote to Congressman Montgomery too, but he's skipped out. I also contacted the governor. How do I get anyone to care? It's a death trap out there."

"This is one of my main issues on the council, and I'm committed to doing something about this problem."

"Thank you," he responded. And within seconds, someone else was talking with her about the school system, class sizes, and the need for more extracurricular activities. Before she could fully respond, another attendee wrangled her into discussing the mayor's proposal for an increase in the hotel occupancy tax, and then another person fired a question about the French-American School's proposal to buy the site of the old golf course to turn it into their new campus, which might or might not increase traffic, might or might not improve the educational quality of the city, might or might not . . .

Every political gathering like this also included a smattering of wackos who dove headfirst into every nutty conspiracy theory that propagated on social media, and she had to speak with them as if she didn't notice their craziness. When she first entered this event, a woman she'd met at another fundraiser breathlessly approached Megan and shared that new evidence proved Helen Keller's entire story was a hoax. "She faked the whole thing!" she exclaimed with wide-eyed conviction.

A cacophony of voices, handshakes, kisses on the cheeks. People wanting her to assist them in a variety of ways. Simultaneously, she anxiously scanned the room for anyone who could help *her*. And not for the typical donors and would-be endorsers who circulated at these events. Instead she needed someone influential enough to get Evina's commutation in front of the president's team.

Very unlikely here, at this important but exceedingly local political event, which felt light-years from Washington. But it might just take one person, who knew the right high-powered DC lawyer, who would be moved by Evina's plight and take up her cause.

She tried to size up those in the room, maneuvering around everyone's agenda while plotting her own. Although not everyone was so calculating, as a few random people seemed to just sincerely want to greet her and tell her it was good to see her again. And she wracked her brain to remember their names.

When she couldn't recall who they were, she fell back on the always reliable observation made with a knowing smile, "So, you still causing trouble out there?" Especially with the men, who ate up her lighthearted but intrigue-laden implication that they were *capable* of causing trouble, up to something mischievous, maybe even mysterious. They loved that shit.

She actually learned that comment from an old boyfriend many years ago. He didn't end up working out, but this line continued to pay dividends.

When had she become this person, who could carry on a seemingly endless series of short conversations with simulated earnestness and mock-focus? She had run for council for the right reasons, and was intent on using her position to better their city. But she knew that to have a truly positive impact, she needed to play this game.

Play this game. Sadly, the phoniness she detested was creeping into more and more aspects of her life. She had noted that officeholders never led their social media bios with their title, but instead first rattled off a series of familial relationships, achingly sending the trite message that their elected or appointed position *always took a second seat to family.* Thus, social media profiles began with "Father, husband, state senator" and "Mother, wife, sister, deputy county land commissioner." Megan wasn't going to totally cave to this fad, so she commenced hers with, "City councilwoman, mother, wife, daughter." Emphasizing her elected position but still showing that *family was important to her.*

What else? She had been asked her favorite color and number by a constituent recently, and she decided to just make something up (green, six) because it was easier than getting trapped in a whole conversation about how she actually didn't have a preferred shade or numeral. Plus, there were all the wholesome things she had to pretend to like because it was blasphemous to say she didn't. Dogs, toddlers, coffee. U2.

Megan glanced at her watch. Forty-seven minutes had passed, but before she could sneak out of this place, there was one person she had to greet in person. He was the biggest reason she'd shown up.

Across the room, Megan saw him break away from another conversation, so she hustled toward him. He smiled as she approached, gave her a hug, and kissed her on the cheek.

"Councilwoman Black! It's good to see you here." He was a large man, tall and wide, with graying hair and jowls that became even more pronounced when he smiled. He wore an expensive-looking pin-striped suit and silver tie, and communicated with a gravelly voice that exuded blue-collar roots.

"Professor Dowling," she started to respond warmly, and then paused to reflect on how absurd it was that she had to woo this guy, to respond using his preferred faux title because that's what everyone did who wanted a political future in this city. For some reason, he seemed to like her, and he'd helpfully endorsed her during Megan's city council race.

Professor Dowling.

Everyone called him that as a sign of respect because he worked at the university. But as far as she could tell, he had never taught a class, maybe never even been inside a classroom. Like *ever*. During the council campaign, when she'd been told to seek his support, she asked one of the local activists what he was a professor of. The response was a dismissive, "Not sure. Does it really matter?" She had then inquired about what issues he cared about, and was told succinctly and unconvincingly, "Good government."

A decade ago he'd reportedly been a staffer in a no-show job in the state capital, but a local newspaper exposé on waste in state government led to an aggressive inspector general investigation. Suddenly, employee salaries needed to be justified, and those dependent on Dowling's political favors stashed him in a new, less visual position at the university. He was rechristened as associate director of government relations for Mountain Hill University, and somehow grabbed the Professor Dowling moniker that no one was brave enough or cared enough about to question.

Since that time, no less than six of his relatives had been hired by the city in various capacities in the department of public works, the parking authority, and elsewhere. A recent news article implied this was another example of government nepotism and cronyism.

But Professor Dowling had dismissed that negative connotation by explaining in the story, "All this shows is that my family is highly committed to public service."

Local political and government leaders knew that he and his family had to be taken care of. He was, after all, chair of one of the state's several "minor" political parties, cleverly branded the Unaffiliated Party. The party sometimes endorsed Democrats, other times Republicans. No rhyme or reason to the choices, except that in the average election 4.68 percent of local voters cast their ballot for the U.P. endorsed candidate on the party's line, probably due to understandable dislike of the two-party system, which made them appreciate the idea of being unaffiliated. Some even inadvertently registered as members of the party, thinking they were choosing to be independent.

Not every state had minor party lines on the ballot that endorsed major party candidates, but Megan had the fortune of living in one of them. And if local politicians ever tried to change that, well, they'd better succeed quickly or else their opponents would have the coveted minor party endorsements in the next race.

After all, 4.68 percent was enough to swing an election. Enough to swing *a lot* of elections.

That's why she was at the U.P. annual banquet. Full of a bipartisan mass of officeholders, candidates, and campaigns buying tables at $1,000 a seat. The party's endorsements were never explicitly for sale, but it was obvious that a major donation to the party was always helpful, and providing jobs to U.P. officials and family members if one won a noteworthy office was a tacit expectation. Meanwhile, it was unclear where any of that money really went. But for the people donating, that was irrelevant.

Not that major parties were above these types of legal cons, not-so-subtly demanding job appointments for party honchos and activists in return for support, soliciting big money payments from aspiring candidates, and then utilizing those funds on preferred vendors with ties to party leadership for GOTV efforts, printing and mailing, and random "consulting" fees.

Before her city council race, Megan had been oblivious to all this. Hell, she'd probably even voted on the U.P. line a few times with the intent of casting a protest vote against the status quo. Now, instead of unknowingly perpetuating the professor's political shenanigans in the voting booth, she was doing so with clear vision at this annual confab. Trying to do the absolute minimum necessary to placate this party leader, kiss the ring, not sell her soul, and escape with some semblance of dignity and hopefully a crucial endorsement when she was up for reelection.

They stood facing each other in the middle of the swirling pool of attendees. "This is a great event," she said. He nodded, but there was something in his eyes that said he wasn't thrilled to be there either. "How're you doing?" she asked.

He lowered his voice. "As I'm sure you know, things are really crazy at the university. I may need your assistance. I think the council's going to end up playing an important role."

Megan knew there was a good chance she'd find the "assistance" he was going to ask for morally objectionable, but there was no harm in hearing him out. "I'm always happy to talk. How can I help?"

"It's hitting my family real hard too. My wife's nephew, Cole, is an assistant softball coach at the school. He's been there awhile but knew nothing about the disgusting things the head coach was supposedly doing. Cole's being targeted now and he's really distraught. We're all worried this is going to turn into a witch hunt and end his career."

"I'm very sorry to hear that, Professor. I understand it's a stressful time. But I'm sure Aaron Montgomery will be a great leader during this crisis." She didn't necessarily believe that, but she didn't *not* believe it either. She really had no idea how Aaron would handle this mess. But Megan knew Dowling was a Montgomery political ally and showing confidence in him would be a good move, especially as a preamble to the request she was about to make.

"I hope so," Dowling said, looking around the room. "The situation is threatening to spin out of control. But if Aaron can steer the university successfully through this disaster, he'll soon be living in the governor's mansion. The board of trustees wanted to make him the permanent president, but I advised him to accept only an interim title. Not good to get bogged down there. One year, quickly right the ship, and then out."

Megan nodded, despite not having an opinion on Aaron's career track. Then she cleared her throat and said, "I actually have a favor to ask, Professor."

"Sure. What is it?" he responded with a cordial tone that gave Megan hope he might actually help her.

"I need to speak with Aaron. It's about something we've already discussed, but he hasn't responded to my calls."

"Well, he's very busy. I'm sure it's not personal."

"I know it's not personal, but this issue is important. *Extremely* important." Aaron was out of Congress and unresponsive but still her best chance of finding someone with DC connections who could point her in the right direction. "If you could just ask him to call me back or meet with me, I'd be grateful."

"I'll do my best. Is it something I can help with?"

She thought about it. Wouldn't that be something? "I'm trying to get a woman's federal sentence commuted. She's a longtime domestic violence victim who was imprisoned on a homicide charge after defending herself against an abusive husband. It's a major injustice. She's a very close friend of mine and has been locked up for years. She's really suffering, and still has decades left unless someone helps her. I don't think she'll survive much longer in prison."

Megan watched him curl his lower lip as he digested this information. Maybe in all his political maneuverings, someone with the right connections owed him a favor. If so, if he could deliver this salvation for Evina, she would take back every cynical, disparaging thought she'd ever had about him and his party.

"I can't think of anyone helpful right now," he said. "But I'll give it more thought, and I'll talk to Aaron. I'll tell him to give you a call."

Tell him. Not *ask* him—that sounded promising. Dowling had outsized political influence and was used to getting his way, even with a former congressman, a university president, a potential future governor.

He gave Megan a quick hug and kiss on the cheek, and then he was on to his next round of conversations with people trying to show their fealty and earn his support for their next elections. Besides the professor's promise to get Aaron to return her call, Megan was no closer to finding a solution for her friend.

But she had now spent well over an hour at this tedious event, and had spoken with the right people as far as her electoral career was concerned. So at least it finally felt politically safe to head for the exit, return to her family, and take a shower.

10
Serena

SERENA STARED at her computer and read the press release from the president's office. She bristled at their failure to seek her input before drafting it, or to even provide her with an advance copy before it went public. Her eyes felt uncomfortably dry as she reread the headline on her screen:

> **Mountain Hill University Hires Firm to Help Promptly Investigate Reports of Sexual Assault**

Serena had no objections so far, and proceeded to review the rest:

> *Mountain Hill University has enlisted C&R Investigations, a leading global provider of investigative services, as an independent third party to help investigate complaints involving former softball coach Rob Dempsey. C&R will begin reviewing complaints immediately, and will also investigate whether other MHU staff and administrators were aware of Dempsey's alleged misconduct and failed to take appropriate measures to prevent it.*
>
> *"We are committed to MHU becoming a shining example of*

Title IX compliance," said Aaron Montgomery, interim MHU president. "We owe it to all those who were allegedly victimized and had the bravery to step forward to ensure a safer MHU for their legacy. C&R will be given unfettered access to all requested witnesses, documents, and evidence. Nothing will be off-limits and their investigation will be completely objective, independent, and transparent."

Serena felt the words were right. But they were just words. She had wanted the university to move fast, but was this too fast? Gillian Fenton was impressive and experienced, but no other firms had even been interviewed.

Her phone vibrated on her desk, and she saw a text from Kayla.

Happy birthday, Mom! Still working to get a sexual misconduct speaker for new student orientation. What about one of the former softball players??

She loved and admired her daughter, but Kayla really had no understanding of the political realities of campus life.

Thanks, Kayla. Great idea, if you'd like to get me fired immediately and lose your tuition support, she quickly tapped back.

Serena heard a knock at her door. She didn't like surprise visits, but her admin must be away from her station. "Who is it?" Serena called out.

"It's me," Drew's voice replied.

Serena rose and opened her office door, and Drew entered past her.

"Great press release, huh?" he said with an encouraging smile. "It's exactly what you wanted. Completely independent firm. Neither of us wanted *me* to lead this mess of an investigation . . ."

"Did you review it before it went out?"

"Yes. Is there a problem?"

"Why wasn't I in the loop? I was intentionally excluded."

She expected him to tell her she was being paranoid, but instead he confirmed her suspicions with an apologetic tone. "The president doesn't trust you. He doesn't see you as a team player."

Before she could respond, she noticed Drew's hands were hidden behind his back. Had they been there the whole time?

"What are you holding behind you?" she asked suspiciously.

He brought his hands out in front and she saw the silver tray topped with a small birthday cake and one unlit candle in the middle. The words *Happy Birthday, Serena!* were written in blue-on-white frosting.

"A peace offering," he said with a grin.

Cake? Their conflict was about the best way to protect sexual assault survivors, and he was trying to smooth things over with *cake*?

"Drew, I appreciate the gesture," she said, as he placed the tray onto her desk. "But what I really need is your support—"

"Absolutely. I'll help you earn the president's trust."

"That's not what I mean. I need your support in helping the girls get justice. I know how these situations play out at schools. Instead of focusing on the victims, it becomes all about political agendas and minimizing litigation exposure. I can't prevent that all by myself."

"Did you read the press release?" he asked.

"Yes, and it's fine."

"It's more than fine. It's great. It's about the victims. Nothing about political agendas or litigation exposure."

She shook her head. "I just . . . find it really hard to believe in any process here anymore. I've seen too much horrendous conduct already and too many people who don't care." She sighed and wondered whether she was overreacting. Maybe she should welcome the university's positive steps that she helped bring about. "I need to get away," she declared. "When this investigation's over, and my daughter finally graduates, then I'm out. I'm not leaving until I make sure this is done correctly and she has her degree, but then I'm gone."

"To do what?" he asked.

Serena looked out the window. "I don't know. Something where I don't have to constantly hope my bosses are acting morally. Where I'm away from all this craziness."

"When you find this place, let me know if they need a deputy general counsel. Look, Serena, just have some cake with me, okay?"

Drew pulled a matchbook from his pants pocket and lit the candle, which she quickly blew out. He then picked up a plastic knife from the tray and cut through the "S" in her name as he began preparing a slice.

She tried not to flinch, but he immediately noticed her flash of discomfort. "Did I do something wrong?" he asked.

"I think I may have told you last year. My parents taught me that cutting the name on a cake is bad luck. They always smeared it out first. It's ridiculous. Don't worry about it."

"Sorry, I forgot," he replied as he turned the blade on its side and ran it across her name. "But why is cutting unlucky and blurring is okay?"

"I have no idea. It makes no sense. But some of these instincts from childhood are hard to unlearn. Anyway, when is the C&R team returning to campus?"

"Gillian Fenton's flying back here tomorrow to discuss preliminary document requests and other logistics with me."

"Good. I'd like her to meet with Ali Tyrell and her father. And I need to be in that meeting so there's a smooth handover. Or will Aaron bar me from that too because he doesn't trust me?"

"No one has told me to keep you away."

"Okay, because Ali hasn't agreed to participate in the investigation, but I think she'll sit down with Gillian informally to meet her and discuss the investigative process. Ali's become the public leader of the victims. If Gillian can gain her cooperation, the others will follow. Then we can really root out everyone who was complicit and make sure they're never in a position like that again. We can't let the Cole Malinowskis on this campus just glide to their next career stops, no questions asked."

Drew nodded in support. "I completely agree."

"Also, Drew, I'm all for trying to 'earn the president's trust,' but if he fucks around with this investigation, I'm going to raise hell," she warned. "Way beyond anything I've done before."

"And I'll raise it with you. But Aaron Montgomery has no reason to interfere. All wrongdoing occurred before his watch. He's going to let them do their job."

He handed her a slice of cake on a paper plate and then gave her a plastic fork from the tray. Serena nodded, then dug the utensil into the dark center. She inhaled the delicious aroma of chocolate, caramel, and sugary white frosting as she brought the cake to her mouth, and tried to use that alluring sensation to temporarily drown out all her concerns for just a moment.

11
Troy

"THIS IS DELICIOUS!" exclaimed one of the managing directors from across the room. "Too bad it takes a multimillion-dollar new client for us to eat this well." Then the MD laughed as others chuckled along.

Troy couldn't remember the conference room ever being so crowded. Managing directors, associates, support staff, human resource professionals, and others milled around and helped themselves to food at the celebratory lunch. Platters of top-quality sliders, a tray of coconut shrimp, chicken parmesan bites, mesclun salad, and assorted cookies. For a company that had for the past couple of years delivered to its employees a constant series of bad news and dim forecasts, with the sprinkling of optimistic rosy projections that never came true, there was finally something for the bigwigs to celebrate.

The long table in the middle could seat about thirty people, with room for two dozen more in chairs around the periphery, and this venue was used every other Tuesday morning for the large New York staff meetings. Anderson generally led them, and the highlight was always when he asked each MD to discuss their new business leads. Troy and his fellow associates watched in bemusement as their supervisors took turns trying to spin their recent networking efforts into promises of generating significant new revenue.

Their attempts ended up sounding like some version of:

My really good law school friend's uncle is a mid-level manager at a financial services company that had a cyber breach, so I'm working my connections to see if we can get a meeting to discuss our cyber security services with them. I think this has huge potential to be a significant engagement for us.

Or:

A California-based restaurant chain has announced plans to expand into the Northeast. So they'll need assistance with background checks on potential vendors and investigations into all sorts of employee issues that may arise. I don't actually know anyone working there, but the general counsel and I have two shared connections on LinkedIn, so I'm reaching out to them to hopefully get us in the door. It's a big opportunity and I'm feeling good about our chances of landing it.

Troy was definitely hungry and interested in taking advantage of this free spread. But currently Emma was talking with some fellow associates near the food trays, and it would be impossible to go over without interacting with her, or awkwardly *not* interacting with her in such close proximity.

The night before, Troy had caught her cryptic social media post that read, "Sometimes in a moment of need you learn that people you trusted are not true friends." Comments below were replete with demonstrations of support, such as "I hope you're okay!" and "Stay strong, Em! Remember, everything happens for a reason!!"

Julia sidled up next to Troy, nodded toward Emma across the room, and whispered, "Do you think she called the reporter back?"

"Doubtful," he said quietly. "But it might be too late anyway. At least MHU came in before the article dropped. That's huge."

Julia nodded. "Huge."

A loud pop cut through the air, and Troy watched Anderson smile as he raised a bottle of champagne. He handed it to an administrative assistant who began to fill a dozen or so plastic flutes, then tried to open more bottles as quietly as she could to avoid distracting anyone from the speech Anderson was launching into.

"I want to thank you all!" he proclaimed, as Luke stood close behind him, no doubt making sure he was at the center of this big win. "If it weren't for all the great work each of you do every single day, C&R wouldn't have its world-class reputation, and we wouldn't be about to embark on one of the biggest assignments in our history. This isn't just about earning profits for our business. It's about doing good in the world. And with this work for Mountain Hill University, we're going to do both in a huge way."

The employees around the room clapped, and Anderson continued, "I want to give special thanks to our newest managing director, who will be leading this investigation. She actually has to head to JFK in a few minutes to fly out to Mountain Hill. Her expertise was *invaluable* in winning this project. Please join me in welcoming former sex crimes prosecutor Gillian Fenton!"

Gillian emerged from the crowd and shook Anderson's hand. He picked up two champagne flutes and handed her one, then they ceremoniously raised them and each took a sip. Anderson gestured toward the packed room, so Gillian nodded and began to speak.

"Thank you, Anderson. Thank you, everyone," she began. "I'm not used to speaking in front of an audience without starting with 'Ladies and gentlemen of the jury,' so please bear with me." She smiled as employees throughout the room laughed supportively, even those like Troy who had so recently heard this line before. "I'm so honored to be part of this great firm," Gillian continued. "To be leading this extremely important assignment for Mountain Hill University, for C&R, and most importantly for the survivors of abuse whose tragic suffering was ignored, or worse, for far too long. We can't undo that, but together we'll find out the truth, help hold wrongdoers responsible, ensure due process for anyone accused, reform the university so this unconscionable behavior never takes place there again, and hopefully provide support and maybe even some closure to the many girls and women who went to that campus to play softball and left with their lives irreparably scarred."

Troy and Julia clapped respectfully, along with everyone else in the conference room. Gillian smiled, then nodded toward Anderson.

"So thank you, everyone, for joining this celebratory lunch," he said. "You've earned it. And you'll continue to earn it, because we have *a lot* of work to do."

Troy noticed Julia silently seething next to him, her mouth agape with anger. "He's not going to mention me?" she whispered in exasperation. She then briskly walked over to where Anderson stood, and Troy braced for the scene she was about to make. But instead she grabbed two champagnes and returned, handing one to him. "I'm going to speak to him again today, and I'm not going to hold back."

"When you walked over I thought you were about to do that now."

"Me too."

Troy suddenly noticed that a lot of eyes were focused on the door, and then he watched as a second reason for C&R to "celebrate" entered the room.

"Why is he barefoot?" Julia asked.

Caleb Lugo wore a pair of faded jeans and a light blue sweatshirt while holding a red book in his right hand. Not the first time he had walked around the C&R offices without shoes or socks, but he was too big a client for anyone to question his decorum. Troy had seen the online reports an hour earlier that the DA's office had decided not to file any charges against Caleb regarding Bianca Velencoso's allegations—a big C&R victory.

Anderson reached out to shake Caleb's hand, but the author wrapped the leader of the New York office in a tight hug. Then he hugged Gillian. "Gillian," he said, picking up a champagne flute, "you always believed in me. Always supported me, even when others were abandoning me. Thank you!"

She smiled. "I'll always be there for you, Caleb. No matter what. Don't ever doubt that."

"Gillian, would you like to say a few words about this excellent development?" Anderson asked.

"Absolutely," she said as she addressed the room for a second time and the attendees watched. "I'm thrilled to hear the DA's office saw this complaint for what it was. I've been prosecuting sexual misconduct cases for almost three decades, and I've learned how to prove a case and how to spot a fake complaint from a mile away. One of the best parts of being a prosecutor is you can decline to charge innocent people, and you actually have more power to help the wrongfully accused than anyone else in society. I'm so glad the Manhattan DA correctly used that power today. No reasonable prosecutor would arrest someone on these facts, especially an individual with your stellar history."

Caleb nodded vigorously. "Thank you, Gillian. And thank you, Anderson. I greatly appreciate C&R's work. Digging up the truth was really a game changer in getting these charges dismissed. I know I can be a little difficult to work with sometimes . . ."

"No, not at all," Anderson responded in mock protest, and they both started laughing, as Troy and the rest of the room watched this show.

"But I have been paying you all a shitload of money for decades. Maybe not at the level of what I hear you're about to get from that dysfunctional university. Nevertheless, I think I've earned the right to be demanding. So, speaking of being demanding, where's Terry?"

"Who's that?" Anderson asked.

Troy's body stiffened because he already knew the answer. Ten feet away, he was about to be called out in front of the firm by one of its major clients.

"Terry. That associate from the Sixteen Foundation event. Talking a big game about his *amazing* connection to a *great* researcher in Spain," he explained with an exaggerated, mocking tone.

Anderson looked confused for a moment, and then finally understood. But before he could offer clarification, Troy decided to assert himself into this impending train wreck of a conversation.

"Troy," he announced, and then took a couple of steps closer to the author and put his champagne flute down on the conference room table. "Troy Abernathy. Not Terry."

"Yes, Troy!" the author responded with a smile. "I guess my recall of names is about as valuable as your research skills. My life was on the line with false charges made by the *least credible human being on the planet* and you came up with a huge goose egg!"

Troy felt a wave of resentment surge throughout his body and mind. He told himself that the man could have him fired in an instant if Troy showed any disrespect, so he needed to stay restrained. But he wasn't going to smile, wasn't going to provide any sign that this was okay. Even though just standing there and taking it probably communicated that anyway.

"Anderson," Caleb continued, "you're not going to bill me for this waste of time, will you?"

"We'll discuss that," Anderson responded with a chuckle. "Considering we saved your neck in the end, I was thinking of charging you double, actually."

Caleb laughed. "And that's why I contest *every fucking invoice* from you people."

Troy was very aware of the room full of C&R employees who continued to watch, many grinning in supportive pretend amusement, no doubt unsure how much of this was pure sarcasm, how much based in truth. He assumed some felt they needed to act as if they found this all charming, the supposedly witty repartee. It was fraught with peril to not give an important MD and their famous client the reaction they sought.

"Okay, *Troy*," Caleb said. "I'll leave you alone. You can step back and return to sucking down the free champagne that I probably paid for. Let me talk with the real hero. Emma Richardson! Where are you, Emma?"

Across the room, Emma glanced toward the door.

"She's over there," Anderson said, pointing. "She's very talented, and as you can see, quite modest."

"Emma, please come here," Caleb said with a syrupy smile.

Troy watched her walk toward the client, taking one careful step after another, her eyes unfocused, her face expressionless. When she reached him, Caleb offered a handshake, which Emma accepted after appearing to consider it for a few seconds.

"Emma Richardson," he said, and shook his head with admiration. "*Amazing* work. If C&R had more employees like you, your parent company wouldn't need to consider filing for bankruptcy. Your current ownership wouldn't be desperately trying to sell to a private equity firm before the ceiling falls in. Your—"

"Okay, okay," Anderson interrupted. "That's enough."

Caleb briefly laughed at Anderson's discomfort, then refocused on Emma. "I see you're an *outstanding* researcher," he said. "I may ask you to help research my next novel."

"Oh?" she asked with a tone of profound innocence. "What's it about?"

"A man wrongly accused of serious misconduct. Anderson told me that's an important cause for you, and you've done some highly beneficial pro bono work with the Innocence Project. Now, because of this false accusation against me, it's a cause that's close to my heart too. I'm really in your debt, Emma. You've given me the most satisfying feeling a man can experience—vindication. So as a token of appreciation, I'd like to present you a signed copy of my latest novel, *Don't Spend It All in One Place*."

Troy continued to observe the proceedings as he whispered to

Julia, "If that fucker getting taken down wasn't going to bring all of us down with him, it would be a lot of fun to watch."

She took a long sip of her champagne. "Indeed."

The author then opened the front cover and began reading, "To Emma. With tremendous appreciation, Caleb."

He handed her the book and the employees applauded, with Troy and Julia perfunctorily joining in. Emma smiled uncomfortably as she held it in her right hand. "Thank you," she said matter-of-factly.

"No," he replied, as he placed a hand on her shoulder. "Thank *you*."

"A signed Caleb Lugo novel, wow," Anderson said. "He doesn't do that often. That's pretty valuable."

Emma nodded, and then seemed to breathe a little easier as Caleb removed his hand from her body. Troy then saw her look around the room, appearing unsure whether her participation was still required, if it was okay to retreat back to the food trays or out of the room.

There was an awkward silence for a few seconds, and then she finally broke it with a deadpan, "So maybe I should sell it on eBay today? In case it soon loses some of that value . . ."

12
Megan

Megan noted the overhead security camera watching her as she greeted Evina with their one permissible hug, the only physical contact they were allowed during each visit. They each had to stand on opposite sides of their assigned table and lean their bodies over the partition in order to embrace. One male correction officer seemed to be watching them particularly closely, no doubt making sure no rules were violated, no contraband was passed from visitor to inmate.

As they sat down across the table from each other, Evina began squeezing and kneading her fingers together, and Megan wished she could hold her friend's hand. Megan glanced at the six-inch scar on Evina's right forearm from a deep cut that had been sutured back together years ago.

"I'm so sorry," Megan said to her friend. "I thought the meeting with Congressman Montgomery was really positive. I didn't mean to give you false hope. But he resigned right after to become MHU president, and now he won't return my calls. Turns out he's just another phony politician."

Evina sniffed a couple of times before looking down at the floor. "It was the most promising sign I've had in so long . . ."

Megan sensed that Evina was fighting back tears and wished her friend would just let herself cry. "I know. I'm sorry."

"It's not your fault. It's really hard to get anyone besides you to help. I need the right person to really care, but I don't know who that would be."

"I've done a lot of research on federal clemency applications this week. Technically it's not a political process and you've submitted your petition to the right place. But the reality is... well... having a major celebrity promote your case would be very helpful."

Evina rolled her eyes. "I certainly don't know any celebrities. Do you?"

"Unfortunately, no. Some of the other people getting commutations have ties to major presidential campaign donors and fundraisers. So that's certainly not us either. I've tried to get media attention as a city council member, but it's just not working. We need to figure out a different strategy."

"I don't know how much longer I can live like this," she replied. "The loneliness, the constant fear, not being free to fight to see my daughter... I need to escape."

Escape.

Megan momentarily evaluated the absurd logistics of a prison break, quickly eyeing the multiple correction officers around the room. She wished it could be as simple as smuggling Evina a nail file in a cake, like on old TV shows.

"Do you think Congressman Montgomery would've gotten this done, if he'd stayed in office?" Evina asked.

"I really don't know. But it sounded promising. He had access to the right people. He said the White House needed his support for the budget vote, and probably other things."

"Do you know anyone else in Washington? Anyone with influence?"

She had been asking herself this question a lot, desperately trying to think of old college classmates or work colleagues who might be in a useful position. But unfortunately the only person she knew who had strong familiarity with the president's inner circle was in no position to ask the current administration for a favor.

She shook her head. "My political contacts are basically all Mountain Hill folks. We're a bunch of minor leaguers. We don't have any sway in Washington."

"Well, someone has to represent us in DC. Who's replacing Aaron Montgomery?"

"The seat's vacant. There's a special election in a couple of months. Hopefully whoever wins will be supportive. But they'll have their hands full with the new role. Even if I can set up a meeting with them, even if I can get them to care, they might not have the time or attention or influence to do anything meaningful for a long time."

Evina wrapped her arms around herself, squeezed as she bit her lip, and then let out a deep breath. "I've already been here a long time. *Eight years*. I can't do this for another long time."

"I know. But don't give up. We'll fight together and figure this out."

Then, for a moment, Evina's eyes brightened. "Megan, what if you ran for Montgomery's seat? Then *you* could be our powerful person in DC..."

Megan emphatically shook her head. She had hoped to be able to seek higher office in a few years, but in her wildest dreams that consisted of winning a state legislative seat. She began explaining the grim reality of the situation. "I barely squeaked by in my city council campaign. There's no support for me to run for Congress. And there's no time to spend a couple of years organizing, building coalitions, doing all that crap. It's a special election in two months. You need to already have a huge grassroots base, donors, name ID, and so much else."

But Evina tilted her head and scratched her forehead to show she was unconvinced. Her friend had a flame of hope now, and she wasn't going to let Megan simply blow it out.

Megan loved the idea of serving in Congress, of being in a real position of influence to assist Evina, and to work on a host of important issues to better her community and the nation. But if she ran, she would surely lose in a landslide. She'd seen this scenario before, when local politicians were too ambitious too soon and suffered overwhelming defeats that ended their careers. It would be a vicious and humiliating experience.

Evina shook her finger while looking intensely at Megan. "Running just for my commutation petition is nuts. I'd never ask that. But if serving in Congress is something you'd want to do, something your family would support, don't let anyone scare you away from trying. This seems like a huge opportunity. For both of us."

Megan remained silent for a few seconds. She knew these types of races were often decided long before voting began, with backroom deals and political power brokers like Professor Dowling doling out key endorsements and ballot lines that made the actual voting virtually irrelevant. Surely other candidates were already working to secure this essential support, if one hadn't closed the deal already.

"Can you put out some feelers?" Evina implored. "Get a sense of what support there is. Maybe you'll be surprised."

She considered her friend's plea. She'd told Evina repeatedly for years that she would do anything to help her, so how could Megan deny her now? It felt fruitless, but restoring Evina's freedom would surely involve relentless pursuit of something that felt like a long shot.

"Okay," Megan said, wondering how she'd even begin. She could gauge what kind of enthusiasm there might be for her by talking with the political, business, and union leaders that she knew. She could hear what they had to say. And of course, Dowling's endorsement would be critical. No way could she pull this off without obtaining backing from his all-important swing party. As much as he and his political machine repulsed her, she would have to reach out to him and ask for a meeting.

"This has to be right for you and your family," Evina said, with what seemed like a look of subtle confidence, a countenance that Megan had probably never seen from her. "It's a huge leap. But I think this is the answer. This is how I get out of here. And this is how you get to be a part of the real big national issues that you're meant for."

Meanwhile, Megan was as far from confident as she could be with this proposal. When it came to running for a congressional seat, the only thing she really did know was that there was so much she *didn't* know. And there was so little time to learn what was needed, while others who were more connected, experienced, and well-financed were surely already making moves.

"I'll talk to people," she responded. "But it's very likely this isn't going to work. If it isn't doable, please don't give up, okay? Because *I* won't give up. As long as you're in here, I'll never stop fighting to get you out."

Evina looked back at Megan and nodded in gratitude. "I promise, Megan. As long as you don't give up, I won't give up."

13
Serena

"This is a *beautiful* campus," Gillian said as she entered Serena's office. "Really stunning."

Serena nodded. It was true. Classic architecture mixed with modern construction, rolling fields on a beautiful landscape, and a brand-new, state-of-the-art student center. The school had it all. Such a perfect facade.

"We're very fortunate to have you here," Serena responded, as she gestured for Gillian to sit in the chair on the other side of her desk. "Having someone with real expertise who's not going to be constrained by the pressures of campus politics—such a breath of fresh air. How did you get connected with C&R?"

"I'm on the board of directors for Caleb Lugo's charity. The author."

"Yes, I'm familiar with his novels."

"It's a *wonderful* organization that supports young, aspiring, underprivileged writers. Caleb's one of Anderson Davis's longtime clients. And C&R is a big supporter of Caleb's foundation." She smiled as she added, "I guess that last fact might be influenced by the preceding one."

"No doubt. But it sounds like a great cause."

"It really is. Anyway, I'm very much looking forward to working with you, Serena. I reviewed all the documentation you sent for Ali Tyrell. Sounds like she's hesitant to do a formal interview."

"She doesn't trust this school. Which is understandable."

"I've dealt with reluctant complainants my whole career. We'll take it slow. I'll explain the process and let her get to know me."

Serena smiled. This was exactly the professional, caring, nuanced approach that was needed. "Right. So I told her this will just be an introductory meeting, and she won't be asked to discuss any details. Just to get her comfortable with you, the process, and what's going to happen next. She and her father have been very vocal in the media. The other victims are following her lead about what to do. I've scheduled four of the other girls . . . women . . . for tomorrow. I'm not sure they'll show. It probably depends on what Ali says to them after this meeting. Hopefully we can gain their trust a little and have a smooth handoff to you as our outside expert. You have all their prior statements and other records."

"Yes, I've read through it all. I've been doing this a long time, so nothing can shock me. But I'm still quite capable of being appalled. And I'm appalled."

"Appalled. Yes, one would think many people here would have been sufficiently *appalled* a long, long time ago. But . . ."

"Speaking of which," Gillian said, lowering her voice even though no one else was in the room, "I didn't want to say it in front of your president, but I loved what you did in that softball field video."

Serena laughed uncomfortably. "Thanks."

"I mean, it was a huge violation of best practices and broke every established rule and procedure . . ."

"Of course," Serena agreed. "Every one of them, I think. If I missed any, please let me know."

Gillian smirked and then looked at Serena with admiration. "But seriously, it's wonderful to see someone so fired up and fighting for these girls and not caring about bureaucratic BS."

Serena nodded. She was starting to really like this woman. Her phone buzzed, and she glanced at it. "Ali's in the conference room now with her father. Let's head over."

Serena and Gillian walked down the hall and into a bright conference room, with one window overlooking the main campus walkway that was now full of students who were either returning to campus or newly arrived for their first semester. Ali stood by the square oak table, looking sullen in the same denim jacket she had worn during their last meeting. Her father stood off to the side, studying his phone. When he noticed Serena and Gillian enter, he thrust it into the pocket of his jeans and walked closer to his daughter.

"Hi, Ali," Serena said tentatively. "Thank you very much for coming back today. Both of you."

Ali and her father didn't verbally respond, as they each turned their focus to Gillian.

"I'd like you both to meet Gillian Fenton," Serena said. "She's a former New York City sex crimes prosecutor with many years of experience, and she's going to lead the investigation. She and her team of experts will thoroughly investigate everything that happened, and she'll be a constant resource throughout the process."

Ali's expression was noncommittal, but Serena thought she saw her eyes open just a bit wider.

"Hi, Ali," Gillian said warmly. "Thank you for meeting with me."

Gillian's body language was kind and open, but also respectful and professional. She didn't extend a hand, not pushing any physical boundaries, but instead leaned her head down and nodded with a knowing look that communicated, *I know this is difficult and I'm here to help.*

Ali simply nodded back, then Darren stepped toward Gillian,

offered his right hand, and shook Gillian's. "Thank you for being here," he said.

"Shall we all have a seat?" Serena asked, and they each took a chair around the conference room table, with Ali on Gillian's right, and her father on his daughter's other side. "Ali, as I mentioned in my email, this is an introductory meeting so you and Gillian can get to know each other. We respect that you haven't agreed to a formal interview. If you do, you're free to bring any advisor or support person you'd like to that meeting. To ensure it's completely independent, no one from the university will be there. Gillian and her team have absolute authority to talk with anyone, ask any questions, reach the findings they think are correct, to hold responsible anyone who's accountable." Serena clasped her hands together and then placed them on the table. "I know you don't trust this school. I know attempts by others to report Rob Dempsey's actions years ago went nowhere, and I am so, so sorry about that. But those days are over. Neither of us will let that happen again. That's my vow to you."

"And please understand, Ali," Gillian followed, "that you're completely in control here. This is your experience, your life. You decide what you tell us, how you tell us. If we're talking, and you'd like a break or to continue on another day, that's completely fine. I don't want you to ever feel pressured. I know speaking with strangers about what happened is hard enough, so if there's anything I can do to make you more comfortable, just let me know. Okay?"

"Thank you," Ali responded softly.

"We're going to speak with as many relevant people as possible. Including Rob Dempsey, if he agrees to talk with us."

Ali shook her head slowly. "He may not remember anything about me. This fucked up my life, but I don't think it was that memorable to him. Especially now that I know there were so many others."

"We'll see about that," Gillian said. "And we're going to talk with as many of those 'others' as we can identify. You're not alone in this."

They were all quiet for a few moments, then Ali turned to her father. "Dad, can you leave the room?"

Darren seemed reluctant to exit, but after a pause he whispered, "Okay," and headed for the door. Before walking into the hallway, he turned to his daughter. "I'll be waiting right outside."

Once the door had closed behind him, Ali looked at Serena and Gillian. "I've spent a lot of years trying to put this behind me. Sometimes trying to forget. Sometimes trying to remember. I'm very concerned about trusting this investigation. I was naive when all this happened. I don't want to be naive again. A lot of us think the university is just going through the motions. Trying to look like they're taking it seriously when in reality they just want to get past this. I'm skeptical that any of this is really about *us*. About what was done to us."

"I'd feel the same way if I were you," Gillian responded. "That's why you decide what you want to do. What's best for you. But I've been doing this a long time, and I think telling us what he did may help protect other people, and that's very important."

The three of them sat at the table, silent for a while. Maybe twenty, thirty seconds, but it seemed much longer. Serena felt increasingly uncomfortable with the void, and had a growing sense she needed to speak soon, and say something. Anything. But she noticed Gillian was comfortable in the silence, and Ali appeared surprisingly calm. So she followed Gillian's expert lead, and the only noises for a little while were the distant voices of passing students, faculty, staff, and other visitors from beyond the window.

Ali finally broke the quiet. "I was only thirteen when all this started." Then the room was silent again. Serena thought about what she'd said—thirteen. Only thirteen years old.

Ali took a deep breath and continued. "I knew nothing. Really nothing. He'd tell me how great a hitter I was. How my fielding showed amazing potential. That with the right coaching I could be a big star. He'd take me into his office alone, show me videos of big-time college softball games, and we'd watch the best players and he'd point out their techniques and he'd say one day that could be me. Then the next summer I was back in the program, fourteen years old, and he gave me all this special attention, telling me how I'd gotten so much better over the past year. It was very exciting for me, because I did love softball. I wanted to be really good at it. I thought I was so lucky."

"Bad people often prey on those who trust them," Gillian said supportively.

"I know that now. So I was sitting in his office, on that brown sofa, watching softball videos after practice. And he asked me if I had a boyfriend. He said I was so amazing I must have a boyfriend."

"What did you say?" Gillian asked.

"I said yes, I did. Even though I didn't. It was getting weird, and I thought if I said I had a boyfriend we'd just get back to softball. And we did. Until a couple of weeks later when he asked me about my boyfriend. Asked me his name, and I made up something, I don't remember what. So then every day after practice I'd be in his office, and I'd be so excited to have his attention but also dreading that he would ask me something personal about this fake boyfriend, and I'd have to lie again. Then he told me he actually wasn't supposed to have players alone in his office, but he'd made an exception for me. Because I was so mature, not like most girls my age. He said that for someone as mature as me . . . age didn't matter."

Ali shook her head and exhaled, and then closed her eyes as Serena sensed Ali might start to cry. And if Serena hadn't been so furious, she might have begun crying herself.

"Thank you for sharing all this, Ali," Gillian responded. "I know it's not easy. If you're comfortable proceeding with a formal interview next week, we'll—"

"I know this isn't the interview yet," Ali interrupted, "and I'm still considering what I should do. But I'm grateful to have someone I can really speak with. Someone who's an expert, who cares."

Serena watched Gillian nod sympathetically. "This is the cause of my life," the former prosecutor answered.

"But I'm not sure this school will ever give you the freedom to use your experience the way you want to. They've always just tried to cover it up. They probably want that now, as much as possible."

"I'm here," Gillian offered as reassurance. "And when it comes to investigating sexual misconduct, I'm not the type who allows anyone to tell me what to do."

"And we would never try to tell her what do to," Serena added. "I fought for an independent inquiry led by an expert with extensive experience. Now we have that."

Ali looked out toward the window, in the direction of the distant softball fields. She was still gazing away from them as she said, "It's been really challenging talking about this. I spoke at the press conference because people need to know how important it is. That was very tough. But talking about the real specifics, going back into those memories, is going to be a million times worse. I'm not sure I want that."

"I totally understand," Gillian said. "You're in control of what you tell us."

"Okay, I'm going to tell you something now. And then I'll decide whether I want to keep talking with you in the future."

"Sure, Ali. That's fine."

"So he eventually put his arm around me in his office, then he kissed me on the head, and I was so embarrassed but also I believed his bullshit about how I was special and mature and he had this unique relationship with me. He asked if he could kiss me on the lips, and I let him. Then he asked if he could touch my chest . . ."

"And what did you say?" Gillian asked.

"I knew it was a bad idea, so I said I couldn't let him because my boyfriend would get upset. The boyfriend who didn't exist. And he just said, 'Well, how about you touch your chest and I touch my chest, and then neither of us are touching the other person so no one can get upset?' And I was stupid enough to say okay, and I went along with it. I knew it was wrong, that he was my coach and he shouldn't be doing this with me. But I didn't know how to say no. Every single day of my life, I think about that and wish I'd been able to."

She glanced toward the side of the room and a look of disgust crossed her face. Serena hoped this feeling was targeted toward Dempsey, and her heart broke as she sensed that the young woman was instead directing it at herself.

"Did this happen more than once?" Gillian asked.

"Yeah," Ali responded. "A few times. Then we were on the sofa one day and he said he had an idea. Instead of touching our chests, how about touching other body parts? And he said I should touch my crotch, and he would do the same thing next to me. And it wouldn't bother anyone because we'd still be just touching ourselves and nothing was wrong with that. It just escalated from there."

Serena's blood was boiling, and she forced herself to stay calm and professional as she thought not just about Ali's experience, about this coach's monstrous conduct, but also about how preventable this all had been for Ali and others. There were numerous warning signs, so many complaints over the years. If just one person had acted responsibly in all that time . . .

"Then what did he do?" Gillian asked.

"Eventually it got to the point that he would actually pull it out. His dick. And ask me to keep sitting right next to him and touch myself. And I would usually pretend I was, with my hand down my softball pants. Sometimes I did touch myself when I thought he was looking closely, because I didn't want to disappoint him." Her face was flushed and she grabbed a water bottle from the table, but continued talking without opening it. "I've spent so much time . . . years

. . . wondering why I agreed to that. I still don't have an answer. But it became a regular thing. And then he said that if anyone found out, he'd be fired and I'd be in trouble and never get into a major college softball program. That terrified me, and I didn't want to be the reason he lost his job. He said so many manipulative things to me . . ."

Gillian sat quietly for a moment as she nodded in understanding. "What else did he say?" she then asked.

"Like, since we all called him Uncle Rob, he said once that he was really glad 'uncle' was just his nickname and he wasn't my real uncle, because since it was just a nickname we could still be together and do things."

Serena could no longer stay silent. "*Where* was the assistant coach during all this? Cole?"

"Coach Cole," Ali replied, and then she appeared to lapse back into silent thought. Serena sensed she was replaying a memory. Finally, she continued, "I never talked to him about anything but softball. But he sure knew I was in that office with the door closed. A lot. And he saw me come out plenty of times. I remember him giving me weird looks, and I'd be so embarrassed. There's no way he didn't put two and two together. It was so, so obvious."

"That's one of the main reasons we've brought in Gillian and her team," Serena responded quickly. "Apparently a lot of people at this school should have known what was happening or did know and took no action to stop it. We want to uncover all that and find out who else is culpable."

"Cole should definitely be at the top of that list," Ali said.

"He is," Gillian assured her.

There was a knock on the door, and as Serena rose, the door opened and Ali's father entered, his face pinched.

"Were you listening out there?" Ali asked accusingly as she stood.

"No," he replied sharply. "But I wanted to know what was happening. I don't like you being alone anywhere on this campus."

Now Gillian stood too. "It's okay. I think we've gotten to know each other a bit. Maybe we can schedule a formal interview for next week when I'll be back with one of my co-investigators. Ali, I really appreciate all you shared. I know it's not easy."

"What I told you . . . that's just how it started. That was only the beginning. There's a lot more."

Gillian nodded sadly. "I figured that. Once someone like him feels emboldened, after all the initial boundary probing, they believe it's safe to take things to the next level. And to use the same tactics with others."

Ali took a couple of steps toward the door, and then turned to Gillian and reached out her hand. Gillian took it, and as Ali said, "Thank you. I really appreciate what you're doing," Ali stepped closer to Gillian and hugged her.

And Serena noted with satisfaction and relief that this ability to connect that Gillian either was born with or developed over her many years of working with sexual assault survivors was exactly what the university needed now.

When Ali and her father had left, Serena nodded in appreciation. "Hearing the way you speak with her, compared to how so many others around here react to these issues . . . My God, it's such a difference. I'm so glad you're here. We have four more scheduled for introductory meetings tomorrow. Hopefully they'll decide to talk to you."

"I hope so," Gillian replied. "I'll be ready."

"I know you will."

14
Troy

"What's the best date you ever had?"

Troy winced as he watched his firm's big client answer the interviewer's question. Even on his phone's little screen Troy could clearly see Caleb's smarminess.

With a mischievous, bad boy grin he responded to the female daytime talk show host on the couch next to him, "How do you define *date*?"

She chuckled, and someone in the 90 percent female studio audience hooted, "Woo-hoo!" which was followed by a few seconds of group laughter and a smattering of applause.

"Well," the interviewer said, and then paused for a second, "that's a fair question. Okay, hang on," she said, pressing a finger to her earpiece. "My producer's telling me the dictionary definition is 'a social or romantic appointment or engagement.' So I like to ask all my guests, what's the best date you ever had?"

Caleb sat there, appearing to be lost in thought. He grinned again. "Define *best*."

So fitting for a man whose career was grounded in the precise and effective use of language. The celebrated author, in front of an audience of fans, parrying the personal question with word games.

The audience released a new round of laughter, with a few whistles mixed in, as the host looked thoughtfully back at her interview subject.

"That's interesting. How *does* one define 'best'? I guess the generic definition is 'most outstanding' or something like that, but let's forget the dictionary this time. The answer is up to you. You decide what 'best' means. So let's try this one more time. What's the best date you ever had?"

Caleb scratched his chin and tilted his head to the side. He then looked straight at his questioner, gave her a quick wink with his right eye, and responded with a sly tone, "Define *had* . . ."

Troy groaned. How did people not find this guy nauseating? And wow, this clip was *not* going to age well. It was probably only a matter of time before the anticipated exposé of Caleb's multitude of sexual misconduct accusations was published. Which might or might not include the author's recent attempts at silencing and intimidating the women who dared make claims against him.

Now, as Troy headed to meet Julia in their duck-adorned safe space, he thought back to their earliest days together. The best date he ever had? Define *date*, define *best*, define *had*.

He and Julia had met at an apartment party hosted by a mutual friend near Union Square. Right away he was drawn to her, the attractive, confident woman with a cute nose piercing whom he overheard telling another woman that she worked for a private investigations firm. She went on to talk about a novel she'd just read. Suddenly she turned to Troy. "I loved this book, but I won't recommend it to you because guys don't read novels."

"That's sexist," he said, shaking his head in mock disapproval. "I avoid book recommendations anyway. If you end up not liking the book, the person thinks you rejected *them*."

Julia thought about this for a moment. "If someone doesn't appreciate a book I love, it's *definitely* a rejection of me."

The apartment was getting more crowded, the room increasingly hot. Julia pushed open a window, allowing a cool gust of air and the sound of car horns to fill the room.

"Then please don't recommend your book to me, because I really don't want to reject you."

The other woman melted away, and Julia looked Troy up and down. "So tell me your story. And proceed with caution. If you lie to me, I'll know it. It's what I do for a living."

He'd had no intention of trying to deceive this woman who piqued his curiosity in so many ways. He told her about his apartment in Astoria, near his uncle's seafood restaurant where he helped with the books, oversaw deliveries, and filled in with the waitstaff. "Not the best use of my legal studies degree. Just please don't run a criminal history search on me," he pleaded with a smile.

"Oh, I definitely will," she replied as she narrowed her eyes accusingly.

"I was young. And all that stuff is being decriminalized anyway."

"Well, you're still young. You should indulge more while you can, before you're too old to blame it on youthful indiscretions."

The following Saturday she texted him in the early afternoon. *Meet me tonight? Lmk if ur free. Up for something nice.*

He replied, *I want to see you but my cashflow situation isn't set up for nice tbh. I don't get paid the big bucks of an international investigations firm.*

I don't either atm. The managing directors keep that for themselves. I'm working to change that, she quickly texted back. Followed by the arm-flexing-a-muscle emoji.

Almost three years later, she was still on that mission, but hadn't come anywhere close to succeeding.

"Anderson opened MHU in Case Tracker," she huffed as they stood facing each other in the lactation room. "He gave himself seventy-five percent origination. Luke got twenty-five percent."

"Luke's not going be happy about that. He's going to—"

"Who gives a fuck about Luke? My point is I received *nothing*!" She paced around the small room, steaming and clenching her fists.

"Are you going to speak with Anderson again?"

"I just did!"

It was clear the conversation hadn't gone well. "So what happened?"

"I knocked on his door, stepped in, and he was cold—made clear he had no time for this. Didn't even offer me a seat. So I was just really direct. I said I saw in Case Tracker that I hadn't been given any MHU origination, that this was a huge matter, and that I was the one who brought it to C&R with *my* professional contact who's now the *president* of the fucking school." Troy raised his eyebrows. "Okay, I didn't say 'fucking school,' but I said the rest. I was respectful, but I was very clear. And he just glared and said, 'Julia, this is the second time you've spoken to me this way. You better make sure it's *the last time*. This investigation is more important than you, than me, than the whole firm. This is an opportunity . . . a *responsibility* . . . to find justice for a large number of sexual assault survivors while ensuring due process for those accused. The fact that you're focused on stats and credit, instead of aiding these women and preventing other girls from being victimized, is frankly just astounding.'"

Troy wasn't surprised, but he shook his head. "What a fucking phony piece of—"

"Right? Like he's not always bullying everyone to take every ounce of origination from every matter he can? I wish I had called him on that, although if I did, security would definitely have escorted me out. But I didn't let it drop. I told him I cared *very much* about the sexual misconduct issues, and I just wanted to make sure my significant contribution to this extremely important assignment was properly and fairly reflected."

"He must have been even more furious that you kept pushing."

"Yeah, but then he started talking with this fake-soothing tone, and he said, 'You will get appropriate credit for this, Julia. I can't say precisely how or when, but I give you my word that you will.'"

"The same bullshit we hear all the time."

"Then he said, 'I'm increasingly concerned your generation really is too focused on themselves, and not the greater good. Our society's going to crumble if everyone grows up feeling irrationally entitled and self-absorbed. My generation would *never even think* of speaking to a supervisor this way, and hopefully after this conversation you won't again either.'"

"*He's* calling *you* entitled and self-absorbed? My God, that's so crazy. It's totally the pot calling the kettle gaslit," Troy responded, as he searched his brain for a strategic insight that would help her cause. "He's never going to agree to give you anything real. Not when it's coming out of his origination. Maybe he'll offer you some of Luke's share, but that won't go over well with Luke, and will just create more problems for Anderson."

"We're going to easily bill millions," Julia bemoaned. "Probably an *unlimited budget*. I can't let them take this all from me."

She let out a frustrated growl as she threw her phone onto the sofa.

"Shhhhh, someone's going to hear you," Troy warned.

"I know you're not supposed to say this, but our lives would be so much better if he just dropped dead," she declared, her voice a notch lower but not quiet enough to calm Troy's fears that their conversation would be overheard. "It's not nice, but it's so fucking true. Then someone at his memorial service can do that thing where they say he was a great investigator, great manager and businessman, but he was an *even greater person*. And everyone nods and smiles like it's an original and poignant and accurate insight. And I'll nod too, Troy! I'm not an asshole. I know how to be fucking appropriate. I'll nod. It'll be a *phony* nod, just like everyone else will be phony nodding, but I have no problem with that."

Instead of following her down this road, Troy suddenly thought of one possible solution, which was actually resurrecting an idea Julia had thrown out days earlier in front of Emma. "Do you really have Aaron Montgomery's cell?"

"I do."

"Then let's fucking call him," Troy said decisively. "Right now."

"Yes," she answered, but he noticed her eyes seemed vacant, her face exuding some hesitance even though her voice was resolute.

"Okay, let's do it," he said encouragingly as she looked up at the ceiling and then back at him.

"I agree. The right move is to call him," she said, but she hadn't reached for her phone yet, which lay on the blue sofa next to her.

"You seem unsure."

"I'm not. Not unsure about calling him. Just not sure what to say exactly. He's a former congressman and now university president. He may be governor one day. I need to be careful. If I reveal any dissention or dysfunction here, he's going to get nervous about C&R and that may destroy the whole opportunity."

"But you know him really well, right? You and your parents?"

"Yes. Absolutely. I know him very well. *Very* well."

"*Very* well? What does that mean?" Troy asked. He had read stories about sleazy congressmen hitting on their female interns. "You like hooked up with him or something?"

"No," she answered immediately, and then paused to think for a couple of seconds. "And fuck you, Troy. Fuck you for asking that. Fuck you for *thinking* that."

"Sorry, it just sounded—"

"I mean, he was a little flirty once in a while, but that's it. He's known my family for a long time. I interned in his office for almost a whole year while I was in college. And my parents are probably the biggest financial backers for all his political campaigns. He knows me personally and likes me a lot. That's the reason C&R got in the door there!"

"How about you start by just thanking him?" he proposed. "You say, 'I wanted to call to personally thank you for retaining C&R on this investigation. We very much appreciate the trust you've placed in us and look forward to helping you and the university.'"

She pondered his suggestion as Troy waited. "Well, that's a little too formal," she said. "But it's the right sentiment. I like starting by thanking him and saying that's the main reason for the call. And then maybe bring up the origination issue as an aside, as if it's not a *huge* deal and I hadn't even intended to mention it."

"Yeah. That's good. You tell him in a casual manner that as a young associate you probably won't receive any of the real sales credit."

"As a young *female* associate," she amplified.

"Exactly," Troy said. He felt hopeful about how this was coming together, and grateful that he might have found a way to help her. "And then you'll be planting a seed. You said he's someone who likes you and your family, and your family has supported him in a huge way for many years. So he won't like that you're being screwed over, and he'll want to do something to help you, right?"

"I think so," she agreed. "I do."

"And if he tells Anderson or anyone at C&R that he wants to make sure you're *properly acknowledged* for this, they'll have to do that."

"Absolutely. He's basically our biggest client now. They want him to be happy. They *need* him to be happy."

She reached down, picked up her phone, briefly held it above her head triumphantly, and flashed Troy an approving grin. She then quickly moved her thumbs across the screen, and then placed the phone to her right ear and waited.

"It went straight to voicemail," she said.

"Okay, well you can—"

She held up her hand.

"Hello, Congressman Montgomery . . . this is Julia McGinnis. I hope you're doing well. Congratulations on your new position . . . I know it's a very *challenging* time for the university, and you're the perfect person to lead MHU through this . . . *situation*. I wanted to thank you for entrusting my firm with this important investigation. We really appreciate the opportunity and won't let you down . . . I'm sure you're *extremely* busy, but if there's a good time when I could briefly speak with you, please let me know. Thank you again, Congressman. Or it's *President* Montgomery now, right? Sorry. Anyway, my parents send their best too. Take care. Bye."

15
Megan

*A*BSOLUTELY, Professor Dowling texted back. *Coffee 4:30 at Finn's?* The quick response encouraged her. *Perfect*, she tapped. *See you then. Thank you.*

It was the next logical step in Megan's evolving plan. Set up meeting with powerful party boss Roger Dowling. Secure his support for potential congressional run. Announce candidacy for Congress. Win election. Use new position to gain presidential support for Evina's clemency petition. Free Evina from prison. Continue to use her national platform to save the world.

She dashed toward the City Hall main doors after a meeting of the education committee, where she continued to advocate for better city support for its public schools. Various citizens milled around the large lobby, and Megan knew most were there to meet with elected and appointed government representatives. Some lobbying their council members, others excitedly securing marriage licenses, and a few attending their third or fourth or maybe even fifth meeting with the planning department as they fought neighbor opposition and bureaucratic red tape to secure variances and other approvals.

As she exited the building and rushed down the steps, a thin man with narrow eyes and overgrown sideburns stood in her way and held up his phone. "Are you going to make a statement about the Caleb Lugo article?"

Megan was used to being asked her views on all sorts of matters that had little or nothing to do with her role and responsibilities. She was a semi-prominent member of the community now, and people wanted her opinion.

"Caleb Lugo article?"

"Yes!" came the harsh response, full of urgency, with a tinge of exasperation.

"I saw something about a European sex worker who accused him of groping her. I think the DA dropped all charges, right?"

"No, not *that* article. The new one. From *The New York Times*. You really haven't seen it?" he asked in disbelief. "Don't you have a staff that keeps you informed about . . . what you need to be informed about?"

Staff.

What did this guy think? That she was in Congress?

"Well, I'm kind of chief cook and bottle washer for my city council office," she answered. "Which keeps me pretty busy. Not to mention raising a family . . ."

He held the phone screen in front of her face, and she looked at the article.

Author Caleb Lugo Intimidated, Paid Off Sexual Harassment Accusers for Decades, the headline read. She perused the first couple of paragraphs, which discussed numerous women the author had allegedly sexually harassed or assaulted. These women had reportedly been aggressively investigated by Lugo and coerced into accepting settlement payments and signing nondisclosure agreements. The article said it had identified several women who had not previously made claims but were willing to speak on the record about nonconsensual sexual interactions with Lugo after they were approached by the paper. None of this was relevant to anything in Megan's life, especially the core issue of Evina's freedom that had dominated her thoughts for almost a decade.

She looked up from the phone. She had read one of Lugo's books a while ago. What was it called again? "Thanks for sharing. Sounds like he's quite a jerk." And hopefully that would be the end of this discussion. She began to walk past him when the man grabbed her right arm in a manner that was awkwardly and surprising rough, taking her by surprise and almost making her stumble on the City Hall steps.

"Excuse me?" she said brusquely, dropping her council member charm for a moment.

"You're not getting it," he said, releasing her arm. "They had investigators look into these women. Finding whatever info they could, including embarrassing photos and videos from their pasts, and then using all that to pressure them into accepting settlements, to stay quiet, so he could keep doing this to others. Lugo's people threatened to send the images to their families and employers if they pursued their claims! It's so disgusting. I mean, I have two sisters and—"

"I get it. It's revolting. Fortunately there's finally been a society-wide reckoning where people like him are being held accountable, and survivors are empowered to come forward—"

"The investigative firm! Did you see the name of the firm?"

"No, I didn't," she said, still confused as to why he was subjecting her to this barrage. "Who is it?"

"The article says that according to two unnamed sources, Lugo's been using C&R Investigations to find adverse information on these women. Information that's been weaponized to silence and intimidate them! C&R!"

Then it all clicked. C&R Investigations. The firm just retained by the university to investigate the horrendous sexual misconduct accusations against Rob Dempsey and cover-ups by others at the institution. The same company that apparently had also helped author Caleb Lugo bully women accusing *him* of sexual assault.

"How can *our university* retain a firm like that?" the man asked with an apoplectic tone.

"It's terrible," Megan agreed. "I mean, was Harvey Weinstein unavailable to conduct the investigation?" The man began nodding vociferously, and she realized that was actually a pretty good sound bite, and she'd have to use that later when she spoke publicly about this development. Which would have to be very soon so she could be one of the first to call for the university to abandon this firm, and she could be seen as a clear leader on the issue. She would need Aimee to draft a statement immediately.

Or maybe she wouldn't have to put out a formal statement in order for her opinion to become public.

"Can you repeat that?"

Megan recognized the young reporter from a local paper, its political beat writer who was assigned to cover city government. A few other people were also starting to congregate around her, now approximately fifteen individuals who listened to what the city council member had to say about this suddenly emerging controversy.

"Which part?" she asked.

"About the university and C&R," he responded. "I don't quote from conversations I accidentally overhear. But if you're comfortable repeating it on the record, I'd like to report what you said."

"Look, I don't have all the facts yet. But there are a lot of serious questions that need to be answered. The university obviously can't retain a firm for the Rob Dempsey investigation that's been working to shield another serial sexual offender from culpability. Not while I'm in office."

"And the Weinstein quote? Can I use that?"

"Sure. Go ahead," she answered.

Another reporter followed up, "So you're calling on President Montgomery to fire C&R?"

She then realized that she hadn't really thought this through, and instead had impulsively reacted from her gut. Now she was suddenly cornered by this phrasing that was the logical extension of her previous comments, but not how she wanted her thoughts to be characterized.

She knew Aaron well enough to understand he would absolutely want to avoid changing firms, because hiring them had been his first big, decisive move as president. He proclaimed the retention of this prestigious investigations practice as a sign that he was bringing real solutions, actual gravitas, and true accountability to the university crisis. He had declared that he thoroughly vetted C&R.

If he was forced to suddenly cut them loose and admit a major error, he would fear looking weak and incompetent. And she knew he hated to be seen as backing down, detested any suggestion that others were showing him up and compelling him to backtrack. He exuded control and wanted to always be seen as being in control.

Challenging him directly was really unhelpful, and unnecessary at this point, as she still held out hope that he would get back to her and provide support or guidance for Evina's petition in Washington. And maybe throw her some help or even his invaluable endorsement if she entered the congressional race. Of course he wouldn't do any of that if he saw her as a political enemy. But had she already gone too far? She also realized she had only read a small part of one article about C&R and Caleb Lugo. Maybe there was more to the story.

"Aaron Montgomery is a strong, smart, caring leader," she responded. "I have absolute confidence he'll make the correct decision."

"And the 'correct decision' is firing C&R?"

"Sorry, that's all I'm going to say right now. I think I've made my position quite clear," she said, even though she knew she hadn't. "Thank you."

She walked briskly down the remaining steps and toward her car amid the warm sunshine of Main Street, hoping her "quite clear" position wouldn't now blow up in her face.

16
Serena

Serena threw the stapler with all her might against the far wall of the office, where it dented the plaster and cracked into two pieces. Then she covered her face with her hands and dropped her head onto her desk.

After several seconds, she looked up but didn't immediately return to the horrendous news article on her computer screen. Instead she gazed at her bookshelf, which displayed the pristine, red and unread spine of *Don't Spend It All in One Place* by Caleb Lugo.

Serena liked his novels very much, appreciated how they dealt with serious topics but always ended with a hopeful message. She had wanted to start this book ever since it was released the previous month. But she had this thing that had prevented her from doing so, another remnant from her childhood. It wasn't just protocols for cutting and smearing names on birthday cakes that shadowed her adult life.

As a young girl and a voracious reader, every time she finished a full-length novel her parents asked how many days it had taken her to read it. She would proudly declare "four" and receive polite claps, or "three" and see their eyes light up. Even less and they would remark,

"You are *so* smart!" or "I bet no other kids your age are reading as much as you!"

There was the time at age eleven when she was home on a snow day and raced through *Wuthering Heights* from dawn to her bedtime, and then announced, "I read this whole book in *one day*!"

The reaction was overwhelming, as her parents both shook their heads in amazement and her mom yelled out, "Unbelievable! You are *incredible!*" She wanted that reaction again, and again. So even now, she involuntarily focused on how many days it took her to read each book, and if a novel lingered too long from start to finish, she had a nagging feeling that she had done something wrong, disappointed someone, maybe the entire world. It just felt like some negative karma would be looming because of this failure to be efficient.

But that meant she couldn't start a new book at night, especially really late, because then that would count as "day one" and she would be wasting a precious day for the stats that lived in her head. Better to begin a novel when she could really devote some time to it during that given day, so she wouldn't risk already being on day two with the clock ominously ticking and far too few pages to show for it.

With all her responsibilities at the university, she'd been regularly working late into the evening and on weekends, and by the time she had a free half hour before falling asleep, it just seemed foolish to read when so little could be covered and "day one" would be squandered.

She knew the whole concept was absurd, but felt powerless to prevent these notable childhood concepts of irrational guilt from influencing her life as a grown woman, no matter how much she wanted them gone. And she was acutely aware that her silly hang-ups were nothing compared to the traumatic youthful repercussions that would surely linger forever for Ali Tyrell. Would there ever be a day in Ali's life when she didn't reflect at some point on her experiences with Rob Dempsey?

Now, before Serena could remove this novel from her TBR list, she was instead reading about the writer himself.

Author Caleb Lugo Intimidated, Paid Off Sexual Harassment Accusers for Decades

It was an extensive exposé detailing all sorts of alleged misconduct. Thoroughly researched, sourced, and documented with on-the-record accounts, incriminating text messages, and excerpts from NDAs. Not unlike the one about the Fortune 500 CEO a few months ago, or the prominent law professor before that, or the affable game show host the previous summer.

Terrible, reprehensible, and increasingly routine. Nothing that would shake her personal world under normal circumstances. But two paragraphs in the middle of the article made her breath stop, her head pound, her spine ache.

According to two unnamed sources, Lugo has utilized C&R Investigations, based in New York, to find damaging information on several women who raised potential claims against the author. Three of the women stated they were presented with potentially derogatory or embarrassing details about their pasts, including explicit photos and videos taken without their consent, by representatives for Lugo in a manner that was meant to intimidate them into silence. C&R offered no comment, citing client confidentiality.

"Caleb Lugo traumatically derailed my life. Then C&R Investigations destroyed my life," said Bianca Velencoso, a Barcelona-based model and actress who accused Lugo of sexual assault earlier this year in New York City. "Anyone who supports that firm is supporting the unethical harassment and denigration of sexual misconduct victims."

Serena heard Gillian's voice in her head, recounting her connection with C&R.

I'm on the board of directors of Caleb Lugo's charity. The author. It's a wonderful organization that supports young, aspiring, underprivileged writers. Caleb's one of Anderson Davis's longtime clients. And C&R is a big supporter of the foundation. I guess that last fact might be influenced by the preceding one.

"I need to see Aaron," she said into her phone. She expected his assistant to tell her he was unavailable, possibly able to fit her into the schedule the next day. She was ready to argue for an immediate meeting, but after a few seconds of silence, the woman responded, "He says to come here now, Serena."

It was just a short walk down Walnut Street to the president's office building, and Serena didn't rush, using the time to get her thoughts together. Clearly C&R needed to be replaced. As much as she had liked Gillian, the university had never really canvassed its other options. No meaningful interviews of other firms. The whole process had been sloppy, and now they would all pay the price of looking incompetent and indecisive as the school that botched this whole situation from the beginning had another high-profile embarrassment.

Nevertheless, all that was the easier part.

The larger problem was that none of these young women trusted the university at all. For understandable reasons. Gillian had just met with Ali and four others in the past couple of days, begun to hear their stories, bonded with them one by one, used her years of experience, compassion, and expertise to gain their confidence. Now they would be told she was gone? Why would any of them agree to speak with someone else now, to open up yet again and relive their traumas with a brand-new investigator?

Somehow, Gillian needed to be involved with the transition to the new team, whoever that would be. She could participate in meetings where a gentle handoff was made. They couldn't just pull the rug out from under these complainants after how perfectly she had connected with them. Serena needed to make sure Gillian wasn't immediately and completely cut off with the rest of her firm.

There was no perfect answer, but it was the least cruel option to have her assist them for just a little longer. Aaron would probably resist that, fearing the optics of a Caleb Lugo board member and C&R employee being associated with this matter for another second. Serena needed to explain the complexity, and convince him to do what was needed for these girls.

She entered the administrative building, rode the elevator three floors, and walked down the hall to the president's suite. She slowed at the admin's cubicle but was immediately waved into the office. Aaron Montgomery held a phone to his ear as he paced behind his desk, with his MHU-purple tie loose and the sleeves of his white dress shirt rolled up. He raised a finger toward Serena.

"Thank you," he said into the phone. "That's very helpful. I completely agree. We need to show we're in control here. If we look defensive, the situation balloons even more. Yes, I know . . . I've also been told some students are holding a rally about this tonight." He paused, listening into his phone, and then let out a brief, exhausted laugh before continuing, "Exactly. A bunch of cross-faded, nonbinary teenagers protesting on the college green won't dictate how we proceed."

Serena cringed at this last line, and wanted to vocally object to the disparaging and offensive characterization of the student body, for whom the university existed in the first place. But before she could decide whether to take up this additional battle, he ended the call and looked at her. "That was our government relations guy, Roger Dowling. You know him?" he asked.

Yes, she was familiar with Roger, although mostly by reputation. Her understanding was that he was some kind of glorified political hack, influential to some extent in local government for some unknown reason, brought to the university as a favor to someone, for something. Or something like that.

MHU continually seemed to be stumbling from one budget crisis to another, but its footprint was still large enough, its total spending and financial influence in Mountain Hill so huge, that it always maintained sufficient room for cronyism. People who were put on payroll and given certain responsibilities without a clear reason for their presence on campus.

"Not well," she replied. "We've crossed paths a little."

"He's really good. He gets this stuff."

"What stuff?"

"We're the latest target for the outrage police. And the media's job is to keep it going as long as possible. More stories, more clicks, more views. First they condemn what's happened here over the past decade. Then they go after the investigators. We replace them, and they set their sights on taking down the new team. Over and over. It never ends. We become a constant punching bag, the symbol of everything that's wrong in this world. It happened again and again when I was in Congress. The media feeds off scandal, and right now we're their soup du jour. We show weakness, and the feeding frenzy grows."

Why was he so quickly dismissing this bombshell, painting it as just part of the media's ongoing quest for titillating content? This was a major author, facing very serious allegations, and there was a real possibility C&R had been complicit. The firm's connection to the university and the Rob Dempsey investigation was far from trivial.

"I'm not sure I follow you," she said. "I agree the media is often irresponsible. But you read the *Times* story, right? You saw what they said about C&R?"

"Yes, and I'm not saying we completely ignore all that. We can't just proceed as planned. But I won't allow us to appear like we're caving either."

"Okay..."

"Unfortunately, Gillian Fenton's no longer an option. She's not just with C&R. She's also a Caleb Lugo board member. She can't be our lead investigator."

Of course, Serena thought, as she stiffened inside with anger and frustration. Gillian was too tainted, probably through absolutely no fault of her own. She was an experienced sex crimes prosecutor who devoted her career to these issues. Doubtful she knew about Lugo's antics while serving as one of many board members on his nonprofit.

But none of that mattered now. She was clearly too tarnished for this assignment. And probably Gillian would prefer to be removed before her involvement set off the inevitable media frenzy, with her name and reputation at the center.

"I agree," Serena said sadly. "She was perfect for the job, but I understand she can't continue now. One thing that's really important, though... She already met with five of the complainants, including Ali Tyrell, who the others are all looking to for guidance. Gillian bonded with these young women who have especially egregious accusations against Rob Dempsey."

"She still can't—"

"I know. Sorry to interrupt, but I understand she can't be the one for us. But I want to stress that it's extremely important, critically important, that she help transition to the new firm. Otherwise we're going to lose these women."

"What do you mean by 'lose' them?"

She felt her implication was so obvious, but apparently an explanation was now required. "They won't trust the process," she said. "Without Gillian, they won't trust the investigators. They won't trust *us*. We'll never get their full stories and learn who else was culpable. We *have* to find out the role of other personnel, like the assistant coach, Cole Malinowski. Law enforcement is just focused on Dempsey. We need to dig deeper, so we can prevent this from occurring again. Here and elsewhere."

He nodded in a manner that flirted with being patronizing but stopped just short, instead indicating through his eyes and slight smirk that she wasn't really understanding the situation and unfortunately he would need to lay out the realities to her.

"Serena, I want this investigation to be successful as much as you do. It's the only way to get the university out from under this mess so it can move on. That's what I was brought here to do. The alleged conduct is atrocious. Unconscionable. But our job isn't to compel these girls to tell their stories, especially if they don't want to. If they don't feel comfortable, for whatever reason, that ends that part of the inquiry. We'll allow the investigators to speak with anyone they want. We won't cover up anything. The chips will fall where they may. But if the potential complainants won't speak with the investigative team anymore, then it is what it is. It's just not our problem at that point. Gillian can't have any contact from this moment forward. Not with us, not with witnesses. That's essential and nonnegotiable."

"But it *is* our problem if they won't speak with us," she pushed back. "We need to learn everything in order to help them heal, and prevent this from occurring again on our campus or wherever the employees involved work next. We know that members of this institution in positions of authority and trust turned a blind eye, and possibly worse, while he was molesting these teenagers. We can't rely on law enforcement figuring all that out for us. We need to learn everything we can, and witness cooperation is essential. If these women won't speak with us because they don't trust us, we need to do everything possible to overcome that. We were building that trust, but I'm afraid without Gillian, after these meetings she had, we'll lose it."

For the moment, Aaron just shrugged. Then he responded, "I was hired to navigate a very complicated path to save this institution from obliteration. That's my chief mission as interim president. Save this school, and get us past this. I appreciate your passion, but I've made my decision."

"This is going to put the new firm, whoever that ends up being, in a very difficult position."

"There's no new firm, Serena."

"What? You're canceling this investigation? That's not—"

"No. Of course not."

"But if it's done without an independent firm, no one will believe the findings. And we don't have the bandwidth internally for what's needed. There are hundreds of interviews to conduct. It'll be a disaster."

"I know all that. We need an independent firm. And we won't start all over with a new one. That would show us to be indecisive and dithering in the face of all these attacks."

"I don't understand."

Again the smirk, and then a sigh, with the implied message that it was an annoyance that she didn't understand and he would have to keep spelling it out for her.

"We're keeping C&R. But Gillian is excluded," he told her. "And anyone else who worked at all with Lugo is banned. It's a big firm and a very prestigious one. They're the gold standard for investigations, going back decades. So a few of them worked with Caleb Lugo? They have hundreds, probably thousands of clients. Worldwide resources. We just use the people who've never been associated with him. Roger proposed this path, and he's absolutely right."

Serena was stunned into silence. This was the worst of all worlds, sticking with C&R sans Gillian. Maintaining a highly problematic firm but throwing away their best asset, as much as Serena knew she had to be disqualified. "I'm intimately familiar with their RFP response," she finally said. "The rest of the firm has little subject matter experience. Without her, they're just a name."

"It's quite a name, though. We were lucky to get them. We fire

C&R, and we'll be laughed at from coast to coast. We'll look even more incompetent than the previous administration if we cut a prominent firm over one client and start over. And it would just embolden everyone who's attacking this school. I'm not allowing that to happen. It would be different if we knew about this before we retained them. But I'm not going to flip-flop now. I was brought here to show decisive leadership, not hide from the woke mob under my desk. This is the way to best manage the situation."

Manage the situation.

So that was the goal. Try to prevent others from making this volatile crisis even more chaotic. Project stability. His plan was for C&R to conduct its investigation. They find what they find. End of story. Checking the box, the big box that shouted that an independent investigation was needed for the university to be seen as diligent and humane and worthy of continuing to exist.

All astonishingly insufficient and unacceptable.

"This is a huge mistake," she said bluntly. "It won't lead to uncovering the full truth. And people will attack us for using Lugo's firm."

He sighed again, looked at his watch, and then focused on Serena. "You have your instructions. And I don't want you speaking with Gillian or anyone else who's prohibited from working with us now. There needs to be a complete break immediately. And don't talk to the media."

Should she threaten to resign? Would that make a difference? More likely it would just be welcomed. And she had no idea how she could possibly afford Kayla's tuition if she was no longer covered as the child of an employee.

"Understood," she said, and then walked out and returned to her office. She slammed the door closed, sat in front of her computer, and began poring over countless news articles from around the country.

For over an hour, Serena reviewed media condemnations of Caleb Lugo and C&R's work on his behalf as she grew more enraged and increasingly determined not to simply acquiesce to Aaron's misguided plan. She noted the plethora of social media posts referencing Lugo's alleged sexual assaults using the hashtag #thishappened. Finally, she closed her browser in disgust and reached for her phone.

Two rings, and then it went to voicemail, so she hung up, waited ten seconds, and tried one more time. Voicemail again.

I need to speak with you, she texted. *It's urgent. Please.*

She stared out the window, watching students, staff, and visitors strolling around campus. After a couple of minutes, her phone vibrated.

"Thank you for getting back to me," she said, her voice shaky.

"There's nothing I can say to you, Serena. Except that I wasn't aware of any of these allegations. I'm as shocked as anyone."

"I know, Gillian."

"And I'm not even allowed to speak with you. I'm totally cut off from MHU." Her speech was rushed, almost breathless. This was a different Gillian, no longer calm and authoritative. "God knows I wanted to help you. But I just can't now. We can't talk anymore. Okay? You'll just get both of us in even more trouble. Please don't make this situation worse."

"I just have one question. That's it."

Silence. Gillian didn't ask what the query was, nor did she prompt Serena to continue. But the former prosecutor didn't end the call yet either.

"Is this going to be a real investigation now?" Serena asked. "Without you. Without whoever else is disqualified. You know the other personnel there. I don't. There's so much at stake. Will there be the right expertise? Can it still be staffed with good people? Or will it just be a bunch of warm bodies thrown here to conduct interviews, bill a lot, and write a passable report? Is this going to be *real*?"

"You know I can't answer that on this call."

"*Why?* Why can't you answer?"

"Because I don't want to be quoted, Serena. I'm not supposed to speak with you."

"I'm not going to *quote* you! I need to know so I can protect these girls."

A few moments of quiet, and then Serena heard a siren come through the phone, emanating from somewhere in the distance on Gillian's end.

"The truth is, I have no idea," she finally answered hesitantly. "I don't think anyone does right now. We're all reeling from this . . . Okay, I need to end this call. Please don't contact me again."

17
Troy

ANDERSON IMPATIENTLY waved Troy into his office as he sat at his desk. "Shut the door," he ordered gruffly. "Sit down."

So Troy did both, as instructed. From his seat, he could see an email still open on the screen. From Luke...

25% origination is unacceptable, and I'm not going to stand for this. It's 50/50 or I escalate to senior leadership. I'm not some associate who you can manipulate and take advantage of.

Anderson caught his glance looking at the screen, and he closed the email quickly just as Troy darted his eyes away. His boss continued to stare at the now empty monitor, no doubt considering whether he should acknowledge what Troy saw.

"Brief window into life as an MD," he finally said with irritation, shaking his head. "Keep this between us. The guy was just coincidentally in my office when this matter came in and now he's busting my balls because he thinks he's entitled to half the origination credit."

And what exactly did you do to bring this in? Troy thought, but of course dared not ask. It was Julia's connection, Gillian's expertise. What was Anderson's contribution? Identifying and hiring Gillian? Wasn't that already in progress before MHU landed on the C&R doorstep?

If Anderson thought Troy had been previously unaware of the multitude of MD battles over origination credit, he was very wrong. Many times Troy had been in a room during a tense conversation in which his supervisors tried in vain to speak cryptically to avoid his comprehension. And he had been exposed to these types of emails in the past too.

He remembered another Anderson/Luke battle from six months ago. Luke had a sizable potential new client that Anderson nixed because they were arguably adverse to a small Anderson client from the previous year. Troy had originally been staffed with Luke, so when Anderson tried to tank the new engagement, Troy was incidentally included on a few of the emails back and forth.

This is NOT a conflict, Luke had written. *And even if it was, you haven't done work for them in over a year. Plus, the total billings were miniscule. That doesn't justify declining this assignment.*

A conflict is a conflict, Anderson responded. *It's not about how big the matter is. Just because you're originating it doesn't make the preexisting client conflict disappear.*

Troy had been walking down the hall later that afternoon when Luke brushed past him and muttered, "Sorry you had to be exposed to that. Amazing how handing him thirty percent of the origination makes a conflict go away."

Now Anderson looked at Troy solemnly. "We all need to focus more on helping our clients, and less on sales credit. Speaking of which, what is going on with Julia McGinnis?"

"She's working very hard. Trying to help the firm."

Anderson clearly didn't appreciate this answer, as he grimaced and tossed a pen across his desk. "Look, it's in her own best interest if one of her fellow associates advised her to tone down the attitude, okay? So you might want to mention that to her. But that's not why I called you in. We need to talk about Caleb. We had to cut all ties with him today," he explained. "After that article we just couldn't have him as a client."

"Okay," Troy responded. Especially while C&R was angling to be bought, it couldn't have a pariah client on its current books.

"So you need to tell that Spanish sub to cease all work immediately. Call now if you have to. I don't care how late it is there. Direct orders from senior leadership. Supposedly this prostitute is looking to do a big interview or speech about the whole matter so she can call for Caleb to be charged by a special prosecutor. We have to stay as far away as possible, or people may think this firm had a bigger role than we really did."

Just as he and Julia had feared and predicted, Emma's actions were now in the beginning stages of devastating the company. One Mountain Hill city councilwoman had even compared C&R to Harvey Weinstein because of its Lugo ties, and social media was all ablaze with her soundbite. Troy also saw online that a student-led MHU protest over C&R's hiring was planned for that evening.

"This story had the potential to be a double disaster," Anderson lamented. "Because we'll lose all of Caleb's business, plus potentially forfeit MHU. But it's not just about revenue. Troy, I want you to know that I'm personally *disgusted* by all these allegations. I've worked for this man for decades and *I had no idea*. I thought it was just Velencoso. One woman. A prostitute trying to get attention. Until that *Times* story came out, I really didn't know how big this was. There was no way I could have known. And of course we had nothing to do with all of the alleged harassment of the accusers that the *Times* irresponsibly tied to our firm."

It wasn't the first occasion Anderson had lied to him about something that was so clearly not true. Troy sat and listened, doing his best not to reveal his actual thoughts. As in the past, he nodded, as if everything he was being told was credible. Maybe that's why Anderson continued to feed him falsehoods with confidence.

"Anyway, we're really fucked now with MHU," Anderson continued.

Troy's heart sank. Julia's huge engagement was about to be wiped out, and Anderson would be free to fire her, as he'd promised. Troy was barely surviving in this place with her. He would be completely lost if she were gone.

"They're canceling our contract?" Troy asked with concern.

"Oh, no," Anderson replied quickly. "I just spoke to their president. They're keeping us."

He handed Troy a piece of paper that contained a news article printout from a local publication near the university. The headline read: *C&R Worked for Lugo, and Now for MHU.*

He started scanning, and quickly settled on Aaron Montgomery's quote in the second paragraph:

> *"C&R is very respected, and I have full confidence in the work they're going to do. This is a large firm, and the investigative team assigned to the university has no connection at all with Caleb Lugo. Not one of them has ever billed an hour to that man."*

"Wow," Troy responded. "That's incredible." He wanted to get up and run to tell Julia.

"Their president told me he doesn't want to bow to pressure. He wants to show strength and proceed with C&R. He asked if we could still do this without Gillian, because she's on the Sixteen Foundation board. And without any C&R staff who *ever* worked with Caleb. Plus, we'd have to show billing records so their board of trustees could confirm all that. And of course I said of course. We just lost a ton of revenue from Caleb. And other clients may drop us. We need MHU more than ever."

Troy nodded. This part was no doubt true. And Anderson didn't say out loud what he was surely thinking, that all this might make

DePalma Capital flee from their potential C&R acquisition. The firm's Chapter 11 filing might be inevitable.

Anderson continued, "The school's facing potential catastrophic liability. Our fees will easily be in the millions. We need to do *whatever it takes* to keep this assignment. This is going to be very challenging, and I'll need your help."

"I'll help however I can," Troy said quickly and sincerely.

"Good. Because I promised Aaron Montgomery, and he's now promised the MHU community and trustees, that we'll *immediately* provide a team of C&R experts who haven't ever billed anything for Caleb. As you know, the problem . . . our huge problem . . . is that over the last thirty years, we basically all have."

"Maybe we can subcontract with another company that specializes in this type of work. A firm with experience in sexual misconduct investigations."

"So they can take half the revenue?" Anderson snapped. "Or more? Come on."

"So what are we gonna do?"

"I'm not sure. Somehow we'll find a way to make it work. I just don't know how yet. But I'm not losing this. And I don't want staffing problems to cost us even *one dollar* of revenue. The reality is we need it all."

Anderson's desk phone rang, and both of them looked over to see "Luke Holloway" on the caller ID.

"I need to deal with this," Anderson explained. "Come back in fifteen minutes. Then we're going to start figuring out how the fuck we staff this thing."

"Sure," Troy answered. And within moments he hurried down the corridor, simultaneously firing off a text to Julia, writing that he needed to speak with her immediately, outside the office. Because what he was about to tell her was too delicate, too sensitive, to be spoken about within C&R's walls, even in their special room.

* *

When he'd first gotten to know Julia, she hadn't disclosed the dysfunctional, toxic side of her company. In fact, she hadn't been truthful in any way about what it was really like to work there. That was back when he was feeling the surge of adrenaline-laced excitement for this intriguing new woman in his life. Before he messed that all up. Before he became CEO of the friend zone.

After those initial Saturday texts, in which she prodded him to meet her in Manhattan that evening, he put on a pair of charcoal slacks and a white-and-blue-checked dress shirt with dark buttons, and hopped on the N toward Midtown. Soon he was facing her at a street corner on a warm May evening. She wore a gray skirt with a black short-sleeve top and matching boots that rose to just inches below her knees.

"You look nice," she said. "I don't know about you, but I've had a stressful week. Exhausting. Definitely need a drink."

"Sounds great."

They entered a nearby bar that was filling up with the evening crowd and sat at the only two available bar stools. She ordered a vodka soda.

"Same," Troy added. Within minutes their drinks appeared, they clinked glasses, and both took a sip.

"What was stressful about your week?" he asked.

She rolled her eyes. "What was *not* stressful about my week? All sorts of insanity. Actually, that's pretty standard where I work."

"So you're really a private investigator?" he asked. Troy saw she was halfway done with her first drink already, and he considered signaling the bartender for another round. He knew he needed to keep the evening's costs under control. He wasn't in a position to blow a couple hundred dollars that night, but he also was fascinated by Julia and didn't want to slow the momentum.

She nodded. "You think I made that up? To try to impress you?"

"No, definitely not. So, do you do . . ." he started to ask, and then paused. He didn't want to sound unsophisticated, but he was trying to understand her work. "Like, undercover investigations? Or . . . ?"

She grinned, looked left and right, then responded in a whisper, "Yeah. I do undercover assignments. All over the world."

Her life sounded dramatically more interesting than his. Impressive and fascinating, while Troy's life was stuck in neutral.

"Are you allowed to talk about them?" he asked quietly. "You must have incredibly interesting stories."

"Things can definitely get pretty unreal. I've seen some crazy shit, that's for sure. I wish I could share details, but these matters are all confidential."

"I totally understand," he answered. "How does one get into this kind of work?" He tried to sound lighthearted, but he was serious. "Being a private investigator sounds a million times better than anything I'm doing."

"Everyone has a different path. It really varies. Maybe after tonight, I'll put in a good word for you. Let's finish this drink and move on to somewhere else. I never like to stay in the same place too long. Just in case."

"In case what?"

She shook her head and finished the rest of her drink.

Within three hours, they were at their fourth bar, seven or eight drinks in, and he was definitely feeling the effects. The world started to slow down, to occasionally spin, as he felt a rush of bliss and levity. Thanks to all that alcohol, the words tumbled from his mouth. He told Julia about his childhood in Queens, attending college upstate, majoring in legal studies but then realizing he definitely didn't want to be a lawyer, and that he hadn't yet figured out what professional path he should take.

She talked about her life, how she grew up in Mountain Hill, had been a congressional intern in Washington, DC, and learned that she liked big city life. For her, the dream was to be based in New York, the greatest metropolis of them all, and now that she was here she was going to enjoy every moment.

Then they walked down a quiet street, unclear about their next destination. She put her arm through his, and he felt an instant wave of exhilaration.

"We should probably get something to eat," he said. "You hungry?"

"Yeah. Definitely. But first, let's stop here."

They paused in front of two large yellow doors adorning an otherwise tan brick building. One of the doors opened, and music from inside blared as two men in suits exited past them to head down the street.

"What is this place?"

"Sounds like a party. Let's check it out."

He looked over the doors and saw the words *Temple Beit HaTorah* in black characters.

"Do you know someone here?"

"That's always possible but not that I'm aware of. I'm pretty sure that's a Bar Mitzvah inside. We should crash it. I know how to blend in at these things."

"I didn't think McGinnis was a Jewish name."

She smiled. "It's not, but I've seen that Drake–Lil Wayne video a million times. Let's go."

"No," he said quickly. "That sounds like a terrible idea. Look, I may not have a lot of money to throw around, but I'm not destitute either. Let me buy you dinner."

"It's kind of job related, actually. I told you about the work we do. We're instructed to do this type of thing periodically to stay sharp."

"To attend Bar Mitzvahs without an invite?"

"To discreetly infiltrate random events without getting caught."

"For real?"

"Yeah, for real."

She gently put her hand around his waist, looked up at him, and then guided him toward the entrance. They walked up a few stairs and into the building where she grabbed a black yarmulke from a tray and placed it on top of his head.

They followed the noise of the crowd down a hallway and into a decent-sized reception hall. A keyboardist was playing a song Troy didn't recognize, and a crowd of about seventy-five people milled around. Hugs, kisses, preteens chasing each other, men in suits and women in conservative dresses waiting at several buffet stations. Two bars strategically placed at each end of the room. She nodded in the direction of one, and he followed her and joined the line of people waiting to order. A heavy man in a suit turned to look at both of them closely. Julia smiled innocently, and he smiled back and then placed his order.

Next was their turn.

"Two vodka shots, please," she instructed, and the bartender placed two glasses on the bar and generously filled them. "Thank you."

She grabbed them both, and then handed one to Troy as she led him away from the bar.

"L'chaim," she said as she clinked her glass against his, and then they both threw back their shots. It was smooth, not some cheap alcohol for sure.

She then walked over to the second bar with him trailing, and repeated the entire process. When they had downed their second shot together, he put more thought into trying to figure her out, and better understand this company she worked for. This was how they were instructed to practice for their various investigation assignments? He wanted to know more.

By now he was beginning to feel the effects of all their drinking in a rapid, overwhelming way. The room began to twist, and it was hard to focus on the crowd of attendees dancing in a circle and holding hands, as a few raised up a boy on a chair.

Julia grabbed his wrist and they stumbled outside and safely down the block. She took a deep breath and shook her head to focus. "We drank a lot," she said, stating the obvious.

"So how often does your company make you do stuff like this?"

"Troy, I was just bullshitting you."

"Which part was bullshit?"

"Dude, I work for a corporate investigations firm. I conduct database research, write reports, and second seat interviews with managing directors. I'm not an undercover agent like in a TV show. I mean, sometimes we have human intelligence assignments that require me to be in the field, but that's very rare. The most undercover part of my job is how professional and content I pretend to act all day."

Now he was living that undercover life too, perennially feigning to be deferential, respectful, and appropriate with Anderson and everyone else who controlled his professional life. And he was about to take that undercover mission even deeper.

He dashed into the elevator, emerged into the office building's lobby, and then headed onto the street where he met Julia on their designated corner.

"Walk with me," he instructed, and they turned down the Midtown cross street, passing a dry cleaner and a deli.

"Spill the tea," she insisted when he remained silent for a few seconds. They paused halfway down the block, the distance from the office providing some assurance they wouldn't be overheard while still being close enough so he could make it back in time.

"MHU is keeping us," he said in a hushed tone. "Anderson just told me."

Her face lit up. "Wow. That's amazing. But what the fuck are *they* thinking?"

"They're thinking that if they say everyone working on this investigation for C&R has never billed on any matter for Caleb, people will accept that. Anderson said Aaron Montgomery told him they don't want to look like they're backing down to outside pressure. I think they know searching for a new firm will drag this out even longer, and they want to get this behind them ASAP."

"I'm sure he also wants to deliver something for my parents before his run for governor. He'll need their financial backing. And he doesn't want to look weak."

Troy nodded. "The challenge now is—"

"Yeah, we're all disqualified. So we're retained but we have no one to work it. Well, besides that issue, I need to step up and make sure I get real origination on this. They're going to bill millions if they find some clever way to staff it. I brought this in. They want to ignore that, but I won't let that happen. Maybe I should call Aaron again. Or have my parents reach out to him . . . Although at my age that's kinda pathetic, right? Yet it might work . . ."

"Don't do anything yet," he cautioned. "There's a much better path."

"What's that?"

"Anderson wants me to help figure out staffing. I need to be back in his office in five minutes. He'll be desperate to find anyone who can work on this. Anyone who hasn't billed for Caleb. He said they have to share billing records with the university so the school can confirm all that."

"So you're Anderson's lackey. What else is new?" she responded, unimpressed.

"I know one person who hasn't billed to him."

"Who?"

"Me."

She looked at him with a confused stare. "You just oversaw all that research in Spain."

"But I haven't put my time in for that yet. I was going to this week. Now I won't. So I'm in the clear."

They were all supposed to enter their billable time in the firm's online system on a regular basis, detailing the client matter, nature of the work, relevant dates, and number of hours, so C&R's billing department could create invoices at the end of each month. Once those invoices were sent out, the time records were indelible, business records that couldn't be altered. Soon MHU would have access to those invoices, to confirm who had spent time on various assignments for Caleb Lugo.

But because Troy hadn't yet accounted for his billable hours in any official recordkeeping, it was as if that work had never happened. And no one would be seeking his time entry now. It wasn't as if C&R could send Caleb a new invoice, after declaring he would no longer be an acceptable client.

"Well, that'll be very good for your utilization stats," Julia responded unenthusiastically. "You won't have to worry about having enough billable hours if you're able to work MHU. But I'm still going to do whatever I can to get what's fair—"

"No. Not yet. Hear me out. Anderson will need to rely on me in a way he never has before. Let me get totally entrenched in this thing. I need to become indispensable. And then when this is really going full-scale, with on-site interviews, and report writing, and all that, when he's really dependent on me to keep it going . . ."

"Then we have the leverage to demand what I'm owed," she finished for him.

"Exactly."

He knew all this totally went against his ongoing plan to stay clear of controversy so he wouldn't get caught in the middle of adversarial and dangerous workplace situations more than was needed. But it was also finally a huge opportunity to really show Julia his gratitude, and his remorse.

"He's going to be furious," she warned, a warning that was tinged with giddy anticipation.

"It's about time we stepped up. We're not kids. We're grown men and women being treated like juveniles. We need to exert ourselves. And you *are* responsible for bringing in this matter. You deserve better. This is our shot to change things around here. We just need to wait for the right moment. And I'm in the position now to help create that moment."

She smiled. She liked this idea. And that made him smile. She placed her hand around his right arm and gave it a light squeeze. Then he had to break the grasp and start rushing back to the office.

18
Megan

They both had a cup of coffee in front of them, sitting across from each other at the professor's preferred table in this downtown establishment, away from other patrons in the corner of the large room. Megan had thought about how she would pitch him, how she would explain why he and his party should back her for Congress. But now that they were face-to-face for the meeting she requested, and he waited to hear what she had to say, an awkward silence festered and she realized she had no idea how to start.

"So..." she began tentatively, "you still causing trouble out there?"

"Always," he replied with a rascally grin.

She nodded and smiled politely, and then realized she needed to dive into the reason for their meeting. If she was going to run for Congress, she knew that over the next two months of this abbreviated special election campaign she would constantly be on the phone for excruciatingly uncomfortable calls seeking campaign donations, running around the district to meet with community groups, issuing policy statements, making speeches, and campaigning door-to-door. But despite all those exhaustive efforts, it was common belief in political circles that this sole individual and the party he controlled, his projected 4.68 percent of the vote, might decide the election. So she could be making all that effort, all that sacrifice, while others laughed at her behind her back, knowing she had no real shot at victory.

How should she proceed? Maybe the best way was to be blunt and direct.

"I'm seriously considering a run for Congress—"

He held up a hand to silence her. "You need to understand," he said as he leaned toward her over the table. "Because of what you said today about the university, I can't endorse you for anything. The party can't endorse you. Not even for city council again."

It was like a kick to the gut. Maddening that it might all be over so quickly, that one man could just whimsically shut the door on her plans, decide who would and wouldn't be a member of Congress, and whether she gained the stature and influence to save her friend. She had feared her comments about the university and C&R would anger Aaron, but she hadn't considered they might also tick off the professor, who worked for Aaron. Or was it vice versa?

"Professor, I'm sure you're as appalled as I am that the university's softball coach apparently sexually assaulted numerous teenage girls," she appealed. "And that many complaints were raised by these girls and their families for years, but nothing was done to stop him."

"Absolutely," he replied. "If it were up to me, I'd cut his fucking balls off. Sorry to be crude, but that's really how I feel about this. I have a daughter. And two sisters."

"And it's essential that whoever investigates this is beyond reproach," she said. "We can't have a firm that's tainted by—"

"Look, Megan, don't lecture me on what's needed. Rob Dempsey is about to be indicted. He'll rot in prison where he belongs. The rest of us need all this to go away. Playing musical chairs with who investigates is going to look amateurish and feeble, and I don't want that for Aaron. I've invested a lot in him. You know, our endorsement won him that first election. No way he gets to Congress otherwise."

She gave him a supportive nod, affirming his boast, becoming a willing accomplice to his attempt to bolster his own ego. And for all she knew, his show of bravado was based on truth, and he had been essential in Aaron winning, as he very well might be indispensable for whoever was to prevail in the upcoming special election.

"Exacerbating this situation like you did today can destroy this school," he continued. "And that would decimate the economic engine of this city. Inflammatory comments like yours will just encourage a bunch of people who went through that softball program to make unverified claims in the hopes of million-dollar paydays. There would have to be massive layoffs to cover all that. I'm not worried about my job. I can take care of myself and go somewhere else if needed. But others won't be as fortunate."

She believed the part about his own employment. He had figured out how to rig the system, cleverly designing a party and fundraising apparatus that was entirely legal and allowed him to mooch off the political landscape to the tune of hundreds of thousands of dollars annually. He would find a way to survive. And thrive.

She leaned in closer and discreetly asked, "You're worried about the nephew you mentioned? The assistant coach?"

The professor nodded slowly, with a look of sadness flashing across his face. "His name's Cole. He's been there awhile and knew nothing of any of this. I've spoken to him, and he's distraught. Devastated. He's having major mental health issues processing all that happened, and he's terrified for his future. He's a finalist at a *major* program for a head coaching job. That's been his dream *for years*. Now he's afraid that school, and every other school, will never hire anyone who worked with MHU softball. Ever."

She wondered how the assistant coach could end up avoiding some blame, as the professor clearly hoped. He was integrally involved in this program for years and knew nothing? "Well, if he didn't do anything wrong, it sounds like a comprehensive independent investigation is the perfect solution. It can clear him."

Dowling scoffed at her analysis. "The more people get worked up about this, the more this whole investigation turns into a witch hunt," he explained. "If the public demands that investigators find widespread wrongdoing, they'll find widespread wrongdoing. They don't want to look like they failed. Not after billing the university millions of dollars. So now you're attacking that investigative firm. Comparing it to Weinstein. You're fueling this crisis. You're making it more difficult for them to clear Cole. And if they do, you're creating an environment in which no one will believe their findings. They're professionals. They're truly independent. Just let them do their job. I want to avoid a situation where the investigators have to take down everyone in their crosshairs to prove they're legit and avoid public condemnation."

"Professor," she began her reply, and again kept a straight face as she used this absurd honorific, "*The New York Times* is reporting this firm assisted Caleb Lugo in covering up sexual misconduct for years and helped intimidate and silence sexual assault survivors. If that's who investigates these allegations, it makes everyone in Mountain Hill look bad. None of us want that."

He took a sip of coffee and then placed the mug back onto the table. "This is a very complicated situation in a lot of ways. It requires skill and nuance to navigate, and I'm trying to help everyone, help this city and this school, come out on the other side intact. I'm advising Cole on how to handle his investigative interview, and we've developed a plan so he can survive all this. You need to let us proceed the way we proceed, and stop undermining our efforts."

"I'm not trying to undermine you. I just—"

"I know you're a relative newcomer to politics," he interrupted. "I've liked you. I endorsed you for council. And not just because I hated that prick you ran against. You can have a very bright future if you play things right."

"And playing things right means . . ."

"Show you're a team player, Megan. Vote for the council's resolution tomorrow supporting Aaron's leadership decisions, including his selection of the investigative firm. I told you I needed your help, and this is what I'm asking for. We have enough support for the resolution to pass, but with the national media going crazy about the *Times* article, and too many people in Mountain Hill buying into that propaganda, we want it to be unanimous. That's very important for Aaron. And me. Then we'll reevaluate your request for our party's endorsement."

She knew what was on the line: 4.68 percent. If she didn't comply, he would deliver that to one of her opponents. Megan was becoming more familiar with the infuriating realities of local politics each day, but one thing she still hadn't mastered was her poker face, so he admonished her with the wag of a finger.

"Don't act like this is some shakedown, Megan. Like you're being asked to do something unethical. All I'm saying is that we can't blow this all out of proportion, make everyone so fired up and crazy that we damage every person on that softball staff and cripple the whole school. That's where it's headed, and you're driving us there with those ridiculous comments."

"I'm not—"

"This is a renowned investigations firm. We need to all just show our public support for Aaron and his decisions, and then let the investigators do their jobs. You're trying to find a battle to fight that doesn't exist, and you're going to end up screwing everyone over in the process. And by the way," he said as his voice grew calmer, "I'm still working on having Aaron call you back. He's just slammed with everything that's going on. He's trying to keep the school together while all the barbarians at the gate want to burn it to the ground. If he can successfully guide the university through this crisis, if he can steer around all the land mines, activists, litigants, and media personalities, and get the university to the other side with its finances and reputation still alive, without looking weak, indecisive, and irresponsible..."

"Then what?"

"If he's the savior, he's going to be the next governor," he answered confidently, as if it would then be a fait accompli. "Very likely he'll be running this state in a couple of years. So, seriously, Megan, it's not a good idea to get on his bad side. Take my advice and support the council resolution endorsing his leadership decisions. Or don't waste your time seeking our party's endorsement, and don't hold your breath waiting for him to return your phone call about helping that friend of yours."

19
Serena

SERENA READ THE EMAIL from Aaron. *Now that he's indicted, I want him removed from paid leave and officially terminated immediately. We'll send out a media advisory with a strong statement today.*

She had no objection to taking this step as the university's human resources director. MHU had to initially put Rob Dempsey on paid leave while the accusations were reviewed and the investigation began. But now that he was indicted, the university could feel legally safe to officially end his employment.

Both Aaron and Serena sought Dempsey's firing, but she felt it was for different reasons. For her, it was the just result of his years of abuse on their campus. However, she feared that for Aaron it was more about closing out this whole situation without really uncovering the extent of their school's misdeeds.

She watched a news video on her phone showing law enforcement escorting the coach down a residential block and into a waiting police car. Two men in dark suits and sunglasses, with several uniformed officers in blue serving in the entourage, guided him into the vehicle, his hands cuffed behind his back. Classic perp walk for the cameras.

Then the video showed a police spokesperson, an older man with a buzz cut wearing a white button-down shirt, standing indoors behind a podium with the state and American flags behind him. "At this time it appears Rob Dempsey acted alone in his heinous conduct. We have not identified any other suspects or accomplices," he said. "We'd like to thank Mountain Hill University, especially interim president Aaron Montgomery, for their full cooperation in this investigation."

They were already talking like they had resolved this matter, she thought. Unfortunately there were no signs law enforcement planned to go after the other university officials and employees who might have enabled the misconduct. Serena knew it was up to her to keep fighting to make sure everyone responsible for Dempsey's actions was held accountable.

Next she saw a video of a middle-aged woman with curly blonde hair in a gray business suit standing in front of the police station, surrounded by reporters. An on-screen chyron identified her as Dempsey's defense attorney.

"This rush to judgment is appalling!" she declared. "My client is being treated like he's already convicted. Rob Dempsey is *innocent until proven guilty*. This is still the United States of America! We're not living in the Kingdom, last I checked. We're confident that when all the facts come out, they'll show he is *innocent*, and *he* is a victim here."

Serena was all for due process, but these last words repulsed her, made her want to vomit. She understood this woman had a job to do, and Dempsey was entitled to a defense. But claiming victimhood? After what he'd done to all these girls?

Her office phone rang, she answered it, and her admin told her that her next appointment was here. It was a conversation she had dreaded ever since that morning's *New York Times* article. She rose and opened her door for Darren Tyrrell, who wanted to speak with her on behalf of his daughter Ali. He had called earlier that day and demanded an immediate meeting right after the university's announcement that anyone associated with Caleb Lugo would be barred from the investigation.

"Darren, please come in," she said, and then closed the office door after he entered. She was trying so hard, risking her career and fighting a lonely fight to help these girls, but Ali's father just stared at her with a look of betrayal.

"So you lied to us, Serena?" he charged. "You said Gillian would support Ali throughout the process. Ali relied on that promise and opened herself up. She's devasted that you're breaking your word. She's not going to speak with any other investigator."

"I'm so sorry. I had no idea what was going to happen. Please, let's sit down and talk this out. I've been trying to support Ali and the other girls ever since you reported this to me."

"And now I see you're just as manipulative as everyone else."

"No! That's not true. You think I'd just sit there while she literally poured her heart out to Gillian if I knew we'd have to change investigators?"

"Ali wants to speak to her. Now."

"I can't arrange that. I'm sorry."

"You'd better try."

She wanted to say that she wasn't in control of this situation, but she had worked so hard to establish the impression that she *was* in control so Ali and Darren could believe in the process. If she said Aaron had instructed her to sever all ties with Gillian, and she disagreed with this decision, then Darren would at best dismiss Serena as irrelevant and seek justice elsewhere.

"Can you just give me a few days?" she pleaded. "I'm going to get some clarity—"

"Clarity . . ." he scoffed.

Serena completely understood his indignation, and felt a surge of guilt and inadequacy for her failure to address it. "I'm going to get a real understanding of what the next steps are and who will be leading them. Please, just give me a couple of days. Okay?"

Before Darren could respond, Serena's office phone rang again and she saw that her admin was calling. "I'm so sorry, excuse me one second," she said as she picked up the receiver.

"There's a man here for you without an appointment," came the high-pitched voice of her young receptionist.

"It's not a good time," she said impatiently. "Who is it?"

"He says his name's Cole Malinowski."

Serena momentarily froze in panic. Then she looked at Darren to gauge whether he had heard and understood the admin's announcement. She instantly saw that he had.

Darren's eyes were on fire as he began breathing heavily. "That's the fucking coach Ali told Gillian about, right? The one that saw her in Dempsey's office all those times and did nothing!"

So, yes, Darren *had* been listening while Ali recounted those events to Gillian.

"Tell him he needs to come back after he sets up an appointment," Serena said quickly into the phone. "He needs to leave."

"No, bring him in," Darren ordered. "Right now."

I've thought a lot about shooting this coach in the fucking head, Darren had said during their first meeting. *Him and everybody else who let this happen to my girl.*

For a moment Darren and Serena just stared at each other, and then the father bolted for the office door and threw it open.

"No!" Serena screamed as she grabbed his right shoulder to keep him from exiting. But there was no stopping him now, as he flung his right arm back forcefully, causing Serena to break her grasp and tumble to the floor. "Call security!" she hollered to her admin, or anyone else who could hear. "Now!"

Darren was out the door and she leapt up and followed, emerging into the corridor by the row of cubicles to see Darren seething in front of Cole, who was wearing gray athletic shorts, a purple MHU T-shirt, and a baseball cap. Cole's eyes were bloodshot, his face unshaven.

"You let this happen to my daughter!" Darren hollered as he pointed a finger at Cole's face. The assistant coach looked shocked and terrified, as he shook his head while he took a step back.

Meanwhile, Serena's assistant shrieked and backed away from the two men. "Someone call security!" she yelled. But no one else was in the area, so this demand, much like Serena's, went unanswered.

"That's not true!" Cole cried out. "I had no idea what he was doing to those girls."

"You could have stopped all of this!" Darren yelled as he shoved Cole hard in the chest, sending his back crashing into the wall. Darren raised a fist as he prepared to strike again, and Serena raced to stop him, flinging herself between him and Cole as the assistant coach raised both hands to cover his head.

"Stop it!" she shrieked, as she braced for Darren to continue his attack, with Serena now in the way of his target.

"Get out of the fucking way!" he commanded with growing rage.

"You need to leave!" she answered. "This isn't going to help Ali. It'll just make everything even worse."

Darren took a couple of deep breaths, seeming to consider her words and decide on his next action. "If you cared about what he allowed that coach to do to my daughter, you'd know that it *can't* get worse."

"Please," she implored. "Please just leave. I promise you, I care. And I'll figure this all out. I just need a couple of days."

Serena braced for his decision, and after a few seconds saw with relief that Darren decided to slowly step away from her and Cole. He then turned and began walking toward the exit down the hall. When he was out the door, she spun around to face Cole, who was still backed up against the wall, his face flushed with fear.

"Why are you even here?" she asked, trying to catch her breath.

"I wanted to speak to you about this investigation."

"Then you should've made an appointment. There's a process in place," she said. "If you have questions about the process, you can schedule a time for me to explain it. Beyond that, you need to wait until you're interviewed."

"I've done nothing wrong," he asserted. "But this is hanging over my head, and this guy and everyone else assumes I'm guilty. I came here because I have the chance to actually lead a major softball program, but they won't hire me if I'm a subject of the investigation. Being a head coach at a school like that is a dream job. It's everything I've worked for. But they said they can't make me an offer unless they're told by MHU I'm in the clear. Very soon they'll just move on to someone else. And the longer this goes on, the more I'm tainted forever."

"Well, you're *not* in the clear," she replied. "There's an investigation. As I said, there's a *process*."

"Process? How are you citing a *process*? You ran onto that field in the middle of practice. You're destroying my life!"

"I just *saved* your life."

"Saved my life? What you're doing drove him to attack me! Have you seen what people are saying about me online? They're acting like *I* molested these girls."

"Maybe you should be glad you still have a job here, Cole. That you haven't been put on leave pending the findings of the investigation, or worse."

"I didn't *do* anything!"

"I don't doubt that," she said. "But the investigation will also look at whether you *should* have done something, considering what you may have known. Or at least what you *should have known*."

He breathed deeply and then bit his lip. "I came here to ask what I need to do to clear my name. But obviously you've already reached your conclusions. You say go through the process. Aren't you overseeing the process? And I heard you just tell this crazy father that you'll 'figure this all out' for him. What the hell did that mean? That you'll figure out how to hang me for all this?"

Serena knew the conversation needed to end. "You have to leave. If you'd like, I can have security escort you out in case he's still outside. But you shouldn't be talking with me like this," she said. "You shouldn't have come to my office without an appointment. An investigator will interview you."

"When?" he asked, not moving. "I'm not just gonna sit around quietly and wait for my day in court while my future is crushed."

"This isn't court."

"No shit."

"The external investigators will interview you. I can't tell you when. Now leave."

Cole moved away from the wall and toward the exit, but before he headed in that direction, he turned to Serena. "I'm not gonna let your 'process' ruin me. I've worked too hard and I've done nothing wrong."

Then he walked away and out the door, just as Serena's admin stepped over to her. "Are you okay? You want me to call security?" her assistant asked, her face slightly twitching with nerves.

It was a little late for that, but they would still need to file a report. "I'm okay," she said without conviction. "And yes, please call security now." Serena then went back into her office and tried to control the trembling inside her chest.

She had very little time and desperately needed to figure out how this investigation could proceed before it all unraveled. She needed a solution, and didn't want to wait for Aaron to provide the new C&R contact. He wouldn't see any urgency in addressing Ali and Darren's concerns. He'd be fine if Ali removed herself from the investigation. One less complaint to consider. One less obstacle before the matter could be resolved with a public statement of contrition and a promise the institution would do better next time.

She had to find out what was happening at the firm, and if she couldn't get a satisfactory answer there, she would have to speak up again. Maybe even publicly. Drew had the info from all the other RFP applicants, the ones who the university had never even interviewed. Maybe she should review them, get a better understanding of the university's other options.

In a flash she decided she needed to reach out directly to C&R as the HR representative from the university and demand to know what the next steps were. The president's office wouldn't approve, but after what she'd just experienced, she didn't care. The free tuition for her daughter handcuffed her, but she decided they couldn't and wouldn't fire her for a call to C&R.

But who at C&R now? Besides Gillian, C&R had sent two other managing directors to the meeting with Aaron—an older gentleman named Anderson Davis and another who looked to be in his early forties, Luke Holloway.

But wouldn't Anderson be banned now too? *Caleb's one of Anderson Davis's longtime clients at C&R*, Gillian had said. And Luke had barely spoken during the meeting. What was his planned role anyway?

So who else was at the firm? She thought about this, and then suddenly recalled Aaron's parting line at the interview:

One more thing. Please tell Julia McGinnis I say hello.

What was that about? Was this part of the reason Aaron had brought them in and now wanted to keep this firm? She sat down in front of her computer, pulled up the C&R website, and searched the directory for Julia McGinnis. Quickly she found the bio and photo of a smiling blonde associate. She appeared to be no older than her mid-twenties and very junior within the organization. Serena then decided to google "Julia McGinnis," but the name was way too common and resulted in a plethora of hits on a wide variety of irrelevant people.

She modified her search to "Julia McGinnis Aaron Montgomery" and saw immediately the woman she was looking for. An article from a local publication dated a few years earlier showed a college-age Julia with two young men standing with Aaron. The title read, *Congressman Montgomery Welcomes New Interns*.

What did this all mean? His former intern worked at C&R. Maybe that helped get them on the radar for this RFP. Nothing necessarily nefarious. But Serena had an overwhelming feeling that finding out more would help her navigate this messed-up situation.

She picked up her phone and dialed Julia's office number that was listed on the website. Serena didn't know what she would say, but it didn't matter anyway because after three rings, it went right to voicemail.

"This is Julia McGinnis at C&R Investigations. At the tone, please..."

She hung up without leaving a message, now feeling she shouldn't have called at all. But this political connection between the associate and the university president was another signal, another warning sign, that continuing the retention of this firm was wrong. She had just narrowly avoided a catastrophe with Darren and Cole, and felt that if this investigation continued on its current path, it would be a disaster at worst, and ineffectively irrelevant at best. The question continued to be what, if anything, she could do about it.

20
Troy

TROY REENTERED Anderson's office, his heart beating fast, still thinking about Julia's pleased smile and hand on his arm. Over the past three years she had become a solid friend, the only real trusted colleague he had at this company. She had done a lot for him, helped prop up his life and steer him in an upward direction, so he relished the idea that he could return the favor and make up for his own past mistakes, while at the same time turning the tables on the man who wielded his authority in toxic and demeaning ways on a regular basis.

Now he was standing in front of Anderson's desk while his boss wrapped up a call. Troy couldn't wait to announce that he could be staffed on MHU work, if his understanding of the current rules was accurate.

"There's going to be an investigation, Troy," Anderson announced with utmost seriousness as Troy took a seat. "I was just informed about it."

Why was Anderson stating the obvious? "I have something to tell you about that," Troy said. "I'm not sure if you're aware, but I'm actually eligible to work on MHU."

"No, anyone who billed for Caleb is disqualified, unfortunately," Anderson explained. "Which is a huge fucking problem. Weren't you listening when I just explained that a few minutes ago? Jesus. Anyway, that's not what I was referring to."

"I never billed anything to him. I coordinated the sub's work in Spain, but I didn't put in my time."

"None?" his boss asked. "Not one hour?"

"No. And you've never given me work for him before," Troy explained. "I'm clear. As long as it's okay that I had that sub—"

"For these purposes, that's not a problem. They explicitly asked for billing records and if you're not on the billing records, it's fine." He swiped his hands together a couple of times to show that Troy had a clean slate. "I'm scrambling to put together a team that can fly out there tomorrow morning. They're demanding to see some of our eligible people in person. We have an unlimited budget and virtually no one to use that budget, so we need a team." Anderson's fist tapped the desk twice in frustration. "We need bodies right away or we lose this whole thing. Okay, so now you're on that team."

"Tomorrow morning?'

"Yes."

Troy was thankful that his proposal to be added to the MHU team had been successful, but he was unnerved at how quickly this was proceeding. Heading out there the following morning with little time to prepare? This wasn't what he had expected or hoped for. Yet he was in no position to object.

"Okay. No problem."

"But that's not the investigation I was referring to," he said while shifting uncomfortably. "Before DePalma Capital will close any deal with C&R, in light of the *Times* article, they want to know exactly what we *did and did not do* for Caleb. They want to know if we did anything unethical, which *of course we did not*. Who knew there would be so many women coming out of the woodwork? I certainly didn't. They're worried about civil liability. Reputational risk. They're concerned that they acquire us and then it turns out to be a colossal mistake. If they pull out of the sale, that's going to be damaging for all of us. Our competitors will obviously all know about it, and our clients will detect there's a potentially serious problem here. We could be thrown into an unrecoverable tailspin."

"When is this investigation starting?"

"Right away. So listen, Troy, you have to keep this between us. They're demanding that human resources immediately conduct a discreet, expeditious, and thorough internal investigation into all services provided by C&R to Caleb Lugo. HR is going to interview people this week. Including you."

"If I'm not in any billing records, why do they want to interview me?" Troy asked.

"I think your involvement is pretty clear from your conversation with Caleb at the conference room reception. Everyone heard it. Tara from HR was there. That can't be undone."

And this just infuriated him. That he would now be in the crosshairs of an HR inquiry because this author had called him out in such an unnecessary, condescending way in front of his coworkers. That he was potentially going to get jammed up because of the man's attempt to embarrass him.

"All right," he said. He noticed that his boss looked particularly concerned, and Troy understood why. There was a lot that had occurred that wasn't appropriate, if Emma's account and the *Times* article were accurate—and he really had no reason to doubt either's veracity. Who knew what else Anderson had done for Caleb over the years. Maybe this "investigation" would finally uncover Anderson's misdeeds.

But what about Troy himself? Had *he* done anything wrong by trying to dig up dirt on one of Caleb's accusers? He didn't necessarily think so, especially considering their firm conducted background research on people all the time. But even if his conscience was potentially clear, had he done anything that *someone else* would think was wrong? Or cite as wrongful because he was an easy target?

"They're not having external investigators conduct the investigation?" he asked. It's what C&R advised other organizations to do all the time. Best to have someone independent, with no stake in the outcome, investigate any potential wrongdoing. It was clearly best practices and, more importantly for the C&R managing directors, it would hopefully lead to the firm receiving the ensuing billable work.

"Please," Anderson answered dismissively. "I mean . . . come on, Troy. I don't have the time, or the patience, for ridiculous comments right now."

So the answer was no. Of course Anderson wouldn't want a real independent investigation that would scrutinize and uncover his actions.

"Here's what's going to happen," Anderson continued. "You're flying to MHU tomorrow for a week of meetings and interviews and then returning here so HR can interview you immediately after."

Troy felt a surge of concern and anxiety. His plan entering the room had been to be assigned to the MHU investigation. But leaving the next morning, with colleagues unknown, to conduct meetings and interviews in a volatile situation, all while human resources planned to question him about his own work, was highly concerning.

He suspected he might be headed for a disastrous week, and assumed there was much more that Anderson wasn't telling him. He had never pushed back with his boss, always responded with obedience that at times bordered on being embarrassingly sycophantic. But if he was going to actually assert himself in this whole process, to show he wasn't someone who could continue to be treated with complete disregard and prepared as a sacrificial lamb on the pyre, he needed to speak.

Something clear, but not too overt. Something that didn't foreclose the option in Anderson's mind that Troy was still acting in the naive manner that he had pretended to maintain so many times in the past, but still showed Anderson that Troy was not powerless in whatever conflict might occur.

"Is Emma going to be interviewed by HR also?" he asked.

Anderson at first just stared at him, and he then rose from his chair and walked around the desk so he was standing next to Troy, right above him, looking down with just inches separating their bodies.

"Why did you ask that?" he responded coldly.

"Well . . . Caleb also talked about her work at the conference room celebration," Troy said softly.

"What does it matter to you if she's interviewed?" he snapped.

"She's . . . she's a friend."

"She's a friend?" he replied suspiciously. "You're asking just because *she's a friend*?"

Anderson was now glaring at him, simultaneously working his intimidation game and clearly trying to read Troy and find out his true knowledge and intentions. Troy looked back as innocently as he could. "We're all a team here at C&R. I care a lot about that team. We all support each other."

"You're really testing my patience. You're lucky you're eligible for this MHU investigation or I might exit you from the firm right now." Anderson's anger then subsided a little and he revealed an instant of concern in his eyes as he added, "And the answer's yes. Human resources will interview Emma also."

Then Anderson decided not to pursue the issue further, perhaps because he didn't want to bring it more attention. He told Troy to arrange for his travel, and that he would be in touch soon regarding which colleagues could join him at MHU.

"I need to find three other semi-competent people who aren't disqualified," Anderson explained. "If you can think of anyone else, let me know immediately. I already told their president that at least four investigators would be on campus tomorrow."

Before heading back to his desk to check the available flights for the next morning, he texted Julia, and they quickly met in the lactation room. He was about to fill her in, but she immediately started talking.

"Aaron hasn't called me back, but my work phone just had a missed call from the main number at the university," she said with optimism laced with irritation. "No message. Maybe it was one of his assistants returning my call on his behalf?"

"Maybe," he replied. "So what are you gonna do?"

"Not sure. I can call his office and hopefully whoever picks up will recognize my name and say they were trying to reach me."

"What about just texting him? He may respond quicker to that."

She ran a hand through her hair in frustration. "I just don't want him to think I'm being weird. And if he then leaves me on read it's going to be really embarrassing. But I do need to connect with him. Anyway, so what happened with Anderson? Did he threaten to fire me again?"

"Not this time. He's busy looking for four eligible people to go to MHU tomorrow. I'm now one, so he needs three more. Not easy."

"Damn, I wish I was able to work on this. I'd be really good at it."

He looked at her skeptically. "You've never interviewed a sexual assault survivor."

"Nor have you."

"I never said I'm going to be good at this. I'm actually really concerned about that."

She shook her head. "I'm great at talking to people who've experienced something terrible. Like when someone's relative passes away, you know how no one knows what to say to them? Everyone gets all awkward."

"Yeah."

Julia leaned toward him as her eyes widened in mock-surprise. She then looked down in simulated sadness and back at Troy, as she placed her right hand on his shoulder and pulled him in for a firm hug. After a few seconds she ended the embrace and offered a sympathetic nod. "Troy, I am so, so sorry to hear about your loss. I'm just *heartbroken*. I know this has to be an incredibly difficult and challenging time. I can't even imagine how painful and shocking it must be. Anything you need—and I mean *anything*—please just let me know. Always remember that your father loved you very, very much and he was extremely proud of you. He was so appreciative of having you as a son, and felt very loved by you."

"So you're good at faking that you care."

"No, I *do* care. A lot of people *care*. But few people know what to *say* in difficult situations. That's what really counts. I know how to make others feel supported. Every single day, I 'like' things on Facebook that I don't even really like. Hell, I 'love' things on Facebook that I don't even really *read*. That may sound phony, but it means a lot to people. It really does."

"You're still on Facebook? That's pretty lame."

"It is but I'm still on it to *support* people. That's my point!"

"Okay, but it's not that simple," he explained. "There's too much going on. Anderson just told me DePalma Capital wants human resources to investigate whatever work we all did for Caleb before they close the deal. I'm going to be interviewed soon."

"Oh, fuck. They're going to ask you about the Spanish research."

"*Oh, fuck?* That's your sensitive, supportive response?"

"Well, I need to think this through. Is Anderson going to make you the fall guy?"

"I don't know. I guess not as long as I'm working MHU. But if he can find a replacement and it helps him to screw me over and say the research was my idea, he won't hesitate to have me blamed for it."

She sat down on the sofa and stared at the duck painting, then turned back to Troy. "First, you did nothing wrong. We conduct background research on people adverse to our clients. That's what an investigative firm does."

"Exactly."

"But it *was* research to undermine a sexual assault victim on behalf of a guy who appears to be the next Matt Lauer. Someone who doesn't understand our profession could think that's really bad. At a minimum it's a major PR risk for new ownership."

"I know."

"Even though you didn't find anything. And where's Emma in all this?"

"Anderson says HR is going to interview her too. But I have no idea how open she'll be. I haven't talked to her since you told her off at the bar."

Julia took out her phone and then placed it on the table in front of her. "Neither have I. Wow, she really screwed us. Okay, stay here while I call back MHU. If I can just connect with Aaron Montgomery, I think he'll want to be helpful to me. Then we'll finally have the leverage to protect ourselves from all these issues."

21
Megan

"How are you voting on the resolution, Megan? We don't want any surprises."

She pressed her phone to her ear as she walked down the hallway toward the city council chambers for their scheduled meeting. She had seen Professor Dowling's name on her caller ID and could have ignored it, but she didn't want to do anything else that might hurt her chances of getting the support of this man and his party.

The proposed resolution was an endorsement of Aaron Montgomery's leadership at MHU. Although not specifically mentioning C&R Investigations by name, it declared the council's "support for President Montgomery and his selected independent investigators to appropriately uncover and address the highly serious allegations of sexual misconduct involving the MHU softball program's former head coach."

Megan felt this resolution was wrong. Having now read the full *New York Times* article, she had no confidence in this firm, nor in Aaron to oversee a proper investigation that wasn't influenced by political considerations. But she told herself she wasn't voting for Aaron. She was voting for Evina's freedom.

"I'm supporting the resolution, Professor. You have my vote."

"Thank you. That'll make it unanimous. Which is really important for Aaron."

Megan knew this council unanimity didn't reflect the Mountain Hill residents at large, from what she heard during conversations with friends and constituents, and comments she read online. Maybe that was why Aaron and his supporters wanted the unanimous vote so much, to tamp down the opposition and project strength.

"And I want you to know," he continued, "we'll remember your support. I can guarantee you'll have our party's endorsement when you run for reelection to council."

Reelection to council.

That wasn't what she sought from him, and he knew that. Reelection to city council would do nothing to help end Evina's imprisonment.

"I'm asking for your support for Congress," she said. This wasn't a time to be subtle. She needed to be clear about what she wanted.

"Look, Megan, I'm not a bullshitter. I always talk straight. We're just not going to be able to endorse you for Congress. You're too new. It's not personal, but it's just not your time yet. We're going to support someone else."

"Who?" she asked, even though it didn't really matter. Without their support, her nascent congressional aspirations would be quickly extinguished.

"I can't say yet," he replied. "But as I said, it's not personal."

She kept hearing those final words in her head as her rage built and she entered the council chamber to take her seat for the meeting. *It's not personal.* She thought about how emaciated Evina appeared each time she saw her in her prison jumpsuit, how she had watched her friend deteriorate before her eyes over the years, locked in a cell, treated like an animal because she had refused to capitulate to her abuser and die. For Megan, this couldn't get more personal. And without Dowling's necessary support, she was once again without a plan, even an unrealistic one, to gain Evina's freedom.

The meeting began, and one by one her fellow council members declared their support for Aaron's leadership and the resolution. Now she was watching one of them, who leaned into the microphone and passionately promised unwavering support to MHU president Aaron Montgomery and his decision to proceed with C&R Investigations to look into all aspects of the Rob Dempsey scandal.

He had the bulk of a former athlete, one who had let himself go as he entered his forties. Still growing in size but no longer because of an athletic training regimen. Instead he wore a too-tight jacket that needed to be taken out, and his face shook fervently as he spoke.

He railed against anyone who attempted to undermine the process and "prolong the community's nightmare." He declared that Aaron was the perfect leader for this crisis, and C&R was an extremely well-respected company. Too many people wanted to throw hand grenades and disrupt any meaningful and prompt resolution of this predicament, but he wasn't going to allow that, he promised.

"Rob Dempsey has been indicted," he pointed out. "He'll be convicted and sentenced to prison. That's the important result here. The rest of us need to support the already-commenced external review so it can do what it needs to do, and then we can move on. We can't let this drag on for years. Although obviously that's what some people want."

He had just masterfully delivered all of Roger Dowling and the U.P.'s mandated talking points. It was all so absurdly choreographed and lacking in principle. But she acknowledged to herself that if Dowling had promised to support her for Congress, *she* would have been the one uttering those words.

Meanwhile, Megan noticed that a number of residents in the gallery did not approve of this council member's speech. Instead she caught frustrated head shakes, exasperated stares, and a notable lack of motion by some residents while others clapped to show support. Dowling had referenced "too many people in Mountain Hill buying into that propaganda" against the university's leadership, and this was clear evidence of that.

Finally, the voice vote arrived, with everyone around the horseshoe table declaring their position on the resolution. Every other member declared "yay," preserving their future electoral viability with Aaron, the U.P., and others who demanded they vote this way. Then came Megan.

"Nay," Megan announced. She might as well vote her conscience. Why should she cave to support these men who had no intention of supporting her, when Aaron wouldn't even call her back after leading her to believe he would be instrumental in gaining freedom for her friend?

The other council members seemed surprised by her vote. Maybe they had been informed that a unanimous decision was expected. A few in the audience rustled in dissatisfaction at Megan's pronouncement, but she did note others throughout the council chambers reacted with surprised gasps and light clapping. She had some support, somewhere, although she couldn't tell from whom exactly.

Finally, the meeting ended and she quickly left the council chambers to head home. She planned to visit Evina the next day, and she needed to have a clear strategy before then. She couldn't show up in the prison visiting room and simply declare that their latest plan was hopeless.

Thirty minutes later she sat on her living room's leather sectional sofa with her husband and communications intern. Sadly, Alan and Aimee were all she had for trusted political counsel as she weighed her next move.

"You should just go public with what Dowling asked of you," her husband said. "It's highly unethical and people need to know about it."

"No one will care," Megan replied. "Local media barely exists anymore. Larger outlets really won't give a shit. Right, Aimee?"

Aimee nodded. "It's just politics as usual," she said. "And really small potatoes to them."

"What are my chances of winning without his endorsement?" she asked. And she received the same answer that Aimee and others provided whenever she asked about the professor's support.

"As a relative unknown," Aimee responded with the confidence of someone who understood politics in a way that was well beyond her years, "really zero. You've barely been on the council. You don't have a large fundraising base, or big name ID, or a committed following."

"I just don't get this," Alan interjected. Although always supportive, he had never been a huge politics guy. The more he learned, the more repulsed he became. He was always there for her, but it was *for her*, not because of any independent interest in government affairs. "This guy just creates a party, gives it an ambiguous name, and then gets to decide if you run for Congress? That's crazy."

"Crazy or not," Aimee said, "it's reality."

"Then let's form our own stupid party," he proposed. "How about the Reality Party?"

They were all silent for a few moments, and then Aimee threw out, "Well, people can create their own ballot lines. You can pretty much call it whatever you want. You just need to have enough signatures."

"Okay," Alan said, nodding. "That sounds promising."

"But hardly anyone votes on those. They're down-ballot, little noticed. It needs to be something unique and noteworthy to galvanize people."

"What kind of names have people used before?" Megan asked, starting to wonder if there was a solution here.

"Names like *Common Sense*, or *For the People. Common Sense for the People. People for Common Sense. Reform* is another one. *People for Commonsense Reform.*"

Megan wasn't a political expert but was learning every day. And it was all too clear that she wasn't going to win this election, make anyone care about her candidacy, with some generic ballot line name that paid superficial respect to vague notions of populism.

She wished it could be the Free Evina Jansen Party. That was her primary issue. But her press conference and other efforts had definitively revealed there was no waiting, sizable, untapped pocket of support for this cause.

Her press conference. What a fucking joke. Standing there, ready to proclaim inspiring words on behalf of righting a terrible injustice. Facing emptiness. Worse than emptiness, because people were there, walking by, not caring at all, going about their lives. Totally ignoring her, ignoring Evina, as they went to work, picked up their kids from school, shopped for groceries, met friends for coffee or drinks. She hated them all for being consumed with their lives and so blissfully uncaring about Evina's shattered existence.

At the time, Aimee had offered her own take. A lesson from her communications professor.

It's not about making people care about your issue. It's about connecting your issue to something people already care about. Rather than trying to get the media to cover your cause, you shape your cause into something the media's already covering.

So that was her answer.

"The ballot line has to be about the university," Megan said. "That's all anyone cares about. MHU, MHU, MHU."

"But what's the ballot line name?" Alan asked.

She didn't have a clear idea, but could sense the feel of it. "I'm not sure. But the sentiment needs to be . . ."

"I like where this is going . . ." Aimee whispered.

"Fuck the piece of shit people who let this happen to those girls," she declared. "And fuck everyone who's playing political games and won't do the right thing now. Fuck all of them." She stopped, looked around the room, and then added for clarity, "That's the ballot line name. Something to that effect."

"But what does running for Congress have to do with any of that?" Alan questioned. "You'd have no role with the university as a member of Congress."

"I'd have a bully pulpit. I'd be the main liaison for federal funding. The last guy in this congressional seat became the *president* of the school."

"I just don't see the real connection."

"It's great," Aimee said supportively. "It taps into the big issue. Seizes on what people are thinking about, and appeals to all those who disagree with the council's vote today. It just needs to be more focused. And we need a real name. Short, succinct, f-bomb free."

"It should be about all the leadership," Megan said. "Cleaning house. Everyone who was leading the school when Rob Dempsey was running rampant. All the human resources people who allowed this to occur under their watch. Everyone overseeing it now when Caleb Lugo's henchmen were hired to clean things up. Yes, that means going after Aaron too, and the *professor*. We need to *clean house*. That's what I want, and I think enough people—yes, *the people*—feel the same way to maybe help us win this thing."

She was fired up, captivated by her own idea that would channel public outrage into helping her, helping Evina. Maybe in the process focus their ire on the men who blocked her path with their cynical maneuvers, false promises, and outright lies.

I'll fight for this, Aaron had told her after she presented Evina's predicament to him. And then he wouldn't even return her phone calls.

"So," she said, "let's figure out the name tonight. And then make a plan for getting those signatures."

22
Serena

She stood before the university president, having been summoned to his office for an urgent meeting. Serena's spine twitched as she braced for him to question her about the near-calamitous physical conflict outside her office. She assumed he would blame her, and she readied her defense.

"Why did you call Julia McGinnis at C&R?" Aaron asked with an intimidating calmness, and she was stung with surprise at this unexpected question about a completely different topic.

Yes, she had made this call. But she hadn't left a message. And the caller ID for all their offices showed the main university number.

As she nervously shifted her hands against her sides and tried to formulate a response, she thought about what his reaction would be if he learned about the email she'd sent that morning to Drew. She really needed to be more careful.

"I don't know who that is," she responded, because she couldn't think of a better answer. "I don't believe I've ever spoken with someone by that name," she added, and that part was actually true.

"She called my assistant and said she had a missed call from the university. So we checked our phone records and it appears that *you* called her."

"If I did, it was a mistake, and I hung up immediately."

He stared at her skeptically, looking like he was trying to understand what she was up to, what her plan was. And she wished she actually did have a plan, other than unfocused hopes of stopping Cole Malinowski and others from being in positions of authority over girls again, and removing C&R from further involvement with the university.

"Look, Serena," he started to lecture, "I was brought in as interim president to get us through this crisis. It's an all-consuming task. I have a million people who want a billion different things from me. My list of phone calls to return is a mile long."

"And I'm here to help," she offered.

"That's the point I'm getting to. You're not helping. I'll just be blunt about that. I understand it would be problematic to fire you. Getting rid of our HR director would look bad, especially after you publicly confronted Rob Dempsey. But if you undermine this school, undermine me, then I can't allow that either. So this is your last warning. If anything remotely associated with you challenges my ability to move the university past this controversy, you're gone. Immediately. It's that simple."

She looked at the intensity in his eyes and understood the contempt he had for her. He was facing so many obstacles, and in his mind, she was another one of them. She wanted to disabuse him of that notion, but felt that she would never be able to do so convincingly.

"Okay."

"I know your daughter benefits *a lot* from your MHU employment. So don't take that away from her."

This last comment sent a sharp pain through her lower back. She tried to ignore the physical discomfort as she nodded and left, her thoughts focused on Kayla. She couldn't allow her actions to undermine her daughter's educational and financial future. But she also couldn't be complicit in covering up years of horrendous misconduct.

With Kayla on her mind, she noted that she hadn't answered her daughter's text from earlier that morning:

I found a perfect speaker for the new student orientation sexual assault awareness talk!

Serena replied while walking back to her office, noting how trivial this issue was now. *Who?*

Kayla texted back right away. *I want to tell you in person! She's awesome. Can you meet me at the water?*

Serena realized that maybe she needed this distraction, any distraction. So she headed to the far side of campus, near the scenic lake and running path. Her daughter walked toward her, wearing gray shorts and a blue T-shirt. The sun glistened off her face, highlighting the usually faint freckles that Serena had adored since she was born.

"It's really nice to see you," she told Kayla. "I needed a diversion. I'm under a lot of stress."

"With the Rob Dempsey situation?"

She nodded. "It's so messed up. What he did. What others allowed him to do. A real investigation should have started by now, but everyone's making decisions based on political and financial motives. When do we finally focus on justice for the victims? It's just heartbreaking."

"Mom, I admire you so much," her daughter gushed, and she felt her child's arms wrap around her body and hold her tight. The warmth, the love, the support—it all rushed through her. Such a contrast from all the negativity she received elsewhere that she wanted to break down and cry. She wished that hug could continue forever, and she made no attempt to move away so maybe it would.

"Thank you," she finally muttered, as Kayla ended the embrace. "I needed that."

"Are you okay?" Kayla asked with concern.

"I will be," she said, trying to appear as if she believed it.

"Your whole career has been about supporting people who

experience misconduct," her daughter said. "You were fighting to help survivors of sexual assault and discrimination way before it became this big national issue. I talk to my friends all the time about how inspiring you are."

"I definitely don't feel very inspiring these days."

Kayla took out her phone from her back pocket and flashed an excited smile. "Okay, well then I have something to inspire you."

"What's that?"

"Our sexual assault awareness speaker."

Kayla coyly held her phone toward herself so her mother couldn't see the screen, and Serena heard the familiar sounds of the electronic pulsing that indicated the initiation of a FaceTime call as a few people walked past them down the path.

"Hi, can you talk with my mom for a minute?" Kayla said toward the screen, which was still shielded from Serena. "She's here with me now."

Kayla then turned the screen to Serena, and she saw an attractive woman in her mid-twenties, with long black hair and olive skin. Serena also observed her own face on the screen, and how haggard and not-camera-ready she appeared. It was quite a disparity between the two.

"Hello," she said awkwardly. "I'm Serena Stanfield, human resources director. It's nice to meet you."

"Good afternoon," the woman responded with a European accent. "Thank you so much for this opportunity. I am very grateful and excited."

Serena tried to step off-screen for a moment as she silently mouthed to Kayla, "Who is this?"

Kayla moved closer to Serena and held up the phone, so that both she and her mother were visible on FaceTime. "Mom," she said giddily, "please meet Bianca Velencoso."

The woman smiled, while Serena's stomach immediately knotted up at the mention of the name and all the trouble it would bring. Just as Aaron and his team were trying to diminish the outside focus on MHU scandals, Kayla had enlisted a speaker who was the center of a national controversy and who had publicly castigated any entity utilizing C&R Investigations. Serena's continued employment was already tenuous, and this woman speaking on campus at an event organized by human resources would surely sink her.

"Bianca Velencoso," was all she could say.

"Yeah, she's the first woman who publicly accused Caleb Lugo of—"

"I know. I know exactly who she is." Serena then awkwardly noted that she was speaking about Bianca in the third person while the woman's live image was right in front of her, and other members of the MHU community continued to move past the public space where they stood. She grabbed the phone from Kayla and fumbled with the device. "How do you mute this? Kayla, I need to mute this call!"

But she couldn't figure it out, and saw the confused look on Bianca's face.

"Mom, what is wrong with you?" her daughter asked with embarrassment.

She knew she needed to explain quickly. Had she been successful in muting the phone? Unclear.

"We can't bring her to campus. That's going to create a media frenzy. It won't be constructive. Her sexual assault allegations are against a major client of the university's sexual misconduct investigator."

"That's why this is the place for her to speak," Kayla replied. "She's going to bring so much visibility to these issues. She's going to call for the Lugo investigation to be reopened with a special prosecutor."

Serena spun around and saw assorted individuals in the vicinity. There was no privacy here, and Bianca continued to look at her with bewilderment. Serena still held the phone, and realized nothing positive could occur while this call continued, muted or unmuted, so Serena tapped the screen to end it and the model's image disappeared.

"What the hell did you just do?!" Kayla called out. "That was so rude!"

"Kayla, there's a lot going on that I haven't explained," she said with a lowered voice. "I don't want to scare you, but I'm very close to being fired."

"Fired? Why?"

"Because I challenged the system, and I'm still challenging it. But I'm literally on very thin ice right now, and if my daughter helps me bring this woman to speak to our new students about sexual assault awareness for an event I'm overseeing, that'll highlight all the controversies with our outside investigations firm, it'll undermine the leadership's investigative plan, and I'll be blamed."

Kayla's previous look of admiration was now gone, replaced with narrowed eyes showing disappointment and scorn. "You don't want her here because she engaged in sex work. Your generation—"

"No, Kayla. Trust me. I don't give a shit about that. There's no ulterior motive. If we bring her to campus, I'll be in a lot of trouble. It's that simple."

"So she shouldn't have a voice? That attitude has resulted in so many victims being silenced. No one wants to stand up."

"I stood up! My God, I stood up. You just told me I inspire you for standing up! But this is just unnecessarily inflammatory. It may feel good, but if I lose my job, and we can't cover your education costs, that's a major problem."

"I'd rather that than be complicit in silencing her!"

"She's not being silenced! There are thousands of other campuses where she can speak."

Her daughter snatched her phone back and then began quickly walking away, shaking her head. Serena thought about chasing after her, and then felt her own device pulse in her bag. She reached in to grab it and saw the call was from Drew. She had emailed him before her talk with Aaron, requesting access to the other RFP responses. She had wanted to review the other options again. But now that request would be the final straw leading Aaron to terminate her.

"Listen, Drew," she said quickly before he could speak. "Ignore my email. Just erase it. Don't mention it to anyone, okay?"

"Sure. I didn't understand the point anyway."

"There is no point," she confirmed. "I realize that. We're all in a bad situation and I don't want to make things worse."

"Serena . . . things *are* worse. Just a few minutes ago, a city councilwoman announced she's running for Congress. For Aaron's seat. And her whole announcement speech was a takedown of the university, C&R, Aaron, everyone who's been in any leadership position over the past few years. Her name's Megan Black."

"I don't think I've heard of her, but sounds like she'll have my vote."

She heard Drew sigh in frustration and concern. "She specifically mentioned incompetence in the general counsel's office. And in the *human resources* department. She said everyone in leadership in those areas needs to be fired immediately. She's not just going after our former president, or Aaron, or C&R. She's coming after *us*, Serena. If this catches fire, if she or some supporter starts mentioning our names, it's going to decimate our reputations. Our careers. We'll be unemployable."

These words instantly initiated an enhanced wave of trepidation. She knew political campaigns were often not about facts, and could serve to just stir people up to vote for a particular candidate, without regard for who was being run over in the process. It was chilling to think that she might be specifically targeted, considering she had had no idea about Rob Dempsey's conduct.

Or maybe that would be the point. She should have known. Even if no one reported it to her, and the former administration intentionally kept her in the dark, possibly she should have been clearer in her messaging to the campus community so that they could come to her with any wrongdoing. Maybe that would have led to one of the girls contacting her, and she could have done something. The accusations from this politician reinforced Serena's own ongoing fear and guilt that she, too, had failed them.

"This woman even has a ballot line that her campaign's collecting signatures for," Drew added, his voice unsteady. "It's called Reclaim MHU, and the stated mission is to 'clean house at Mountain Hill University and replace all current MHU employees who had oversight responsibilities involving personnel in the MHU softball program and legal and human resources departments.'"

Serena understood it was probably only a matter of time before the campaign or others in the community looked into the real names of the people who had failed to prevent these atrocities. Her identity was already somewhat public from that viral video. Would that protect her? Or just make her easier to target? Even worse than the threat of Aaron firing her, this public shaming might be disastrous for her life and career.

"She wants to take us all down," Serena said. It was frightening, but also understandable. "Maybe we should reach out to her. Explain the situation."

"We'll need to speak with Aaron first," Drew insisted. "We need to find out how he wants to handle this."

"Drew, he's going to feel he's not responsible for the past because he just arrived on campus, and everyone who predated him is fine to target."

"She's firing at him too. For retaining C&R. Let's talk to him."

"You always want to wade through 'proper channels' whenever there's a problem."

"And you never do."

"If I'd listened to you at the beginning, Rob Dempsey would still be running our softball program and molesting girls."

"That's so wrong, Serena," he replied as his voice cracked. "How can you say that? I would never have let that continue after you came to me. You know me better than that."

Did she? Increasingly, she didn't trust the judgment or intent of anyone here. "Fine, let's talk to Aaron. But you need to realize that the best way to dig ourselves out of this mess is to cut ties with C&R."

"Aaron will never do that. He's too invested in them. He won't back down. It's just not the way he responds to these things."

"I know. And that may be what he feels is the best course for him, but it's absolutely not for you and me, or the university. It's going to be terrible for the rest of us."

She looked out onto the lake as a couple of joggers swept by her.

"Let's talk with Aaron before you do anything," Drew implored. "Please, for once just listen to me."

"Okay," she said reluctantly. "Just this once."

23
Troy

"You like fucking me more than the other girls?" she had asked him through blurry eyes. Julia flashed a mischievous, flirty grin that lasted no more than a second and was quickly replaced by those same eyes closing as her head arched back and she let out a *mmmm* noise followed by a short exhale. The meaning was unclear, but Troy instantly narrowed it down to either a sign of pleasure or a snicker.

Meanwhile, Julia's question hung in the air, and he froze, physically and mentally, as the alcohol continued to flood his head, and her bedroom appeared to occasionally move around him. There had been no other "girls" in a little while. He considered how to respond, what answer would be the correct one that would be truthful and quick and not kill the mood. But then he realized she wasn't acting as if she awaited a serious response, so he whispered softly in her ear, "Absolutely."

Just the latest awkward near-misstep since they entered her Upper West Side apartment. Their drinking had continued, and even escalated, since taking advantage of the free shots. The rest of the night had been a blur of excitement as they hit a couple of more bars and ended up in a K-Town private room with a bottle of Ketel One and a few mixers, sharing a microphone as they stood and screamed at each other the lyrics of assorted cheesy pop songs.

They were both highly intoxicated, and he was connecting with her more and more, trying to focus on being himself, go with the flow, not screw this up. They talked more about how unsatisfied he was with his current job, she made exuberant declarations that she would help with his career plight, and she offered more coy allusions to secret missions for her investigations firm, never clearly revealing whether she was being accurate or fanciful.

They reveled in their shared acquisition of free drinks earlier that evening, making stupid jokes about how they should repeat that adventure soon, maybe make it a regular thing. He drunkenly suggested they find out where all future Bar Mitzvahs in Manhattan were taking place, and charge potential party crashers seeking a quick free drink for the info. She approved, and threw out the idea that they create an app, call it Open Bar Mitzvah, and earn billions.

When they were finally back at her place, kissing and stumbling and fondling and almost completely undressed, she made some casual remark about having her period. He murmured something in response about how they therefore couldn't have sex that night.

"Why not?" she asked quizzically.

"That's what I've been told."

Julia rolled her eyes, then grabbed a blue towel from a nearby chair and tossed it on the bed, covering part of her lavender floral bedsheets. She then lost her footing for a moment and lurched forward, regained her balance, pointed at the towel, and declared, "Voilà!"

Then there was a blur of frenzied activity, her body entangled with his as he fought off the effects of all that alcohol to stay present and competent through it all. It might have been just a few minutes after her question about "other girls," or maybe as much as a half hour later, when he lay beneath her as she rode him while facing away toward the head of the bed. He was admiring her body and getting off on her moans when he started to consider whether her moans were actually sobs.

"Hey," he said, reaching out for her torso and pulling her down next to him. "Are you okay?"

He looked at the tears rolling down from glazed eyes onto her cheeks. Beyond concern, a panic gripped him that he might have done something wrong. He was trying to think logically and assess the situation. But he had had so much alcohol that it was challenging to think straight, except for the stark realization that she too had consumed a crazy amount of vodka and therefore maybe he shouldn't be in her bed.

"Why are you crying?" he asked with rising alarm.

She shook her head, and then wiped her eyes with her right hand. "I don't want to talk about it," she finally said softly.

This made him even more paranoid, fearful that he had crossed some line, done or said something that had resulted in this reaction. "Okay," he responded, "but can you just tell me why you're crying?"

"I don't want to," she snapped.

"Was it something I did?" he asked, her refusal to explain helping to feed the growing panic in his gut.

"I said I don't want to talk about it."

The tears had largely subsided but remained on her face, glistening in sadness as she stared up at the ceiling. "I need some water," she whispered.

He rose and took a couple of unsteady steps, placed a hand on the nearby wall for balance, and worked his way into the kitchen where he took a black mug from the counter and filled it with water from the sink. Back in bed, sitting next to where she lay, he handed it to her, and she sat up to drink, spilling some on her chin.

His chest thumped as he thought about what he might have done to cause this. Not knowing was tearing him apart, and then he saw fresh tears start flowing down her face, putting him in an unbearable state of guilt and anxiety. "Why are you crying? Tell me," he implored.

"Oh my fucking God!" she exclaimed as she turned toward him and some of the water splashed onto the towel beneath her. "I told you three times I don't want to talk about it. What the fuck's wrong with you?"

He instinctively leaned away from her, startled by her verbal lashing, as he longed for the Julia from earlier. But she was no longer acting in that lighthearted spirit, laughing and spinning stories that intrigued and entertained. He tried to figure out where he had gone wrong, and what he should say or do. He wanted to find a way to bring her back to the person she was before, but even more, he yearned to understand his own culpability as worst-case scenarios flashed through his head. How could he be sure she hadn't been too intoxicated to consent to having sex with him?

"*Okay*," he shot back with extra emphasis, to show he was being agreeable to her demand. "I was just trying to understand if I did something that hurt you."

"I didn't say you did."

"But you didn't say I *didn't*."

She opened her mouth in exasperation. "I'm sorry. I didn't realize that while I was hysterically crying I needed to be more sensitive about *your* feelings. My bad."

"I just think that if you told me what's wrong, then we could—"

"Get the fuck out of here!" she ordered. "You are unreal. You just don't stop."

"I'm just trying to understand why you're crying. And I don't want to leave you like this," he insisted. "I think if you just told me why—"

He abruptly stopped talking as she extended her right arm and pointed firmly toward her apartment door. "I don't want you here anymore."

He reviewed his options, and recognized that prodding her again for an explanation was certainly not a good one. So he nodded, began to put on his clothes, and then when fully dressed he looked back at her, naked under her sheets, her body turned away from him but the angle still allowing him to observe that her eyes were closed.

"I hope we can talk another time," he said, and then headed for the apartment door.

He texted her the next day, asking if she was okay. He had to wait five painful days to receive her response:

Troy, let me be very clear about the other night. Me crying had nothing to do with you. But you being incredibly insensitive while I was crying, when you could have just been supportive and comforting, and instead you kept selfishly badgering me, that had everything to do with you.

I'm very sorry, he replied. *Can I please see you again?*

No, she answered. *I need someone who will be sympathetic when I'm down, not just willing to party with me when I'm up. I'm not saying you're a terrible person, but I could never be with you again.*

OK. Again, I'm very sorry. I wish you well in everything.

TY. Hope you get out of your uncle's restaurant one day.

This last comment struck Troy as a mocking slight, maybe a well-deserved one. He felt terrible and confused about how this all had ended, and quite possibly Julia did too. Because three months later he received an email from C&R—his first interaction with Tara from HR. She wrote that they had been told he had a strong background in legal studies and writing, and might be interested in a position as a junior associate with the firm. That his information had been shared by one of their current associates, Julia McGinnis. Tara asked whether he was interested in coming to their offices for an interview.

Now, almost three turbulent years later, he was headed to MHU with three colleagues assigned by Anderson. Troy's boss had apparently scoured the company to find anyone still eligible to work this matter. Dave Carlson and Rick LeBeau were two husky men in their late fifties from C&R's Security Risk Management practice, which boasted how it "helped clients anticipate and respond to a myriad of facility, operational, and employee security challenges." If a client was concerned about organizational threats, physical security, and other related needs, they were the go-to guys, able to expertly analyze office plans for security weaknesses and create effective countermeasures against terminated employees who might look to harm their former employer.

None of these services had anything to do with the university's current problems, but their lack of specific experience in that area was irrelevant because similarly, their work had never been needed by Caleb Lugo, so Anderson seized on their availability.

Troy hadn't previously worked directly with either of them but had seen them at office staff meetings, in the C&R hallways, and at the annual holiday party. Dave was a little larger with a salt-and-pepper beard, while Rick's head was shaved and he sported a goatee with stark blond color that was no doubt attributable to hair dye.

As they sat together near their airport boarding gate, Dave whispered to Rick and Troy, "Now we'll be stuck for God knows how long on this crazy Me Too case. What a clusterfuck. I read how this coach really liked blow jobs from fourteen-year-olds. Definitely not *my thing*. Girls are so annoying at that age. Who wants to deal with them any more than you need to?"

"That's probably why he had them suck his dick," Rick quickly responded. "To get them to *stop talking*, you know?" And they both immediately burst into deep-voiced chuckling, as Troy closed his eyes and sensed the looming disaster they would be facing once he and these two men began client meetings and interviews with sexual assault victims.

Troy then interrupted the laughter by declaring, "I think it's best if I do most of the speaking during the interviews." Even though he felt incredibly uncomfortable and inexperienced about conducting any interview, especially with someone who'd been sexually abused and was dealing with years of trauma. He wasn't sure how he could avoid unintentionally saying the wrong thing. But these two were an even worse option.

Before either of them responded, the fourth member of their group returned from purchasing some food for the flight, carrying a plastic Hudson bag. Marissa Zhong was in her mid-thirties and dressed in a charcoal jacket and matching skirt. An experienced certified public accountant, she'd been leading numerous, complex audits on behalf of C&R's financial investigations team. Again, nothing that crossed paths with their noted author client, so she too was in the clear. Just like the SRM guys, she had no experience with sexual misconduct investigations, but C&R couldn't afford to be choosy. And she did add a female to the team, which was no doubt important for appearances' sake, if not more.

"Handing off all my other work was not easy," she said as she took a seat and began scrolling through her phone. "Some clients not thrilled. And my origination this quarter is going to take a big hit. Then of course I'll get blamed for that."

"Same," Rick commiserated. "I was supposed to do a walk-through at a school in Toledo tomorrow to review their active shooter security precautions and train their personnel. Who did we end up sending instead?"

Dave shrugged. "I think someone from the Chicago office. It's so messed up how they can't find people to staff this MHU investigation, but they just laid off three guys in that office for low utilization. All three could have boosted their utilization and saved their jobs with MHU, but they're banned because they helped Caleb Lugo with some minor matter a decade ago, so they're fucked!"

"I know," Marissa responded. "The firm RIFs a whole bunch of people so our current expenses look better compared to the declining revenue, then we get MHU, which is a huge boost to our salability, but now we have no one to staff it. Meanwhile, I've been reading all the materials on this coach. There's so much he's accused of. It never ends. We're going to be at this school for eternity. My other clients are going to drop me if I can't figure something out."

They had all been told by Anderson to clear their calendars, that they would be billing virtually nonstop for the foreseeable future on MHU, and nothing could get in the way. As the firm scrambled to identify any able body to contribute to this highly lucrative matter, it was a pretty big success that C&R had been able to field a team of four somewhat presentable professionals on such short notice, whose names would not be found in any Caleb Lugo billing records.

"You ever deal with an asshole like this coach?" Rick asked his female colleague.

Marissa nodded. "In college I had a professor who cornered me during office hours. I just said, 'Awww, you want to have a baby with me?' He backed off quick."

Troy wanted to get out of there immediately, off this team, away from this assignment. He should have billed his time to Caleb Lugo and disqualified himself from this debacle. After nearly three years of trying to stay out of harm's way, he had voluntarily introduced himself into the fray and feared he would soon pay a heavy price. He had seen declaring his eligibility for MHU work as his shot to help Julia and better his own situation, but maybe he had miscalculated.

The four of them soon boarded their flight and then shared an Uber to the hotel that abutted campus. From his room on the fifteenth floor, Troy had a clear view of the commotion feeding into the school's main arteries. Students, staff, and faculty walked briskly while a few stopped to sit on benches or stand and converse with others who filled out the MHU universe.

He looked in the mirror at his navy suit, the best one he possessed. The same attire he had chosen for the Sixteen Foundation fundraiser earlier that month. As he straightened the red-and-gray tie, he noted it was almost time for the four of them to meet in the lobby. From there, they would walk to the nearby administrative building for the first of numerous meetings and interviews with university officials, current and former players from the softball program, staff with oversight over the activities of the former coach, and more. Their work, which they were in truth woefully unprepared for, would be dissected and criticized by various groups associated with the school, plus local and national media, activists, and political leaders.

If they performed perfectly, if they utilized decades of relevant experience to conduct a flawless inquiry, they would likely still be torn apart by those seeking to do so. The fact that none of them actually possessed this necessary experience, and they would surely be far from perfect, meant this was a likely catastrophe in the making.

And in the midst of it all, he had to fly back to New York later that week to be interviewed for C&R's own internal investigation.

He felt the key to surviving this all, successfully helping Julia, and having them both come out thriving or at least moderately well in the end, was taking this one step at a time. So it was time to proceed to the next step—meeting the main MHU contacts for their work, Deputy General Counsel Tim Durso and Human Resources Director Serena Stanfield.

24
Megan

It was probably the last non-campaign activity Megan would engage in until Election Day, which was just eight weeks away. There was so much to do, an absurd amount of money to raise, and a seemingly endless number of people, organizations, and interests groups with which to try to gain favor. But she needed to see Evina.

As Megan had done countless times, she went through the whole screening process—removing her shoes, emptying her pockets, sending her bag through the machine, walking through the metal detector. Then she had to stand with her legs wide and arms out as a correction officer patted her down. She hated how this had become robotic, normal, a part of life that occurred over and over for years. One day she would visit Evina without needing a security screening, without Evina being confined in a dungeon for defending her own life.

Megan now looked at her friend, who sat facing her across the table in the visitation room. Evina's eyes looked heavy, her face even more drained of life than usual. But Megan saw a tiny spark of hope in her face as soon as she delivered her news.

"I'm doing it," Megan informed her. So there was no turning back now. "I'm running."

Evina slowly shook her head with admiration and appreciation. "Oh my God. That's amazing."

"It's a longshot. But if we can pull this off..."

"After the trial, my lawyer said something like one percent of convicted defendants are successful on appeal. And unfortunately I wasn't in that one percent," Evina replied thoughtfully. "I understand the campaign's a long shot, but it's gotta be greater than one percent, right? Our odds are going up."

Megan smiled. Speaking of odds, it was time to tell Evina her campaign strategy, and Megan braced for her disappointment that none of it involved rallying people to see the wrongful injustice in her conviction.

"*A lot* of people are furious about how MHU covered up for their pedophile softball coach."

"I know. Just like people in a position to help me didn't care, officials at the school weren't moved to do something either."

"Right. And a growing segment of the district is also outraged that MHU hired an investigative firm that blackmailed and harassed Caleb Lugo's sexual assault victims. The other candidates are all defending the school and trying to curry favor with the political machine that backs the MHU leadership. No one in the congressional race is speaking for all these voters who are justifiably furious."

"So you're going to speak for them."

"Yes, I'm going to hammer that issue over and over until I win this thing. That's how I'll hopefully earn the power to help you from DC. I'm sorry the campaign won't be focused on your cause. It's just that—"

Evina waved her hand to stop her explanation. "No, I understand. Please don't apologize. People don't care about me. If they did, I'd have been released years ago. Too many just see me as a manipulative bitch who murdered her wonderful, innocent husband, and then lied about years of abuse. The prosecutors and his family created that narrative during the trial, when they had all the power and I had none. Running your campaign on that issue is a dead end."

"People may not care, but *I care*," Megan assured her. "And if I win this election, I'll have the platform to hopefully make the people in Washington who control this process—"

"To make *them* care?" she asked skeptically.

"To make them act to get you out of here," Megan clarified. "Aaron Montgomery told me that as a congressman he had leverage with the White House because they needed his support for close budget votes and things like that. Plus I'll have more ability to drive this story in the media."

"So we're betting that a majority of the voters will be drawn to your message."

"We don't even need a majority, Evina. The Democrats and Republicans will each have their candidate. Plus there'll probably be other independent campaigns. I have my first candidate forum in two days. I just need a plurality of the vote, more than anyone else running. Even if I get less than a majority, we win if I'm the top vote getter."

"And let's say this all works. If you win, if you're elected . . . what kind of time frame are we talking about to . . ."

"I have no idea, but you'll be my biggest priority. When anyone powerful needs my support for anything, this will be the main issue I'll demand *their* support for."

"So we could be talking years."

"Maybe," Megan conceded. "Or maybe there's some razor-thin vote on a big appropriations bill right away, or a tight House leadership race. Then my vote will be crucial and the price will be helping get you clemency. Or possibly once I'm in Washington I get exposure to the right celebrity who has a large platform to advocate for you. The president signs commutations regularly. We just need to get your petition in front of the right people so you're on the next list."

Evina actually smiled for a moment. "Eight weeks?"

"Yeah," Megan responded. "Eight weeks. If I win this election, if I'm a congresswoman, I'll find a way to get you out of here."

"And if you don't win?"

Megan had no idea what course to take if she lost. But she wasn't going to say that, and she had too much to tackle right now to worry about fallout after a possible election defeat. It was an issue for another day, one she might be able to completely avoid if she ran this race successfully.

"Then we'll find another way. We'll come up with plan B. Or C, or D. Whatever letter we're up to now. But I like our current plan, so let's stay focused on that. All right? I need to get back on the campaign trail."

"Okay. I trust you. And I'm incredibly appreciative. I'm so lucky to have you as a friend. I'd be lost without you, because it's so hard living like this. I lay awake at night wondering if I'm destined to be here for decades, and I know I don't have that in me. I just can't. I keep thinking about how I could've avoided killing him that night. Then I wouldn't be here."

"You wouldn't be here because you'd be dead. You defended yourself. That's not a crime. That took real strength, Evina. We need to get the right people to recognize that." Megan saw how miserable, defeated, and near-hopeless Evina appeared again, with her gaunt face, thinning hair, distant eyes. "You filed your clemency petition not that long ago. We've just begun to fight for that," Megan declared with as much confidence and strength as she could muster.

Evina nodded. "I love you so much. You're the greatest friend. I'm still alive and fighting because of the strength you've given me."

"No, Evina. You give *me* strength. Every single day. Seeing you persevere and keep battling against enormous obstacles. I love you. You're my best friend. We're going to keep fighting until you're free, so neither of us is going to ever give up. Okay? *Neither of us.*"

25
Serena

Serena headed straight up the stairs to the third-floor conference room, where she had attended the earlier C&R interview with Gillian Fenton, Anderson Davis, and Luke Holloway. Now the team had magically transformed through the power of scandal and desperation to a new group—Troy Abernathy, Marissa Zhong, Dave Carlson, and Rick LeBeau.

Drew entered the room just after she did, and she took a look at this new lineup and shook their hands as they each introduced themselves. Troy was young. How young? Too young? Hard to tell. He was gracious and professional, but how much relevant experience did he have?

Marissa didn't have the flaw of Troy's youth, but her CPA background seemed highly unhelpful. Although it might take a CPA to calculate the school's potential civil liability. Or what they'd be paying C&R in investigative fees.

The other two men seemed more grizzled, seasoned. But grizzled and seasoned with what? Expertise in security and threat management was surely important in many contexts. But what about in this area, which was the only one she really cared about?

She decided to just be blunt. "Do you each have experience with sexual misconduct investigations?"

"Absolutely," Dave quickly responded.

"Many," Rick added. "Weren't those part of our RFP response?"

She nodded. "They were. But that response didn't include anything about the four of you. So that's why I'm asking. Have you each conducted sexual misconduct investigations before?"

"Of course," Dave reassured her.

Marissa added, "We were chosen for this team because of our experience, and we're grateful for the opportunity to assist the university."

She noted that Troy was silent, maybe because he was the junior member of the team. Or was it for some other reason?

"Is Gillian Fenton still working for C&R?" she asked him.

"Yes, she is," he replied.

"Have any of you spoken with her about her meetings with the complainants? She really connected with them, and it would be good if she updated you about her conversations before you interview them."

These remarks were greeted with silence, and Serena wondered if that was because they were unsure what the correct answer was. Unsure if they were supposed to have had spoken with Gillian, regardless of whether they actually had.

"We were told she couldn't be involved in our work," Troy finally explained. "President Montgomery instructed my boss, Anderson Davis, that anyone who—"

"Yes, yes, I know," she interrupted with frustration. "But I think touching base with her informally would be beneficial."

"But if you haven't," Drew said, "maybe let's not now?" He looked at Serena, his eyes subtly imploring her not to push this issue. "It might cause more trouble at this point."

"Should we seek clarification from Anderson? Or President Montgomery?" Troy asked.

She knew Aaron would never go for this, as much as it would be helpful and meaningful for Ali Tyrell and the others. Even though connecting with Gillian about her meetings was prohibited, she hoped the C&R team now in her presence had been smart enough to discreetly do it anyway. But that appeared not to be the case, unless they were just acting that way to avoid confessing to violating the rules. One could dream.

"As you all know, this is a complicated investigation," Serena instructed. "In addition to complainants who've experienced years of trauma, there are many individuals who were around all the softball activities in one role or another, and people who worked in various other parts of the university, who may have had the opportunity to prevent this years ago. We need to understand why they didn't report anything during this time. It's essential to learn what they were aware of. And what they *should* have been aware of."

"No problem," Troy responded. "We're reviewing all the documents, and we'll be ready for the initial interviews tomorrow."

Every instinct told Serena she couldn't rely on this group, they weren't the right people for this assignment, and they weren't equipped with the proper sensitivity and training for such an undertaking. "Before I trust you all with commencing this investigation," she said, "I need to ask one more question. Are you really capable of conducting this inquiry with the proper expertise and staffing that's necessary for a wide-ranging sexual misconduct investigation involving potentially hundreds of interviews and dozens of sexual assault survivors?"

They were all silent, and she sensed they were unsure which of them should respond. Serena stared directly at Troy, for some reason picking him out of the group, and asked, "What's your answer?"

"I think so," he said. "I do. I definitely think so."

And that answer told her everything. *I think so.*

Enough bullshit, enough deception, enough bait-and-switch promises of stellar personnel. Enough, enough, enough. A new firm had to be brought in, one that wasn't tainted and compromised, one that didn't have some political connection to the university's president. This might delay the process and cause a new round of public criticism and controversy, but finding a new firm was now essential.

She quickly ended the meeting and then headed to the president's office, with Drew once again trailing her. When she got there she just pushed open the door, walked in, and saw Aaron sitting at his desk, fixated on his phone.

"We need to replace C&R," Serena insisted, as Aaron returned an irritated look. "Right now."

"We're not doing that. They're on campus already," Aaron responded sharply. "You have to work with them or I'll find someone else who can."

"Who cares if they're on campus?" she replied. She was no longer concerned about being deferential to her new boss. She still feared being fired and losing the tuition support for Kayla, but the consequences of staying silent were too high. "I just met with their team. They're completely wrong for us. A CPA, a couple of security guys, and some kid who's a junior associate. I asked about their capabilities and I got a very inadequate response. This associate just said—"

"They're experienced investigators from one of the most prestigious firms in the world," Aaron interrupted. "If we fire them, we'll look weak, and it'll take a month or more to identify a new firm. Then the new investigators will take time to get up to speed, and the media and the public will castigate us for our indecision and delay. I'm not allowing that. We move forward. Expeditiously. Let's be thorough, but let's do this as quickly as possible and get past this."

"I strongly, *strongly* disagree," she replied as he stood and took a step toward her. "They're going to make things worse, not better. They aren't going to be able to make the complainants feel comfortable participating in this process. And I won't sit silently by while this university once again—"

"What does *that* mean, Serena?" Aaron barked as his voice rose in anger. "I told you before that I won't allow you to undermine me and the university. It sounds like you're threatening exactly that. So think *very carefully* before you speak again."

She took a moment to consider his words and what she should say or do next. She wasn't going to cave to him, but she also knew she needed to be cautious. Serena had been focused on how the new C&R team would be detrimental for Ali and the other victims, but that obviously wasn't a priority for Aaron. Maybe she should instead appeal to the situation's political ramifications. She and Drew had discussed talking with Aaron about the new congressional campaign that was targeting them all, so possibly this was the time for that.

"It's not just about C&R being ineffective without Gillian," she said. "This city councilwoman who's running for Congress is using their hiring as—"

"I can handle Megan Black. Don't worry about her. I have a strong plan for navigating this crisis, and she or anyone else who gets in the way will face serious consequences."

"Let's go, Serena," Drew said, and she knew he was trying to save her from her next response, to protect her from herself. She reluctantly decided to follow his lead, but before she reached the door, the president spoke again.

"One more thing. The C&R investigators have to interview Cole Malinowski tomorrow. We need that completed before there's another blowup like what happened with that girl's father. Cole's lawyer is saying he's being deprived of an opportunity to tell his story in a prompt manner. And she's not wrong."

"We can't tell our outside investigators what order to interview people in," she said. "We'd be interfering with—"

"Just tell them to interview Cole Malinowski. Tomorrow. That doesn't compromise their independence. Stop catastrophizing everything, Serena!"

Catastrophizing everything? Their star softball coach had molested teenage players, multiple members of the administration had covered up his behavior, and the firm brought in to investigate had been actively combatting allegations against another serial offender. So many victims might have been spared a lifetime of trauma if she'd been able to effectively catastrophize all this sooner.

"I'll suggest to the team that they interview Cole Malinowski tomorrow. But I can't instruct them what to do. That decision needs to be made independently by our *independent* investigators."

She hoped this minor pushback showed she wouldn't just blindly follow his instructions. But as soon as he replied "fine" and walked back to his desk, she realized that in reality she had totally caved to his wishes.

As she headed with Drew out of the building, she shook her head in frustration and disappointment. "These people are not the right people," she insisted. "And interviewing Cole now isn't correct either. Investigators should speak with him *after* they gather more information from others, so they can first learn where he was before, during, and after these sexual assaults. Ali Tyrell already started telling me and Gillian that Cole was almost surely aware of everything. At a minimum, the investigators need to fully interview her before they speak with Cole."

"They can always reinterview him later," Drew responded.

"There's only one chance to have that first interview," she warned. "And what if he doesn't agree to another? His lawyer wants to get him interviewed before we really know all the facts."

What were her options? She could go directly to the board of trustees with her objections. She could speak publicly, say the university once again wasn't doing what was needed to take these allegations seriously. But the response would be that it had hired a top firm and given experienced investigators independence to conduct an inquiry.

"You met the new team, Drew. You feel comfortable with them?"

she asked as she paused walking to stare at him, and he stopped moving too. "Truthfully, do you?"

He nodded. "I do. These situations are always problematic. There's no magic solution. Rob Dempsey's been indicted, he'll spend decades in prison, and we've retained prominent investigators to look into any cover-up and failure to act. Yes, this hasn't been smooth, but these things never are. You can't get a perfect resolution. That's just not real life. We can't rush the investigation, but we shouldn't delay it either by casting aside C&R. We're all doing our best to figure out this mess and save our school."

She wished he was as troubled as she was, or at least troubled at all. Maybe the threatening language from Megan Black had gotten to him and made him feel a need to rally around the university's response.

"I'm going to base my decision on Ali Tyrell's response to her interview. If she's comfortable, if she feels she can appropriately speak with this team and they're taking her story seriously, then I'll stand down. But if she doesn't believe in them, then there's no way they can be effective, and they need to be replaced."

"Just promise me one thing," Drew cautioned. "Please."

"What's that?"

"Speak with me first before you do anything rash. Okay? Give me a chance to talk you out of it."

"We'll see," she answered noncommittally. "I may not want to be talked out of it."

26
Troy

As soon as Troy uttered those words to Serena Stanfield, he knew he'd fucked up in a huge way.

I think so. I do. I definitely think so.

Wrong answer. That much should have been obvious before he spoke, but in the midst of all the stress and confusion, it took the instant reaction on Serena's face to make his mistake terribly clear. It wasn't so much a look of being shocked or appalled. Instead, it was a knowing glance, as if she'd just solved an important, ongoing question—that she finally had clarity about a complex situation.

With those words, he had told her everything—that this wasn't the best investigative team, that he wasn't at all comfortable in this high-pressure, challenging role. That if the university sought a top-notch investigation operating with appropriate sensitivity and understanding, they weren't the right personnel.

There was really no right answer, however. He hadn't been comfortable with the exaggerations offered by the other members of his team. Telling Serena they'd handled these types of matters before, when in fact none of them had. He didn't feel right echoing these boasts, but he hadn't intended to potentially tank the whole mission either.

Troy had been a part of so many C&R pitches, either in written proposals or in-person meetings, when he and his colleagues had been forced to stretch the truth in order to land a potentially lucrative assignment. Okay, well not *forced*. No one forced them. But if they wanted to stay employed, they needed to either bring in business or be staffed on a project that someone else originated, and stretching one's credentials was often essential in the consulting world.

But this felt different, more egregious, and unsettling in a way he had never before encountered. Lying about having interviewed sexual assault victims, when the people who really had done so were prohibited from taking part, seemed like crossing a new line. And besides the lack of morality, the risk appeared to be much higher than with other matters. Wouldn't someone eventually press them on the details? How would that play in such a high-profile situation?

He knew his colleagues' answers came back to the millions that C&R was expected to bill—the blank check from MHU. The teetering financial status of their company, the need to show immediate revenue to entice their new buyers and avoid seeking Chapter 11 protection.

However, when Serena posed the question, he couldn't bring himself to unequivocally play along, nor could he summon the moral courage to speak the truth. He was stuck in this purgatory where he was pacifying no one, and betraying everyone.

Troy expressed all this to Julia in a late-night phone call as he lay in his hotel bed and nervously anticipated the next day's interviews. He had been reviewing the university-provided documents about prior complaints on his laptop, making sure he was familiar with every appalling detail before the questioning of witnesses, when he took a much-needed break to call her.

"I'm trying to handle this all correctly," he lamented. "But it's really tough."

"I know," she commiserated.

"I really messed up with my answer. I'll make sure to do better next time. If I'm given a next time."

"Well, MHU hasn't fired us yet. So Anderson hasn't fired *me* yet. Just be very careful what you say. There's so much at stake."

"Yes, too much. And as if this situation wasn't chaotic enough, I just got told I have a new interview scheduled for first thing tomorrow morning with one of the assistant coaches. There's hardly any time to really prepare."

Troy wondered whether he should just resign, give up on a career with C&R, stop trying to play savior for Julia. But then what would he do next? He had no other good option.

Then he thought about the reality of what they were investigating. Numerous young women who had been sexually assaulted by their trusted coach. School officials who potentially knew about the misconduct and allowed it to persist. Possibly other university personnel who actually weren't responsible in any way, and who were relying on a thorough investigation to provide proper due process and clear them from the nationwide outrage.

"Am I crazy to hope we can actually do some good here?" he asked Julia. "In addition to protecting ourselves? I mean, there's a lot of bad shit that went down on this campus. I'm starting to interview some of the victims soon. I'd like to actually help them. I wish we could just focus on that, instead of all the drama about origination credit, proper staffing, and pending layoffs."

"Listen, Troy," she began sympathetically, "you mean well. You're not like the others, who just focus on maximizing their own profit. But . . ."

"But what?"

"Please don't get your hopes up that these girls are going to get some justice from our toxic shitshow of a company. Understand that realistically . . . that's not likely. And it's not your fault. Just do your best."

He thought about her words, and knew his stress extended well beyond these issues. "It's also hard to focus on what I need to do tomorrow, when I have this interview back in New York looming over me. I have no idea if I'm a target because of the Caleb Lugo research. I'm really going in blind."

"You just need to stand up for yourself and explain you did nothing wrong. Remember, we're not powerless. With my connection to Aaron, and C&R needing you on the MHU team, we have some good leverage."

"Has Aaron called you back?"

"No, but I took your advice and texted him. He wrote back today that he's sorry he hasn't returned my call, but things are very hectic. He said he'd call soon."

The next morning, the C&R foursome met in the hotel lobby and walked across the street to the administrative building, where they were set to occupy two conference rooms throughout the day and begin interviews.

He was paired with Rick for now, while Dave partnered with Marissa. He entered one of the conference rooms with Rick and they took seats at the far end of the table. Rick took out a yellow notepad to document the interviews, while Troy pulled out his laptop and plugged it into a nearby outlet.

"Okay, first up, Cole Malinowski. So, Cole, let me ask," Rick started with a mock question as he stroked his goatee with no one else but Troy in the room. "Were you covering up for this pervert, or were you just fucking clueless the whole time? Because those are the two options." He then laughed and leaned back in his chair, before releasing a self-satisfied sigh.

"How about I begin the questioning?" Troy suggested. It wasn't as if he had interview experience in similar situations, or really any other high-stakes scenario, but he wanted to stave off a quick disaster.

"Sure, that's fine. I'm billing all day either way."

There was a knock on the door, and Troy stood and walked over to open it, welcoming in Cole Malinowski and a blonde-haired woman in her late sixties. Troy had seen photos of Cole on the university website, with the assistant coach sporting some variation of the MHU purple athletic shirt. Now he wore a dark suit and blue tie, looking ultra-professional.

"This is my attorney, Katherine Barbato," he said with a rushed, anxious tone. Troy noted Katherine's stern demeanor, and how she appeared serious and intimidating already.

"I want to be clear," she began, "that my client did nothing wrong and is under no legal obligation to be here. But he wants to help the school he loves, and he wants to clear his name, so he's willing to answer your questions."

"Thank you both for meeting with us," Troy responded. "Please have a seat."

Troy and Rick were then on one side of the table, facing Cole and his attorney.

"I'm Troy Abernathy and this is my colleague Rick LeBeau," Troy continued. "The university retained us in response to the sexual misconduct allegations against former head softball coach Rob Dempsey. We're speaking with many people he coached or supervised, and we appreciate your cooperation."

"I've been trying to get interviewed and tell what I know since this began," Cole said, shaking his head in frustration. "The whole thing has really messed up my life. I'm not comparing myself to those girls and what they experienced. Obviously I can't even imagine how they're doing. But everyone's assuming I'm somehow responsible, and my name's being dragged through the mud on social media and in my professional circles. I've worked so hard for years to earn my dream of leading a major softball program, and another school was about to hire me for that. They were just going to conduct a few reference checks, and then this all blew up. So I'm in limbo, and I don't know where my life and career go from here."

Troy nodded. "Why don't you start by telling me about your background. How did you start working with this program, and how long have you been employed at MHU?"

"I attended college here. Loved it. I was captain of the baseball team. After graduation, I played in the minor leagues for a couple of seasons, but that wasn't going anywhere unfortunately, especially after I suffered a pretty bad knee injury. I knew Coach Rob when I played here, and he asked me to return to campus and help with the softball program. I worked with him for about ten years, rising to the position of his main assistant."

Troy was about to ask his next question when Rick interjected, "So here's the thing, Cole. You were obviously real tight with Coach Rob, right?"

"What do you mean by 'tight'?"

"You worked with him regularly. You were his right-hand man. You ran the program with him."

"Yeah, that's all true."

"So your position now is that," Rick continued, leaning forward skeptically, "over this entire decade, working with him, watching him interact with all these girls, you knew nothing? You saw nothing that made you just a little suspicious?"

Cole was silent and turned to his lawyer for a moment. She nodded, then Cole responded, "Who said I saw nothing?"

Troy looked up from his computer screen and struggled to understand his implication. "You're saying you *were* aware of improper activity?"

"Yes."

"Can you give us specifics?"

"There were occasions over the years when he would become a

little too friendly with some of the girls in our summer program. At first it was little things, like he'd be uncomfortably close to certain players, in their personal space, complimenting them a lot. Then sometimes I didn't know where one of the girls was and then she'd suddenly be back on the field. And the time she was away would coincide with Coach Rob not being around. I remember all that very clearly. One of them was named Ali—"

"Ali Tyrell?" Rick cut in.

"Yes," Cole confirmed. "I actually saw her go into his office, when he was already in there. This was years ago. I don't remember exactly when. I stayed nearby. My office was down the hall, and I kept peering out and waiting for one of them to exit. Finally she did, and walked quickly past my office. I looked out and her hair was messed up, no longer in the neat ponytail she always had. Then I saw his door opening again, so I ducked back into my office, and he walked by. I only saw him for a couple of seconds that time, but he was adjusting his clothes, tucking in his shirt. Stuff like that."

Troy was typing quickly, and Rick was taking handwritten notes.

"Was this the only time you observed anything like that?" Troy asked.

"Absolutely not. There were similar occurrences over the years."

"How many?"

"I don't remember exactly. At least half a dozen with different girls. Always around his office."

When Troy reviewed the MHU-provided information, he had seen how every documented allegation had led to a finding of no responsibility, or the matters were dropped, usually in conjunction with a settlement payment and a nondisclosure agreement. He had carefully read every page and was confident that none of this paperwork had reflected Cole being a whistleblower in any way. Which led to Troy's obvious follow-up: "So why didn't you report this?"

Cole squinted his eyes and turned his head slightly to the side, as if he was surprised by this question. "What are you talking about? I did. Multiple times."

"There's no record of that," Rick insisted. "Who did you report it to?"

"Serena Stanfield. She runs human resources."

Troy's mind did a silent double take as he heard this name. "When did you first make a report to her?"

"I don't have the exact date. Years ago."

"Was it in writing?"

"No. I went to her office. I told her I found this behavior very disturbing and I was concerned about the safety of the softball players."

"How did she respond?"

"She said she'd look into it. I don't know what she did after that, but this conduct continued, and I went to her office several more times over the next few years to let her know what I'd seen. And each time she just thanked me for the information and said she'd follow up."

"Did you document these discussions?" Troy asked. "Did you put anything in writing? Email?"

"No, but in hindsight, I wish I had. I thought speaking directly with the HR director was the right action."

"Was anyone else present when you spoke with her?"

Cole shook his head. "No, but I just thought of something."

"What's that?" Troy responded.

"There are CCTV cameras all over her office building. You can just pull the footage. I'll try to figure out the dates."

"When was the last time you reported an incident to her?" Rick asked.

"Probably a year ago."

"These cameras all have thirty-day cycles, and they don't preserve footage beyond that period," the expert in security risk management explained. "There's no way that footage is still available."

"Oh really?" Cole said. "That's too bad."

Troy's eyes connected with Cole, and he saw how the assistant coach's mouth curled up a bit to demonstrate purported disappointment at this latest development. Troy just nodded for the moment, but in his mind he tried to figure out if any of this was potentially credible. Multiple attempts to report these incidents? Over the course of years? And yet no records, no witnesses, except for Serena who would no doubt deny they ever happened.

Nevertheless, this was a significant development, and they had to follow proper investigative protocols. The new information had to be brought to university leadership immediately, and they would need Serena to recuse herself from overseeing the investigation. What else? If they didn't handle this correctly, C&R would be blamed. *He* would be blamed.

"When Serena Stanfield didn't act on the information you brought to her, why did you keep going to her? Why not try someone else?" Troy asked.

"I just figured the HR director was the right person to approach. It's maddening. I mean, so much went wrong here," Cole explained as he looked earnestly at Troy and then Rick. "So many people just ignored this whole situation for years. But I didn't. I tried to help."

"Did you speak with Rob Dempsey about your concerns?" Rick questioned. "Or try to intervene when he was alone with one of the girls?"

"No. If I could go back in time, I absolutely would. But you have to understand, it was a really tough situation. I didn't have any proof he was doing something wrong, and he was my boss. It seemed like the responsible thing was to report it to HR, like we're told to do."

"I think we need to pause this interview," Troy said, and looked at Rick who nodded his agreement. "We'll be speaking more, but based on what you told us, we need to talk with other administrators about how to proceed."

"Okay," Cole said, rising. "The more you investigate, the more you'll see that those who had power to do something failed to act. If you ask me, all leadership personnel who were here before this became public need to be removed. That lady has the right idea."

"What lady?" Troy asked.

"The lady running for Congress. Megan Black. The one who says we need to reclaim MHU. She's absolutely right. Hopefully people will listen."

27
Megan

POLITICAL CAMPAIGNS move fast. Campaigns for Congress, especially so.

In just two days, Megan had cobbled together a small team of people to hopefully galvanize public support and shepherd her through the strange, roller-coaster process. Aimee served as her campaign manager, and Megan had retained a fundraising chair and communications director. She even had a volunteer driver, taking her from event to event.

Once she announced the Reclaim MHU ballot line, there was an instant surge of volunteers and donations, many coming from people across the country who knew nothing of her or her district, but were outraged by the media narrative about Rob Dempsey and the inadequate administrative response.

She was trying to balance running this race in a sincere, honest manner with practical steps needed to win this election. Her campaign sent out an email blast to potential supporters, asking for fundraising support. The email declared that the campaign was "$14,576 from our goal!" and it was essential that they hit this mark "by tomorrow's deadline!"

She had asked her new fundraising consultant where the $14,576 figure had come from. He told her that people responded best to an arbitrary, specific number that sounded reachable, and this was the phantom figure he came up with. Standard fundraising practice. And what about tomorrow's deadline? What deadline was this? Again, she was told this was a fiction utilized to foment urgent action.

Yesterday evening she spoke at her first campaign town hall in a large meeting room at the local VFW site. Over 150 people in attendance listened to her recite the numerous ways MHU leadership, past and present, had failed their community.

The microphone was in a stand in front of her, but when she got to the key part, she removed it from its metallic hold, placed the device closer to her mouth, and strolled a few steps toward the front row of the audience.

"That's why," she urged, "we must reclaim our beloved university. Too much is at stake, and the nation is watching. The *world* is watching. I haven't given up on MHU. Have you? No, I didn't think so. I love MHU. And we can still save it. We're *going* to save it, because it's too important for us to watch it fall apart from scandal and incompetence."

Audience members nodded, and then a few of the local residents began to applaud. Some even stood as they contributed to the ovation, so she raised her voice into the microphone and continued, "We need to completely clean house. For the hardworking employees who aren't responsible for these horrors, we're on your side. But for the leadership and their negligent and incompetent human resources staff who failed to protect our daughters, for the current president who's playing political games during a time of tragedy, my message is clear: *Throw them all out*. Now. We need to *reclaim MHU*. If you choose me as your next congresswoman, I'll make sure we do."

She got the desired result. Cheers, enthusiasm, people lining up to speak, take selfies, offer to volunteer, spread the word, and collect signatures for her ballot line. Several told her they had just made online campaign donations on their phones.

She shook some more hands as she made her way to the exit, walking with two campaign volunteers toward the waiting black SUV that would take her to the next campaign stop. But standing outside the vehicle under an illuminated streetlamp was a familiar, albeit unexpected face, who solemnly looked at her and asked, "Can you talk for a moment, Megan?"

"Certainly, Professor," she replied, and nodded to her escorts, indicating they should enter the car so she could talk outside in semi-privacy.

"Aaron asked me to speak to you."

"Why doesn't he call me?"

"Because your campaign is viciously and unfairly attacking him."

"He wouldn't call me back *before* my campaign became critical of him, so don't use that as an excuse."

He nodded. "Listen, Megan, you can't keep saying this stuff. You just can't."

"You don't have leverage over me. I'm not seeking your endorsement anymore, *Professor*," she replied, emphasizing the last word with as much sarcasm as she could muster.

"Here's my point," he explained. "Aaron won't allow you to keep trashing him and his legacy. You need to understand that if you don't stop *immediately*, he'll have no choice but to fight back. You're not the only person targeting him, and just like with the others, he's going to have to come after you. Hard. Very soon. So please back down *now*. Spare us all this unnecessary conflict, okay? It doesn't help anyone."

"He's going to come after me? With what?"

"Everyone has something."

She shook her head. "Good luck with that. I'm happily married with two kids. I pay my taxes. My life's completely socially acceptable."

"Okay, Megan. It's your decision. But before you proceed, think about Evina Jansen."

She had remained poised throughout this conversation, standing up to this political power broker without wavering, but she now felt a sudden jolt of concern in her gut that she sensed was completely transparent to this man.

Instead of threatening her, why couldn't Aaron just promise to help Evina, in return for Megan standing down? Maybe they felt this would be more startling, more likely to have an immediate impact. She could ask for an explanation, but she knew that would make her concern even more obvious, and he would think they had this potential power over her.

In any event, she wasn't going to let this asshole intimidate her, the way he did to all the other local politicos who cowered in his presence and groveled for support. Her campaign, predicated on her opposition to MHU leadership, was only in its infancy but so far a clear success. It provided the first real hope she would be able to free Evina since she left Aaron's office. She wouldn't change course or back down now.

She didn't respond to his foreboding comment. Instead she turned away, entered the vehicle, and instructed the driver to head to the next event.

Now, the following evening, she sat alone in the back seat of that same SUV, parked outside the high school that was hosting the first congressional candidate forum. Megan wanted to review her notes one more time, think over what she wanted to say as she usually did before a public appearance, but instead she stared at her phone and the broadcast that had just begun.

She had been alerted by several supporters that Aaron had announced a live television interview with a national news network to address many of the "issues and distortions" that had circulated regarding his leadership and other related topics. In particular, a statement from a university spokesperson said Aaron would "discuss how untrue characterizations and outright lies were being used by certain individuals for political advantage in a manner that was harmful to the university and our democracy." She sensed this was going to be the return strike the professor had warned about, so she needed to see it live.

The interview began, and Megan watched on her phone as Aaron sat in a chair wearing a crisp blue suit and red tie, and his female interviewer began asking him questions about the continuing MHU crisis.

"Let's talk about the investigation," she prodded.

"Absolutely," he quickly responded. "We have one of the *top* investigative firms in the world, C&R Investigations, sending their best people to *independently* investigate all allegations of sexual misconduct in the MHU softball program. We'll release their full report publicly when they complete their work, subject to any necessary redactions to protect witness confidentiality. We're being completely transparent and responsible, because what happened on this campus *under the previous leadership* is unconscionable."

"You say top investigative firm . . ." she began to follow up.

"It unquestionably is. There's no debate about that."

"Yes, and apparently Caleb Lugo would agree," the reporter responded with a challenging tone, and just a little bit of snark. "Because when he wanted to dig up dirt to silence his sexual misconduct accusers, he chose that firm also."

Megan looked at her watch. Just a few minutes until she needed to enter the building, greet the organizers, start shaking hands, get ready to be introduced. Not a lot of time, but she had to see this interview through to the end, so she could understand if and how she was targeted, and be able to respond knowledgeably to whatever he said if she was asked about it inside.

Aaron nodded to the interviewer. "I'm very glad you brought that up. People are distorting this issue in disingenuous ways."

"So what's the undistorted version?" the reporter asked.

"A worldwide investigations firm, just like a worldwide law firm, has many clients. *Many* clients. If a couple of people in one part of the firm assisted a problematic person, that doesn't take away from the extraordinary work conducted by others throughout the company, who have had stellar careers and nothing to do with Caleb Lugo."

"But how do you know—"

"We've ensured that every individual assigned to the university's investigation has never billed so much as one second to Caleb Lugo. The people raising that issue want us on the defensive. They'll criticize anyone we bring in. They can always point to someone at any major firm who once upon a time worked for someone objectionable. We're just not going to play that game. We have horrendous, egregious allegations to investigate, and we brought in the best people in the world to do that."

The interviewer nodded, and Megan wondered how she was going to follow up on this assertion. Aaron's spin was far too simplistic to just be accepted. Was this the only firm available? Why not select a company that *didn't* work to support a serial sex offender? And it wasn't just that they were Lugo's advocates in some way. They had actively uncovered embarrassing, potentially nonconsensual images to tarnish, intimidate, and blackmail the women who were risking it all by coming forward. There was so much with which to push back.

But the journalist decided not to take any of those paths.

"Let's turn to city council member Megan Black," she said instead, and Megan felt an uneasy rumbling work its way through her stomach at the mention of her own name. Simultaneously, there was a knock on the car door, indicating she needed to enter the debate.

She waved her hand and snapped, "Not yet!" She could see that Aimee was outside the door, and it was too dark to quickly tell if she was alone. Megan hoped no one else had been on the receiving end of her uncharacteristic rudeness, especially not a constituent or an event organizer. But she was glued to her phone and couldn't take the time or attention to fully explore who was outside.

"Yes, let's . . ." Aaron replied, and Megan heard something ominous in his tone, although it surely came off benevolently firm to any neutral party viewing the interview.

"She's running in the special election for your congressional seat, and she's creating a new ballot line, Reclaim MHU. She's already surged to second place in an online poll while campaigning on a platform of 'cleaning house' throughout the university. She's saying the current leadership is part of the problem. And as the top of that leadership, that includes you."

"Naturally."

"You haven't directly addressed this, so what is your response to Megan Black's campaign and the many people who seem inspired by it?"

Megan watched Aaron sigh, as if he didn't want to say what he was thinking. She knew this was all calculated so he could seem sympathetic, to appear as if he deeply regretted having to go negative but that it just couldn't be avoided.

"Here's the thing about Megan. She's a relative newcomer to politics. She just got elected to the Mountain Hill City Council a year ago."

"So you think her attacks are based on inexperience?" the interviewer asked.

"I wish I could say that," he explained with a sad nod. "I wish that *inexperience* was all we were dealing with."

All we were dealing with. What the hell was he talking about? She braced for his answer.

"What do you mean?" the reporter asked as she leaned toward him.

"First of all, it's heartbreaking and maddening that Megan would use horrific sexual misconduct allegations involving teenage girls for her own political benefit. It's also unfortunate that when it comes to Megan Black, this type of unethical, shameless behavior isn't surprising."

Another knock on her window, this one louder. Another quick wave of the hand. She couldn't stop viewing her phone now.

"What else are you referring to?" the journalist asked.

"The full story is a long one," Aaron said. "But here are the key points. There's a woman named Evina Jansen who's in federal prison for murder. And it wasn't just *a* murder. It was a torture killing. The victim, her husband, was stabbed in the back, dragged across state lines, and thrown in a ditch. Really horrendous."

Now Megan sucked in her breath and held it, her eyes wide open. She had braced for him to attack, to try to undermine her reputation and her campaign for Congress, and she'd steeled herself for this and felt ready to fight back. But she hadn't expected Aaron to stoop to tossing Evina into this scrum, for her friend to be on the receiving end of attacks in a national broadcast from a powerful man, while Evina sat in a lonely prison cell, defenseless.

"I remember reading about that," the reporter commented. "About a decade ago?"

"Exactly. She's tried to appeal her conviction and sentence in every possible way. Which is of course her right. But there was no merit to her attempts, and they were denied by every court that heard them. It wasn't limited to the brutal murder—which was of course bad enough—but even before that, the state removed her daughter because of rampant child abuse. And this woman, Evina Jansen, is the childhood friend of Megan Black."

"You're certainly not blaming Councilwoman Black for the acts of a childhood friend, are you?" the reporter asked. "If each of us were responsible for what the people we grew up with did later in life, we'd all be—"

"Of course not. But here's what she is responsible for. When I was still in Congress, right before the university appointed me interim president, Megan came to my office, using her status as a member of the Mountain Hill City Council, and urged me to advocate for the White House to commute this woman's sentence. First of all, there are countless people who are more deserving, such as nonviolent drug offenders from impoverished communities who are unjustly incarcerated for decades."

Megan gripped her phone harder with both hands as she listened. Where was he going with this?

"I think the politicization of the clemency and pardon process has been well-documented," the interviewer followed up.

"Absolutely," Aaron answered. "But it wasn't so much about using her power to advocate for an undeserving convict. The even larger problem was the way she did it."

"How was that?"

"She wanted me to withhold my vote on the upcoming budget for leverage. Use my solemn vote as a member of Congress to get her childhood friend, a convicted murderer, an unrepentant child abuser, out of prison."

"You fucking liar!" Megan called out, even though she was alone in the car.

"She urged me to hold up the *entire national budget* for this convicted killer. It was just so crazy. I've seen a lot in DC, and it was the most unethical move I've ever witnessed."

The phone shook in her hands as full panic set in. This new, fabricated narrative threatened to quickly define both Evina and Megan as immoral, dangerous women. She needed to immediately and forcefully respond to all these distortions.

The world needed to know that Evina never hurt her daughter. She had been unable to protect her from an abusive husband. She had killed him in justifiable self-defense. She had been wrongly convicted, no matter what the courts said. Had Megan wanted Aaron to use his influence to set her free? Absolutely. To use his power as a congressman to help one of his constituents. What was wrong with that?

And she hadn't suggested the budget leverage idea—he had proposed it. He had thrown it out there so casually, as if it was no big deal. Now he was portraying it as a sign of how unethical she was.

"If I had gone along with Megan's scheme and stalled the federal budget," Aaron continued, "that would have meant delaying or stopping much-needed support for so many projects and programs in our district, including at this university. Holding up those funds would have had a cruel, harsh impact on many Mountain Hill citizens. But she didn't care about the people in this district who she would hurt. And now she wants to *represent them in Congress*? As someone who held that seat for a decade, I find that to be a highly disturbing prospect. With my current university position, I won't endorse anyone in this race. But I have to say . . . I believe I have a duty to say . . . that our next congressperson can't be Megan. I love this district too much to quietly let that happen."

The banging on the window again startled her, and she quickly turned in that direction. She tried to focus her eyes, but everything was a blur of fear, anger, and guilt. Guilt because her attempts to help Evina had now so suddenly, spectacularly backfired, with her cause quickly tarnished, and tied to allegations of unethical behavior on a national broadcast. All her success in building this campaign and taking on Aaron had led not to freeing Evina, but to him launching a powerful missile to destroy her.

The door then swung open, and Aimee put a hand on her shoulder to guide her out of the car. "We need to get inside, Councilwoman. I know Aaron Montgomery's interview isn't over yet, but there's no more time." She led Megan into the building, and Megan felt as if she stumbled through the entrance. Or was that just in her mind? Aimee told Megan to focus on the upcoming candidate forum, not anything else.

Aimee guided her down a corridor and into a small room, maybe a teachers' lounge of some sort. Megan collapsed into a chair, and Aimee knelt down next to her and placed a soothing hand on her arm.

"He wants to derail your focus on him and the university," Aimee advised. "Don't let him succeed."

"He's succeeded," she whispered. "I can't think straight. I can't go out there like this."

"You'll be escorted to the auditorium in a few minutes. I know it's tough, but you need to just think about the candidate forum. In a very short time you've captured so much support. He's coming after you like this because your message is *working*. Don't let him stop you now."

"They'll bring up what Aaron said about me and Evina. I need to come up with a clear answer."

"You tell the truth about Evina," Aimee urged. "And how you're her best friend and trying to save her life. It's your truth versus Aaron's lies."

Megan watched Aimee stand and look at her phone as an increasingly alarmed look swept her campaign manager's face. Aimee was intently reading her screen, with her eyes unblinking and her breath deepening.

"What is it?" Megan asked.

"The White House just released a statement," Aimee said softly, and showed Megan her phone. "You may be asked about it, so you'll need to read it quickly. There's not much time."

Megan looked at the phone and noted the image of the White House seal above a few lines issued in the name Chief of Staff Brad Connelly. On behalf of the president, he was disavowing any involvement in this building disaster.

> To be clear, the White House was never approached in any way regarding this commutation request, and we would never negotiate for support on the federal budget by promising to grant or withhold presidential clemency for a murder conviction. There is a legal, nonpolitical process for such requests that must be followed.

The timing was too quick, Megan thought as she continued to review the statement. It was so obvious there had been coordination between Aaron and the White House. But she surely could never prove that. Panic continued to overwhelm her as she kept reading, finally coming to the paragraph that cut out her heart:

> The White House has never at any point entertained this petition, and based on our understanding of the merits, or lack thereof, we don't expect to ever consider it in the future, especially in light of apparent attempts to subvert the clemency process. Because of the legal, factual, and ethical shortcomings, we don't believe this petition has the merits for the president to ever grant Evina Jansen clemency.

Just like that, it was over. Before the full development of her campaign, before Election Day, before she could really implement her strategy to use her position as a congresswoman to earn support from the White House.

She still needed to debate. She'd be led in at any moment. But her soul was no longer in it, and she certainly wouldn't be able to perform the way she needed to. She had already lost, no matter what happened at the candidate forum or in the voting booths. She wanted to just leave, bury her head somewhere, not have to face the world.

And while she acknowledged that, in reality, she couldn't escape, she also thought of her friend, who would soon learn about this news, if she hadn't already. Hope was the one thing that kept her alive. Hope that her miserable situation might soon receive a merciful act from Washington that would free her. Now with that hope seemingly shattered, what might she do?

Moments later Megan walked in a haze to the high school auditorium, being led by some people she didn't recognize, shaking hands and exchanging words she didn't really process. All the while, she was consumed with wishing that the professor had been more specific with the threat he had delivered on Aaron's behalf. She hadn't understood the magnitude of what they might do. If she had, she would have immediately capitulated and held her fire. Absolutely. If she had truly comprehended their plan, she would have done anything they wanted to forestall this result. Now it was too late.

28
Serena

I THINK SO. *I do. I definitely think so.*

Serena heard those words over and over in her head for forty-eight hours. All day. All night. In her dreams and when she was lying awake unable to sleep. They confirmed everything that she already thought.

She finally decided that she was done asking for permission to do something about it. She would make her case one more time to Aaron that this firm was completely inadequate for the monumental task for which they were retained. She would attempt to do this in a nonthreatening, logical way that would maybe appeal to some sense of reason and good faith that she hoped he had.

Then, if he didn't agree, she would have to act on her own. Maybe contact the board of trustees. Possibly just announce C&R's firing herself. At some point she needed to stop cowering in fear of the consequences of taking drastic action, as daunting as those concerns might be.

She arranged with Aaron's admin for a 9:30 a.m. meeting with just the two of them. But when she entered the president's office at the scheduled time, Aaron stood with Drew, who looked even more uncomfortable than usual. Serena wasn't sure why Drew was there, but she decided to just forge ahead.

"I'd like to discuss C&R again," Serena began. "When I met with their new team and asked about their capabilities, the response was extremely concerning. I didn't have a chance to fully communicate this to you before, so I'd like to lay out the specifics as to why they're completely inappropriate for—"

"You're off the investigation, Serena," Aaron replied. "Completely and immediately. Drew will be the university's sole point of contact. You're to have no interaction—"

"Wait!" she snapped. "What's happening? Why are you—"

"You've been implicated. That's all I can say."

"*Implicated?*" she asked with disbelief. "Implicated in *what*?"

"At this point, that's all I can tell you. I've decided not to interim-suspend you during the course of the investigation, but if you have any contact with witnesses or the investigative team, you'll be terminated for cause."

Her mind was spinning. "I have a right to know what this is based on."

"No, Serena," he said. "You don't. You know that. Giving you more information could compromise the investigation. If you fight me on this, I'll have you removed from campus."

Serena tried to figure out what "implicated" could mean. Obviously either someone had lied about her, or Aaron had misunderstood information and made a reckless rush to judgment. Or maybe she was being targeted because she was seen as a troublemaker, not simply focused on pushing this investigation through to completion ASAP. Serena knew she had just one card to play.

"I'm the whistleblower," she said firmly. "And this is retaliation. That's illegal."

Aaron shook his head. "This is in no way retaliation. Our reasons are logical and well-documented. I can't share them, but this is the only way to proceed. Our general counsel's office concurs." He looked at Drew, who silently nodded.

"Really, Drew?" she exclaimed.

"Yes," he responded, avoiding eye contact. "I'm sorry, Serena. This is for your own good."

"You can both say whatever you want," she countered. "But I know what's really happening. This university has covered up the Rob Dempsey misconduct for years and—"

"Before I ever got here," Aaron interjected.

"Yes, before you ever got here. But this institution covered it up, subjected God knows how many girls to sexual abuse, until I put a stop to it. Now your job is to protect this school and limit its liability. You're sidelining me as punishment, and to stop me from uncovering the truth."

"That's not what's happening at all. I have no stake in what's revealed during this investigation. I want everything out in the open, so we can properly address it, help those who've been victimized, and then move on as an institution that continues to thrive while protecting all of its people."

"I think my lawyer may frame it differently," Serena responded. Even though she didn't have a lawyer. But as HR director she had dealt with plenty of attorneys who initiated complaints and lawsuits against the university. Now she'd need to reach out to one of them so they could be on her side. "And the public will see it differently."

"Serena, you're not being fired. You're not being suspended. You have your job and salary. And your daughter's tuition support."

"As long as I step aside and shut up, right? So it's not just retaliation. It's bribery too?"

Drew then spoke for the second time. "A witness says you've known about Rob Dempsey allegedly sexually abusing teenagers for years."

Her eyes widened. "What? That's absurd! Who said that?"

"The witness says they directly and specifically reported suspicions about Rob Dempsey to you, and you failed to act."

Aaron looked disapprovingly toward Drew but didn't interrupt.

"Who's this witness?" she asked, her voice growing louder. Both men shook their heads. "Tell me who it is," she commanded. "This is a blatant lie, and I need to be able to respond to it."

"You'll have that opportunity," Aaron explained. "The investigators will interview you at the appropriate time. But you can't oversee an investigation when you're named as someone who ignored years of the very misconduct that's being investigated."

"Serena, of course I don't believe it's true," Drew said. "But you know we need to take this step."

This was convenient, way too convenient, for a university president who obviously wanted her out of the way. Now he would have a clearer path to make sure the bare minimum would be done to get to the truth, so this whole situation could be expeditiously placed in the rearview mirror.

Serena knew that Drew meant well. But he wasn't a fighter, wasn't going to put his career on the line. He would manage the investigation, allow it to run its course, and acquiesce to the university's demands that the matter be closed as soon as possible.

And what if this false accusation had a larger intention than just to sideline her? What if whoever orchestrated it wanted the investigators to reach a finding that she was responsible? Or maybe that would just be the threat that was held over her head to stop her from making their whitewash difficult.

"It's Cole, right?" she asked. "Cole Malinowski. Is he the one who said I knew what was going on?"

"We're not disclosing the identity of the witness," Aaron responded.

"Well, I know he was just interviewed. He's trying to save his own ass by shifting the blame to me, and he blames me for bringing this whole matter out in the open."

"On that note, let's end this conversation," the president said. "Please leave, Serena."

"Am I right? Is it Cole?" she asked, looking at Drew. She knew from his darting eyes that she was correct.

"I can call security and have you escorted from campus and immediately terminated," Aaron declared. "You're pushing this when I told you not to. You're now undermining and interfering with the investigation."

She looked out the large window on the far side of the room, observing the flow of life, the students, faculty, and staff going about their lives on this vibrant campus. She wouldn't let the latest iteration of administrators compel her to shut up and join the massive deception that had been occurring for years. The previous president and general counsel had falsely portrayed the university as having no problem that needed to be uncovered. Now the current administration was working to send the dishonest message that it *was* all being uncovered.

Serena then had a thought. A potentially irrational thought. But the world she worked in was irrational, so it might also be an accurate one. She looked straight at Aaron. "Did you tell Cole to say this?"

"What?!"

"Come on, Serena," Drew quickly said, looking visibly upset. "I've supported you all this time, but this is just too much. It's too crazy. Please."

"You did, didn't you?" Serena didn't take her eyes off Aaron. "I told you I wouldn't sit silently by while the university conducts this inadequate investigation. Then you said Cole needed to be interviewed right away, and now I'm removed from the whole process, which you wanted all along."

"Leave this office immediately," he commanded, "or you'll be fired and taken from campus."

"Please listen to him," Drew implored. "Don't make this worse."

Serena was cornered. Powerful people were targeting her. She needed to defend herself but had no idea how. In addition to this outrageous false allegation, which was likely planted by the president, she also had to contend with the public accusations against HR personnel at the university by Councilwoman Megan Black.

"Okay," she told Aaron, acquiescing to his demand. "I'm leaving."

She headed back to her office, fell into her desk chair, and swept a fresh piece of cinnamon gum into her mouth. She would love to call Cole, or better yet find where he was and confront him in person. She could ask him to repeat his account to her face, dare him to tell her what he had said to the investigators. Berate him for lying in a pathetic attempt to save himself.

But she could never realistically take that path. It would be classic witness interference by the human resources director. A clear violation of law and policy.

Her other thought was to fire C&R. Right now. Just do it. Email Anderson or Troy, or whomever else was the best point of contact, and say their contract to investigate was being rescinded. Then she could announce publicly that a new RFP was being issued to find a replacement investigator.

It would be instant national news because of the high-profile nature of this whole sordid mess. But Aaron would quickly reverse the announcement, and he would have to say publicly that she lacked the authority. It would embarrass all of them, no doubt end her career, and probably accomplish nothing. Furthermore, it would appear as if she just squashed investigators because they received negative information about her. As with her fantasy confrontation with Cole, she'd be taking a dangerous step that would lead nowhere and almost certainly end up severely damaging her life.

Serena stood and paced around her office, wondering if she had any good options left. She recognized that if she failed to act, those who sought to harm her would easily succeed. She needed to find a way to take back this university from those who were using it for their own political and financial ends.

Reclaim MHU.

No wonder that slogan had caught on so well, so fast. The institution was beloved throughout Mountain Hill, despite what a horrifying embarrassment it now was. So many locals grew up nearby, worked for the university, and sent their children here. They desperately wanted to preserve the school for all it did for the community and all it could still be in the future.

Megan Black.

The woman who had initiated that campaign, attacked Aaron, unabashedly taken on the leadership. And by going after leadership, she repeatedly questioned who was running human resources during the years of sexual abuse. Designating Serena as a culprit, even if she didn't do so by name.

Last night Serena watched Aaron attack Megan. *The enemy of my enemy is my friend,* she thought. On her own, Serena didn't have the power and leverage to take him on. She needed help. Maybe she and Megan could join forces somehow or at least connect, compare notes, and strategize. Their goals seemed to have so much in common. Maybe she should reach out to her.

But no. As tempting as that all was, it was probably a foolish idea. Megan Black's campaign had painted the whole situation with such a ludicrously broad brush, calling for everyone to be thrown out, inciting people to "clean house." News reports had quoted Megan as condemning MHU's "negligent and incompetent human resources staff," implying Serena as HR director needed to be tossed aside too, even though Megan surely had no idea who Serena even was.

And what if Aaron's charges were correct? That Megan had tried to get him to manipulate a key budget vote in order to politicize the clemency process and help free a child abuser who murdered her spouse? Aaron making the accusation didn't mean it was true, but his allegation was so specific, so detailed. It clearly wasn't fabricated out of nothing.

Contacting Megan Black was too problematic. No way could Serena trust her, some rando politician, potentially just as self-serving and conniving as Aaron. Plus, Megan might publicize Serena's outreach, try to gain even more attention by weaponizing it.

But there was another woman who might be an ally. Despite its own obvious risks, this option somehow felt safer.

She picked up her phone and pressed Kayla's name.

"Mom, what's going on?"

She never called her daughter during the day. A few texts back and forth occasionally, but not phone calls. And there hadn't even been that since their dustup a few days ago, so Kayla would know this was important.

"Hi, Kayla," she responded. "Where are you? I need to see you right away."

"It's not a good time. I have class in a few minutes. And I'm still really mad about the other day."

"We need to talk about that."

She heard her daughter sigh. "I don't want a lecture from you."

"I'm not looking to lecture you. But I want to—"

"Want to what?"

"I want to talk with Bianca Velencoso. Can you arrange that? Or at least text me her number? It's important."

After a few seconds of silence, Serena heard a short laugh filled with exasperation and frustration. "Absolutely not," Kayla replied, and then immediately ended the call.

29
Troy

Troy took a late-night flight back to JFK after an intense week of MHU interviews and meetings, then jumped into an Uber that crawled through construction-related traffic to his apartment. He got up early the next morning and tried to look as fresh as possible in suit and tie, dreading the day that lay before him. He needed to survive being debriefed by Anderson about the MHU investigation, interviewed by Tara from HR about the C&R/DePalma Capital investigation, and questioned by Julia about all that was occurring and what their next steps should be. And if that wasn't enough, he had to then fly back to MHU for his most high-stakes interview yet.

"Tell me what happened on campus," Anderson commanded from his desk as soon as Troy entered the office.

Anderson was still officially barred from the case, but MHU was confirming that only through billing records while publicly announcing that no one who worked for Caleb would assist the university. It was irrelevant for MHU and the public what origination credit Anderson received, since that was an internal stat not shared with clients. It similarly didn't matter how intricately involved he was in the planning, as long as he didn't enter any billable time.

"We interviewed a bunch of the employees, including the assistant softball coach, Cole Malinowski. The other interviews didn't lead to much, basically people saying they knew nothing, saw nothing."

"Right," Anderson scoffed.

"But Cole told us he warned the human resources director *for years* that Dempsey was acting inappropriately with girls."

"Wait, *Serena*? Serena Stanfield?"

"Yes."

"She's the one who hired us." Anderson began tapping the desk in frustration. "Oh, shit. That's not good."

"No," Troy agreed. "If it's true, it's terrible."

"Regardless of whether it's true, she now has to be a subject of the investigation. So Serena can't oversee it anymore. Our whole retention is precarious anyway because of the Lugo bullshit. Now a new university point of contact may want to narrow the scope, or even get rid of us as the investigators."

"I hadn't thought of that."

"You *need* to think about that, Troy! You need to make sure it doesn't happen. There's *way* too much at stake. DePalma Capital will be looking at this quarter's revenue to make a final decision. We're counting on the MHU billings. You better not fuck this up. So what did you do after the assistant coach gave you this info?"

"I told their deputy general counsel," Troy responded nervously. "Drew Kosick. He thanked me and said he'd take it to the president. Then Drew informed me he was our sole point of contact. They've given me no indication they're looking to move on from us."

This seemed to pacify Anderson, at least temporarily, as he slowly nodded. "There's growing pressure for them to do that, though," he said.

"I know."

"Although if they do fire us, at least I'd then get to fire Julia," Anderson said with an unamusing attempt at gallows humor. "Listen, Troy, during our careers we all face important tests, and this is yours.

If you can't keep us retained at MHU with our full budget, you still may be able to keep *your* job. But you'll have shown you don't have what it takes to really make it here. You want a successful career at C&R? This is your chance."

"I'm doing everything I can. We're flying back late this afternoon. I'm interviewing the first of the complainants. The one who's been very vocal in the media."

"Okay, good," Aaron responded. "Who's your co-interviewer?"

"We still just have the same three others on the team, right?" Troy asked.

"Unfortunately they're all we have for now. If we can't find anyone internally soon, we'll have to get a few inexpensive ex-cops and sub them out. That still cuts into our profits, though. But otherwise we're leaving a lot of money on the table by not billing as many hours as we can. It's a problem either way."

"All right, so we have Rick, Dave, and Marissa."

Anderson thought about these names, and then asked, "Who has the most experience with sexual misconduct interviews?"

"They all have none," he answered, surprised Anderson hadn't already asked this question before assigning them.

"Great," Anderson responded in frustration. "Okay, take Marissa. If you're interviewing a girl about fucking her softball coach, it's best to have another female in the room."

"The allegations don't involve actual sexual intercourse. She's alleging that—"

"I'm obviously using the term in a general sense," Anderson snapped. "What the hell is wrong with you? Imagine if MHU knew how dense you can be. They'd fire us tomorrow for putting you on the team."

The man thrived on ruling by fear, belittling Troy and others whenever he could. Instead of responding directly, Troy decided his best course now was to change the topic.

"I'm going into the interview with Tara from HR in a half hour," he explained.

Anderson nodded and then gave Troy a serious stare. "Okay. Remember, we did nothing wrong. You managed some research for a client. You had a sub gather intelligence on an adverse party, like we do all the time. We had no idea he was *allegedly* a serial offender of some sort."

Troy noted how Anderson emphasized *allegedly* as if the matter could be referred to the Innocence Project. He said the word as if Anderson hadn't been central to the whole strategy of intimidating and defaming Caleb's many victims.

"I'll let you know how it goes," Troy answered, and then left the room. He walked down the hall toward his cubicle, stopping halfway and ducking into the lactation room. Julia sat on the sofa, waiting for him.

"We need to make sure Emma tells HR everything Anderson made her do," he said.

"No, Troy!" she shot back, rising.

"I'm done working with him. I just can't take that man anymore. He threatened to fire you again if we lose MHU. As damaging as the *Times* article was, no one yet knows the real truth, which is even worse. This is the best way to get him out of our lives forever."

"You said you'd confront him once you were embedded at the university!"

"I still can. But I also think this is a good way to proceed."

She shook her head. "I don't trust Emma. And we can't trust Tara from HR either. Plus, Emma's last meeting with her was terrible, when she got the PIP from Anderson. Asking Emma to reveal all to Tara would be a *huge* mistake."

Troy pulled out his phone to see how much time he had before the interview. Twenty-four minutes. "I can't even think straight. I'm so stressed. Fuck. After this HR interview, I have to fly back to MHU for my first interview with one of the softball complainants. She's the woman who's all over the news. I have to interview her about being molested by her softball coach, and even without all this other insanity, I'm not comfortable with that. I'm just not."

"I know," she said, putting a sympathetic hand on his arm. "She may cry, so you need to be prepared for that. We know you're not really good when women cry."

"Are you trying to help me, or make me feel worse?" he quickly responded while pulling away from her.

"Help you. Of course."

And he knew she meant that. Even if she wasn't.

"If Emma tells HR what she told us, Anderson won't be able to survive that," Troy argued. "Instructing a young female associate to collect hardcore revenge porn for a client? Using it to blackmail, intimidate, and harass sexual misconduct accusers, to pressure them into silence? He'd be done."

"We'd all be done," Julia charged back. "The HR report will go to DePalma Capital, and they'll bail on the whole deal. Then all our competitors, clients, and potential clients will know DePalma ran away from us because of what they learned during their due diligence. They'll suspect it has something to do with the *Times* article and they'll be right. And maybe more specifics are leaked, and possibly that becomes public. And that pushes MHU over the edge to fire us. This isn't just C&R's big matter, this is *my* big matter. Something like this won't come my way again anytime soon."

Troy shook his head at her logic and then responded with agitation. "Stop deluding yourself that this is your ticket to some great career advancement. You're getting zero origination credit. *Zero percent.* And your secret weapon university president won't even return your calls. He cares more about attacking some local congressional candidate than helping you. You won't be losing anything if we do what's needed to take down Anderson, because you have nothing to lose. And if somehow we can keep MHU but get rid of Anderson, then that solves your origination problem."

"No, then Luke will take it all. Luke's as bad as Anderson, maybe worse. He's the future Anderson, the younger version."

They were both suddenly quiet, letting their mutual arguments soak in, as Troy contemplated his next move. Then he placed a call on his phone, put it to his ear, and after a few seconds began speaking. "Are you in the office? Can you talk with me and Julia?"

Julia sighed and placed a hand on her forehead in disapproval, as Troy heard Emma's voice tentatively respond, "When? Now?"

"Yeah, now. It's urgent. I promise we're not looking to argue with you. We need to all talk."

"Okay," she responded with hesitation. "In the usual spot?"

"Yes."

He put the phone back in the inside pocket of his suit jacket. "She's coming over. I wanted to make sure she didn't think we were looking to berate her or something."

"Not that she doesn't deserve it."

"Have you spoken to her since the Gin House?"

"No. You?"

He shook his head. Thirty seconds later, the door opened and Emma stepped into the room, looking uncomfortably at her two colleagues. "So what do you want?" she asked as she closed the door.

"I'm being interviewed today for the HR investigation that DePalma Capital demanded," Troy said.

"So what do you want from me?" Emma asked.

"Anderson told me you're being interviewed too. I wanted to say... I think it's really important you tell everything about what he did with you. The whole story."

"And for the record, I strongly disagree with him," Julia interjected.

"No shit," Emma snapped. "You made your feelings real clear at the Gin House. Troy, I guess you changed *your* mind."

"Not about going public. I still think that was a mistake. But it's done. This is different. It's an internal investigation, and when you're interviewed we need them to know the truth about—"

"I already spoke with Tara from HR. I had my interview this morning."

"And you told her what he made you do?"

Emma stared back at him for a few moments. "No. I need this job, and I know what this company will do to me if I speak up. I've seen how they retaliate."

Troy understood her fear, but felt exasperated by her timidity now after having run to the media earlier. "What happened to 'all these things I just accepted as inevitable are actually unacceptable'?" he asked with frustration.

"I pointed that reporter to women who wanted to tell their stories. And they did. But it's not safe for me to tell *my* story."

"Then this inquiry will conclude Anderson did nothing wrong, and he'll stay the New York office head, and this kind of stuff will happen again and again," Troy said. "You have the ability to stop all that and make him pay for what he did to those women and how he treated you."

"You want him to pay for how he treats *you*, Troy. And you want to steer this investigation away from the research you oversaw for Caleb. Don't act like you're trying to help me."

"All those things are true. Please, Emma. Please go back to HR. Tell them everything he did. This investigation is meaningless without your account. I know it's tough. I know it's scary. But you'll be fighting back for yourself and so many others. You'll be helping to right a tremendous wrong. You tell the whole truth, and C&R will *have* to fire Anderson for what he did."

Emma turned toward Julia, then back to Troy. She stood there in silent thought for a few seconds before softly stating, "I need advice on this."

"From who?" Julia asked.

"The only person I respect in this whole fucking company," she said, and Troy ran through the various C&R personnel in his head, trying to figure out who she was referencing. "Gillian. She's the only one with good intentions. She got screwed over, just like I got screwed over. I got forced to do these terrible things for Caleb Lugo, and then because of that work I'm banned from actually *helping* sexual misconduct victims at MHU! Gillian would understand all this, because she got fucked over too."

Troy silently noted that the person she cited as her only respected colleague had been working there for about a minute and a half. But he couldn't think of a better answer. Gillian was a former prosecutor, an expert in all sorts of misconduct matters, someone who hadn't been entrenched in their warped culture for years.

"This is all a really bad idea," Julia cut in. "None of us will be helped by it. It'll just make our whole situation worse."

"Based on your reaction to me last time, I really don't care what you think, Julia."

"Emma, I've always been a friend to you. It's only when you decided to do your reckless rogue investigator thing that I—"

"We don't have time to rehash this," Troy interrupted. "I'm being interviewed in about twenty minutes. I'll be asked what I know. You want to consult Gillian? Fine. Let's call her. Is she here today?"

"Yes, I just passed by her office. She's there."

"Okay, should we all go there now? Or ask her to come here?"

Emma shook her head. "No. I'm going to speak with her by myself." She then left the room, and Troy was once again alone with Julia.

"Maybe if we worked together," he said, "we could find interesting, rewarding jobs in a calm place. With decent salaries and a positive, supportive culture. A healthy environment."

"Sure, Troy. We can definitely do that. Unless you're looking to have a career in the *real world*."

"There just have to be places that are better."

"But those companies aren't hiring *us*. Especially not now, with Caleb Lugo a national pariah and our résumés virtually declaring we were his foot soldiers. Whether we like it or not, this is the place for us. We need to make it work. If I can just get this MHU origination—"

"Enough with the origination credit. Please!"

"If I can get it," she continued, "we're talking millions in revenue. Revenue that will transform C&R's financials for this quarter and the whole next year. That'll make the acquisition by DePalma Capital a reality. Save the company. I won't just be a fungible junior associate they can shit all over. This'll put me on a whole different level. And I'm taking you up there with me."

The door suddenly opened and both of them halted their conversation as Emma reentered the room.

"Did you speak with Gillian?" Troy asked.

"Only for a minute," Emma responded. "I just told her the beginning, and she was very concerned. She said to bring both of you to her office immediately."

30
Megan

THE MEDIA actually showed up this time, Megan noted. Reporters, cameras, regular citizens stopping in front of City Hall because they observed the hubbub as they walked by.

Megan and her campaign were reeling nearly forty-eight hours after Aaron's counterattack. The first, most immediate consequence of Aaron's accusations was a drying up of the fundraising spigot, with the initial surge of online donations dramatically slowing, and a couple of large potential donors telling her fundraising consultant they wanted to wait and see how this new controversy developed before committing their funds.

An online poll that morning showed her dropping to fourth place, fifteen points behind the leader. These online polls were notoriously unreliable, but the same survey, two days earlier, had showed her in second. Now that supposed support for her candidacy had supposedly evaporated.

She struggled to comprehend all this and figure out what actions to take while simultaneously dwelling on the agonizing reality that her campaign strategy had just completely ruined her friend's life. She needed to speak with Evina, console her, and apologize. Beg for forgiveness.

But Evina hadn't called yet, and it was so hard to get away from the tornado of this congressional race, especially while knowing that any fleeting hopes of resuscitating Evina's public image and maybe turning the whole campaign around would be further undermined by leaving the trail for a prison visit at this crucial time.

She no longer had the luxury of focusing her campaign on MHU. Not with Evina's reputation and battle for freedom thrust into the national spotlight. Instead Megan spent the past two days defending herself and Evina from Aaron's allegations, making it a focus of every opportunity to spread the truth, whether in front of community groups, speaking at public forums, working the room at a senior citizen center, or talking to the media. She fought tirelessly to push back against this new narrative before it would irrevocably define her and Evina. But the result so far was an increasingly lackluster response and a growing sense that she had lost her initial momentum and was headed for a decisive defeat.

So she decided to hold a press availability on the steps of City Hall, with Aimee once again setting up the lectern. But while the last attempt on that site had produced resounding silence, she now had people's attention, for better or worse.

"I want to speak about my dear friend Evina Jansen," Megan declared. "She grew up in Mountain Hill, like many of you. She married a horrible man who preyed on her, abused her, and nearly killed her multiple times. Here's one example. A year after their marriage, he became enraged after she received a text from a male coworker. He grabbed her phone and pummeled her in the head with it over and over. She needed twenty-three sutures in her scalp. I was in the hospital with her. I saw the bloody wounds. I watched her clutching her head in pain.

"A domestic violence counselor in the hospital advised her to discretely pack a bag that she could use at a moment's notice if she needed to quickly escape the house the next time he became violent.

And you know what happened? Her husband found that bag and saw the change of clothes and toothbrush inside. He threw her to the floor and squeezed her neck so hard that she couldn't breathe and lost consciousness.

"I could spend all day with you, detailing every attack, every sadistic assault. I know all this because I've been her friend through all of it, and I saw the physical and emotional toll of these beatings. I saw how she tried to leave him, and he kept stopping her, blocking all avenues of freedom and her will to pursue them. This brutality was her unescapable reality for years."

She paused for a moment and saw that the crowd of reporters and other onlookers were listening. Not necessarily supportive, but not hostile either. Curious, potentially interested. They seemed to want to hear what she had to say.

"He abused their infant daughter, and to her own horror, Evina was powerless to stop him. So CPS took her child away. Because of what *he* did. Not because of any allegation of mistreatment by Evina Jansen. Evina endured so many beatings from this man, and then on the night of the final beating, he violently assaulted her in a drunken rage. Striking her repeatedly, ripping her clothes, intent on murdering her. So she had two choices: kill him in self-defense or die at his hands. It's a decision I hope none of you ever have to make. What she did took tremendous strength and courage. But she was unfairly convicted by a system that didn't care. Now she's been locked in a cell for eight years and faces decades more in prison."

A female reporter standing in the front row began to speak, but Megan quickly held up her hand to stop her. She wasn't finished with her statement yet.

"I sought help on Evina's behalf, including from then-Congressman Aaron Montgomery, because he was our representative, and his job was to help the citizens of this district when they were wronged. I explained Evina's tragic predicament to Aaron in his DC office. And

I want to be very clear about something. *He* suggested he could help get her sentence commuted by using leverage in an upcoming budget vote. *He* proposed this. Not me. He's now lying and saying I made that request, when in fact it was completely, one hundred percent something he recommended."

As the reporter in front began to speak again, Megan guessed what was coming. The natural follow-up was whether Megan had opposed this plan, objected to using that kind of political maneuvering to help one individual through the supposedly nonpolitical commutation process while potentially holding up budgetary support for this district and the whole country. She had expected that question, and was ready to answer. Or at least try.

"Councilwoman Black, I have a question about the Rob Dempsey scandal and the MHU investigation," the reporter said instead.

"Okay," Megan responded tentatively, surprised by this redirection.

"Many of the alleged victims have expressed reluctance to speak with the university-appointed investigative team because of their ties to Caleb Lugo and their attempts to silence the victims of his reported sexual misconduct. You've been vocal that the firm should be replaced. Ali Tyrell, who has taken on the role of unofficial leader for these women, has said publicly that she may refuse to speak with them and encourage others to do the same. Yet if they don't talk with the investigators, it'll be nearly impossible to determine who else at the university is responsible for allowing the sexual abuse to continue unabated for years. So what's your advice to Ms. Tyrell and the other survivors about whether to sit for interviews with C&R Investigations?"

"I've been really clear that this firm needs to go," Megan answered. "Now I'd like to get back to—"

"Yes, but should Ali Tyrell and the others speak with them if the firm continues their university-sanctioned investigation?" the reporter followed up. "Or should they refuse?"

"I can't tell them what to do," she replied.

"Why not?" another reporter asked.

"It's a personal decision. From everything I've read, they've experienced terrible trauma from a man in a position of trust who abused that trust. They have the right to choose the correct path for themselves. I won't try to tell them what to do."

She was trying to sound gracious, deferential, and understanding, but she sensed from the uninspired faces in front of her that this answer had come off as weak and noncommittal. Yet she wasn't looking to discuss MHU.

"I'm here to talk about the dangerous, immoral fabrications of Aaron Montgomery," she explained. "He's trying to protect his job by falsely smearing a domestic violence victim who's currently in prison for the crime of saving her own life!"

A male reporter toward the back of the crowd raised his hand, and she pointed toward him to take his question.

"What's your opinion about whether these women should cooperate with the investigation?"

"I've already answered that."

"No, you haven't. You said you don't want to tell them what to do. But why can't you express your opinion? You've certainly expressed your opinion about the other aspects of this situation."

"I'm just not here to address that today."

"What about the assistant coaches who worked under Rob Dempsey?" another asked. "Should other schools refuse to hire them? Even if they haven't been found responsible for misconduct, does working with him and failing to stop this behavior show they can't be trusted?"

She had no idea how to respond to these questions. "We need a thorough investigation before anyone can fairly address that," she said. "By someone other than C&R. Overseen by a president other than Aaron Montgomery. Now, I'd like to address the situation with

Evina Jansen and the immoral lies of Aaron Montgomery. I'll take any questions you have on those issues."

The reporters were silent, as the citizens who had paused to watch this presser started to move on, one by one. Megan looked out at the people in front of her, and saw complete apathy about Evina and her plight.

"Then shame on all of you," she declared to the media and local residents in front of her. "Because she's one of you. She could be you. And you've all abandoned her."

31
Serena

As Serena walked past the site of the new student center, she noted the preparations underway for the big grand-opening ribbon-cutting event the following evening. Risers constructed, sound system and lighting assembled and checked, the celebratory banner hung behind the podium in front of the building.

She didn't plan to attend. She didn't want to interact with Aaron and his people again if she didn't have to. And by the time the ceremony was actually held, she would certainly not be welcome there.

Instead she kept walking to the edge of campus and down a narrow block full of low-rise buildings that housed many of MHU's undergraduates. After Serena arrived at her destination and walked up to the third floor, she fumbled with the key Kayla had given her and then unlocked the door of the small off-campus apartment. A ragged tan sofa that looked like it had been rejected by Goodwill graced the middle of the room, with a small brown coffee table in front of it. A collection of photos was haphazardly taped to one of the white walls next to a school pennant.

There was only one course of action left for her. She had to blow things up again, just as she had on the softball field. It wasn't safe not to do so. Not while she was being targeted by Cole, and Aaron, and Megan, and God knows who else.

The gateway to accomplishing that was Kayla. So she waited in her daughter's apartment for an hour, and then another. She paced around, stared out the window, and then sat on the tattered sofa. She had never invaded Kayla's personal space like this, but she now had no alternative.

Finally, Serena heard the turn of the key in the lock, so she rose before the door opened. "I'm in here," she warned, because she didn't want to scare her daughter. But if she had provided more advance notice, Kayla might not have agreed to meet. Not after the way she had ended their conversation by the water and their last phone call. Not after ignoring Serena's multiple texts and calls after that. "It's Mom."

Kayla opened the door and tentatively entered the apartment. "What are you doing here?" she asked accusingly. "I gave you that key for emergencies. It's not right for you to—"

"It's an emergency. I want us to call Bianca Velencoso right now. I'm not asking. I'm telling you. Call her now."

She watched her daughter think this over. "And if I say no?"

"Come on, Kayla."

"Is that 'Come on, Kayla' from my mother or the human resources director?"

"Both. I've rethought your idea to have her speak about sexual misconduct at new student orientation."

Kayla stepped further into the room and looked at her mother with skepticism. "What about your concerns about being fired?"

"I'm a sitting duck right now. If I don't do something quick, something big, the new president will destroy me. I'm sorry if that sounds paranoid."

Kayla slowly reached into the back pocket of her jean shorts and withdrew her phone. "Actually, from what I've read about him, that doesn't sound paranoid at all. Look what he just did to that city councilwoman."

Her daughter sat down on the sofa and Serena joined her, and then watched as Kayla initiated a FaceTime call. As grateful as she was that Kayla was following her instructions, Serena hadn't expected to be on camera. Her mind felt scattered and she had thrown her outfit together quickly. Wearing an unwashed pair of tan slacks and a ten-year-old blouse surely wasn't the attire for a video call with a model.

"Can we just do a regular phone call?" she entreated.

But then it was too late, as Bianca's tanned, flawless oval face flashed onto the screen. Serena could see that only Kayla was visible to Bianca as the actress said, "I wasn't expecting to hear from you again, Kayla. Your mother seemed very upset you were speaking to me. Standing up for myself is leading to a lot of hostility from people like her."

Serena quickly grabbed the phone from her daughter and positioned it in front of her so she and Bianca could see each other. "I'm right here. And I'm so sorry. I don't have any hostility toward you. I swear."

But Bianca wasn't placated by this response. Instead her face shook a little in agitation as she responded, "Don't try to bullshit me. You ended that call as soon as you found out who I am. And I know why. I looked you up online after. You were the one who hired the firm that Caleb Lugo used to dox me. To ruin my career, crush my life. You rewarded them with this huge contract at your university."

Serena anticipated that Bianca would blame her for retaining C&R, and had readied her response. "I've devoted my career to fighting discrimination and sexual misconduct on campus. I've overseen countless sexual harassment investigations, and I'm constantly trying to help people who've been victimized. That firm wasn't my call. I swear. I have limited power. I'm trying my best, but as you know there's a lot of adversity when you want to do what's right."

Bianca scoffed and looked toward Kayla while shaking her head.

"Have you seen the video of me running onto the softball field to confront the coach who was abusing girls here?" Serena asked.

Bianca's body language relaxed a little as her posture seemed less stiff and she delicately pointed a finger toward Serena. "That was you?"

She nodded. "We're all on the same side. I'm fighting from the inside. And I'm losing that fight. So I need your help."

"What do you want?"

"I know Kayla talked to you about being our sexual misconduct speaker at new student orientation. I'd like you to still do that."

Then the fire was back in Bianca's eyes. "Speak at Mountain Hill University? I'm disgusted by your school! It's shameful how your university let that softball coach molest all those girls *for years*. It's unconscionable how your officials covered it up. And even if you're not responsible for hiring C&R, your president definitely is! Do you understand what this firm did to my life?"

"I know what they did..."

"But do you *understand*? I needed to support myself as a struggling actress. I had to find a way to earn money to survive. And they exposed my private affairs to the world. To everyone! My family, my friends, the whole industry that will never take me seriously now. I had to explain this all to *my parents*! To my *grandmother*! They told me they're disgusted by me! I'll never recover from this."

"I'm so sorry, Bianca."

"So sorry? You're still paying the firm that did this! Using them to pretend to care about sexual assault survivors like me. Your president is supposedly going to run for governor. He should never have *any* position of authority. His support for C&R is horrific. He should be *fired and condemned*! Goodbye, Serena. I don't have time for you or your school."

"Wait!"

"Mom, just let her go, *please*," Kayla begged.

Serena saw that Bianca hadn't ended the call yet. She needed to talk fast before she did.

"Bianca, I'd like you to speak to our campus. It's important."

"Did you hear what I said? Why would I help your school?!"

"I'm not asking you to help our school. Not the way you mean. I want you to talk here and say exactly how you feel about everything you've been through, and everything our university is doing."

Bianca paused with a surprised look as she narrowed her eyes and stared back at Serena. "Is this some kind of trick?"

"No, I promise. I'm on your side. And I want you to speak to the students here."

"If I speak to your students, I won't hold back. I'll tell them all the disgusting things that were done to me by Caleb Lugo and C&R Investigations. I'll tell them your president is condoning all that by giving millions of dollars to the people who helped Caleb Lugo attack me. I'm sure you don't want me to do that."

Serena knew this would lead to national media coverage of Bianca's remarks and end any hopes of Serena peacefully coexisting with the new administration. Yet they had already made it clear that they were engineering her downfall, and she had to take extreme measures to fight back.

"I want you to do all that," she whispered. "I don't want you to hold back. Can you speak at our sexual assault awareness event tomorrow afternoon? You can join by Zoom. I'll send you the info."

"You won't try to censor me? I can say anything I want?" she asked skeptically.

"Yes, I want to give you a platform to speak the truth. I think you'll inspire people in a significant way. And maybe lead to real change."

"That is tempting," Bianca said thoughtfully. "I want a forum to call for a special prosecutor. And your campus is the perfect place.

But considering everything you've said, everything your school has done . . . I don't want to join your Zoom tomorrow."

"Please, Bianca. Just think about—"

"I don't want to join your Zoom," she declared again. "I want to be there in person."

32
Troy

"So Caleb Lugo told you a woman accused him of sexual assault, and you offered to conduct research in Spain on her to assist him?" Tara from HR asked, her long, graying hair flopping in front of her glasses as she accentuated the final words of the sentence. Troy was taken aback by how she phrased the question in such an accusatory manner, even though the firm coordinated research to protect their clients in high-stakes matters all the time.

They were in conference room B, the same one where he, Julia, Anderson, and Luke originally met to start drafting their MHU proposal. It was windowless and relatively small, with one stark black table, a few chairs, and a whiteboard on the wall. The physically tight environment added to his growing recognition that he was trapped, caught in processes much larger than him by people who didn't care about his well-being.

"Yes. Anderson was right there," Troy said defensively. "Caleb Lugo asked both of us to help. It was standard background research on an individual who was adverse to a client."

She put her pen down and stopped writing for a moment. "It's standard for you to dig up dirt on women who experienced sexual misconduct in order to silence them?"

He flinched at the characterization, which he felt was an unfair exaggeration. Troy's panic grew as he realized her phrasing probably indicated how she would describe his work in whatever report she authored after her investigation concluded.

He really wanted to tell her about Emma's experience with Anderson. Otherwise, Troy might be singled out to DePalma Capital and then excised from the company so they could feel satisfied that their deal could proceed.

Right before the HR interview, he, Julia, and Emma had hurried into Gillian's office, with her array of courtroom sketches adorning the wall, depicting her trial days in the DA's office.

"Tell me exactly what's going on," she said sternly, staring at Troy.

"There's a human resources investigation into our work for Caleb Lugo," Troy answered. "DePalma Capital's demanding it in advance of their possible acquisition of C&R. They're concerned about the potential reputation and litigation exposure. I'm not sure if Emma has told you—"

"I quickly gave her the main points just now," Emma said. "We didn't discuss the details yet."

"Okay," Troy said, addressing Gillian. "Then hopefully you understand that what Anderson made Emma do for Caleb was wrong, and it's important for Emma to share that with human resources as part of this investigation."

"Then what happens if this information's revealed publicly?" Gillian asked. "By DePalma Capital, or someone else?"

"I don't know," he replied. "I guess then we're all in a bad situation."

She shook her head in frustration. "You need to hold off for now."

"I'm speaking with HR in a few minutes."

"You can tell HR what you did. What you saw. But it's not for you to speak about what other people experienced."

Was this correct? He had relevant, important information about problematic behavior. Exactly the type of actions that HR was purportedly investigating. But she was more senior than him, and giving him direct instruction. Violating that could make things even worse.

"I need to escalate this," she said. "Right away."

"What does that mean?" he asked. "Where are you escalating this?"

"I don't know yet," she answered. "But this is obviously a huge problem that goes well beyond your meeting with HR today."

Meanwhile, Emma nodded, as if this all made sense. She clearly admired Gillian, and felt her guidance and decision-making were sound. Troy looked at Julia for her take, and she announced with exasperation, "Just to be clear, I think this is all a mistake. Our company has severe problems, but if we let DePalma Capital know the real story, it'll be very bad for all of us."

Gillian pointed a finger in Troy's direction as she commanded, "Everyone just hold any further action or discussion about this. I need a few minutes, and then I'll find the right course to take. Now, out of my office, all of you."

Troy was the first to leave, already a couple of minutes late for his interview. It was scheduled two floors above Gillian's office, and three floors above his own cubicle, where his small travel suitcase was packed and ready for his flight to MHU.

Now he wondered what steps Gillian was taking, as he thought about how to answer this question from the HR investigator.

It's standard for you to dig up dirt on women who experienced sexual misconduct in order to silence them?

"Of course not," he asserted. "We generally don't handle these types of matters."

"But you thought it was important this time?" came the follow-up.

"I don't make decisions about what clients we help or what matters we accept," he explained. "I'm an associate. Not an MD."

"So you do what a managing director tells you?"

"Yes. That's my job."

"So if a managing director asks you to help undermine a sexual assault survivor and damage her reputation and her life, you follow instructions? No matter what?"

Each question was making this worse, more stressful, increasingly obvious that this investigation was going to paint him in a terrible light. "Tara, I didn't know Caleb Lugo was sexually assaulting all these women. At the time, he was a long-standing, reputable client of the firm. Starting way before I was hired."

"Yes, I know that."

"At his charity event, he asked Anderson and me whether we could conduct research in Spain on a woman who he said was falsely accusing him of groping her. That's all we knew."

"And you told him you would."

"Yes."

"And you did."

"Right, but that research didn't lead to any relevant information. None of it was used in any way."

"So you want credit because your work was unsuccessful? DePalma Capital wants to understand what assignments C&R undertook to intimidate and silence sexual assault victims. It sounds like you admit you tried to do that. Have you or anyone else at C&R targeted any other women?"

He wasn't sure how to respond. He didn't know what was safe to reveal. "Have you spoken with Anderson Davis?" he asked.

Tara shook her head. "I ask the questions, not you. And I don't reveal who I've interviewed. Don't you conduct investigations as part of your job? I'd think you would understand that."

Troy took a sip from the bottle of water in front of him. He wasn't even thirsty, but he needed to stall for a few moments and give himself a chance to consider what to do. He knew the real objectionable tasks, the ones that really fit into what this investigation was about, could only be revealed credibly by Emma. But he now had instructions from Gillian not to provide any information about Emma's role, and Emma hadn't agreed to be outed at this point. Plus, Julia firmly felt revealing all would tank the DePalma Capital deal, plunge C&R deeper into its current fiscal crisis, and potentially ruin its reputation regarding sexual misconduct issues, just as it was gearing up to bill millions to MHU.

They would be unemployable elsewhere, at least in a good job, at a respectable company. They would be known as the C&R associates, the Caleb Lugo lackeys, the untouchables. But if he stood silent, HR might look to hang him to save the rest of the firm. He had to make his own decision about what to do.

"You need to speak with Emma Richardson again," he said desperately. "Please."

"Emma Richardson?" she asked, searching through various papers that lay in front of her.

"She's another junior associate you interviewed. Caleb Lugo thanked her at the conference room reception. You gave her a PIP earlier this month."

She smirked and then nodded. "Oh, right. She's the one with the utilization problems. Wants to get paid a New York corporate salary and just do *pro bono* work."

"Emma's actually an extremely hard worker and very smart."

"So what's your point? What's her involvement? It seems you're trying to distract from my questions whenever I touch a nerve. *Talk to Anderson Davis. Speak to Emma Richardson.* It's about time you were fully honest and open about what *you* did."

Troy glanced at the digital clock on the wall. He needed to head to the airport very soon and he was running out of time. But if he left before this was finished, Tara would call him back for a follow-up interview and he wanted to put this behind him. He was stressed enough about his MHU work, particularly the interview with Ali Tyrell.

"I'm not looking to distract. I'm trying to supply you with the full story. Anderson and Emma have important, relevant information."

"What information do they have?"

"I think it's best if they answer that question."

She shook her head in frustration. "No more games, Troy. Cooperation with this investigation is a requirement of your continued employment at C&R."

He knew the firm couldn't fire him today. He was still needed at MHU. But his value would disappear as soon as Anderson could recruit a replacement.

"I'm answering your questions to the best of my ability," he replied.

"Then answer this," she ordered. "Why don't we see any time entries for your work with Caleb Lugo? Were you trying to hide your involvement?"

The answer, of course, was yes. But not trying to hide it from his own company. He'd been hiding it from MHU, with Anderson's consent. Was it safe to explain that truth to Tara, when she was reporting all to DePalma Capital? Probably not.

"It was hardly any time," Troy explained with a slight wave of his hand for emphasis. "Just a few hours contacting the sub and reviewing his research, which amounted to nothing useful."

"You clearly left this off the billing records so it wouldn't be discovered. But apparently you forgot about all your emails showing your work on this, which I've reviewed. And Lugo's *recognition* of your work during the conference room reception."

"I wasn't trying to be deceptive. It was just a few hours. It was a crazy time, and I just didn't get to enter them. And I knew he wasn't going to pay for it anyway after we cut ties with him as a client."

"Isn't utilization your main performance metric?"

"Yes."

"And you didn't want to bill and show this utilization?"

"As I said, it was a negligible amount of time."

"That doesn't make any sense. First Emma's obsessed with pro bono," she replied with annoyance, "and now you're treating a paying client like his matter's pro bono. How do you all expect to get paid if we don't charge anyone anything?"

"You need to talk to Anderson," he insisted. "And Emma. I've told you everything I did. There's nothing left."

She looked at him skeptically, and Troy couldn't wait to leave the room and be free from this inquiry.

"Okay," she said. "I know you have to head to MHU, so I won't keep you longer." He felt a wave of relief, which was quickly extinguished by her next comment. "We'll talk more when you return."

But he didn't want this interview hanging over his head anymore. He needed to get it over with.

"Do you have a lot more questions? If it's just a few, I can stay a little longer and answer them now."

"We'll talk more as soon as you're back," she repeated ominously.

This was exactly the situation he had hoped to avoid. Being interrogated about his role with Caleb Lugo enough so he was rattled just before his high-stakes interviews at MHU, but still not being able to put the whole HR interview in the rearview mirror. It threatened to consume him, just as he needed all his composure for the interview with Ali Tyrell.

Troy rose and walked toward the door, exited, and closed it behind him. He took a deep breath and considered texting Julia, but there was another associate standing in front of him.

"Emma . . ."

"Gillian hasn't gotten back to me, but I've been thinking about what you said. About stopping Anderson and holding him responsible for what he did to those women. And to me."

He couldn't control the smile that spread across his face. This was the answer to so many of his problems. Exposing his toxic boss for what he was. Detouring the investigation from focusing on Troy's own work.

"So you're going back in? You'll tell HR what happened?"

"I need something from you first," she replied. "Before I take this leap."

"Sure. Anything."

"I want a promise..."

"A promise of what?"

"That Julia will give me fifty percent of her MHU origination credit once Anderson's taken down."

His heart sank. This origination competition was out of control and threatening to consume them all. He knew Julia would never agree. She didn't want Emma speaking with HR anyway. But he'd have to try and convince her to give Emma something. Maybe not 50 percent. Would Emma settle for a third if Julia was willing to part with that?

"I can't... can't speak for her..." he stammered. "I can call her and ask..."

Emma then let out a short laugh and patted him on the shoulder. "That was a joke, Troy. I don't want her fucking origination. I want to make sure Anderson's never in a position to do anything like this again. I know I'm risking my career by speaking up, but that's the only way to stop him."

She then stepped toward the door, opened it, and walked into the interview room. "Funny joke..." he whispered sarcastically as the door closed in front of him.

"What's a funny joke?" a male voice behind him asked impatiently.

He turned and saw Anderson, who eyed him suspiciously. Troy didn't even try to come up with a credible answer, as he was much more concerned with his boss finding out Emma was speaking to HR again.

"HR just interviewed me. Now I'm heading to the airport for MHU. Tara said she's going to continue my interview when I return."

"Forget about that for now. No more HR interviews for anyone about our Caleb Lugo work."

Troy didn't know if this was good or bad news. Was it a lucky break or more cause for alarm?

"DePalma Capital doesn't want this inquiry anymore?"

Anderson shook his head. "C&R just received a legal demand from Caleb's lawyer, insisting we immediately halt this investigation. They're saying we're providing confidential client information to DePalma Capital and violating the terms of his contract."

Troy understood the author wouldn't want additional details of C&R's work for him revealed to anyone, especially considering the inevitable risk of leaks as more people learned additional scandalous info. Not while Caleb was fighting to salvage his existence and potentially facing the appointment of a special prosecutor who might authorize his arrest.

"How does he know about this investigation?" Troy asked.

"I have no idea," Anderson responded quickly, and then walked toward the door of the interview room. Troy knew he couldn't let him find out Emma was in there, at least not before she had a chance to reveal her story. Emma had already been highly reluctant to talk, and if Anderson intervened, she might never build up the nerve to do so again. Plus, once Anderson understood what she was doing, he would surely employ all sorts of intimidation tactics at his disposal.

"Wait, don't go in there."

Anderson stopped and turned. "Why not?"

He needed to come up with a convincing reason. But he could think of none. Yet he had to stall him for as long as possible. He had to say something that would guarantee Anderson wouldn't immediately open that door.

"I know what you did to Emma," he said calmly, even though

inside he was a cauldron of nerves, terrified of the consequences of challenging his boss for the first time. He didn't want to expose Emma like this, but maybe showing Anderson that Emma wasn't alone in this knowledge would make him less likely to retaliate against her.

"What did you say?"

"I know what you made her do."

"I have no idea what you're referring to." Anderson let out a deep exhale and then took a step closer to Troy. "And who the fuck do you think you are to talk to me like that?"

Troy had crossed a line. A line that could never be uncrossed. So there was no point in backing down now. He was pretty sure Anderson couldn't fire him, not if his boss understood Troy was willing to tell all if necessary. Not while Troy was still needed on MHU and scheduled to imminently conduct a critical interview.

"I know everything," he asserted. "All the sexual assault victims you helped threaten and blackmail. The revenge porn you coerced Emma into finding. The *Times* article only had a small part of the story and didn't specifically name *you*. But I know the whole truth. In today's world, careers of men much more powerful than you are routinely ended for doing much less."

Anderson shook his head and curled his lip in scorn. "First of all, you don't even know what you're fucking talking about. Emma's on a PIP and barely has a job here, so I guess she's willing to lie about me to save her own ass. And you've got to be the most gullible fool I've ever met to believe her bullshit. You just made a *huge* miscalculation."

Maybe he had made a miscalculation. It was too soon to tell. But he had already succeeded in stalling Anderson from entering the interview room. He was buying Emma time to tell her account to HR, and he had to find a way to keep extending that time.

"I believe her," Troy responded, already picturing himself back in his uncle's restaurant, assisting with the books and waiting tables, his hopes of becoming a successful investigator shredded and unsalvageable.

"Listen, Troy. You're lucky I don't have the time or personnel to replace you at MHU today. You're lucky I have to deal with this demand from Caleb's lawyer. Otherwise—"

"And what if I say I'm not going to MHU?" he replied.

"Then I have no reason to keep you employed. And the other members of the MHU team will probably fuck up the Ali Tyrell interview, costing us the cooperation of the other complainants and a shitload of business, maybe even the entire assignment. In which case I'll be able to fire Julia too. Is that what you want? Extinguishing both of your careers and the financial viability of this company?"

He knew Anderson was right that refusing to head to campus might be disastrous for them all. He had to go. There was no choice. But first he still needed to earn Emma a little more time.

"Even if I go to MHU today, what you did with Emma, and with Julia . . . It's just—"

"Get to the fucking airport!" Anderson roared, extending one hand and pointing down the hall. "Now!"

Before Troy could respond, the conference room door flung open and Tara looked out with concern. "What's going on?" she asked. "Is something wrong?"

Troy peered into the room and saw Emma seated inside, her head turned to look past Tara into the hallway. Anderson obviously saw her too. "Is that Emma Richardson?" he snapped. "She already interviewed with you. Why is she back?"

"I don't know yet," Tara replied, and Troy's heart sank upon hearing those words. "She said she had more information to provide. So we're about to do a second interview."

Anderson's eyes opened wider with recognition of the situation. "All interviews need to stop immediately," he ordered. "We have a legal demand from Caleb Lugo's lawyer saying we're breaching the confidentiality provision of his contract by providing information to DePalma Capital. Our legal department's speaking with his counsel now."

"Okay," Tara responded, and then turned to Emma, who was still seated inside the room. "You heard what he said. We can't talk anymore today."

Emma rose and walked out from the conference room, briefly locking concerned eyes with Troy while avoiding Anderson's gaze. She then headed down the hallway and disappeared around the corner.

Anderson glared at Troy. "Leave for the fucking airport immediately, or I swear to God my next move will be to terminate you. We'll do it right now. HR's already here, so we have everyone we need. You even *think* about calling my bluff for another second, and you're career's finished."

So Troy didn't think for another second. He immediately turned and left, following the path Emma had walked moments earlier. He grabbed his travel suitcase from his cubicle and raced down the stairs, into an Uber headed to LaGuardia.

Troy's chest thumped as he pulled out his MHU notes to prep for Ali's interview in earnest. But he couldn't really concentrate as he thought about the C&R investigation, and realized who must have tipped off the author.

Gillian.

She had professed her loyalty to Caleb at the Sixteen Foundation event. *You've always been there for these kids. And you've always been there for me. So I'll always be there for you. Always.*

And then the sex crimes prosecutor had backed him at the conference room reception. *I've been prosecuting sexual misconduct cases for almost three decades, and I've learned how to prove a case and how to spot a fake complaint from a mile away.*

Gillian had been burned and embarrassed by her new employer, yanked from a high-profile assignment that she changed jobs and left a stellar career as a prosecutor to lead. She had said she needed to "escalate" the info Emma provided. Now he knew to whom she escalated it.

If Caleb now succeeded in stopping this investigation, would DePalma Capital run from the impending deal? And then would the threatened massive layoffs occur as part of the financial fallout? Hopefully not, although acquisition by a private equity firm often meant reorganization and cost cutting, so possibly he was screwed no matter what happened.

Regardless, right now he needed to focus on the upcoming interview. He was terribly unfamiliar with direct questioning of witnesses. Most of his work had been database research and report writing. He had no experience in this particular subject matter, and felt highly uncomfortable asking a woman about sexual assaults by a softball coach when she was a teenager.

Plus, he knew Ali and her family were already hostile to this investigation and wanted Gillian to conduct it. The university's HR head was probably working to get their firm fired, and a local congressional candidate and much of the media continued to attack them and university leadership for retaining C&R. Now he would be the face of all that, with Ali able to report to whomever she wanted that the C&R interview was a terrible experience, and he would be named as the chief culprit.

He took the three-hour flight, and then disembarked and walked to the ground transportation area where his interview partner, Marissa Zhong, waited for him after having flown in from the West Coast. She was a star CPA, financial fraud investigator, and the perfect person to uncover complex monetary misdeeds by sophisticated con artists and unethical CFOs. None of that applied to the MHU investigation.

"Sixty-five percent chance this interview's going to be a major train wreck," she stated dolefully.

She was the numbers person, but his instincts matched hers. "I know. We need to show Ali Tyrell we're conducting a solid investigation. Even if no one else wants to help us do that."

"Agreed. Jeez, if we could just go back in time," she mused, "and work on one Caleb Lugo matter, we wouldn't have been thrown into this mess."

They took an Uber to the university. It was almost time for their 5:00 p.m. interview, so they couldn't even stop by the hotel, drop off their bags, and decompress. They entered the office of Deputy General Counsel Drew Kosick, and after a few niceties, he led them to the conference room where their most important interview was set to begin.

The same room where he had met the HR director, Serena Stanfield. The meeting where he had stumbled to express the most basic assurance of confidence and competence, and it was a marvel that he was still employed and on this campus.

A minute later, Ali Tyrell walked in, the woman he had prepped for, the one he'd seen on television in Anderson's office, speaking at the rally while Julia first presented this incredibly lucrative opportunity. He had expected her to be there with a lawyer, and her father, who had also been very vocal throughout this process.

But she walked in alone, wearing gray slacks, a white button-down shirt, and a denim jacket. She couldn't have been much younger than Troy, maybe by three or four years. Troy's career had so far been full of disappointment and frustration, but as his eyes met Ali's, and she gave him a stoic nod, he was overcome with the greatest sense of failure he had ever experienced.

Failure to be in a position to really right the wrongs that occurred on this campus, to actually provide something meaningful for Ali and all the others who had their lives derailed by a predatory coach. Failure to protect them from the educational, political, and corporate entities who now desperately looked to secure their own agendas amidst the fallout.

And there was so much more.

Failure to successfully support Emma, having just convinced her to agree to an interview that exposed his colleague to all sorts of retaliation, even though it was aborted before she was able to provide meaningful information.

Failure to really help Julia, to be there for her in any notable way, either when she shed tears with him in her bed or when she yearned for his help as the bosses at C&R took advantage of her.

Failure also to stand up for himself, to successfully push back against Anderson, the way he had promised when he crafted his plan to use the MHU leverage for their benefit. Failure to be strong, and self-sufficient, and not in constant fear that the next workplace controversy would end his career.

It was now so clear that all of his intentions had failed, because his efforts had led him to this moment. Still under Anderson's thumb, targeted by his own HR department, the point person for this large-scale investigation that half the nation seemed to be intent on condemning.

"Hello, Ali," he said as he offered his hand. "I'm Troy Abernathy. Thank you for meeting with us."

Marissa introduced herself and shook Ali's hand, after which Ali declared, "I want to renew my request for Gillian Fenton to conduct this interview."

"Unfortunately she's not part of this investigation anymore," Troy answered.

"Because she was on the board of that charity?"

He nodded, and then Marissa told her, "Anyone associated with Caleb Lugo won't be involved with our work here." She clearly meant this to be a reassuring explanation, but Ali wasn't satisfied.

"Gillian just supported his charity for young underprivileged writers," she said. "That's different than the investigators who helped him blackmail sexual assault survivors. *Those* are the people who need to be banned, not her."

"I can't control those decisions," Troy explained. "But Marissa and I are here to interview you, if you're okay with that. We're trying to find out the truth about what happened so people can be held responsible and this school can better protect the members of its community in the future."

"So neither of you worked for Caleb Lugo, I guess? That's why you're allowed to be here?"

"That's right," he answered as quickly as possible, knowing if he delayed even for a moment, his conscience might get the better of him and force him to deviate from this response. The only response that would be acceptable.

"Never," Marissa said with a tone of pride, as if her moral fabric prevented her from assisting such an immoral deviant.

"There are so many people at this school who failed us," Ali said sadly. "Coach Rob never could have gotten away with this by himself. The assistant coaches who allowed it to continue. The human resources and legal staff who just covered it up and silenced the accusers. The leadership who only wanted to protect the university's image and didn't care about me and all the other girls."

"That's what we want to uncover," Troy said. "That's why we're here."

"But part of me sees you as just more of the same. It's so frustrating. I keep waiting for some sign that any authority associated with this school will actually have enough concern, competence, and morality to really investigate what went on here. I want to trust someone to do that. I desperately want to. But I'm not going to be naive again and just blindly trust. Not after all I've been through."

"How about we all sit down and talk?" Marissa offered.

"Right," Troy added. "No formal interview yet. Let's discuss your concerns. They're all very understandable."

He sensed that at any moment she'd see through them both, understand that their calm and authoritative demeanor masked a backdrop of chaos. She would then walk out the door, effectively putting an end to this whole investigation.

Ali took a seat on one side of the table, and Troy and Marissa sat across from her. "We want to help," he said. And this was completely true. Even though he felt their best efforts would never amount to anything meaningful.

Ali looked at him skeptically, as if she had heard some version of this line from so many others in the past. "It just seems like everyone cares about something besides me and the other Coach Rob survivors. No one really cares about *us*. I think Gillian did. But she was the only one."

Marissa shook her head. "That's not true. We do this for a living because we care. Our firm is in this business because it cares."

"The firm that tried to ruin anyone who accused Caleb Lugo of sexual assault?"

"The people who worked on his matters have nothing to do with this investigation," Troy's colleague insisted. "President Montgomery required that, and C&R supported his decision immediately."

"Troy, let me ask you," Ali began, turning toward him, and his heart began to pound as she put him on the spot. "There are a lot of people who want to believe that the university, and your company, are capable of doing what's right. There are also many who think it's all a show to make money for your firm and save the school's reputation. One woman is even running for Congress on that platform."

"I think unfortunately things like that are normal in a high-profile matter such as this," Troy said, even though he had no idea if any of this was normal. But it seemed to be a reasonable response.

Ali sat there for a few moments, seemingly deep in thought. "The new university leadership is saying we can trust you. Maybe having a proper process with your firm could be beneficial. And it might calm my father down. I can't even bring him on campus now without worrying he'll do something crazy again. But . . ."

"But what?" Troy asked.

"I know what happened to me is not my fault, but I keep thinking that if I wasn't so naive then, I'd be living a normal life now," she explained. "Instead of sitting here with you, and going to therapy because of the trauma this coach caused. So I'm determined never to be naive again. I know part of not being naive is making sure I'm direct about what I want and expect from people. I wasn't that way before, but I've learned that I need to be. I've become a big believer in looking people in the eyes and asking clear questions. So I'm asking you. Will this be a thorough investigation by experts? Is C&R the correct firm for this? Can we trust you and your colleagues?"

I think so. I do. I definitely think so.

That was the answer he had given the last time this question had been posed to him. Lacking in veracity, completely unsatisfactory, a pathetic attempt at smoothing over an anything-but-smooth situation. He couldn't make that mistake again.

Ali locked eyes with him, just as she said she wanted to. He wished he could help her, protect her, do the right thing. But he also knew he never could, not the way things were currently set up. Not in this lifetime. He wanted to tell her all that, to be completely honest, but that too was impossible. So instead he looked back at her and displayed the most confident and compassionate expression he'd ever mustered as he immediately and succinctly reassured her:

"Absolutely."

The reality was that life had put him in a position in which the only person he could potentially help in a meaningful way was Julia. There was no hope of being a benefit to anyone else, so he had to focus his efforts on her. It was finally time for him to return her favors, atone for his sins, and truly be there for her.

As the MHU investigation now teetered on the brink of collapse,

Julia's future hung in the balance. He needed to do everything in his power to preserve and safeguard her path to success. Then he could know that at least one person, one woman, had been protected and supported by his actions.

Absolutely.

As he let that decisive word sink in, and watched Marissa nod in confirmation next to him, he also realized that in order to really deliver for Julia, and protect himself and Emma, there was one more thing he needed to do. One phone call he needed to make.

33
Megan

MEGAN DESPERATELY needed to talk with Evina, find some way to stop her from viewing the situation with complete hopelessness, as Megan did. And she feared Evina would consider all this to be Megan's fault. Which it was.

She had hoped Evina would phone her so Megan could try to console her and apologize, but over the past three days since Aaron's interview, Megan had received no calls from state prison. She knew she needed to visit Evina in person.

But there was simultaneously the small matter of her being in the midst of a heated special election campaign for Congress, which had been on an upward trajectory until this latest attack. People in Mountain Hill knew not to cross these powerful men, but she had ignored that conventional wisdom and was paying the price. She told herself that if she couldn't counteract the damage they'd inflicted, she at least needed to find a way to damage *them* in return.

How? She wasn't sure. Earning a seat in Congress and representing Mountain Hill on the national stage might give her a platform and the influence to support a well-crafted strategy to take them down. But first she needed to win.

"I'm going to undo this," she told Evina with as much confidence as she could muster, staring solemnly from across the table in the prison visiting area. Even though she feared there was in reality no solution available. "I'll find a way. Don't give up."

"Undo what?" Evina asked with confusion.

Fuck, she doesn't know, Megan thought. She had assumed her friend would have found out about the latest developments, especially the White House's statement that she would be ineligible for clemency. Now Megan would have to break the news to her, and she had no idea how to begin that horrible task.

"I'm sorry. I thought you knew. Aaron Montgomery publicly attacked me for seeking his support for your petition. He said I asked him to hold up the whole federal budget until the White House granted your release."

Evina sat silent for a few moments. She didn't look disappointed or upset by this news, but Megan hadn't communicated the worst of it yet. She was trying to ease into it, hoping this method would be less cruel.

"Did you really do that?" Evina asked.

Was she asking this accusingly? Or with appreciation? Unclear, but her tone communicated a disbelief that such a major national stand would be considered on her behalf.

"No, I didn't," Megan said, and then lowered her voice in case others could overhear. "I asked for his help, and *he* made that offer. Not me. At the time I had no problem with it. I'd still have no problem with it."

"But then you started attacking him, so he had to fight back against you. And me."

"I went after him because he completely blew me off and ignored all my follow-up. He wasn't going to help. So we needed another plan, and I realized that focusing on the university was the way to win this election and then help you. I had to find an issue that enough voters feel strongly about."

"Because they didn't feel strongly about me being imprisoned for defending myself against an abusive monster," she replied sullenly.

"No, unfortunately they didn't. But listen, I need to tell you the rest." She heard herself whimper as she summoned the strength to continue, and her eyes began to mist. Evina seized on Megan's visceral distress to suddenly reveal her own alarm, as her mouth opened and her eyes grew wider.

"What's the rest?" she asked softly.

Megan clenched her hands together tightly, and then leaned in toward her friend. "The White House said . . . in response to Aaron Montgomery's allegations . . . that they'll never consider your clemency petition."

"No, Megan . . ." Evina gasped in disbelief.

"I'm so sorry. I never thought they would . . . or could . . . do something like that."

"No!" Evina shouted, as correction officers from various parts of the room focused their attention on her.

"I'm sorry, Evina, but this isn't the end. People are fickle. Politicians are fickle. We can still rally public opinion and get a future administration to consider your petition."

"A *future* administration?" Evina cried out in disbelief.

"I'm not done fighting. We're not done fighting."

"No!" she screamed again, this time slamming her fist onto the table and then leaping up to a standing position. Evina looked around at her surroundings, which had been her environment for years and threatened to be so for decades. She shrieked with all her might as Megan stood too, and correction officers swiftly grabbed Evina and forced her down to her knees.

Evina began howling in anguish as two burly men in uniform held her in place on the ground. Another turned to Megan. "You need to leave with me immediately," he said as he roughly pulled her by the arm toward the visitors' exit.

At first she resisted, struggling to free herself from his tight grip. "I need to stay with her!" she shouted, hoping this would appeal to some sense of compassion and reason. But it just led to a second correction officer seizing her other arm, and both of them pulling her away as Megan's heels dragged across the floor's dark blue tiles.

Just as she reached the door, she was able to focus her eyes one more time on Evina, collapsed onto the floor, surrounded by correction officers, no longer yelling. Three men continued to hold her down as others worked to clear the room following Evina's outburst that they responded to as a security threat.

She took in Evina's state of despair and hopelessness, and one thought suddenly consumed her mind.

I'm going to fucking kill him. Just as Evina had to kill Logan, I need to kill Aaron.

She was roughly escorted out the visitors' entrance to the prison, and she stumbled toward her car. Then Megan was back in her dark gray Honda Accord, driving into the dusk with Google Maps programmed for the main administrative building of Mountain Hill University. As she drove, she noted how free she was on the road, able to head anywhere, breathe the air if she rolled down her window.

Things that Evina might never again experience. Things that Megan would surely never experience again if she went through with her violent, unformed revenge fantasy. So she needed to be realistic. She wasn't a killer.

But she was going to confront him—immediately, aggressively, publicly. Megan knew from local media reports that he was set to speak at MHU's student center grand opening, and she should be able to make it to campus just in time. He had attacked her and Evina from the safety of a television studio with a reporter who lacked the knowledge or dedication to push back on his false narrative, and Megan had made her own statements defending Evina since then, which had been received with a collective community shrug.

She had to demonstrate that he was a manipulative liar, willing to destroy Evina's life for his own political advantage. What she needed now was a massive, public takedown to put him in his place and reset the public dialogue about Evina's plight and Megan's role in helping her.

She continued to develop her plan as she sped alone toward the university, crafting her wording, anticipating his responses. All the while wishing she was already on campus, because she couldn't wait to train her sights on Aaron and unleash her fury.

Megan was shaken out of her focused planning by a text message popping up on her phone, which she had placed on the black dashboard mount extending from the air vent. She was driving fast, straight down the highway, and knew she absolutely shouldn't review text messages. But she noted peripherally that it was from Aimee, so she clicked on it while keeping one eye on the road.

Megan—check out this video from the university. Just happened an hour ago.

So she tapped on the link and considered pulling over to the side of the road to watch, but instead decided to just keep moving, not wanting to miss her opportunity to catch Aaron while he was exposed in a public setting. The video began streaming, and she tried not to look directly while driving, thinking that if she just focused on the sound it would be like listening to the radio.

But she found herself compelled to look. There was a woman speaking in front of a crowd on what appeared to be an indoor stage. The video was from a local news site, and the words on the screen read, *Bianca Velencoso speaks to undergraduates at Mountain Hill University.*

She felt her car slightly swerve, and the dashboard flashed an image of a cup of coffee with a warning that read, *Driver Attention Level Low. Time for a Break.* Which provided yet another thing for her to look at instead of the road.

Meanwhile, the woman talked from a podium, and shots of the audience showed a roomful of youthful, enthusiastic supporters. She spoke with a Spanish accent and telegenic, movie star poise as she described how author Caleb Lugo sexually assaulted her in his New York City apartment and how his powerful friends and allies, including his high-priced investigative firm, worked to embarrass and silence her and others he preyed upon.

"Caleb Lugo met me in Spain at a charity event," she said. "I had read his books. I was a fan. I'm sure he'd never heard of me, as I was a struggling actress in my country. He told me to contact him when I was in New York. So I did, and we went out to dinner, drank some wine, and then headed back to his apartment."

Eyes back to the road. Megan knew she definitely needed to stop her car if she was going to continue viewing the speech. But she also felt that time was of the essence and stopping was emblematic of defeat. So again she tried to keep her attention on the highway in front of her, and focus her ears on the audio.

"And I'll be honest with everyone," Bianca declared. "I saw this as a business transaction. There's no longer a need for me to hide that, now that his goons have outed me in the media. And I thought he understood that too, but when I asked him for payment before proceeding any further, he got furious. *Really* furious. He started screaming, 'Do you know who I am? You think I need to *pay* someone to fuck me?!'"

The next voice Megan heard was the automated warning from Google Maps, the female narrator telling her the Route 48 exit was quickly approaching on the right. She blinked to focus, realizing she was in the far left lane and needed to get over quickly. Route 48, which she had campaigned to fix as a city councilwoman, but after nearly a year in office she had been woefully unsuccessful in getting any kind of consensus among city leaders. The dark roads, the lack of lighting, the twists and turns and potholes and flooding every time it rained.

As she maneuvered her vehicle toward the rapidly upcoming exit, Bianca Velencoso kept talking. "Then he shoved me down on the sofa, and I was on my back. He undid his pants, pulled up his shirt, and forced me to start giving him oral sex. I told him no, and he put one knee on my shoulder, holding me down. I fought to get up but couldn't. His weight was just too much. And he was yelling at me, 'You're a fucking whore! I should have known. You're a disgusting fucking whore!'

"I tried to push him away," Bianca continued, "but then he slapped me hard, twice across the head, and began pulling my hair so hard that a clump ripped out in his hand. So I stopped fighting and did what he wanted, with his knee painfully digging into me. It went on for a couple of minutes, although it seemed much longer. Then when he finally finished in my mouth he let up and lay down next to me. I grabbed my purse and ran for the door."

Megan was too busy with her own enemies to get invested in Caleb Lugo's comeuppance, but she admired Bianca's bravery and passion. She continued to take in the speech as she maneuvered down Route 48, squinting to make out the dark turns.

"I told the police and the DA that he sexually assaulted me, but they did nothing. They said I should have reported it immediately, not months later. One detective said I had a motive to lie because I had asked Caleb Lugo about auditioning for a role in his next Netflix series when we first met in Spain. No one took me seriously. He was famous and influential, and I'm nobody. I'm not from this country, and I speak with a foreign accent. I was alone with this. I also worried that if they found out I engaged in sex work, no one would ever believe he did this to me, and it would end my acting career. And that's exactly what happened, when Caleb Lugo's investigators targeted me."

Megan heard booing from the audience, and outraged shouting.

"They dismissed my case, and it seemed there would be no justice for this man," Bianca told the audience. "Until all these other women came out against him. Now many people believe me. And speaking here, with everything that happened on this campus, is the perfect forum. Because when I faced Caleb Lugo's wrath for daring to report that he attacked me, his investigative firm tried to cripple me. They wanted to embarrass me. Shame me. Make it so no one would believe me. Now that firm, C&R Investigations, is working here, for *you*. Investigating *your* softball coach's actions with teenagers who were too young and powerless to escape his manipulative grooming. This should be unacceptable to anyone who truly cares about these girls."

The road was growing more treacherous, more confusing, and for a minute Megan tried to only half listen, to be responsible by focusing on the actual driving. But her attention returned almost fully to the woman's words when Megan heard her declare, "And that's why the president of this university, Aaron Montgomery, should immediately resign or be fired. He has violated the trust of this institution and the many victims of sexual abuse on this campus."

Megan heard more raucous applause and then the ping of another text from Aimee.

This story is getting a LOT of coverage.

Megan looked up and slammed on the breaks to avoid hitting the car in front of her. The last few minutes had been a blur, but she now saw that she was near the university. She had spoken about the school so often, so publicly, without having actually set foot on its terrain since her council campaign.

She parked on the street just off the main campus area, then quickly headed toward the college green. She asked a couple of undergraduates where the new student center was, and one of them pointed down the street toward the athletic fields.

Bright lights emanated in the distance, and as she drew closer she could see a crowd mingling near a stage set up in front of a pristine new five-story structure. She worked through the people, assertively nudging some away and weaving through any open space she could identify, until she reached the front of the audience.

About twenty feet from her, mingling in the crowd, Aaron was shaking hands while wearing a gray suit and a purple tie with the MHU insignia. Megan knew she needed to come across passionate but in control. She had right on her side and that hopefully counted for something, if she could utilize it correctly.

She noted that he caught a glimpse of her approaching before she could speak, and he turned to face her, a look of irritation flashing for an instant before he gazed in her direction with arrogant confidence.

"You lied, Aaron," she charged. "You offered to use your vote to help Evina Jansen's cause. You said you believed in it. I never suggested that to you."

People around them began turning in her direction, surprised by the confrontational nature of her words. Despite Bianca Velencoso's inflammatory campus speech earlier that day, the ambiance at this student center event had been ostensibly friendly and celebratory until Megan spoke.

"Welcome to Mountain Hill University," he responded. "I know you're not very familiar with our campus. It took a political campaign for you to grace us with your presence."

She ignored his comments and reiterated her initial accusation. "You were the one who suggested utilizing your budget vote to—"

"To assist your friend, a convicted murderer? You really want people to believe I'd hold up a national budget and stall needed funding for this district and our university to get an unrepentant killer and child abuser out of prison? I never spoke with you again after your unethical proposal because I thought that was the best way to avoid embarrassing you. But you have no shame, and here you are. Please, Megan, I know congressional campaigns can make people sink to new lows, but this is too much. Even for you."

She thought about all she could say to defend Evina, to show how unethical and manipulative Aaron was. People were watching, some holding up their phones and surely capturing video of the confrontation. She wanted to detail Evina's life. How she had grown up in a fractured home, with an abusive father, and then fallen prey to a man who repeatedly assaulted her, choked her, burned her.

How many times Evina had been in fear of death, and facing the even greater terror that he would physically harm her daughter. So she finally killed him, stabbed him in the back, took the brief opportunity to strike before it was too late.

Morally justified in every way, even though the police and courts said he hadn't been an imminent threat at that moment. But she couldn't get away—she had tried repeatedly, and he had always pulled her back into his life, through threats, through apologies and promises to never hurt her again, through vows that if she left him he would make sure she never saw her child again. A threat that, even in death, he was following through on.

Now Aaron was calling Evina a murderer, a child abuser, in front of a crowd who had no idea what the truth was. Megan longed to defend her friend, make the case for why she was a good person who had taken action to save her own life, who deserved freedom just like everyone around her who amicably gathered to welcome a new building on their campus. She could endeavor to think of a smart way to do this, to succinctly and effectively make the case for Evina, and tear down Aaron in the process.

But the echoes of Bianca's speech still resonated in her mind, and Megan suddenly realized that defending Evina in this moment would not be beneficial. It would contribute nothing to Evina's fractured cause of gaining freedom. Bianca's speech reminded her that the only issue the public really cared about today was the university's softball scandal. The fallout from that tragedy dominated people's attention, and it represented Aaron's one glaring weakness.

Focusing on that issue had quickly transformed Megan from a

rookie city councilwoman, spurned by the city's biggest power brokers, to a tremendous force with growing public support. It was a campaign message so effective that Aaron had felt the need to sink incredibly low to fight back.

He had launched his counterattack, rocked the foundations of her campaign and devastated her friend's life. Her instinct had been to battle him on this issue, to defend herself and Evina. But she now recognized that this change of topic was exactly what Aaron had been looking for. She'd been a fool to grant him that wish.

Her campaign was now sinking, and she understood that what was killing her chances at victory wasn't actually Aaron's allegations about her role in trying to secure Evina's freedom. The downslide had started when she deviated from her winning issue to engage Aaron on his selected topic. For better or worse, most voters didn't really care about that. And therefore they stopped caring about her and her campaign.

After hearing Bianca Velencoso attack Aaron on this very campus, Megan realized more than ever that publicly accentuating her Reclaim MHU ballot line was the winning move. It angered some but endeared her to others, and inspired a significant portion of the city in a way that most likely would never earn her a majority of the special election vote, but could very possibly give her a plurality, and therefore a seat in Congress. The media was already feasting on Bianca's attack, and now Megan needed to take advantage of the moment, ride the surging wave that this woman from Spain had just fueled.

Aaron was highly unethical and skillfully manipulative, and she couldn't let him control the debate. She needed to just follow her planned message and not deviate, no matter what. After all, this was the advice he had provided during her city council campaign.

Have a winning message that galvanizes voters, and stick to it. People will try to throw you off your talking points, but don't let them. Just keep repeating your message.

And Aimee had recognized Aaron's strategy before the candidate forum. *He wants to derail your focus on him and the university*, she had said.

"Your shiny new student center can't mask that countless girls were sexually assaulted here, and you're doing your best to orchestrate a sham investigation."

"That's absurd."

"And all this happened under your watch!"

"My watch?" he exclaimed, stepping closer to her. "I was in Congress. I wasn't part of the administration then. I took this position to save this school."

"You were intimately familiar with how this school was run, who was in charge, and you had a responsibility as the representative of this district to make sure claims of sexual assault were being handled in a responsible, thoughtful, and fair way. There are federal regulations that require it. You were our federal representative. But you did nothing."

Was this a stretch? As a congressman should he have been more intimately familiar with the institution's Title IX response? Her mind was racing too fast to know for sure, but one thing she did feel certain about was that, true or false, after what he had done, such an accusation was definitely fair game.

"Your friend is a convicted murderer and you were an accomplice to her unethical plan to escape justice," he asserted, his voice rising. But she stared at him and refused to budge, and she began speaking louder too, making sure all who were watching, including the people raising their phones to record this altercation, could hear her clearly.

"Our university needs to *clean house!*" she declared. "Together, we can *reclaim MHU!* Reclaim it with a real president. Reclaim it with human resources staff who are caring and responsive, not derelict in their duties like the current incompetent officials. Reclaim it with an impartial investigative firm that isn't earning its profits by silencing sexual misconduct survivors. Bianca Velencoso was right when she spoke here earlier today. It's time for you to go."

She received a collection of angry shouts, with at least one man screaming that she needed to shut the fuck up. Megan was on Aaron's turf, after all. But she also heard a few people around her begin chanting, "Clean house!" and when she turned she realized the words were coming from multiple locations, gaining steam, getting louder, as the tone of the chant became increasingly full of indignation and resentment.

Megan looked back to gauge Aaron's reaction, hoping to see him mortified, embarrassed, showing signs of weakness and defeat. But instead she saw him standing solemnly next to the professor, who whispered in Aaron's ears for a few seconds. Then the president nodded, and two uniformed officers from the MHU Police Department approached Megan, with one instructing her to leave or face arrest.

She had already been dragged away by law enforcement once today, and she didn't need to experience that again. But before she voluntarily departed, she turned to the crowd with their multitude of cell phone cameras pointed toward her and declared, "You want to *clean house*? You want to show Aaron Montgomery and his cronies that the years of ignoring the anguished cries of our daughters are *over*? Support me on Election Day, and I promise we'll finally end their reign of terror on this campus and *reclaim MHU!*"

The crowd response was explosive, with angry epithets directed at Megan mixed with chants of support. Amidst the frenzied disorder, she felt with undeniable clarity that she had just engineered a solid boost to her campaign, getting it back on track with the energy of a bullet train.

However, she then imagined Evina's reaction when she learned about this altercation, when whatever prison access to news included the inevitable stories and videos. She would learn how Aaron had continued to trash Evina's name and her quest for freedom, and that Megan had decided the best course of action was to *change the subject*.

But Megan had come to the tragic conclusion that Aaron and his team had effectively crushed any ability to free Evina now, and the fallback plan had to be to seek revenge against those responsible. She knew the best way to do that wasn't by shouting about Evina's life in front of a crowd, in a congressional district, that just didn't care. True vengeance would first require the acquisition of actual power, and the way to achieve that would be to win this election. Only then would she have the strength and influence to deliver Aaron the merciless retribution that justice required.

34
Serena

"Drew, are you alone?" she asked into her work phone. Again uttering this question before heading over to his office, but this time in response to *him* calling *her*.

How many times recently had she feared it was her last day of employment? Yet she was compelled to take actions that increased the odds of that being true. Maybe now that day had finally come.

"Just come over, okay? Right now."

His answer was as firm as Drew could be. The lack of a direct response to her question told her the answer was certainly no. This would be no casual conversation with her coworker. Not after yesterday's speech by Bianca Velencoso.

She walked to Drew's office and opened the door without knocking, and saw him standing there in conversation with their university president, as both paused to look at her.

"Close the door," Aaron commanded, and she did as she was told.

She didn't like how they stared at her, how she had to wait even these few seconds to find out what consequence they had in store. The uncertainly was highly unnerving.

"Just get to the point," she said flatly.

"I want to talk with you," Aaron said. "And this will be our last conversation."

"Why is Drew part of this?"

"He's a witness."

"A witness to what?"

"To make sure you don't fabricate what's said."

While Aaron appeared stern and intimidating, Drew looked as if he wished he was anywhere other than in this room for this meeting. His usual nonconfrontational self, once again thrust into an adversarial situation Serena had enflamed.

She resented him for his weakness, his failure to take a side and take a risk. "That's you, Drew," she said coldly. "Always a witness. You're a great . . . *witness*. One day you'll actually have to act and not just be a witness."

She saw how crestfallen he instantly became, with his eyes looking down to the floor as he muttered, "That's unfair, Serena."

"Today's your last day working here," Aaron then announced. "You've been undermining my attempts to save MHU since the day I arrived. Allowing that woman to speak to our students and publicly tear down this school is unconscionable for a university official. It all ends now. We're going to talk, and then security will remove you from campus. Permanently. I don't want you ever setting foot here again."

"This is retaliation," she shot back. "Retaliation because I spoke the truth. All these people around you are literally pawns in your game of chess, but I won't be a pawn. You can escort me off campus, but then you'll hear from my lawyer."

Then the expression on Aaron's face changed to one a few degrees more cordial, as he held up his right hand in a seeming effort to turn down the temperature of their growing confrontation. "I'm not looking to go to war with you, Serena. I have way too many fights on my hands. And the investigation is actually proceeding well now, despite your attempts to subvert it. Ali Tyrell is cooperating, and the others are following her lead. I know I said their participation wasn't essential, but after Bianca Velencoso's speech attacking my leadership so publicly . . . these girls showing trust in the investigative process was crucial."

"We're asking you to resign, Serena," Drew said. "Just resign, and find somewhere else you'll be happy. It's obviously not here. The university will pay you six months severance. Salary and benefits."

She didn't want to abandon this school, but she also recognized they were determined to force her out, one way or another. If they fired her, she could bring legal action, which they surely wanted to avoid. But it was something she would rather avoid too.

"Two years," she responded.

Aaron shook his head. "We can't do more than a year."

"Two years," she said, holding firm. "And full tuition for my daughter until she graduates."

He was silent for a few moments, as was Drew. Serena knew the amount of money she proposed was insignificant to the school. They were going to pay C&R millions, and settle lawsuits with a growing number of sexual assault victims that would easily cost the school nine figures. Her financial demand was monumental for her, but not so for them. They were after something besides money.

"One year. I'm not giving you a day more than that. But we'll cover your daughter's full tuition," Aaron said. "And you'll need to sign an NDA."

A nondisclosure agreement. This was how they kept people quiet. This was how they covered up the misdeeds and scandals, year after year after year. But she understood why people signed them. Just as she now would.

Getting away from this place. One year's salary. Not having to be concerned ever again about paying for Kayla's college education, a worry that had hung over her life since she was a toddler.

The university wanted her gone, and wanted her silent.

Get off the field, bitch.

She'd have to accept this deal. There was really no other viable option. Although there was one more, important concern. Always another concern.

"What about being *implicated*?" she asked, emphasizing that last word, just as Aaron had done when he first used it against her.

Aaron looked for a moment at Drew, and then back at Serena, before answering, "I'm confident once this agreement is signed, that will no longer be an issue."

"No longer an issue? You said this statement was made to the investigators. That can't just be withdrawn and magically erased!"

"It can and it will," Aaron responded casually, as if he was talking about a minor clerical issue. "After this agreement is signed, no one will have an interest in belaboring that issue."

There was relief to know that this attempt to frame her—because that's what it was—would now disappear. But also anger and disgust at this acknowledgement that he was in control of that absurd allegation. She no longer had any doubt that he or one of his people had planted that suggestion with Cole, so the young man could save himself and take her down, or at least establish intimidating leverage over her. Although she could certainly never prove any of that.

Fifteen minutes later, she had signed their agreement and placed a copy in her bag.

"I'm going to walk to my car now by myself and drive home," she declared. "I won't return, but I also don't want to be escorted off campus. If anyone tries to do that to me, I'll raise hell."

"Fine," the president responded, and she turned and left. Probably to never be in the same room with either of those men again.

She headed down the main campus walkway, toward the staff parking lot where her vehicle awaited. What would happen to this institution now that she would no longer be there? What official would fight for those needing an advocate who wouldn't be influenced by campus politics and other impure motivations?

Serena knew she was abandoning this school, where she had attended college and spent years as an employee. She loved MHU, and wanted so badly to be able to help it realize all of its potential, and to stop the careers of those who were using their positions to prey on others, or whose advancement was predicated on their silence in the face of horrible misdeeds.

But one year's severance. Escaping all the toxic stress and grief. Having college tuition all covered. She was paying a price for all that, a price that would no doubt eat away at her conscience for years. Selling out with the signing of that NDA. But what was the alternative?

She sat in her car, not yet starting the engine. She reached into her purse for a stick of gum to help alleviate the stress, to provide just a little spark of comfort as she sorted this all out. Despite her regrets, she was alone and safe. So she grabbed a peppermint stick, knowing that whatever brief sneezing reaction followed would be contained within the privacy of her vehicle.

She began to unwrap it, but before she could place it in her mouth, she felt her phone vibrate on the seat next to her. It displayed a number with a Colorado area code, and she decided to answer.

"I'm sorry to call you again, Serena," the woman said. It was the athletic director who had inquired about hiring Cole. Serena had since looked her up online and saw she was legit. "But our leadership is anxious to make a decision on the softball coach position. If we don't soon, it'll really hurt recruiting, and we believe we have a great shot at making the Softball World Series this year."

"What would you like from me?"

"Is there any update you can give us regarding the investigation and Cole Malinowski?"

"I actually just left my position at Mountain Hill University," she replied, feeling odd saying it out loud to this stranger.

"Oh, really? Are you going to another school?"

She knew she couldn't tell the truth. She would need to be evasive, or just make something up. "No. I've decided to head out on my own," Serena said. "I'm starting a human resources consulting practice."

This idea had just popped into her head as she was talking. Maybe it was actually a good one. With the severance package, she would have some time to try it out, see if it actually worked.

"Congratulations. That sounds great," the athletic director replied. "We'll probably need your services in the future. We have so many issues here. But for now, can you please tell me anything about the investigation? We really need some guidance."

"There's nothing I can say about Cole. It's all confidential."

"How about off the record? Is there a reason we shouldn't hire him? If he failed to act while girls were abused, we need to know."

Serena started the engine. There was a process for all this. Formal complaints, an investigation, interviews, the review of evidence, a detailed report with findings and analysis. It would violate so many principles of due process to subvert all that. Plus, she had just signed a nondisclosure agreement, and violating its terms might jeopardize all the benefits she was set to receive.

Yet after all Cole had done, the impulse building within her was tough to resist. *Being a head coach at a school like that is a dream job*, he had told her. *It's everything I've worked for.*

"Off the record?" she asked as she shifted her car into drive, even though she knew there was no such thing as *off the record* in a situation like this.

"Yes."

"Off the record, you should absolutely *not* hire him. Based on what we've learned, that would be a huge mistake."

"Thank you so much, Serena. I'm very grateful. We definitely won't now."

35
Troy

THE C&R CONFERENCE room table was laid out for another celebration, covered with trays of various lunch foods, bottles of champagne, and plastic flutes.

Julia stood next to him once again, as she and Troy surveyed the events unfolding around them. But he was not in a celebratory mood. Even two weeks later, he kept seeing Ali Tyrell look at him and nod in response to his misleading assurances about their investigation. She deserved better, but he had to accept the unfortunate reality that, for Ali, he could never deliver better.

"You see Caleb's arrest video?" Julia whispered. Troy nodded and she continued, "Twenty-seven counts of rape, sexual assault, and forcible touching. Police walking him out of his house, whimpering in handcuffs. I can't stop watching. Love it."

After Bianca Velencoso's speech at Mountain Hill University, a special prosecutor had been appointed. And even more women had quickly followed the media barrage by making their own public claims against the author. *The New York Times* had been publishing daily follow-up pieces with sordid details of new allegations.

Troy had watched the video, seen the author with his arms behind his back, choking back tears, trying to duck his head away from the cameras that seemed to be everywhere. An attorney for Caleb had tried to intervene, to tell the police that they shouldn't be parading him publicly, that this was improper and inhumane, and that once he received his defense, he would be exonerated.

Defending Caleb Lugo would be no easy task, but he had a skilled, loyal attorney fighting for him. Troy knew the author was highly fortunate to have experienced former sex crimes prosecutor and former C&R managing director Gillian Fenton in his corner.

Fortunately, so far C&R's name hadn't appeared in any more of the *Times* exposés. "If there's any justice in this world, he'll die in a jail cell," Julia added.

Then Anderson spoke as the C&R employees stood around to listen. Despite the festive atmosphere, he appeared melancholy, tentative. "I, uh, want to thank everyone who made the last thirty-seven years the most wonderful career I ever could have asked for," he said, and then paused, trying to contain his emotions. "It's been quite a ride. But it's time for me to go. I talked it over with my family, and we agreed that with DePalma Capital now set to lead C&R's next chapter, it's the right moment for me to step away. I never saw myself as the type to be happy in retirement. I've loved this work too much. But I'm going to do my best to embrace it, and hope for the best."

He then raised a champagne flute and declared, "To the best investigative firm in the world! It's been the honor of my life to be a small part of its success." As the employees around the room began to applaud the outgoing boss, Anderson strolled around the room, shaking hands and receiving enthusiastic well-wishes, hugs, and kisses on the cheek.

As he grew closer, Troy knew he would have to say something graceful in front of the other employees. But the last thing he wanted was to utter one more phony, obsequious pleasantry to this man. Finally Anderson was upon him, and Troy instinctively reached out to shake his hand.

"I hope everyone in your retirement treats you as well as you've treated people here," he said.

Anderson paused to consider his comment, his face stoic. "You're never going to last here, Troy," he then whispered. "You'll be out on your ass within a year. Guaranteed."

Troy knew it was very possible Anderson was correct. He would have to do everything in his power to be successful, to prove him wrong. Meanwhile, Anderson was already moving on to receive a slew of good wishes from other employees, and Julia began tugging on Troy's arm. "Luke wants to talk," she said. "Come with me."

He followed her out the door, around a corner, and down the hall, where he saw Luke entering his office. When all three were inside, Luke closed the door. "Thank God that man is finally gone," he said.

"So far I'm a *huge* fan of our new owners," Julia gushed. "Forcing that asshole out right away . . ."

"Yeah," Luke responded. "I guess the HR investigation helped them see this was needed."

Troy shook his head. "No. That investigation had nothing to do with this. Caleb's lawyers were able to put an indefinite hold on it."

"So how did they know to get rid of him?" Julia asked.

"I called them," Troy announced. "I just called DePalma Capital and asked for their CEO, and she got on the phone with me. I told her everything. About Anderson, Caleb, Emma, all of it. She was particularly interested and concerned in light of Bianca Velencoso's speech."

"Jesus, Troy," Julia quickly responded with disbelief. "You could have tanked the whole deal. Ruined everything. And why didn't you tell me?" She seemed particularly disappointed that her C&R confidant hadn't kept her in the loop.

"DePalma Capital wanted to acquire C&R, but they were concerned about the firm's inappropriate conduct. That's why they asked for the HR investigation. So I gave them what they were looking for. Serving up Anderson as the chief culprit, which he was, so DePalma could remove him and feel better about their acquisition. And I didn't tell you because . . . I was concerned you wouldn't approve."

"You're right, I wouldn't have approved. But it worked. You did it. Wow." Julia shook her head in amazement. "He's so fucked," she then added gleefully.

Luke laughed. "Oh, he's not fucked. He's devastated about being kicked out, but he's got a huge buyout coming with the sale of the company, as long as he's not terminated for cause. It was in his contract. And they can't terminate him for cause because too many high-profile clients would find that disturbing after working with him for years. It would just lead to more questions about what he did wrong. Plus, DePalma Capital doesn't want him suing and trashing us publicly. So he's getting a large golden parachute, and he was going to retire in a few years anyway. I'm sure he'd like to be leaving on his own terms, and that really hurts. But he'll be fine. More than fine."

"Okay, but why did you want me in here?" Julia asked.

"We need to talk MHU. We still have no idea how we're going to actually staff this. We need to figure that out. Almost the whole firm's still banned because of their Caleb Lugo work. Our SRM guys are great at what they do, but let's be honest, they're walking time bombs on a large, highly sensitive sexual misconduct matter. And if we sub out the work, we lose all that revenue. We need to figure out a solution immediately."

"Right," she responded, and then looked at Troy to see if he had an answer. But at the moment he couldn't think of one.

"Also," Luke continued, "Anderson's origination is now unaccounted for. It has to be reassigned."

"Yes, I'm *very* aware of that," she said.

"So let's start with the origination. Look, I don't want to fight you, Julia. Let's end all this dysfunctional conflict about sales credit. How about we just split it fifty-fifty, okay? If we can actually find competent bodies to staff it, we're going to bill millions. We'll both end up in great shape."

Troy watched Julia as she stared back at Luke. Maybe she was thinking the same thing Troy was wondering. What was Luke's contribution to merit half of the origination? He had been in the room when Julia brought it to Anderson. He had forced himself into helping craft their proposal and attending the MHU pitch meeting. Why should he get fifty percent just for that?

But Luke was an MD. He had leverage over her. And his offering to concede fifty percent of the origination credit for a multimillion-dollar assignment to a junior associate was monumental and unprecedented. She'd be foolish to turn down this offer.

"I think you should have forty," she finally responded.

"Julia, you taking sixty is just—"

"No, I'll get forty also."

"I don't understand."

"I want us to give my guy Troy here twenty. If he hadn't gained the cooperation of their main complainant, who's advising everyone else to participate in the investigation, this whole assignment wouldn't exist for us anymore. And if Troy hadn't called DePalma Capital, we'd both still be begging for Anderson's scraps. He should get twenty."

But Troy felt he didn't deserve it. His biggest contribution had really been deceptively assuring Ali Tyrell that their firm had the resources and competence to shepherd this incredibly important investigation, that she and the other complainants could put their trust in C&R, in him. He had done this for Julia, to support her. Gaining financially would only exacerbate his guilt.

But what was he supposed to do? Say no?

"That's sixty percent of the origination going to associates," Luke said disapprovingly. "The other MDs will not be happy."

"Credit should be based on what you accomplish, not how old you are," she explained. "Your age shouldn't matter."

Luke nodded. "Okay, fine," he said reluctantly. "Troy, with Anderson kicked out, I stand to inherit some of his other clients, so I do owe you something as a thank-you." He then reached onto a shelf near his desk and pulled down a bottle of scotch, opening it and then taking out three glasses from a drawer. He poured and handed one each to Troy and Julia, and then raised his glass in the air. "To the bright future of C&R Investigations!" he declared.

Julia raised her glass and started to respond, but her phone began pulsing on top of Luke's desk. Troy saw that the screen read *Aaron Montgomery* and then looked at Julia to gauge her response.

"Holy fucking shit," she exclaimed. "He's calling me back!"

She snatched the phone from the desk, tapped it, and held it to her ear. "Hello, this is Julia McGinnis."

Troy could hear Montgomery's voice booming through Julia's phone. "Julia, good afternoon. This is Aaron Montgomery. I'm so sorry for the delay in getting back to you. I'm not always great with returning phone calls when things are busy, and, well, as I'm sure you know, things are *very* busy."

"Oh," she started innocently, as if she had barely noticed his delay, "I totally understand. No worries, President Montgomery. I just called to thank you for retaining my firm. And to assure you we'll do a great job for the university."

"Thank you, Julia," Troy heard the man say. "The initial meetings have gone well, and the complainants are saying they'll proceed with C&R, so that should stop some of the obnoxious critics who are looking to tear down this school for every decision we make. And to be frank, that probably saved my job too after all the heat I've been getting. You may not be aware back in New York, but there's a crazy congressional candidate constantly attacking us, a Spanish prostitute showing up on campus and calling for my firing, and other rogue employees getting in on the act. But you know I'm not the type to back down. One by one, we're making these obstacles go away. So hopefully within a year we'll have this all behind us and can move on."

Julia then nodded emphatically, even though Aaron couldn't see that. She bit her lip to contain her exuberance. "Thank you so much, sir. We won't let you down."

"I have no doubt. And please send my best to your parents. As you know, I'm always very grateful to them."

"Absolutely. They're your biggest fans. They're already talking about fundraising events for your governor campaign," she said.

"Thank you, but of course I can't discuss that now."

"Of course. I'm sorry."

"No, it's fine," he said with a laugh. "Take care, Julia."

She placed the phone down and looked at Troy with a brightness he had never seen before on her face. It was a look of relief, contentment, and excitement about the future. "Can you believe this?" she asked with a smile. "An actual happy ending. The good people triumphant. The bad people vanquished. It's like we're living a fucking Caleb Lugo novel."

She then stepped toward Troy and wrapped her arms around him, squeezing tight, and he placed his hands on her back and felt her body against his. The warmest, most satisfying hug he had ever experienced.

36
Megan

Six Weeks Later

Evina: *What if you ran for Montgomery's seat? Then you could be our powerful person in DC.*
Aimee: *It's not about making people care about your issue. It's about connecting your issue to something people already care about.*
Aaron: *People will try to throw you off your talking points, but don't let them.*

SHE HAD FOLLOWED all their instructions. And now here she was, overcome with an aching numbness that prevented her from basking in the ebullient gathering that surrounded her in the campaign's hotel suite. Her mass of supporters mingled downstairs in the ballroom, waiting for her to appear and deliver a victory speech.

Her husband hugged her, and then both of her sons embraced her too. All telling her how much they loved her, how proud they were, how much good she would do for their community and the nation in Washington. What a monumental accomplishment to get elected to Congress, let alone without major party support.

"The ballroom is packed," Aimee excitedly told her. "It's nuts down there. Everyone loves a winner!"

Everyone? Surely not everyone. The majority of voters had actually cast their ballot against her. The Reclaim MHU platform energized many, but was also divisive and scary to others who relied on the university for their businesses, their jobs, their children's education. What did "Reclaim" really mean? It was up for interpretation, and some viewed it as a problem, and an unnecessary threat to the current university president, who was their long-time former congressman.

Her campaign hadn't been enough to take down Aaron, even with Bianca Velencoso weakening him with her speech. Ali Tyrell publicly announcing that she'd cooperate with his investigators meant that for now he would stay as university president.

Bianca had undermined Aaron's public authority, and made Megan's path to victory apparent and possible. But then Ali had helped resuscitate the man. In the end, this all meant that she could never get a majority of the vote. But in a multi-candidate race she hadn't needed a majority. 43.57 percent. That's all she received. And it was enough.

"Professor Dowling just called my cell," Aimee announced, holding up the phone with the mute function visibly enabled. "He said he tried to reach you a couple of times and you didn't answer."

"That's right."

"What should I tell him? He's an important potential ally for the future. You'll definitely want the U.P. endorsement when you run for reelection."

She grabbed Aimee's phone, unmuted it, and placed it to her ear. "Yes?" she said impatiently.

"Is this Megan?" the professor asked.

"It is. What do you want, Roger?"

"Megan, first of all, I want to congratulate you. I've seen a lot in my years, but not someone pulling off a victory like this as an independent candidate."

"Thank you," she replied plainly.

"Whether we like it or not," he continued, "we're now going to have to work together. You'll be in Congress, and we're running the university. Aaron asked me to call you and propose a reset."

"A reset? What does that mean?"

"Let's start over, Megan. Clean slate. Lots of times, political relationships start off rocky. Back in the day, Aaron and I fucking *hated* each other. Oh my God, the battles we had. Now we're . . . well, you know."

He was actually trying to patch things up. It was such a ludicrous concept, after what they had done to Evina, that she decided he must be insane. Or she was. Or this whole system was.

It showed how insignificant their attack on Evina had been to them. Just part of a campaign, like other campaigns in the past and the future. *It's not personal*, he had told her at the U.P. banquet, and again before the city council vote. For them, it was just one of countless political skirmishes that could then be followed by handshakes, followed by more skirmishes, with changing alliances and strange bedfellows and all that.

Megan also realized this meant Aaron and the professor didn't think she had been serious about the substance of her winning campaign, which had focused on excoriating and replacing the MHU leadership. They must assume she just adopted that issue as part of an inauthentic, calculated political strategy. And she reminded herself that was not true.

Rage pulsed throughout her body and her breathing grew heavy. Aimee looked on with concern, but so far no one else in the room seemed to notice. She had been silent for a while, for how long she didn't know. But it had been long enough that the man on the other end decided to talk again.

"Aaron could be an important ally," he explained. "Despite all the recent campus shenanigans, I still believe he can be the next governor. You're our new congresswoman. Together the two of you would be unstoppable. If you'd like, I'll have him call you."

Here he was again, dangling this phone call from Aaron. The call she had yearned for. The call that never came. Now it sounded like Aaron really would call her if she just provided the green light. But the thought of ever speaking with him again sickened her. She wanted to respond with some stinging rebuke, a caustic rejection of this proposal that would send a powerful message that she irrevocably despised them.

However, that would be unwise. Not unwise because she needed them, but unwise because it would prematurely warn Aaron that her entire existence, including all this newfound political power, would now be focused on targeting *him*. Best to wait for the right moment to strike, when she had a fully developed plan, when he least expected it.

"Sure," she responded. "I'll give you back to my campaign manager Aimee Guzman to schedule that call. She'll be serving as my chief of staff."

Aimee's eyes lit up as she retrieved her phone from Megan. Then Megan took out her own device, which had been pulsing nonstop in her bag. So many missed calls, texts, and social media notifications.

She perused them for a minute, and then Megan's phone lit up with the one call she absolutely had to take. The number indicating a call from state prison.

Rob Dempsey had just pled guilty, agreeing to serve decades in prison to avoid a public trial where all his misdeeds would be revealed in horrifying detail. In New York, Caleb Lugo had been arrested for numerous counts of sexual assault, and a prison cell hopefully awaited him too.

Two monsters destined to be incarcerated, removed from society, no longer able to use their power and position to prey on the vulnerable. But this prison outreach was from a third inmate. Not Rob Dempsey. Not Caleb Lugo.

"Evina . . ." Megan began to say.

"You've won," she gasped. "You really did it. I'm so proud of you."

"Thank you," Megan responded, knowing her victory had come with an incalculable cost. A cost that Megan then saw was not fully realized by her friend.

"And I thought more about what you've said. People are fickle. Opinions change. I've fought too hard, for too long, to give up now. With an advocate like you in Washington, I won't give up. Your victory gives me hope that one day soon I'll be free."

When Megan had last been able to visit Evina, and in their several phone conversations since then, she had tried to put her best spin on the catastrophic events that had doomed Evina's clemency petition. But she also kept wondering whether all these attempts at positivity had been a mistake. The more she ruminated on recent events, the more she knew for sure that with the White House's public statement and the associated public trashing of Evina's life, the whole situation was horribly unsalvageable.

The White House's position wasn't the type of thing that could be just walked back, especially not for someone like Evina Jansen, who offered no benefit to the current administration. And future administrations would view her similarly. Her clemency could never happen now.

"It's going to be very challenging . . ." she began, trying to balance setting realistic expectations while not ending Evina's will to live.

"Right, but when you're in DC, everything will change. I believe in you. You'll find a way to get my clemency granted. And then I'll come visit you in your congressional office. We'll have a glass of champagne together. I can't wait for that day."

"Evina, I'll never stop fighting for you," she replied truthfully, as she tried to think of some plausible action or series of events that would lead to her freedom. But Megan truly could think of nothing. So as revelers all around her celebrated this victory, she instead silently dwelled on the nothingness, as it enveloped her whole being and suffocated her soul.

The only ounce of comfort she could find was in knowing that for this injustice, unlike so many injustices perennially raging around the world, there was a specific, responsible individual who could be blamed and targeted for retribution. "I love you, Evina," she finally added. "You're not alone. We'll keep fighting. I'll visit you tomorrow."

When the call ended, Megan's head pounded with guilt, anger, and fear. She was suddenly being led out of the room, down a flight of stairs to the stage where hundreds of supporters and members of the media awaited her victory speech. She knew she had to address the crowd, but she wasn't sure she could voice a word.

She was backstage with her inner circle—her husband, her sons, Aimee, and a few other devoted campaign aides. Someone was at the microphone, telling the swelling crowd that their congresswoman-elect was about to take the stage.

Now she was at the podium, surveying the men, women, and children in front of her. Celebratory music swelled while people applauded, held up their phones to record video and take photos, and shouted words of enthusiasm. In the back of the room, a dozen or so attendees stood by the bar, taking the opportunity to refill their drinks while the lines were temporarily shorter and the alcohol still flowed.

As she was about to address the audience, with a large "Reclaim MHU" banner hanging behind her, she kept thinking of Evina all alone for decades in a prison cell, and of the man who ensured that's where she would stay. But Megan needed to silo those thoughts, stop obsessing over them, not let them derail her victory speech. Because if she was going to use her new position to exact vengeance, she needed to be seen as a strong, confident leader.

So she commanded herself to stop thinking of all that. Just for fifteen minutes, long enough to make this speech and get off stage. She summoned all her strength and composure, looked out upon the gleaming faces, and felt her husband and sons close to her body, proudly standing right behind her.

It wasn't enough to help her stop thinking of Evina, but it was sufficient for her to be able to display her best version of a telegenic smile and boldly proclaim in triumph, "Thank you, Mountain Hill!"

Acknowledgments

There are many people who were instrumental in turning this story from an unfinished Word document into a complete, published novel. I'm very grateful to Brooke Warner and the amazing teams at SparkPress and SparkPoint Studio, including Crystal Patriarche, Addison Gallegos, Tabitha Bailey, and Maggie Ruf. Thank you to everyone at Simon & Schuster who is responsible for the skillful distribution of this book.

Thank you to the remarkable beta readers who reviewed early drafts and provided critical feedback – Peggy Wang, Julia Denardo Roney, Jeanne Samet, and Mia Lee. I'm greatly appreciative to author Jacqueline Friedland for her very helpful publishing insights and advice.

Thank you to the nation's Title IX community for all of your indispensable work in response to sexual misconduct allegations such as those in this book. You have the most challenging, thankless, and important jobs on campus.

I'm incredibly fortunate for the loving family who has been in my corner since childhood. My parents Gary and Linda and my brother Steve have supported me in good times and bad throughout my life. Their thoughtful ideas for improving and revising this novel were vital in reaching the final version. Having a mother who was a high school English teacher continues to pay dividends.

To Jen Buchwald, I love every moment we spend together, whether we're traveling to Paris and Bruges, reading and talking about novels on the couch, or hosting open bar events for friends and family. Your meticulous, creative, and clever revisions of this novel were invaluable and pushed me to become a better writer.

To Samantha and Jake, I'm continually inspired by your creativity, passion, kindness, and humor. As a responsible parent, I told you both that you weren't old enough to read my books. But hopefully you're reading them anyway when I'm not looking. If so, I would love to hear your thoughts.

About the Author

photo credit: Suzanne Claire Photography

DAN SCHORR is a sexual misconduct investigator at his firm, Dan Schorr, LLC, and an adjunct professor at Fordham Law School. Previously, he served as a New York sex crimes prosecutor, the Inspector General for the City of Yonkers, and an adjunct law professor with Tsinghua University in Beijing, China. He has been a television legal analyst for Good Morning America, CNN, Fox News Channel, Law & Crime network, and elsewhere. Schorr lives in Rye Brook, New York with his wife and two children. His debut novel *Final Table* was the Indie Excellence Awards Winner in Literary Fiction. *Open Bar* is his second novel.

Looking for your next great read?

We can help!

Visit www.gosparkpress.com/next-read
or scan the QR code below for a list
of our recommended titles.

SparkPress is an independent boutique publisher delivering high-quality, entertaining, and engaging content that enhances readers' lives, with a special focus on commercial and genre fiction.